AMERICA: BEWARE!

THE #1 STAR
OF BRITISH HORROR HAS COME TO SCARE THE
LIVING DAYLIGHTS OUT OF YOU

#1

"HERBERT SEEMS TO RACE EAGERLY,
ZESTFULLY, TOWARD EACH NEW HORROR!"
—STEPHEN KING,
in *Danse Macabre*

#1

"HIS IMAGES OF VIOLENCE ARE POWERFUL ...
HIS STYLE PARALLELS STEPHEN KING'S."
—RAMSEY CAMPBELL,
in *The Penguin Encyclopedia of Horror
and the Supernatural*

#1

"A UNIQUE VOICE ... HARD-HITTING AND BLOODY."
—DOUGLAS E. WINTER, in *Faces of Fear*

#1

"A MAST
—*Library J*

D0204585

THE FACE OF EVIL

Halloran stepped back, horrified at the countenance that stared up at him.

The skin was withered and deeply rutted, like wrinkled leather left in the sun; and its coloring, too, was of old leather, except where there were festering scabs that glinted under the flashlight. Most alarming of all were the eyes. They were huge, lidless, bulging from the skull as if barely contained within their sockets; the pupils were cloudy, a fine membrane coating them, and the area around them that should have been white was yellow and patchworked with tiny veins.

"It's you," came the sibilant whisper...

SEPULCHRE

Novels by James Herbert

THE RATS
LAIR
DOMAIN
THE FOG
THE SURVIVOR
FLUKE
THE SPEAR
THE DARK
THE JONAH
SHRINE
MOON
THE MAGIC COTTAGE
SEPULCHRE

SEPULCHRE

James Herbert

JOVE BOOKS, NEW YORK

This Jove book contains the complete
text of the original hardcover edition.
It has been completely reset in a typeface
designed for easy reading, and was printed
from new film.

SEPULCHRE

A Jove Book / published by arrangement with
the author

PRINTING HISTORY
G. P. Putnam's Sons edition / July 1988
Jove edition / August 1989

ISBN: 0-515-10101-X

Jove Books are published by The Berkley Publishing Group,
200 Madison Avenue, New York, New York 10016.
The name "JOVE" and the "J" logo
are trademarks belonging to Jove Publications, Inc.

PRINTED IN THE UNITED STATES OF AMERICA

10 9 8 7 6 5 4 3 2 1

CONTENTS

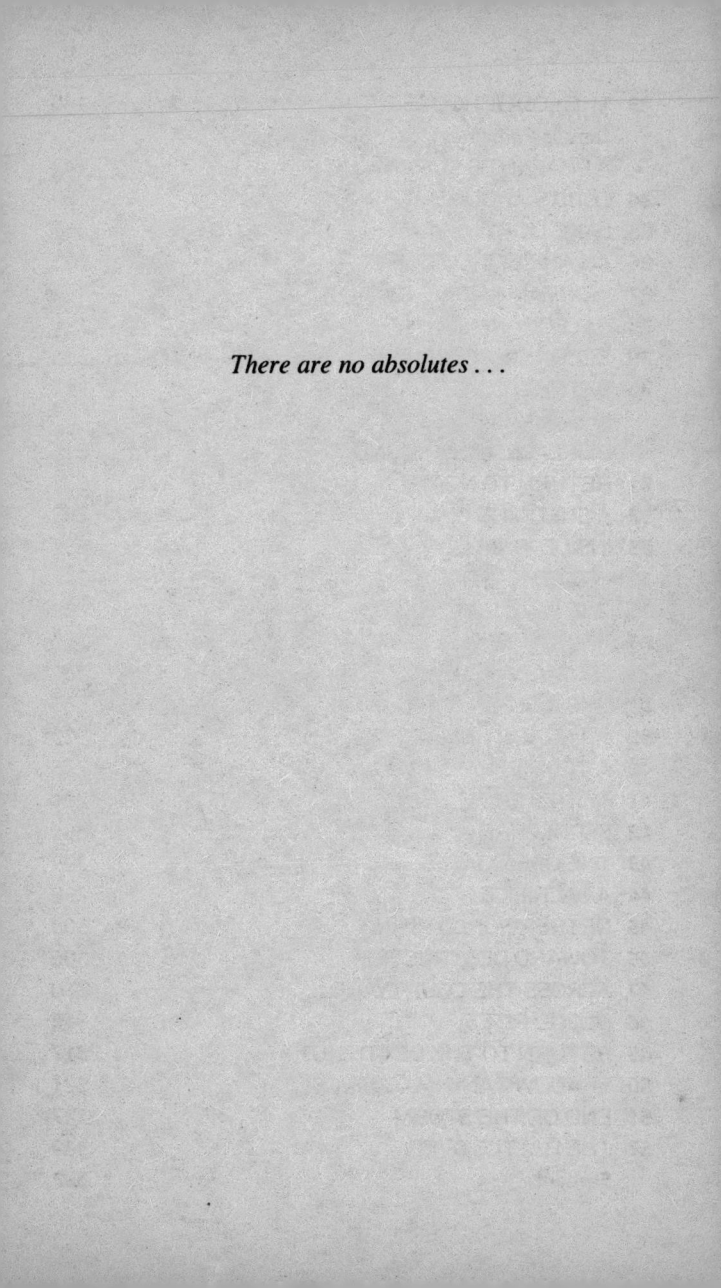

There are no absolutes . . .

'And the Lord God said unto
the serpent, Because thou hast done this,
thou art cursed above all cattle, and
above every beast of the field; upon thy
belly shalt thou go, and dust shalt thou eat
all the days of thy life.'

Genesis 3:14

The Sumerians

Three thousand years before the birth of Christ, the first real moves toward civilization emerged from southern Mesopotamia, around the lower reaches of the Euphrates and Tigris rivers. Because the land was between two rivers—*Sumer*—the people there were called Sumerians.

Their ethnic origins have never been explained.

This race of people made three important contributions toward our advancement—four if you count the establishment of firmly governed communities.

The first two were these:

The measurement of time in hours, days, and months; and astrology, the study of the stars' influences, which eventually led to the science of astronomy.

But the third was most important of all, for the Sumerian high priests discovered a way of making man immortal. Not by eternally binding his spirit to its earthly shell, but by preserving his knowledge. These high priests devised the written word, and nothing invented since has had a greater effect on mankind's progression.

Yet little is known of these people themselves.

By 2400 B.C., they had been swallowed up by surrounding, less enlightened tribes, who absorbed the Sumerian culture and spread it to other lands, other nations.

So although their achievements survived, the Sumerians' early history did not. For the kings, the princes, and the high priests destroyed or hid all such records.

Possibly they had good reason.

1

MORNING DUES

The man was smiling. Halloran was smiling and he shouldn't have been.

He should have been scared—bowel-loosening scared. But he didn't appear to be. He seemed...he seemed almost amused. Too calm for a sane man. As if the two Armalites and the Webley .38 aimed at his chest were of no concern at all.

Well, that wisp of a smile on his unshaven face would spirit itself away soon enough. This "eejit's" reckoning was coming, sure, and it was a terrible unholy one.

McGuillig waved his revolver toward the van parked in the shadows of trees just off the roadside.

"Your man's in there."

The harshness of his tone made it clear he held scant patience with Halloran's manner.

"And your money's here," Halloran replied, nudging the bulky leather case on the ground with his foot.

McGuillig watched him coolly. When he'd spoken on the phone to the operative, he'd detected a trace of Irish in Halloran's voice, the merest, occasional lilt. But no, he was pure Brit now, no doubt at all.

"Then we'll get to it," McGuillig said.

As he spoke, rays from the early-morning sun broke through, shifting some of the grayness from the hillsides. The trees nearby dripped dampness, and the long grass stooped with fresh-fallen rain. But the air was already sharp and clear, unlike, as McGuillig would have it, the unclean air of the North. Free air. Uncontaminated by Brits and Prods. A mile away, across the border, the land was cancered. The Irishman regarded the weapon he held as the surgeon's scalpel.

Just as McGuillig, brigade commander of D Company,

Second Battalion of the Provisional IRA, watched him, so Halloran returned his gaze, neither man moving.

Then Halloran said: "Let's see our client first."

A pause before McGuillig nodded to one of his companions, a youth who had killed twice in the name of Free Ireland and who was not yet nineteen. He balanced the butt of the Armalite against his hip, barrel threatening the very sky, and strolled to the van. He had to press hard on the handle before the back door would open.

"Give him a hand," McGuillig said to the other Provo on his left. "Don't worry about these two: they'll not be moving." He thumbed back the Webley's hammer, its *click* a warning in the still air.

All the same, this second companion, older and more easily frightened than his leader, kept his rifle pointed at the two Englishmen as he walked over to the van.

"We had to dose up your man," McGuillig told Halloran. "To keep him quiet, y'understand. He'll be right as rain by tomorrow."

Halloran said nothing.

The back door was open fully now and a slumped figure could be seen inside. The older Provo reluctantly hung his rifle over one shoulder and reached inside the van along with the youth. They drew the figure toward themselves, lifting it out.

"Bring him over, lads. Lay him on the ground behind me," their commander ordered. To Halloran: "I'm thinking I'd like to see that money."

Halloran nodded. "I'd like my client examined."

McGuillig's tone was accommodating. "That's reasonable. Come ahead."

With a casual flick of his hand, Halloran beckoned the heavyset man who was leaning against their rented car twenty yards away. The man unfolded his arms and approached. Not once did Halloran take his eyes off the IRA leader.

The heavyset man strode past Halloran, then McGuillig. He knelt beside the prone figure, the Irish youth crouching with him.

He gave no indication, made no gesture.

"The money," McGuillig reminded.

Halloran slowly sank down, both hands reaching for the leather case in front of him. He sprung the two clasps.

His man looked back at him. No indication, no signal.

Halloran smiled, and McGuillig suddenly realized that it was he himself who was in mortal danger. When Halloran quietly said—when he *breathed*—"Jesus, Mary. . ." McGuillig thought he heard that lilt once more.

Halloran's hands were inside the case.

When they reappeared an instant later, they were holding a snub-nosed submachine gun.

McGuillig hadn't even begun to squeeze the .38's trigger before the first bullet from the Heckler & Koch had imploded most of his nose and lodged in the back of his skull. And the other Provo hadn't even started to rise before blood was blocking his throat and gushing through the hole torn by the second bullet. And the Irish youth was still crouching with no further thoughts as the third bullet sped through his head to burst from his right temple.

Halloran switched the submachine gun to automatic as he rose, sure there were no others lurking among the trees, but ever careful, chancing nothing.

He allowed five seconds to pass before relaxing. His companion, who had thrown himself to the ground the moment he saw Halloran smile, waited just a little longer.

2

ACHILLES' SHIELD

The sign for Achilles' Shield was as discreet as its business: a brass plaque against rough brick mounted inside a doorway, the shiny plate no more than eight-by-four inches, a small right-angled triangle at one end as the company logo. That logo represented the shield that the Greek hero Achilles, if he'd been wiser, would have worn over his heel, his body's only vulnerable part, when riding into battle. The name with its simple symbol, was the only fanciful thing about the organization.

Situated east of St. Katharine's Dock, with its opulent yacht basin and hotel, the offices of Achilles' Shield were in one of the many abandoned wharfside warehouses that had been gutted and refurbished in a development that had brought trendy shops, offices, and "old style" pubs to lie incongruously beneath the gothic shadow of Tower Bridge. The company plaque was difficult to locate. To spot it, you had to know where it was. To know, you had to be invited.

The two men sitting in the fourth-floor office—a large, capacious room, because space wasn't at a premium in these converted warehouses—*had* been invited. One of them had been invited many times over the past six years.

He was Alexander Buchanan, a suitably sturdy name for an underwriter whose firm, Acorn Buchanan Limited, had a "box" on the floor of Lloyd's of London and company offices near Fenchurch Street. Acorn Buchanan's speciality was K & R insurance. Kidnap and Ransom.

The person with him was his client, Henry Quinn-Reece, chief executive and deputy chairman of the Magma Corporation PLC. He looked ill at ease, even though the leather sofa on which he sat was designed for maximum comfort. Perhaps he did not enjoy the scrutiny he was under.

The scrutineers were three, and they were directors of Achilles' Shield. None of these men did or said anything to relax their prospective client. In fact, that was the last thing they wanted: they liked their interviewees to be on edge, and sharper because of it.

The one behind the large leather-topped desk, who was in charge of the meeting, was Gerald Snaith, Shield's managing director, officially titled Controller. He was forty-nine years old, a former major in the SAS, and had trained soldiers, British and foreign, all over the world. His main service action had been in Oman, his exploits largely unknown to the public because, after all, that particular conflict—or more accurately, the British Army's participation in it—had never been recognized officially. A short man, and stocky, his hair a slow-graying ginger, Snaith looked every inch a fighting man which, in truth, he still was.

In a straight-backed chair to the side of the Controller's desk sat Charles Mather, a Member of the Order of the British Empire, a keen-eyed man of sixty-two years. Those keen eyes often held a glint of inner amusement, as though Mather found it impossible to treat life too seriously all the time, despite the grim nature of the business he was in. Introduced to clients as Shield's Planner, personnel within the organization preferred to call him the Hatcher. He was tall, thin, and ramrod, but forced to use a cane for walking because of a severe leg wound received in Aden during the latter stages of that "low-intensity" campaign. A jeep in which he was traveling had been blown off the road by a land mine. Only his fortitude and an already exemplary military career had allowed him to return to his beloved army, sporting concealed scars and a rather heroic limp; unfortunately a sniper's bullet had torn tendons in that same leg many years later when he had been General Officer Commanding and Director of Operations in Ulster—hence the stick and early retirement from the British Army.

The only non-English name among a very English assemblage was that of Dieter Stuhr, German-born and at one time a member of the Bundeskriminalamt, an organization within the German police force responsible to the federal government for the monitoring of terrorists and anarchist groups. Stuhr sat alongside Snaith at the desk. Younger than his two colleagues and four years divorced, his body was not in the same lean condition: a developing paunch was beginning to put lower shirt buttons under strain, and his hairline had receded well beyond the point of no return. He was an earnest, overanxious man, but supreme at organizing movement, finances, timetables, and weaponry for any given operation, no matter what the difficulties, be they dealing with the authorities in other countries (particularly certain police chiefs and high-ranking officials who were not above collusion with kidnappers and terrorists) or arranging "minimum-risk" life-styles for fee-paying "targets." Within the company he was known very properly as the Organizer.

He bore an impressive scar on his face that might well have been a sword-scythed wound, perhaps the symbol of machoism so proudly worn by dueling Heidelberg students before and during Herr Hitler's rapid rise to infamy; but Stuhr was not of that era and the mutilation was nothing so foolishly valiant. It was no more than a deep, curving cut received in his childhood while falling off his bicycle after freewheeling down a too-steep hill outside his hometown of Schleiz. A truck driver ahead of him had been naturally cautious about crossing the junction at the bottom of the hill and Stuhr, an eleven-year-old schoolboy at the time, had neglected to pull on his brakes until it was too late. The bicycle had gone beneath the truck, while the boy had taken a different route around the tailboard's corner catching his face as he scraped by.

The scar stretched down from his left temple, and curved into his mouth, a hockey-stick motif that made his smile rise up the side of his head. He tried not to smile too much.

Gerald Snaith was speaking: "You understand that we'd need a complete dossier on your man's background and current life-style?"

Quinn-Reece nodded. "We'll supply what we can."

"And we'd have to know exactly how valuable he is to your corporation."

"He's indispensable," the deputy chairman replied instantly.

"Now that is unusual." Charles Mather scratched the inside of one ankle with his walking stick. "Invaluable, I can appreciate. But indispensable? I didn't realize such an animal existed in today's world of commerce."

Alexander Buchanan, sitting by his client on the leather sofa, said, "The size of the insurance cover will indicate to you just how indispensable our target is."

"Would you care to reveal precisely what the figure is at this stage of the proceedings?"

The question was put mildly enough, but the underwriter had no doubts that a proper answer was required. He looked directly at Quinn-Reece, who bowed assent.

"Our man is insured for fifty million pounds," said Buchanan.

Dieter Stuhr dropped his pen on the floor. Although equally surprised, Snaith and Mather did not so much as glance at each other.

After a short pause, Buchanan added unnecessarily, "A sizable amount, I'm sure you'll agree."

"I dread to think of the premium involved," Mather remarked.

"Naturally it's proportionate to the sum insured," said the underwriter. "And I'm afraid the discount on the premium to Magma, even if you accept the assignment, will be accordingly low. Ten percent instead of the normal twenty."

"I imagine, then," said Mather to Quinn-Reece, "that we are discussing the safety of your chairman."

"As a matter of fact, no," came the reply. "The person to be insured doesn't actually have a title within the company."

"We can reasonably assume that he doesn't serve the tea, though," Mather said dryly. "I'm sure Mr. Buchanan has already informed you that a target's name never appears on any document or insurance slip concerning such a policy, even though documents will be lodged in various vaults—we demand total secrecy for security reasons, you see—but can you at least tell us your man's role within the corporation? We'll come to his name later, if and when there is an agreement between us."

Quinn-Reece shifted in his seat, as if even more uncomfortable. "I'm afraid I can't tell you that either, not at this stage. Once a contract is agreed, then Magma will give you all the necessary information—on a need-to-know basis, of course."

"We're well used to such discretion," Snaith assured. "In fact, we encourage it. But so long as you understand that nothing—absolutely nothing—must be withheld from us should we decide to take on the job."

"I understand perfectly," the deputy chairman replied, nodding his head gravely.

I wonder if he really does, thought Snaith. That every part of the target's life would be delved into, his wife, family, friends, his habits, recreations. Whether or not he has a mistress. Especially that. A mistress (or mistress*es*) was always a weak link in any operation of this sort because usually the target himself tried to cover up that particular side of his activities, would even endeavor to elude his own protectors for the occasional tryst with his woman. Shield would also have to know how the target was regarded as a man—stubborn, soft, fit, unfit, loving, harsh, conformist or otherwise, and so on (intelligence was assumed if he was worth insuring in this way). If married with children, what kind of husband was he, what kind of father? Snaith and his operatives would need to know his precise movements, every hour, every minute of the day and night. Were these movements regularly reported both inside and outside the corporation? Would the media ever be informed in advance? He was already aware of the employee's value to Magma—an incredible fifty million pounds—but what was the nature and value of his function? All these questions, and many more, would have to be answered before Shield could begin to devise a specially tailored security cover. Even then, no such protective system could ever be foolproof, not where terrorists were concerned. But one question had to be answered at the outset.

Snaith leaned forward on his desk, his fingers interlocking, thumbs turning circles around each other. "Why now?" he asked. "Why do you feel this member of your corporation needs protection at this point in time?"

"Because," Quinn-Reece replied blandly, "he told us so."

This time Snaith and Mather did not refrain from looking at each other.

"Your man has received a warning, a threat?" asked Mather.

"Not exactly."

Dieter Stuhr, who had been jotting down odd notes throughout the proceedings, rested his pen. "Is Magma involved in some venture that could put your employee at risk?"

"Not at this moment."

"It has been in the past?" Stuhr persisted.

Buchanan quickly spoke up. "Gentlemen, I'm sure you're all well aware of the Magma Corporation's undoubted prominence in the commercial world. It has widespread international interests in the mining, industrial, and energy sectors, with assets of over six thousand million pounds and an annual turnover of something like forty-five thousand million pounds. It would take you a whole day to study the list of subsidiary companies the corporation owns."

"Thank you for the information, Alexander, but what the hell has that to do with what we're talking about?" Snaith inquired bluntly.

"Only that you may rest assured that Magma is not involved in any enterprises that might be considered, er . . ."

"Shady?" Mather obligingly finished for him.

Stuhr smiled way past his left eyebrow.

"Questionable," Buchanan allowed.

"I'm sorry, I didn't mean to imply . . ." Stuhr, still smiling, began to say.

"That's quite all right, I understand," said Quinn-Reece. "You need to be fully in the picture, as it were. Let me put it this way: the man we are discussing has certain . . . abilities" —he stressed the word—"that companies whose commercial activities are similar to our own might well envy. In that respect, he could always be at risk should one of those rival companies, shall we say, become *over*envious."

"They could always pay more than you for his services," suggested Mather, becoming somewhat intrigued by their prospective client.

"If," Quinn-Reece replied almost slyly, "they knew of his existence." He smiled at the three men facing him, pleased with their rapt attention. "I'm sorry to sound so mysterious but, you see, our man has unique skills that would be virtually impossible to match. Not that our competitors would ever have knowledge of them because those skills are kept secret even within our own organization."

Mather rested his hands over the handle of his cane. He glanced toward a huge window, a gull catching his eye as it swooped by, wings dazzling white in the cold sunshine. "This sounds, uh, quite interesting," he said, returning his gaze to the deputy chairman. "Yes . . . interesting indeed. Would you care to elaborate?"

Quinn-Reece held up his palms. "Again, I'm afraid not. At least, not until you agree to the assignment. I know that puts you in an awkward position, but we have our own security requirements. There is also one other matter that might not meet with your satisfaction."

Stuhr's pen was poised once more.

"The man we're discussing," Quinn-Reece went on, "already maintains a strong protection unit around him."

"Ah," said Mather.

"Bodyguards?" inquired Stuhr.

Quinn-Reece nodded.

"Are they well-trained?" asked Snaith.

"Reasonably so, I believe," replied Quinn-Reece.

"Then why does Magma need our services?"

The deputy chairman looked at Buchanan.

"That's a priority condition of Acorn Buchanan if we're to take on the risk," said the underwriter. "These personal bodyguards may well be proficient, but my company would feel more comfortable if Achilles' Shield were running the show."

"It's no problem," commented Stuhr. "I can work out an effective operation into which they can be absorbed. First, though, we would have to ascertain just how good these men are, and how trustworthy; and they would have to recognize implicitly our authority over them."

"Naturally," agreed Quinn-Reece. "Your company would have complete control."

"That's fine then," said Snaith. At least he thought it was fine.

Buchanan cleared his throat. "There is yet another factor, Gerald," he said.

The tone of his voice hinted that Snaith and his colleagues were not going to like this one.

"I've already explained to Mr. Quinn-Reece and his chairman that it's Achilles' Shield's practice to have at least three operatives in direct contact with the target, so ensuring a too-friendly relationship never develops between protector and protected."

"It's our way of making certain," Snaith told Quinn-Reece, "that if our precautions fail and our client is abducted, then negotiations between the kidnappers and our man won't be hindered by personal involvement."

"I can appreciate that," the deputy chairman responded.

"Unfortunately," Buchanan went on, "the Magma Corporation will allow only one of your men to cover the target on a close basis."

"Good Lord," said Mather, while Stuhr muttered under his breath, *"Verflucht!"*

"That's impossible," Snaith quickly asserted.

"Please understand that the condition only applies to internal security," said Quinn-Reece anxiously. "Whatever outside arrangements you care to make are entirely up to you. You see, we're dealing with a matter of utmost secrecy here. The fewer people who know of our man's role within the corporation the better as far as Magma is concerned."

"I can assure you of absolute confidentiality," Snaith insisted.

"I've no doubts on that score. But this person is one of the prime reasons for the corporation's success throughout the world. Our secret weapon if you like. We have no wish for that secret—nor even the fact that we *have* a secret—to be exposed beyond key executives within the organization itself. If you are to take on this job, your man must be governed by that same secrecy."

"You mean even we in this room are to be excluded from this knowledge?" a surprised Stuhr asked.

"That is the case."

"It's highly irregular," huffed the German.

Quinn-Reece was no longer ill at ease. He actually enjoyed laying down this last condition because it reminded him of his position within Magma and the strength of his corporation: imposing Magma terms was part of normal business negotiations and home ground to him. He began to feel less intimidated by these three Shield people, more bullish. Besides, he was a shrewd judge of atmosphere and knew they were already hooked. Perhaps the talk of secrecy was close to their own clandestine hearts. And obviously the financial inducement was irresistible, for Achilles' Shield fees would be in direct ratio to the premium paid.

"Irregular," he admitted, "but as far as the chairman and myself are concerned, fundamental."

A silence followed in which the Controller, Planner, and Organizer considered the implications of such a condition.

"For what period of time is the insurance cover?" Mather finally inquired.

"No more than a few weeks at the most," Buchanan promptly answered.

"Reason?" asked Snaith.

Buchanan turned to Quinn-Reece, who replied: "Our man feels there will be no risk after that."

"He's somewhat remarkable," said Snaith.

"Yes, that's quite true. Are you interested in the assignment, gentlemen?" Quinn-Reece searched each face.

"You'd be making our task very difficult," Snaith told him. "But yes, it sounds like an interesting job. Finding the right operative might be tricky, though—our people are used to working as a team."

"Oh no," said Mather mildly. "I don't think there's any problem at all in that respect, Gerald. I think we have exactly the right chap, don't you?"

Snaith stared blankly at his Planner for a moment. Then understanding dawned in his eyes. He opened his mouth, but before he could speak the other man nodded his head.

"Yes," Mather said. "Yes, I think he'd be ideal."

A shade reluctantly, Snaith had to agree.

3

MAGMA

Halloran stopped for a moment to gaze up at the twenty-four story building. Impressive, he thought, and impressive it was, rearing up between staid, gray city blocks like a massive glass and bronze sculpture, tinted windows impenetrably black, its metal structure reflecting the morning sun so that multifaceted surfaces glowed a deep gold. Exterior elevators slid up and down the smooth walls, pale faces staring out from the capsules, watching the human patterns moving below. All corners—and there were many—were gracefully curved, the outermost buttresses adding a fortlike strength to the architecture, an image abetted by the different levels of the main building, some recessed, others outcropping.

Magma's headquarters was not a place to be easily stormed, Halloran mused. Yet for all its stunning grandeur, emphasized by the mostly uninspiring drabness of London's financial sector, there was something . . . something brooding about this edifice. Its surfaces dazzled a metallic luster that seemed almost overpowering, too forceful for the surroundings.

He stood there awhile longer, studying the Magma building, oblivious to the office workers scurrying around him, before crossing the road and going inside to leave the crisp coldness of the early spring air for the sterile coolness of the air-conditioned foyer.

Mather was already waiting for him, seated in the middle of a row of beige lounge chairs and facing a huge circular reception desk. Men in light-blue, epauletted shirts roamed inside the circle, banks of television monitors behind them, monochrome offices and corridors displayed on the screens. Other screens were imbedded in square pillars around the vast

concourse, these providing a variety of information for anyone
passing through: foreign exchange rates, the general market
report, company news, active shares, leading shares, traded
options, U.S. Mint, new issues index, and even BBC news
headlines.

The area bustled with life. Escalators carried visitors and
staff up to and down from the floor above, while elevators
around the glass walls took passengers to the heights. Digital
payphones were mounted on low tables set before the rows of
lounge chairs, there for the convenience of waiting business-
men. Lush palms and plants together with kinetic sculptures
constructed from the same material as the outside walls gave
the concourse a slightly less formal air. Long glass display
cases contained examples of rock strata, while others held
samples of ore and minerals, crystals, even semiprecious
stones, all exhibits of the earth's contribution to the Magma
empire.

Halloran noticed several informal meetings taking place
around the floor, discussions conducted *sotto voce*, the under-
tones adding to the complex's general buzz. Who'd need an
office with a setup like this? he wondered. Maybe the roving
security guards who were very much in evidence were also
there to discourage noncompany personnel from such practices.

A marble-clad wall, the large rectangular slabs needing no
other decoration than their own subtly hued textures, brought
the wide reception area to an end; several doors and a central
elevator system (obviously provided for those whose vertigo
somewhat reduced the joy of viewing the city panorama while
rising above it) were spaced along the wall.

Mather had spotted him and was rising from his seat, one
hand pushing against his cane for support. Halloran went forward to meet him.

"Rather splendid, isn't it?" said Mather as they drew near.

"Even better than Changi airport," Halloran replied, shaking the Planner's hand.

"Good to see you, Liam. Sorry about the Irish operation."

Halloran nodded, said nothing.

"Let's check in and get our instructions," suggested
Mather, turning away and limping toward the circular reception desk. Halloran followed, still taking in the scene around
him.

A receptionist watched their approach and, when they reached him, asked with no curiosity at all: "Can I help you?"

"Mather and Halloran—to see Sir Victor Penlock. Ten o'clock appointment."

If the uniformed receptionist was impressed that they were there for a meeting with the corporation's chairman he gave no indication.

"Company?" he inquired.

"I think you'll find that information isn't necessary," Mather told him.

The receptionist, a youngish man with spectacles and a distinct lack of charm, sat at his desk and tapped computer keys. Green lines of type reflected in his glasses, and soon he appeared satisfied, although there was little change in his demeanor.

"You'll need ID tags," he told them, and punched more keys on a machine concealed from view beneath the counter. When his hand appeared once more it was holding two yellow strips with Mather's and Halloran's names typed individually in capitals on each. He slipped them into plastic clips and passed them over.

"Attach these to your lapels, please. You need to go up to the eighteenth. You can take the scenic route to twelve, then transfer to an interior elevator for the rest of the way. Or if you prefer, you can take the interior express straight up to the eighteenth." He pointed at the elevator banks beyond the reception circle.

"I rather fancy the scenic route," said Mather brightly. "What d'you say, Liam?"

Halloran smiled as he clipped on his name tag. "Fine by me."

They crossed the busy floor to one of the capsule elevators, Mather chattering like a child looking forward to an amusement-park ride. They saw one of the elevators discharging its load and headed toward it, Mather quickly pressing the button for the twelfth floor once they were inside so that they would be alone.

The older man's mood became serious, although he peered through the thick glass, looking for familiar landmarks as the elevator rose above the streets.

"What went wrong, Liam?" he asked.

Halloran, too, watched the shrinking streets, the broadening view. "My guess is that our client died at the time of kidnap or soon after. We already knew from his company's medical report he had a weak heart. He'd suffered a minor heart attack two years before."

"But you didn't know he was dead before you went in with the money."

Halloran shook his head. The Thames was coming into view, its surface silver in the bright sunshine. To the west was St. Paul's, to the east the Tower of London; other landmarks, gray in the distance, were beginning to appear. "I had the notion. They would never let me speak to him on the phone, told me I had to take their word for it that he was in good shape. There was little choice."

"Thugs," said Mather. "Murdering IRA thugs."

"They consider themselves to be at war."

"Kidnap and murder? Indiscriminate bombings? A strange war."

"There's never been a normal one."

The older man glanced at Halloran. "I know you too well to imagine you have any truck with the IRA."

Halloran watched a dragonfly helicopter inching its way along the river, keeping strictly to its assigned route where an air accident could cause the least damage, as it headed for the Battersea heliport.

"I read your report," Mather said to break the silence. "Why the Heckler & Koch? An Ingram is more compact, easier to conceal."

"Our own man had to examine the client—I needed accuracy so that he wouldn't get hit. And I didn't know how many I'd be up against, so I had to have the choice of switching to automatic. It was a pity for them their victim wasn't a well man—their organization could have been a lot richer."

"And a pity his company didn't call us in earlier as more than just negotiators. He might not have been abducted in the first place under our protection." Mather shook his head with regret. Then: "At least publicity was avoided."

Halloran smiled grimly. The last thing Achilles' Shield wanted was attention from the media, always preferring to remain anonymous, not only in name but in role also. Too many Members of Parliament were fighting to introduce a bill banning K & R organizations such as Shield, condemning them as an inducement to kidnap rather than a deterrent. He had removed their client's corpse from the scene of the shooting, leaving it by the roadside in another county to be discovered by others. Because of that, the two incidents hadn't been connected—at least, not by the public. The authorities on both sides of the border, who had cooperated with Shield before on similar K & R operations, had turned a blind eye (although the Garda naturally hadn't been happy about the killings on their territory).

"Here we are," Mather said as the elevator glided to a smooth halt. The doors sighed open and the two men stepped out.

They found themselves in another reception area, although this was far less impressive than that on ground level, and much quieter. Through the windows to their right they could see a wide, open terrace, white tables and chairs placed all around, the building itself recessed here to provide a spectacular viewing platform over the southern half of London. It was empty of observers at the moment, the sun too feeble to take the chill from the breeze at that altitude.

A few people sat inside, though, waiting in the beige loungers, while Magma staff wandered through, some carrying documents, others collecting the visitors and leading them off to second-stage elevators or into corridors branching from the lobby.

The desk on this level was set into the wall and stationed by only two blue-uniformed men. A girl was standing by the counter talking to one of them. On seeing Mather and Halloran emerge from the elevator she broke off conversation and hurried over.

"Mr. Charles Mather?" she asked, smiling engagingly.

The older man raised a hand. "And this is Mr. Halloran," he said, indicating.

"I'm Cora Redmile. Sir Victor sent me down to fetch you." She shook hands with both men.

She was slender, dark-haired, her eyes a muddy brown flecked with green. Mid or late twenties, Halloran guessed. Her smile was mischievous as she looked at him.

"I hope you enjoyed the journey up," she said. "Some visitors are quite unsettled by the time they reach the twelfth floor."

Halloran only smiled back, and for a moment uncertainty flashed in her eyes.

"Absolutely splendid, m'dear," Mather answered. "Marvelously clear day for spying the landscape. You should make people buy tickets."

The girl gave a short laugh. "Compliments of Magma. If you come with me I'll take you to the eighteenth. Mr. Quinn-Reece is waiting with Sir Victor."

"Up to the aerie. Splendid."

Still smiling, the girl turned away and they followed her to the row of interior elevators.

Inside and on their way, Mather said: "You'd be Sir Victor's personal secretary, I take it."

"No, not Sir Victor's," she replied, and made no further comment.

"Ah," murmured Mather, as if satisfied.

Halloran leaned back against the wall, feeling the slight headiness of blood pressured by high speed. He caught the girl looking at him and she quickly averted her gaze.

"My goodness," said Mather. "We're fairly shifting, aren't we?"

"I can slow us down if you prefer," Cora told him, anxiously reaching for a button on the console.

"Not at all. I'm rather enjoying the experience."

She smiled at Mather's glee, her hand dropping back to her side. Once again, her gaze strayed to Halloran. In his dark tweed jacket, with its leather elbow patches, his check shirt and loose-knitted tie, he should have resembled a country squire; only he didn't. Far from it. And there was something about his eyes . . . He looked like a man who could be cruel. Yet there was a quiet gentleness about him too. Cora was puzzled. And interested.

"How many security men does the building have?"

Halloran's question took her by surprise. There was a softness to his voice also, the slightest trace of an accent. West Country? No, Irish. With a name like Halloran it had to be.

"Oh, I think Sir Victor has all those details ready for you," she answered quickly, realizing she had been lost for a moment.

He looked at her steadily. "You know why we're here?"

Now she wasn't sure if there was an accent at all. "Yes. I'll be assisting you."

Mather raised his eyebrows at Halloran.

A small *ping* as the elevator came to a halt. The doors drew back like stage curtains to reveal a sumptuous lobby, its thick carpet a deep mauve, hessian walls the palest green. Ceiling lights were recessed so that soft glows puddled the corridors leading off from the open area. Strategically placed lamps and spotlights compensated for the lack of natural light. A wide chrome and glass desk faced the elevators, and the girl sitting behind it rose as soon as their feet sank into the lush carpet.

"Good morning. Sir Victor is ready to see you. May I arrange some tea or coffee?"

"Tea would be very nice," said Mather.

"Any preference?"

"I'll leave that to you, m'dear, though I'm partial to Earl Grey."

"Earl Grey it is." She raised her eyebrows at Halloran, who said, "Coffee, black, no preference."

"If you'll follow me," said Cora, and led them into the corridor beyond the high-tech desk.

There were no doors, but display cases were set into the walls on either side, each depicting the corporation's worldwide industrial and mining activities, either photographically or as models: a vast borate minerals open-pit mine, Mojave Desert; a hydrofluoric acid plant, UK; a pyrite mine, Spain; gold, silver, and emerald mines, Zimbabwe; open-pit copper, South Africa; oil and gas wells, UK and global. And more: tin, uranium, diamonds, coal, low-grade ores, all manner of base and precious metals, some, like molybdenum (a silver-white metal), that the two men had never even heard of. Toward the end of the corridor was an encased back-lit map, bright red circles indicating areas of exploration and research around the world; there were a lot of red circles.

It was something of a relief when they arrived in a wide area flooded by daylight, both men feeling that they had just emerged from an educational passage in a geological museum. If visitors to Magma's chairman were meant to feel overawed, perhaps even intimidated by the time they reached his office, then the ruse was effective.

"Nothing like flaunting it," Mather quietly remarked to Halloran.

"The Magma Corporation is very proud of its many interests," said Cora with no hint of reprimand in her tone.

"So it seems." Mather smiled sweetly at her.

Broader corridors stretched left and right, glass-walled

rooms with vertical blinds, most of these open, on either side. Sounds buzzed from them: muted conversations, ringing telephones, clattering typewriters. But Cora crossed the open space before them, going to a wide double-door which looked so solid that Halloran wondered if she had the strength to push it open.

It opened with ease. She stood back to allow them through.

Now they were in an office shared by two secretaries; one could have modeled for *Vogue,* while the other, with her heavy-framed spectacles and wire-frizzed hair, might have looked well on the cover of *Science Today.* Both were busily involved with word processors; they barely glanced up.

Directly ahead was another large door. Cora went to it, tapped once, entered. A brief announcement, then she turned and beckoned Mather and Halloran through.

4

THE NEED FOR SECRECY

The chairman's office was high-ceilinged, the wall at the far end mostly tinted glass; it looked disconcertingly easy to step off the edge into open space. The chairman's oak desk was almost as wide as the room and the only traditional piece of furniture present. The rest comprised black leather and chrome, with dark ash units around the walls. The chairman himself was as imposing as the rest of the Magma building.

Sir Victor Penlock was tall and slim, with silver and gray hair aplenty, and no sign of relaxed stomach muscles. He wore a gray double-breasted suit, the material of which had a subtle sheen. His face was sharp, light blue eyes keen. His grip was firm when he greeted first Mather, then Halloran, shaking their hands, studying their faces. He spent a second longer studying Halloran's. "I understand you haven't yet met Quinn-Reece," he said to him.

The deputy chairman came forward. "I'm told you'll be particularly suited for protection cover of this kind. You prefer working on a one-to-one basis."

"We'll see," Halloran replied, disliking the clamminess of Quinn-Reece's hand.

"I beg your pardon?"

"We'll see if I'm suited after I've spoken to the target. We don't appear to know much about him."

"My apologies for that," cut in Sir Victor. "But there are reasons." He indicated chairs. "Please, won't you sit down, then perhaps we can put you fully in the picture."

The chairman took his place behind the desk, and the others found themselves seats around the room. Cora, Halloran noticed, sat in a chair by the wall as though she were an observer of the meeting rather than a partaker.

"By the time most new visitors to Magma reach my office," Sir Victor began, "they've become aware of the corporation's numerous activities throughout the world, so it should be unnecessary for me to give you a detailed lecture on our size and strength. Suffice it to say that we're recognized as a major force as far as mining, industrial, and energy interests are concerned. No doubt you've taken note of the various companies that form our group. They have their own identity because for the past twenty years we've practiced a decentralized system of management which encourages the profitable development of individual companies inside their own industries and locations. Between them, they either produce, process, and fabricate most prime metals—anything from aluminium to zinc—as well as manufacture industrial, construction, and engineering products and chemicals; or they may supply raw materials for energy, principally coal, oil, gas, and uranium."

He paused. "I said I wasn't going to lecture, didn't I? No matter—I *am* leading up to an important point. So, you have an idea of what Magma and its companies are all about. We employ over eighty thousand people throughout the world, twenty thousand of those in the UK."

There was a light tap on the door and a woman in a pale blue uniform shirt and dark blue skirt brought in a tray of tea and coffee. Sir Victor waited for the beverages to be distributed and for the door to close again before continuing.

"As a corporation involved in enormous investments both here and abroad, we have two considerable problems. One is that large fluctuations in currency exchange rates give us immense difficulty in predicting the economic environment in which long-term investment decisions will come to maturity."

Halloran caught Mather's eyes glazing over and hid his grin behind the coffee cup. Sir Victor's diction was crisp and clear, yet nothing could prevent the words themselves entering the brain as a drone.

"Unfortunately, the lengthy lead times from feasibility study to commercial operation mean that decisions have to be made today concerning the next generation of mining projects. In other words, we have to decide now what will be best for Magma in, say, seven to ten years' time. You'll appreciate just how difficult that might be."

"Yes, yes," Mather appreciated. "I should think you'd need to be a fortune-teller to do that."

Mather smiled broadly, but Sir Victor and his second-in-command regarded him soberly.

"You're nearer the truth than you might imagine," said the chairman.

Mather's eyebrows arched and he shot a look at Halloran.

Sir Victor leaned back in his chair and swiveled it sideways, his head turning away from them to examine the view outside. It was an odd gesture, almost as though he was suddenly reluctant to face them directly. Yet his manner was uncompromising when he spoke.

"What I'm about to tell you, gentlemen, must not go beyond these walls." He turned back to them, his eyes boring into theirs. "I must have your solemn promise on that."

Mather was quick to respond. "My company has already given assurances regarding confidentiality."

"I'm not referring to Achilles' Shield. I mean Mr. Halloran and yourself. This matter cannot even be discussed within your own organization. May I have your word?"

"That would be highly irregular. If our assignment is to be watertight, we must have every cooperation from—"

"You will have that. In full. But there are certain details which are not essential to your planning that must not become common knowledge"—he held up a hand against Mather's protest—"even among a select few. In fact, there aren't many inside the Magma Corporation itself who are privy to this information. I can promise you, though, your security arrangements will not be affected to any significant degree."

"I shall have to confer with my senior colleagues," Mather said dubiously.

"Let's agree."

All eyes went to Halloran, who had spoken.

"It can't do any harm." He placed his empty coffee cup on a small table by his chair. "But there are conditions. If anything illegal is involved here, then we're out. And you must tell us everything—no little details held back. If we don't like what we hear, Shield withdraws. Simple as that."

Quinn-Reece looked set to bluster, but his chairman smiled.

"That sounds reasonable," Sir Victor remarked. "Thank you for being so direct, Mr. Halloran; it saves time. Are you in accordance with this?" He aimed the question at Mather, who smiled too. He was used to Halloran's bluntness. "I suppose I have no objections," he answered, as if wondering to himself.

"Very well." The chairman appeared to relax a little. "A moment or two ago you suggested we might need a fortune-teller to predict safe investments for the ongoing profitability of the corporation . . ."

"A mild joke," put in Mather. "I noticed you didn't laugh."

"Nor would we. Would you be surprised if I revealed that despite all the highly sophisticated research methods, our extensive statistics for forward planning, explorations of new territories, satellite surveys using microwave, ultraviolet and infrared radiation, structural analyses, advanced computer calculations—all that, and more—much of our new growth depends almost entirely on the special ability of one person?"

"I'd be very surprised," Mather replied without hesitation.

"As our competitors would be if they knew. As would the press, and of course our shareholders. Yes, I suppose such a revelation would create amusement in some quarters. And great personal risk to our man from others."

"Your rivals? Surely not?"

"When the stakes are so high, and discovery of fresh raw materials diminishing so rapidly, access to new fields proving more and more difficult and expensive, there develops over the years a competitively cutthroat situation—and I use that term literally."

"Is this why you want your man so heavily insured?" asked Halloran.

Sir Victor nodded.

"He's already received threats?"

"Not exactly."

Mather interrupted. "Look here, can we slow this down for a minute? I'm not clear at all on just what this employee of yours does for Magma. Are you saying he's some kind of exploration wizard? And isn't it time we were told his name? All this non-identity business is only serving to compound my confusion."

Halloran knew the older man's mind was far too sharp to be fogged by anything said so far; this was merely the Planner's way of drawing out basic information that so often prospective clients were reluctant to convey.

"'Exploration wizard' is not entirely correct, although 'wizard' might be appropriate in some respects." Sir Victor allowed a small laugh between himself and his deputy chairman. Again Halloran found the girl, Cora, watching him closely.

"Gentlemen," said Sir Victor, his tone serious once more. "It's time you met your—how is it you refer to them? Target? —yes, it's time you met your target. I think then all will be made clear. At least, I hope that will be the case."

With that, he stood and indicated a door leading off from his office. Mather and Halloran rose too, both more than a little curious.

5

THE WHITE ROOM

He was tired. He'd had to leave Ireland discreetly, traveling south by road to Wexford, hiring a boat to take him from there across to a point just outside Newport, Wales, the journey made in the dead of night. The sea had been rough, but that hadn't bothered Halloran unduly. No, it was disappointment that had dragged his spirits down, exhausted him.

He hated to lose a man. The negotiations for the release of the kidnap victim had gone on for weeks, with Halloran using all the techniques he had learned over the years dealing with terrorists such as these: when to play tough, when to appease, when to hedge, when to sound innocently confused. Anything to gain more time and information. The first priority was always to retrieve the client unharmed—unharmed as possible, anyway, the capture of his or her abductors a minor consideration. If that wasn't possible, then it was vital that the kidnappers did not get their hands on the ransom money. That would make them too careless with their victims' lives in future snatches. It would also upset whoever was supplying the money.

Terrorists, as opposed to the normal criminal (if there was such an animal), were always tricky to deal with because they were invariably neurotic, unpredictable, and given to bouts of violence toward their captives and quite often those negotiating the release. The IRA were different. Oh, they had all those faults, and others not mentioned, but they could be cool and calculating—and sometimes more cruel because of it. There was no trust in them, and no trusting in them. They were a conscienceless and dangerous entity.

Which was why Halloran was so often chosen to deal with them.

But this current assignment with Magma puzzled him. Not as to why *he* had been chosen to handle it—he worked best alone, when he didn't have to rely on others—but more specifically, why the corporation had allowed only one protector working on the inside. For the incredible amount of money paid to insure the target's life, he should have had a small army around him, even though he had four bodyguards of his own. Could keeping secret his function for Magma be that important? Apparently so.

They were in yet another elevator, the access to which had been in a small antechamber next door to the chairman's office, and were rising toward the twenty-second floor. Quinn-Reece was no longer with them, having excused himself to attend another meeting elsewhere.

"Two floor buttons only," remarked Mather, looking at the panel set by the doors.

"This is a private elevator and only travels between the eighteenth and twenty-second," Sir Victor explained. "A limited number of employees are allowed to use it."

"And the twenty-third and -fourth?"

"Living quarters and machinery rooms, the latter being at the very top."

What price a sky-high penthouse in the heart of the city? Halloran silently mused. And whose penthouse? The chairman's? Maybe the target's, if he really was that important to the corporation. There were a lot of questions still hanging in the air.

The elevator walls were a glossy black, the occupants' reflected figures like shadowy ghosts around them. The overhead light was subdued, and it would have been easy to imagine they were traveling below the earth's surface rather than up toward the clouds.

Movement stopped, a subtle sensation, and the doors parted. The corridor beyond was as gloomy as the elevator's interior.

A heavyset man stood opposite, close to the wall, as if he had been awaiting their arrival. His arms were folded across a broad chest and they dropped to his sides in a token gesture of attention when he saw the chairman.

"He's ready for us?" asked Sir Victor, stepping from the elevator first with no deference to Cora's gender or courtesy toward his guests.

The man nodded. "He's waiting." There was just a hint of civility in his voice, his accent American.

From his thick-set stature and uncomfortable appearance in his business suit, it was easy for Mather and Halloran to surmise that this man was one of the bodyguards. His hair was long, incongruously (considering the staid suit) tied into a tail behind. Sullen eyes set in a pudgy face flicked over the visitors. At first, Halloran had thought the man's cheeks were unusually ruddy, but when he moved closer he realised that a patchwork of thin, livid scars emblazoned both sides of his face. Without further words the bodyguard led the way along the corridor, keeping at least six feet ahead of the entourage. The walls on either side were bare and dark, and Halloran brushed fingers against one side, feeling a coarse material: the covering was black hessian. It was unusually cold in that corridor, yet the gloom was beginning to feel stifling.

They turned to the right, a large double-door facing them. Its surface, like the elevator walls, was glossy black, and for one startling moment Halloran had the impression of apparitions approaching them. As the bodyguard leaned forward, extending both hands to grip the separate door handles, his spectral reflection leaned closer as if to snatch him. Both sides of the double-door were pushed open, the bodyguard standing aside to allow the party through.

The room was huge and almost blindingly white.

"Welcome to limbo," a voice said.

6

FELIX KLINE

The man who had spoken wasn't what Mather or Halloran expected at all.

He didn't look worth fifty million pounds. He didn't seem like someone whom a multinational, first-league corporation could possibly be dependent upon. He looked nothing like a genius, and nothing like a wizard.

He was something of a disappointment.

At first their eyes had been stung by the unexpected dazzle, the abrupt contrast between gloom and astonishing brightness. But as they blinked away the irritation, they were gradually able to take in their new surroundings. There were no windows, and there was no furniture apart from a low, moderate-sized dais in the center of the luminously white floor. If there were other exits around the room, they could not be discerned against the white walls, at least not until their eyes had become accustomed to the glare. Even the high ceiling was of white light. The whole effect was of vast and empty space that served to make the figure sitting on the edge of the dais seem even more insignificant.

He was wearing jeans and a blue sweatshirt chopped off at the elbows, his legs stretched out before him, ankles crossed, his hands behind him and flat against the surface of the small platform. He grinned at the group standing in the doorway.

"The sudden change wipes your mind clean, doesn't it?" he said. Then he laughed a peculiar high-pitched giggle. "That's the idea, y'see. A blank mind, a clean slate; a white sheet, waiting to be filled with images. I can make everything black if you prefer?" He looked at them with eager expectancy.

"Not just now, Felix," said Sir Victor quickly. "Not if you don't mind. I want to introduce you to Mr. Mather and Mr.

Halloran from Achilles' Shield, the company I discussed with you."

The man addressed as Felix stood and ambled over to them, hands tucked into the back pockets of his jeans. He was well below average height, about five-three, his shoulders slightly rounded so that he appeared to stoop. His age could have been anywhere from twenty-five to thirty-five. His curly hair was dark and unkempt, his complexion swarthy, almost yellowish. And his eyes, above a hooked nose, were large and pitchy, as deep and shiny as oil pools.

"Let me guess," he said, grinning again, and looking over their heads.

There was something odd about his eyes, and Halloran couldn't quite figure out what.

He stepped before them, lowered his gaze. "You," he said, stabbing a finger at Mather. "You're Mather. You're the Organizer—no, no, the *Planner,* that's what you're called, right? Am I right? Course I'm right. Damn right. And you . . ." He faced Halloran.

His grin dropped away for an instant.

The grin was back, but humor was lacking. "And you are Halloran," he said more slowly, less excitedly. "The Muscle. No, no, not just that. A bit more than that. Shit, you're a cold bastard."

Halloran returned his stare and realized what was bothering him about the smaller man's eyes. The pupils were unusually enlarged. With all the dazzling brightness around them, they should have been almost pinpoints. Smack? Could be. He seemed hyped up.

"This is Felix Kline," Sir Victor interposed. "The person you've been engaged to protect."

If Mather was surprised he didn't show it. "I'm very pleased to meet you, Mr. Kline."

"That you are," agreed Kline. "How about you, Halloran? You pleased to meet me?"

"You might grow on me," replied Halloran.

The girl stepped in quickly. "There are lots of arrangements to make, Felix. These gentlemen will have to know your day-to-day movements, your plans in advance, how best their people can cover you twenty-four hours a day."

"People?" snapped Kline. "We agreed only one. Halloran's it."

"He'll need backup," said Mather, beginning to get annoyed with this volatile young man. "He can't keep his eyes on you every minute of the day and night. There has to be outside protection."

Kline was still watching Halloran. "All right. You take care of that, Cora—you know my movements better than I do. Give the details to Mather, he's the brains. I want to be alone with Halloran for a while. If he's going to be my constant companion we'd better get to know each other a little. What d'you say, Halloran? D'you have a first name?"

"Liam."

"Yeah? I'll call you Halloran. It's okay for you to call me Felix." He smiled then, and suddenly looked like an innocent. He turned to the chairman of Magma. "Listen, Victor, I need to see you later about Bougainville."

"Copper?" asked Sir Victor.

"Uh-huh. Think so. A source we haven't tapped yet."

"That's good news if you're sure."

Kline was irritated. "I can't be sure. You know I can't be *sure!*"

"No, I'm sorry, of course not," the chairman appeased. "We'll discuss it later. When you're ready."

"Okay, okay. Now leave me alone with Halloran. We've got things to discuss. You come back when you're through, Cora."

They left, only the bodyguard lingering by the door. Kline snapped his fingers, then pointed, and the heavyset man followed the others, closing the double-doors behind him.

"Mystified, Halloran?" said Kline, walking backward, away from him, toward the low dais at the center of the room, his white sneakers squeaking against the shiny floor. "Yeah, I bet you are. How come a little creep like me can tell a big wheel like Sir Victor what or what not to do?" He hopped onto the platform and stood with legs apart, thin arms folded across his chest.

"I'd be interested to find out," said Halloran, remaining where he was. His voice sounded hollow in the empty space around them.

"Yeah, and I'd be interested to find out about you. You bother me, Halloran, and I don't like that."

Halloran shrugged. "You can always ask for someone else. There are plenty of good operatives at Shield who could take my place. But if I bother you, you might be more prepared to do as I say. It's your life I'll be protecting, remember."

"Could I forget?" He dropped to the floor again and sat on the edge of the dais, elbows on knees, his body hunched. "You got questions you want to ask?"

Halloran walked over and sat next to him. "Tell me exactly what you do for Magma. That'll be useful for starters."

Kline laughed, a quick explosive sound. "You mean the old boy hasn't told you? Probably wanted to lead you into it gently. Okay, Halloran, sit there and listen—you're about to be educated."

He was on his feet again, skittishly pacing up and down before his one-man audience.

"I welcomed you to limbo, right? Well, that's what this room represents. Nothingness. A void. Nothing to distract, nothing at all to interest. Not unless I do this!"

He darted toward the dais, reached for something behind Halloran. He held the rectangular object in one hand, and Halloran saw it was a plain white remote-control unit, even the buttons colorless and unmarked so that it had been almost invisible against its resting place. Kline aimed the sensor cells and thumbed a button.

The room was instantly plunged into total darkness.

Halloran moved instinctively, changing his position on the dais, going to his left. He heard a dry chuckle from somewhere in the inkiness, an eerie scratching sound that stiffened the muscles of his back.

"A different kind of void, isn't it?" came Kline's voice.

Halloran twisted his head, hopelessly trying to locate the source in the pitch black.

"It's full of things," Kline said, and this time he sounded close, almost by Halloran's shoulder.

"Bad things," Kline whispered in his ear.

Halloran rose, reached out. Touched nothing.

"And now we do this," said the voice.

Halloran squeezed his eyes shut against the burst of light from one of the walls. He opened them cautiously, giving his pupils time to adjust. Some distance away an unmarked relief map of South America glowed.

Light reflected off Kline, who stood six feet away to Halloran's right. His hand, holding the remote, was extended toward the brightly lit map. He shifted his aim.

"Now this," he said. *Click*. Another map. North America by the side of South.

"This. This. This." Kline used his arm as a pointer, turning slowly, maps of different countries appearing one after the other, lining the upper halves of the walls, all the way around. India, Africa, Spain, Australia, Indonesia, Alaska, many more, plus sections of land or islands he didn't immediately recognize. They illuminated the room, large, detailed murals in greens and browns, with seas unnaturally blue.

Kline was grinning at him, his face and body a kaleidoscope of soft colors.

"Satellite photographs," Kline told him. "We're looking down at Mother Earth from outer space. Now look at this." He carelessly aimed the remote at one of the relief maps. A button clicked. The map became an incredibly detailed flat study, exactly in scale to the one it overlaid, but with towns, villages, rivers, and mountains clearly marked. "Something else, right, Halloran? I can tell you're impressed."

Click.

The pictures around the wall disappeared, shut off together save for one. An island.

"Know this place, Halloran? New Guinea." The relief zoomed up, the left side growing out of frame. The map froze again. "Papua New Guinea, a steamy hellhole. But rich in certain things."

He watched Kline return to the dais, a shadowy, back-lit figure that somehow exuded electric energy. The small man squatted in the middle of the low rostrum, ankles crossed, crouching forward toward the screen.

"Copper, for one," Kline said, his eyes intent on the bright picture. His voice became dulled as he concentrated. "My deed for the day as far as Magma's concerned. It already has a copper mine down there, but it's running low. Did you know the demand for copper is up ten percent after the long recession? No, guess you didn't. Why should you? Shit, I hardly care myself. But old Sir Vic does, him and his cronies. Big money to them, y'see. Well, looks like I found 'em a new source, quite a ways from the established mine. Did that this morning, Halloran, before you arrived."

Halloran stared. "You found them copper? I don't understand."

Kline laughed gleefully, smacking the platform beneath

him with his free hand. "And who can blame you? You're like the rest: no concept of the mind's real power. Reason is mankind's disease, did you know that? A wasting away of senses. So what do you care? A dumb bodyguard is all you are."

"So educate me a little more."

Click.

Total darkness once again.

Halloran softly walked to a new position.

Kline's disembodied voice came to him. "All this black worry you, Halloran?"

He didn't answer.

"Make you wonder what it's concealing? You know you're in an empty room, you saw that when the lights were on. But now you're not so sure. Because you can't see anything. So your own mind invents for you."

A chuckle in the dark.

"You can hear me, so you know I'm here, right, Halloran? 'Bout six or seven feet away? But if I touch you . . ."

A cold finger scraped Halloran's cheek.

". . . now that scares you. Because reason tells you it doesn't make sense."

Halloran had instinctively gone into a crouch. He shifted position again, heard his own feet scuff the floor.

"Scares the shit out of you, right?"

A finger prodded his back.

Halloran moved again and kept moving, reaching out for a wall, something solid on which to get his bearings. His stretched fingers touched a face.

Then brilliant light forced his eyes shut.

"You were helpless. I had you cold."

They were on the platform once more, Halloran steadily forcing his jarred nerves to settle, Kline sitting beside him, grinning, his oil-slick eyes watching. Halloran could smell the other man's sweat, could see the damp patches beneath his armpits.

"Sure, you had me cold," he agreed. "What was the point though?"

"A tiny lesson about the unreality of reality. You asked me to educate you some more."

"That wasn't what I had in mind."

Kline giggled. "Fear was something I put into you. And you did feel fear."

"Maybe."

"Yet you knew it was only me and you in here. A little guy like me up against a trained heavy like you. Unreasonable, wouldn't you say? The darkness overcame your reason, don't you see? Made you vulnerable."

"I admit I was disoriented."

"Much more, I think."

"It hasn't helped me understand anything. I don't see what it had to do with finding copper on a map."

"Perhaps it was a demonstration and a test at the same time." The coarseness had left Kline's voice and his manner had subtly changed, the banter all but gone to be replaced by a cool mocking. "A silly game, yes, but I wanted to gauge your reaction to, as you put it yourself, disorientation. My life appears to be in your hands, after all."

"Let's get on to that later. Talk to me about copper in New Guinea. How did you locate this new source?"

"Through my mind, of course. Intuition, second sight, sixth sense, extrasensory perception—call it what you will. I look at maps and I perceive hidden minerals and ores. Even stores of raw energy. I can tell where they can be found beneath the earth's crust. Oh, I don't mean to boast—I'm not always right. Seventy-five percent of the time I am, though, and that's good enough for Magma. Oh yes, that's more than good enough for Sir Victor Penlock and his board of directors."

Halloran slowly shook his head. "You find these . . . these deposits with your mind? Like a diviner locates underground springs?"

"Huh! Finding water beneath the soil is the easiest thing in the world. Even *you* could do that. No, it's a bit more involved. Let's say scientific geological studies and even carefully calculated estimations point me in the right direction. I'm given an area to look at—it could cover thousands upon thousands of square miles—and I totally shed irrelevant matters from my thoughts. This room helps me do that: its emptiness cleanses my mind."

He waved a hand around at the room. By using the remote control a few moments before, Kline had dimmed the light considerably, rendering the walls and floor a pale, cheerless gray. Halloran could now see faint lines where the screens were imbedded. He also noticed tiny sensors strategically and discreetly positioned to pick up commands from the console held loosely in the other man's hand. The room was ingenious in structure and design.

"Can you understand why I'm so valuable to the corporation?" asked Kline, gazing down at the floor and massaging his temples with stiffened fingers as though easing a headache. "Have you any idea how fast the developed countries are using up our resources—fossil fuels, minerals, metals, timber, even soils? We're rapidly running them down. World-wide we're searching and digging and consuming. We've gotten greedy. The big corporations don't believe in restraint: they've always done their utmost to supply the demand, with no cautions, no warnings, nothing to upset the flow of cash into their silk-lined pockets."

He raised his head and there was something sly about his smile when he looked at Halloran.

"Now they're getting scared. The harder new sources of raw materials are to find, the more concerned they get; the more expensive it is to scour those materials from the earth, the more jittery they become. That's what makes me Magma's biggest asset, why I'm so precious to the corporation. Even fifty million pounds would hardly compensate for my death."

Halloran rose and walked away, his hands tucked into his trouser pockets, head bowed as though he were deep in thought. He turned, looked back at the small watching figure.

"That's some story you're asking me to swallow," Halloran said.

Kline's cackled laughter shot across the room. "You don't believe me! You don't believe I can do it! All I've shown you and you think this is some kind of game. Wonderful!" He pummeled his feet on the white floor with the joke of it.

Halloran spoke calmly. "I said it's hard to believe."

Kline became still. "You think I give a shit what you believe? All you have to do is protect me, nothing more than that. So maybe it's time I found out how good you are."

His thumb worked the remote-control unit once more, and a buzzer or a light must have alerted the man outside the double-door because one side opened and the bodyguard stepped through.

"Halloran here doesn't think you're up to much, Monk," said Kline. "You want to give him a little workout, introduce yourself?"

Monk wasn't smiling when he approached.

Halloran still faced Kline. "I don't do auditions," he said.

"In that case Monk's liable to break your arms."

Halloran sighed and turned to meet the other man who was ambling forward as if he intended to do nothing more than shake the operative's hand. But there was a certain, recognizable, gleam in Monk's eyes.

He took the last two yards in a crouching rush.

To find Halloran was suddenly behind him.

Monk felt Halloran's foot planted squarely against his rear end, a hard shove propelling him further forward, the action one fluid movement. All balance gone, the bodyguard skidded to his knees, reduced to a clumsy scrabbling figure. He came up in a crouching position.

"Bastard." The curse was high-pitched, almost a squeal, as though his voice box was squeezed somewhere too low in his throat.

"Jesus, it speaks," said Halloran.

The bodyguard ran at him.

"Felix, call him off!"

It was Cora's voice, but Halloran didn't bother to look toward the doorway. He had no wish to hurt this lumbering ape-man but at the same time it was too early in the day to be playing silly games. He stepped aside from the charge again and brought his knee up into the bent man's lower ribs, using only enough force to bruise and upset his victim's breathing for a while.

Monk went down with a *whoosh* of escaping air and spittle from his open mouth. To give him credit, he immediately began to rise again, his face red and glowering. Resignedly, Halloran prepared to jab a pressure point in the man's neck to bring the contest to a swift and relatively harmless end.

But Cora strode between them to confront Kline. "Put a stop to this, Felix," she demanded. "Right now."

Halloran caught the brief flash of rage in the small man's

eyes before it was suppressed, and Kline beamed a smile of the innocent.

"Only a test, Cora," he all but simpered. "No harm done. I needed to know how good this guy was, that's all."

"He wouldn't have been recommended to us if he wasn't any good," she replied, her tone modified by now. She turned to Halloran. "I'm so sorry, this should never have happened."

Monk was clutching his sore ribs with one hand, looking from Halloran to Kline, awaiting further instructions.

"Wait outside," Kline snapped, obviously displeased with his man's performance. Then, to Halloran as Monk left the room with less ease than he had entered: "You move pretty fast."

"If he's your best, you've got problems," said Halloran.

"Oh, he's not my best; he's my ox." Kline rose from the dais, a quick feline movement. His eyes seemed even darker than before and glistened with some inner thought. "No doubt there are matters you will have to discuss with Cora concerning my future safety. She's my personal assistant—no, much more than that—so feel free to confide in her absolutely. Now I need a shower; I'm beginning to stink."

"You and I have a lot to go through," Halloran said to him.

"Tell it to her. I need to rest." It was a command, and Halloran frowned.

The girl touched his arm though, and he looked down at her. Kline was already walking away, heading toward a far corner of the room. He clicked a button on the unit he was still carrying, and a door that had been virtually invisible before slid back.

"Felix really does need to rest for a while," Cora said as they watched him disappear through the opening. "His special gift often leaves him quite exhausted."

Halloran had noticed the perspiration stain low at the back of Kline's sweatshirt as well as those beneath his arms, and his frown deepened. It was cool in the room, almost uncomfortably so. And when he had touched the small man in the darkness, Kline's skin had been cold.

He remembered that moment, remembered the shudder that had run through him.

For when his fingers had reached out and felt Kline's face in that total darkness, they had touched ridges and creases, dry, wrinkled skin that had no place on the features of a comparatively young man.

Reason told him he must have been mistaken, the shock of the moment creating an illusion, the sudden blinding light instantly wiping the image from his mind.

But now that thought—that *feeling*—had returned. And Kline, himself, had warned against reason.

7

KLINE'S PREMONITION

Cora picked at the salad, her interest centered on Halloran rather than on the food before her. The riverside terrace was beginning to fill with office workers on early lunch break, the fine weather after such a dreary winter proving an attraction. A pleasure boat filled with pink-faced tourists cruised by, the Thames a slaty blue again after months of sluggish grayness. New buildings lined the bank across the river alongside old decaying warehouses. There was still an edgy chill in the air, but it only served to make the new season more fresh, a cleanness in the breeze sweeping away the dregs of winter.

Halloran was winding his way through the circular tables, holding the two drinks chest high to avoid nudging heads and shoulders of other diners.

She watched and she was just a little afraid of him. The casual way in which he had dealt with Monk's aggression made her wonder how lethal he could be if the situation were desperate. Yet at first glance he seemed anything but a violent man. He was tall, but not massive, his body lean, certainly not muscle-bound. Even his clothes were casual, nothing sharp or self-conscious about them.

That was at first glance. Take another look and notice the pale blue eyes, the warmth in them that could turn to a bleak coldness in an instant. She'd seen that happen when he'd been introduced to Felix. And Felix had been aware of it, too.

That worried her, for Felix might need this enigmatic man, no matter what mutual dislike had already sprung up between them. There was something about Halloran's quiet strength that was totally reassuring: he was a man to feel safe with—unless you were his enemy.

Cora thanked him with a smile as Halloran placed the gin

and tonic in front of her; she deliberately left it there, aware that she'd taken the first one too fast (to Halloran's surprised amusement). His own was a whiskey with ice, and he put it to one side as he tucked into his ham salad. She tried a dismal attack on her own food once again but gave up after a few mouthfuls.

"I don't seem to be very hungry today," she said, and wondered why it sounded like an apology. She lifted her glass and drank, finding the gin more sustaining than lettuce and cucumber.

Halloran nodded and took a healthy sip of his whiskey to keep her company. His smile was gentle.

"What part of Ireland were you born in, Mr. Halloran?" Cora asked, the sinking warmth from her second drink already beginning to relax her.

"Call me Liam," he replied. "I wasn't born in Ireland. My parents were Irish, but I was born here in London, although I grew up in Kilkenny. My father was a captain in the British Army, and spent much of his time abroad while Mother and I stayed on my grandfather's farm."

"And did you eventually join the army?"

"It was a natural enough thing to do." He put down his knife and cut pieces of cheese with the edge of his fork. "I need to know a good deal about your employer, Miss Redmile. His private life as well as business."

"Cora."

"Okay—Cora. Tell me about him. Tell me how long he's been your boss."

"I joined Magma about five or six years ago, but I haven't worked for Felix all that time."

He encouraged her with a nod.

"Felix took me on as his PA three years ago. I don't know why. He saw me when I was delivering some documents to Sir Victor's office one day from my department on the sixteenth. The documents were urgent, and I interrupted their meeting. Apparently he asked about me, and the next thing I knew he'd put in a request to have me as an assistant. I wasn't even sure who he was at that time, although I'd heard rumors."

"Rumors?"

"Yes. No more than office gossip. Felix Kline's presence at Magma has never been official; you won't find his name mentioned in company papers, not even on a pay slip or tax statement."

"Isn't that illegal?"

"Not if he's never been employed by the Magma Corporation. As far as the outside world is concerned, he could just be paying rent for the penthouse suite."

"Except I bet even that isn't on record," suggested Halloran.

"The official resident is Sir Victor himself."

"So Kline's role for the corporation really is that secret? Your board of directors is afraid that he'll be nabbed by the competition?"

"More than that. There are over a hundred thousand shareholders of Magma, most of them UK-registered: imagine their reaction if they found out their corporation was guided by a mystic."

"It's a relief to hear you say that. I was beginning to wonder if I was the one who was out of touch with modern business practices."

Cora laughed and he was glad. She had been tense ever since she'd taken him away from the white room, as if the minor tussle she'd witnessed between himself and the heavy had upset her. Later, in the daylight, he'd noticed a faint darkness beneath her eyes, like smudges under the surface skin, the look of someone who'd recently found sleep difficult. Maybe she was concerned for her employer, worried because the danger to him was considered serious enough to warrant hiring a K & R agency, despite the fact that Kline already had his own bodyguards.

"I gather—and this might sound naïve given all I've learned so far today—that Kline has achieved fantastic results for Magma."

"That's an understatement." Cora smiled at him before sipping from her glass.

"When did the corporation discover his talents?" Halloran left his fork on the plate and leaned forward, resting his folded arms on the edge of the table. "I mean, just who approached who?"

Now she avoided his eyes. "I'm not at liberty to say. I'm sorry, Liam, but my instructions are to supply you with information relevant only to your protection plans."

"Is there a reason for that?"

"The same reason that just one person—you—will be allowed to stay close to Felix: secrecy, discretion, call it what you like. The less people who know about Felix Kline, the easier Sir Victor and others will feel." She was suddenly anxious. "I'm not assuming too much, am I? You have accepted the assignment."

"Oh yes," he replied softly, and again there was something disconcerting in his eyes when he smiled. "But there are certain ground rules he'll have to agree to." Halloran reached into the inside pocket of his jacket and drew out a folded sheet of paper. "A simple list of dos and don'ts," he said, handing it to Cora. "Make sure he reads through it today. If Kline's willing to go by them, call Shield later this afternoon, talk to Mather."

"And if Felix isn't willing?"

"Then we've got problems. Possibly Shield will turn down the assignment."

"May I see the list?"

"Of course. You'll be part of the setup."

Cora unfolded the sheet of paper and ran her eyes over the lines of type. She nodded her head. "It all seems straightforward enough."

Halloran reached over and tapped the corner of the paper. "Point three there. Does Kline have a chauffeur?"

"Yes. One of his bodyguards. Janusz Palusinski."

"Is Palusinski familiar with antikidnap driving techniques?"

"I . . . I don't know."

"It's important."

"I'm sorry, I really have no idea. Palusinski has been with Felix a lot longer than I have."

"Okay. If he isn't he'll have to spend a day or so with one of Shield's drivers. He'll need to learn the handbrake turn, the reverse turn, how to break through a roadblock—that kind of thing. None of it's too difficult to master for an experienced driver. Until then, I'll do any driving for Kline."

Cora looked down the list again. "Covert signals?" she asked.

"We'll work out a system of identifying each other with code words. Handy for telephone conversations, knocking on doors, and the like. We'll arrange nonverbal signals too for emergencies where words either won't help or might put us at risk. Nothing fancy, just simple signs. There'll be other key words for use in a kidnap situation, words that will let us know if Kline is hurt, the number of abductors, maybe even clues to his location if he's aware of it himself. If he sticks to the rules there shouldn't be any need for those."

Cora shivered, caught by a breeze skimming off the river. "This is scary," she said.

"Sure it is. But that's how it should be—scary enough to keep you both on your toes."

"That isn't very reassuring."

"You're hiring my company for Kline's protection, not for giving false comfort. I've got to be frank with you, Cora: if an organization, be it terrorist or hoodlum, is out to get someone, it's virtually impossible to prevent them from at least making the attempt—and that's usually when people get hurt. We can only do our best to minimize the risk. But if it's any consolation, it's far easier to assassinate someone than it is to kidnap them."

She visibly paled.

Halloran leaned forward again and gripped her lower arm. "I didn't mean to alarm you. We *are* only talking about a kidnap-and-ransom situation here, aren't we? Nobody's threatened his life?"

Cora slowly shook her head and Halloran withdrew his hand.

"What is it, Cora? What's upsetting you? As I understand it, all we're going on is a 'feeling' Kline has that he's in some kind of danger, with no hard evidence of that really being the case."

"You don't know Felix, you've no idea of his psychic ability. He has powers . . ." Her voice trailed off.

"Yeah, I know—powers that are secret." Halloran looked away from her, toward the river. "Well that's between Magma and Kline. My only interest is protecting a man made of flesh and blood, someone as vulnerable as the rest of us. But if he knows something about this particular predicament he's in—or imagines he's in—he'd better tell me. What is it that's frightened him so much, Cora?"

She bowed her head for a moment. Her fingers curled around the base of her gin glass, which was now empty; she twisted the glass, sunlight glistening off its rim. A group at a nearby table laughed at a shared joke. The microphone voice

from a pleasure-boat guide drifted over the terrace parapet.
Cora's fingers became still.

"For the past week," she began, her voice low and hesitant, aware of the people around them, "Felix has been troubled by some kind of premonition. Nothing substantial,
nothing he can recognize. A dream, a nightmare, one that he
can never remember when he wakes. But he knows it's a
warning to him, a precognition of sorts that won't fully reveal
itself to him. It's made him distraught. No, more than that—
Felix is terrified."

"He didn't look that way to me," commented Halloran.

"He'd never show those feelings to an outsider. Felix is a
very private man."

"You're telling me he's had a premonition of his own
death?"

She gave a shake of her head. "No. No, something worse
than that."

A shadow fell across the table, startling them both. A barman collected their empty glasses, transferring them to a tray
of others.

"Lovely day," the barman said, turning away without waiting for a reply.

The girl looked across at Halloran. She said nothing more.

8

BODYGUARDS

Snaith wasn't happy.

"You mean Magma is going to all this bother because their man—this chap Kline—has had a premonition of some sort?" He glared at Halloran as though it were his fault.

Halloran himself seemed preoccupied. He scratched the back of his fingers against his jaw. "That's how it is," he said.

Snaith rested back in his chair, one hand still on the desk, fingers drumming a beat. "Ludicrous," he pronounced.

"Not to the corporation," said Mather, sitting in an easy-chair opposite Halloran, his bad leg stretched out before him. Now and again during the briefing and planning meeting he would absentmindedly rub his kneecap as if to ease the pain of the old wound. "They have great faith in this man's ability; I don't think it's for us to dismiss his foreboding so lightly."

Dieter Stuhr, sitting at one end of the Controller's desk, tapped the blunt end of his pencil against the large notepad in front of him. "Personally, I don't see how that affects us anyway. What goes on between Kline and the Magma Corporation is their affair. We should treat this like any other job."

"Of course you're right," agreed Snaith, "but this business bothers me. It's"—he shook his head, frustrated—"it's not logical. What kind of man is he, Liam?"

"Changeable," came the reply. "I'd say he's highly unstable—neurotic, in fact. He's going to be a problem."

"I see." Snaith's expression was grim. "Well, we've dealt with prima donnas before. And his personal bodyguards? What's your opinion of their worth?"

"I was only introduced to one. He wasn't very effective."

Nobody in the room asked him how he'd reached that conclusion; they accepted his word.

Mather consulted a notebook. "I have the names of the other three here. Let me see now, yes—Janusz Palusinski, his driver, then Asil Khayed and Youssef Daoud. They're described as personal attendants, which I suppose could imply anything."

"Good Lord," exclaimed Snaith. "Arabs?"

"Jordanians."

"And the first? Czech? Polish?"

"Janusz Palusinski—Polish."

"And the one you met, Liam?"

"Monk. He didn't say much."

"Theodore Albert Monk," Mather supplied from his notebook. "According to the Magma files, he's American."

"That's some mixed bag," commented Snaith.

"Apparently Felix Kline picked them up on his travels. They've all been with him for years."

"The driver might need some training," suggested Halloran.

"That's being taken care of," Snaith told him. "Kline's PA, Miss, uh—Redmile, rang me earlier this afternoon to arrange it. Dieter?"

"I've got him booked in for tomorrow. We'll lease Magma one of our own specials—for Palusinski to train in and to use afterward. Kline's own vehicle doesn't have enough protection facilities; body and windows are bulletproof, but that's about it. I'll want to keep Palusinski for at least two days, Liam, to make sure he really knows what he's doing when he leaves us, so it looks like you're Kline's chauffeur until then."

Halloran nodded.

Snaith spoke: "Miss Redmile also confirms that her employer agrees to the list of conditions regarding his own actions in the forthcoming weeks. I understand you had lunch with her today?" He was looking directly at Halloran. "Apart from their business relationship, what is she to Kline? Is she his mistress?"

Halloran took time to consider the question. Finally, he said, "She could be."

"She's that type?"

"What type?"

"The type who beds her boss."

"I wouldn't know."

"But she's a looker."

Halloran nodded.

"Let's assume that's the case, then."

Mather noticed the brief flare of anger in Halloran's eyes and was puzzled by it. Liam usually held his emotions totally in check. "I don't see that it's entirely relevant, Gerald," Mather put in. "After all, Kline isn't married, and there's no mention of other girlfriends—or boyfriends, for that matter—in the dossier from Magma."

"She could be a weak spot," Snaith replied. "He might put himself at risk if he knows she's in danger. There could be other possibilities, also. Has she been checked out?"

"I have her file right here," said Stuhr. "Charles brought it back from Magma earlier today, so I've only managed to glance through it. She sounds pretty solid to me. Raised in Hampshire, an only child, father a university lecturer, mother a local general practitioner, both now deceased. Attended private school until eighteen, bright—seven Os and three As—but never went on to university. Rents an apartment in Pimlico, has a substantial sum of money in her bank account—what's left of the proceeds from the sale of her parents' home, plus a little of her own savings. Magma is her first and only job apart from a bit of summertime temping when she was still a student; she worked her way up in the organization, and I think she is wonderful." He took a black-and-white photograph from the file and held it up for the others to see.

Snaith didn't smile. "Dig deeper over the next few days. Find out who she socializes with, boyfriends, lovers, her politics, religion—you know the kind of thing. She's close to the target, so we can't take chances."

Snaith paused, ran fingers through his short ginger-gray hair.

"Now," he said, looking around at all of them. "Our friend Mr. Kline. Just what the hell do we know about him?"

"Hardly anything," answered Stuhr. "It took me all of half a minute to read through his file."

"Hmm, that's what I was afraid of. This bloody secrecy can be taken too far."

"Oh, I don't think Magma is to blame," said Mather. "When I spoke with the chairman this morning it became very apparent that the corporation doesn't actually *know* too much about Felix Kline's background. I got the impression that so long as the man continues to make them money, they're not particularly bothered."

"Would somebody please tell me just what it is he *does* for Magma?" complained Stuhr.

"Sorry, Dieter," said Snaith, "that isn't necessary for you to know. Their terms, I'm afraid, so don't sulk. What does his file tell us?"

Stuhr made a snorting noise, but didn't argue. "Like I said —there isn't much. He was born in Israel, arrived in England eleven years ago, began working for the Magma Corporation almost immediately—"

"A Jew with two Arab companions?" interrupted Snaith.

"They're not all bitter enemies. He moved into the penthouse suite of the Magma building when it was completed about five years ago. He also has a country home in Surrey, by a lake, two thousand acres of pastures and woodland. I need hardly say that's a huge amount of land to own in the Home Counties. He's obviously a very wealthy man. Unmarried, doesn't drive, doesn't smoke, drinks a little, no mention of drugs—but there wouldn't be—doesn't gamble. That's about it."

"What?" said Snaith incredulously. "There must be more."

Stuhr reached for a file lying beneath Cora Redmile's. He opened it and indicated the single sheet of paper inside. "I told you there wasn't much to read."

"It must give his birth date, where he was educated, his employment before Magma. Isn't there anything about his social activities? It's essential that we at least have some idea of what those are."

"He doesn't appear to have any if this document is anything to go by."

"Charles?" Snaith appealed.

Mather waved a hand. "That's the situation, I'm afraid. Even in conversation the chairman gave nothing away. Naturally I probed, but got nowhere. As I said, they seem to know little about the man themselves, and I think that's of Kline's choosing; perhaps part of his own terms of employment was his complete privacy on all personal matters. If he'd already demonstrated how good his abilities were, I don't suppose the board objected too much."

"All right. I'm not happy, but let's accept the situation for what it is." Then Snaith asked hopefully, "I suppose his salary isn't in there somewhere?"

Stuhr grinned and shook his head. "Not even a hint."

"We could find out from other sources, but let's not waste our time. In fact, there's a lot more information we could uncover if we took the trouble, but we'll take the assignment at face value. Our contract will be signed later today—we're moving fast on this one. Liam, you'll be Kline's constant companion as of eight o'clock tomorrow morning. Dieter, I want a report from you on terrorist and kidnap activities during the last year. Obviously anything relevant to Magma or its subsidiary companies is what we're after."

Stuhr made a note. After the meeting he would spend some time at the data-processing machine, using a special access code to link up with another company that specialized in maintaining and updating the activities and whereabouts of known worldwide terrorist groups on computer.

"I'll do some checks on Magma's rivals, also," the German said, "see if there are any areas where competition has become overfierce."

"Good. We're looking for enemies, business or otherwise. But if Kline is as neurotic as Liam says, this whole affair could well be a waste of time and effort. The man might be suffering from a severe case of paranoia." The Controller managed a grim smile. "Still, that's his and Magma's problem—Achilles' Shield gets paid either way. What do you have for us, Charles?"

Mather stopped rubbing at his knee. "It's all fairly straightforward. For the time being we'll allocate four operatives to work with Liam, our inside man. Two to a team, working six-hour shifts around the clock. We'll also keep a backup here on alert. Any preference as to whom you want, Liam?"

Halloran shook his head.

"Very well. As requested by Magma, our teams will keep at a distance. They'll maintain a constant patrol around the Surrey estate's boundaries—as usual, we'll inform the local police to save them from getting into a tizz."

"Will our people be armed?" inquired Stuhr.

There was a pause. Snaith preferred his operatives to be "kitted" against "severe hostility," but it was illegal for private bodyguards to carry weapons in England (a law that was constantly abused, particularly by foreign visitors to the country).

The Controller came to a decision. "Liam will take with him to the estate whatever hardware he feels is necessary. I'm reluctant to sanction anything that will harm our special relationship with the police and Home Office, so our patrols will be unarmed for the time being. However, should there be any definite moves against our client, then the situation will be reconsidered. Although we'll have to rely on Liam and Kline's own bodyguards to take care of internal surveillance, we'll need a detailed report on the security system of this place . . ."

Stuhr made another note.

". . . and the Magma building itself. The latter worries me considerably. Too many people in and out all day. However, we can plant an extra couple of our men in the lobbies of the ground and twelfth floors; naturally Magma's own security people will have to know they're there. We'll have a surveillance team outside at night, front and back, when Kline's in residence."

"The building worries me, too," said Halloran, and all eyes turned toward him. "It's a glass and metal fortress, but it's vulnerable."

"Then let's hope nobody tries to get at the target before we're operational," commented Mather. "Now that would be amusing."

Snaith didn't find that prospect amusing at all. Not one bit.

9

ENTICEMENT

Ah, good, at last he is approaching the boy.

The boy is nervous but he speaks with bravado. He is pale, the boy, and looks unwashed; no doubt the rumpled plastic bag he carries contains all his worldly goods. He is perhaps sixteen, perhaps seventeen. The English believe that is too young to be without family, without a home; would that they knew of the orphans who freely roam the streets and market-places of Damascus, boys who wander alone, others who prowl in packs, stealing, begging, and joining lost causes because they will supply them with guns. Pah! The self-important British know nothing of such things.

The boy is smiling. An unsure, nervous smile. He is lost in this huge railway station with its throngs of blank-eyed strangers. He would be even more lost in the city itself should he step outside. Now he assumes he has found a friend. If only he realized. Hah, yes, if only the boy understood.

Ajel, be quick, Youssef, do not linger on this plain of shuffling travelers and vagrants. Policemen patrol, they search for runaways such as this one.

Now he is hesitant. The boy is uncertain. Perhaps it is the dark skin he does not trust. The English nurture such intolerances, instill them in their young.

Talk smoothly, Youssef, my friend. He looks around, the movement casual, nothing more than a glance at arrival and departure times, a constantly changing pattern high on the station wall: but Youssef really looks to see if he and the boy are being observed. You are not, my friend; I, Asil, have already looked for you. I am the only one who is interested. Besides, a man talking to a *shab* is familiar to these surroundings. Nobody really cares. Life is too personal.

He places a reassuring hand on the runaway's shoulder and the boy does not flinch away. Perhaps money is mentioned. Ah, I see the boy nods. He has all the boldness and the stupidity of the unworldly.

My friend turns away and the boy follows. They walk side by side. Not close, not like lovers, but like associates in sin. I see it in your eyes, Youssef, the gleam that shines from your dark soul, even though outwardly you are calm. And the boy swaggers; but this is a self-conscious posturing, an arrogant affectation.

I must quickly go to the car. I must be ready in the darkness of the backseat. The boy will hardly feel the needle's sting; he will only sense my presence when it is too late.

Then, for him, sleep. A long, deep sleep.

And when he wakes—our pleasure and the master's sustenance.

Hurry, Youssef, *ajel*. I suspect that same gleam is now in my own eyes. My body is already aching.

10

INTRUDER

Monk was surprised. Nobody was due this time of night. Leastwise, nobody'd told him.

The elevator was humming though. Faint, but it was on its way up. Sounded like the one from the chairman's suite. No way could it be Felix's elevator, the one that slid all the way down to the basement. Nobody else had the code for that. Even the chick, Cora, had to wait till it was sent down for her.

Monk was momentarily distracted by Cora's image. The image was naked from the waist down.

Sound's stopped. It'd traveled no more'n four stories. Yeah, from Sir Vic's den. Who the hell—?

Monk heard the doors open.

But no one stepped out.

The bodyguard laid down his magazine and rose from the chair at the end of the corridor. He released the restraining hoop on his shoulder holster but stayed where he was, awaiting developments.

No mood for fuckups tonight, he told himself. It'd been a bad day already. He'd been shown for a jackass that morning, a clumsy meatloaf, and he was in no mind for surprises tonight, even if some jerk had made a mistake in coming up to the twenty-second. Just step outside, lessee the color of your teeth.

Still no one. But the doors weren't closing, and that wasn't right.

Monk crept down the corridor, one hand on the butt of his pistol, a big lumbering man who nevertheless approached the elevator silently, soft carpeting helping his stealth. The corridor was gloomy-dark—the way Felix liked it—and mellow light from the opening ahead stained the floor and opposite wall.

The door should've closed by now. Unless someone had a finger on the OPEN button.

Monk drew out the Smith & Wesson.

He paused, the opening only two feet away. There were no shadows in the glow that spread from it.

He braced himself, readied to spring forward and sideways, gun arm pointed into the lift. But he thought better of that tactic. Monk wasn't stupid. His bulk was too good a target.

So he got down on his hands and knees and crawled forward, gun barrel almost alongside his nose, elbows digging into the deep pile. No one expected to see a face appear below knee level.

He was at the very corner, easing his massive head past the shiny metal ridge, the interior of the elevator coming into view. His gun hand was no more than a few inches ahead of him.

Nobody there. It looked like there was nobody there after—

A hand grabbed his hair and yanked him forward onto his belly. A leg straddled him and crushed his gun into the carpet. Iron fingers still dug into his hair, making the roots scream. Something slammed hard into his neck, and his thoughts became unsettled dreams.

Janusz Palusinski sat at the kitchen's breakfast bar slapping butter on bread with a carving knife whose blade was at least nine inches long. Beside his plate was a tumbler half full of vodka.

He checked his wristwatch, parts of tattooed numbers showing at the edge of the broad strap, then sawed off chunks of roast beef, the red meat rare almost to the point of being raw. As he cut he wondered if Felix—*mój pan,* he mentally and with more than a degree of cynicism added—would scream in his sleep tonight. A terrifying sound that stilled the blood of anyone who heard it. What did the man dream of? What fears possessed him when he slept? How close to total madness had he come? But no. Janusz must not even have a negative *thought* about his master. Felix would know, he would sense.

Felix, Felix, Felix.

Just the name could cause an ache inside Palusinski's bald head.

The Pole wiped the back of his fist across his forehead, the knife he held catching light from overhead in a sudden flare. Normally the kitchen lights, like all the others in the penthouse, would be kept low by dimmer switches, but at present Felix was sleeping, he wouldn't know. Yet sometimes he did . . . Sometimes he would accuse them all of things that he should never have been aware of, and they would cringe, they would cower, they would be craven before him. Still Felix— O lord, master, and oppressor—would make them suffer, sometimes the punishment cruel, other times involving a mere few hours of discomfort. Palusinski often felt that the two Arabs enjoyed that part of their servitude. Monk's brain was too curdled to care either way, *blazen* that he was.

But Janusz was different, he assured himself. Janusz was aware of certain things . . . The others were fools. No, the Arabs were not fools. They believed . . .

Palusinski gulped neat vodka, then unscrewed the mustard-jar lid. He dug in the tip of the carving knife, sunk it four inches, then spread the dollop it came out with across the cut meat. He slammed another thick slice of bread, also lavishly buttered, on top, pressing down with the flat of his hand so that yellow goo oozed from the sides.

Twenty minutes before the gorilla was to be relieved, he told himself as he raised the overflowing sandwich and barged his mouth into it. Monk—a good name for an animal such as he. Hours of sitting watching an empty corridor was a fitting task for such an *idiota*. But for Janusz it meant five hours of misery to look forward to. A torment. Another torture imposed by Felix. Even pain was better than boredom.

What was it that had made Felix so nervous? The man was mad, there could be no doubting that. But a genius also! No doubting that, either. *Gówno!* No doubt at all. But why afraid now, *mój szef?* You, who lives in shadows, who distrusts the light unless it is for your purpose. What fresh fear haunts you now, *mężcyzna* of many dreads?

Palusinski chomped on meat and bread, lips glistening from the surplus of butter. He stilled his jaw to gulp vodka, seasoning the mushed food in his mouth with fire. His eyes were small behind the wire-framed spectacles he wore, their lids never fully raised, like blinds half-drawn in a room where secrets were kept. They were focused upon the rim of the open mustard jar, everything else a soft periphery; yet his eyes were not seeing that rim with its sliver of reflected light, for his thoughts were inward, perhaps examining those very secrets within that room of his mind. He sat, slowly munching, as if mesmerized.

Something snatched him from the introspection, though. And he didn't know what.

A sound! A movement? Palusinski was puzzled. He was sensitive to intrusion. Months of living rough, sleeping in ditches, eating raw vegetables dug from the earth, always with his eyes darting left, right, afraid he would be seen, what would happen to him if they found him . . . all that, even though it had been many years since, had attuned his senses for the slightest shift in atmosphere.

His grip tightened on the knife. Someone was in the room beyond.

Monk? He would never disobey Felix's orders to watch the corridor one floor below until Palusinski took over. Unlikely, then, that Monk would desert his post. Youssef and Asil? No, they were not due to return that night, they had the country house to prepare for their precious lord and master's visit. Then who?

Palusinski slipped off the stool and reached inside his jacket, which was draped over a chair back. His hand came out with a thick, round metal bar, its length matching the blade protruding from his other fist. He crept over to the light switch and extended finger and thumb to turn it counterclockwise. The light in the kitchen faded.

From where he stood the Pole could see a broad section of lounge beyond and he cursed the shadows out there, the darkness of the furnishings, the blackness of the walls. He could wait; or he could venture out. He had the patience—skulking and hiding in the old country had instilled that in him—but he also had a duty. To Felix. He must *never* fail in that.

He held his breath and, armed with the weapons, moved toward the open doorway.

The danger—*if* there was someone out there—would probably be from either side of the doorway where a person could lurk safe from view. Which side? Always the dilemma.

Which side would an assailant strike from? *If* there was someone there . . .

He crouched low and ran through, counting on surprise,
the knife held at hip level, tip pointing upward, ready to
plunge or swipe. Palusinski turned as soon as he was clear,
thrusting one leg back for balance and for leverage so that he
could spring forward or withstand an assault.

There was no need. Nobody hid outside the kitchen doorway, not on any side.

But somebody was behind the long black couch nearby.
Only Palusinski, sensitive to intrusion though he was, neither
saw nor *felt* the shadow that rose up from it.

He may have felt fingers tilt his head to one side so that
certain nerves in his neck were exposed, but if so, he didn't
remember later. He definitely did not feel the edge of the
stiffened hand chop down, fast and silent to deaden those
nerves. Nor would he have felt the shock traveling along their
roots toward a certain terminal inside his brain. The journey
was too swift for that.

Kline was within himself.

He swam in blood vessels amid cells that changed from red
to scarlet around him, through narrow passages, breaking out
into round caverns, swept on by a bubbling tide that never
stilled, toward a source that was no more than a distant rhythmic echo somewhere ahead in the labyrinth of busy tunnels,
the rush to the sound as exhilarating as it was terrifying.

There were other things racing with him that were alien to
these passages, black misshapen forms that were there only to
disease and destroy; but these parasites themselves were steadily destroyed, attacked by globules that engulfed, swallowed,
digested. And these defenders decided that he, too, was foreign, had no place alongside healthy corpuscles, that he was
an interloper, a danger, up to no good. Even though it was his
own body he journeyed through.

He screamed at the giant lumps to get away, to leave him
alone, he meant no harm. But they were programmed to fight
to the death all that was not right in the system and had no
minds of their own. Two attached themselves to him as he
was flushed through into a wider tunnel, and he felt the burning of his own back, his arm, acid seeping into him.

Yet he was so near, the rushing even faster, moving in

contractions, the steady beat louder, louder still, becoming a thunder, the rapids leading to a fall, the fall to be mighty and devouring. And that was his desire, no other yearning possible to him now: he wanted to be consumed by the mountainous heart.

Instead these blind, ignorant creatures, organisms that knew nothing of other things, were eating him. His body was decomposing under their chemical excretions.

Nearly there, nearly there.

He could hear the hysteria of his own laughter.

Nearly there.

The noise ahead—*THUD-UP THUD-UP*—deafened him, filled him with dread. *Elated* him.

Nearly there.

Nearly swallowed.

It wasn't too late.

He would make it.

Be absorbed by the heart.

THUD-UP THUD-UP

There . . . !

But not there.

Drifting back, drawn away, consciousness the carrier. Floating upward, a soft retreat . . .

An abrupt awakening.

There was someone with him in the bedroom. Kline opened his mouth to call out, but something clamped hard over it. A hand. A strong, threatening hand. He felt the extra weight on the bed. Somebody, a shadow among shadows, kneeling over him.

Another hand encircled his throat.

"Someone else and you could be dead," Halloran whispered close to his ear.

11

A DANGEROUS ENCOUNTER

Halloran glanced into the rearview mirror.

The blue Peugeot was still there, keeping well back, at least four or five other cars between it and the custom-built Mercedes Halloran was driving. His own backup, in a Granada, was directly behind him.

He reached for the radio transmitter mounted beneath the dashboard and set the transmit button.

"Hector-One," he said quietly into the mouthpiece.

"Hector-Two, we hear you," came the reply through the receiver. "And we see the tag."

Kline leaned forward from the backseat, his face close to Halloran's shoulder. There was a bright expectancy in his eyes.

"Turning off soon," said Halloran. "Stay close till then. Out." He replaced the instrument.

"We're being followed?" Kline asked, nervousness now mingled with expectancy.

Cora, next to him in the backseat, stiffened, and Monk, who occupied the front passenger seat—riding shotgun, as he liked to think of it—shifted his bulk to look first at his employer, then out the tinted rear window. His fingers automatically went to the revolver at his waist.

"No need for that," Halloran warned. "And use the side mirror if you want to spot them."

"Nobody can see in," Monk protested petulantly, already aggrieved with Halloran for having made him look so useless twice the day before.

"They can see shadows through the glass. Face the road and take your hand off that weapon."

"Do it," snapped Kline. Then to Halloran: "Which one is it?"

"The light blue. A Peugeot, a few cars back. It's been on our tail since we left London. My guess is it took over from another car that picked us up in the city, probably close to the Magma building." In fact, Halloran had felt uneasy long before he'd arrived at Magma early that morning to take Kline down to his Surrey home for the weekend. Yet he'd been unable to spot the "tag" until they were into the outskirts.

"Are you sure?" asked Cora, resisting the urge to look over her shoulder at the traffic. "This road is a main highway south—most of these cars have probably been with us for miles."

"Cora," said Kline, "if he says we're being followed, that's it—I believe him." Halloran's easy penetration of Magma's security system the night before had impressed him. By wearing clothes that had merely resembled the security guards' uniforms, Halloran had strolled into the basement parking lot, hidden until most of the day staff were leaving that evening, then found his way to the upper floors using the outgoing rush as cover. Nothing more than a stroll against the tide. Then a vacated room, a broom closet, or a toilet—Halloran hadn't given him details—until nighttime, then through to the chairman's suite, locked doors only slowing him down, not barring him. Observation cameras? No problem. Only certain corridors and halls were monitored that late at night and, at an agreed time, Shield had created a minor diversion. No more than a motorbike messenger thumping on the glass main door to attract the attention of the two security guards on the monitoring desk. The messenger had waved a package in his hand, and one of the guards had gone to the door while his colleague watched from the desk, poised to press an alarm button that would alert the other two security guards patrolling the building as well as the local police station should anything untoward occur. So his eyes had been on his partner and the messenger outside (the latter insisting that delivery forms had to be filled in and signed before he released the package) and not on the screens behind him. The ruse had allowed Halloran to negotiate the more exposed locations without being seen. Naturally a risk was involved, but human reaction being what it is, the risk was slight. The rest of the journey had been simple (simple, that is, for someone like Halloran): the private elevator, the "pacification" of Monk and Palusinski, the entry into his, Kline's, bedroom. No big deal (and heads were already rolling in the corporation's office that morning as specialists from Achilles' Shield revised Magma's security arrangements).

Someone else and you could be dead. Kline remembered Halloran's words. Not quite that simple, Halloran, he thought. No, not *quite* that easy.

He smiled, and Cora was puzzled by the sudden burning intensity in his eyes.

The Mercedes was slowing, the left indicator blinking. Halloran turned the car off the main road, then picked up speed again, their surroundings soon vignetting into green fields and hedgerows, with few houses between.

Cora noticed Halloran occasionally glancing into the rearview mirror, but his reflected eyes betrayed nothing. He had warned Monk not to look back, and she herself followed the instruction. Their car maintained a steady speed, and still Cora could not detect from Halloran's manner whether or not they were being followed.

Several minutes passed before he reached again for the radio transmitter.

"Hector-One."

"Hector-Two. Over."

"Tag's still with us, keeping well back."

"Yeah. We made out three occupants. Want us to block them?"

"No. No offensive until we're sure. There's a village ahead. Pull in somewhere and let 'em by. Follow at a distance and come up fast if they make a move. Out."

"Will do. Out."

Houses quickly loomed up, then they were into the village, a hamlet really, only a few houses on either side of the road. Halloran saw the small filling station and knew where his backup would pull into. He checked the mirror as the Granada slowed into the driveway. The blue Peugeot soon came into view, and he put his foot down a little to give them cause to hurry.

He had taken a more circuitous route than necessary to Kline's country house, but now they couldn't have been more than fifteen minutes away. If these people were hostile, he wanted them to make their play soon, before they were too close to home. He preferred to keep trouble off the doorstep.

He eased up on the accelerator, inviting in the possible pursuer. The Peugeot increased speed, coming up fast, beginning to fill the rearview mirror.

Halloran had faith in the "hardened" vehicle he was driving. The door panels, trunk, roof, and engine compartment were armored with Kevlar, aluminum oxide ballistic ceramic tiles, which was lighter than the old-style heavy steel plate that tended to render a vehicle clumsy and so impede its performance. The windows were of layered bullet- and blast-resistant glass, and the tires were compartmentalized and self-sealing so that speed need not be reduced should they be punctured by bullets. Even the gas tanks, main and reserve, consisted of separate cells that would limit the outbreak of fire should they be pierced.

The French car was directly behind now, only feet away from the Mercedes' reinforced bumper.

"Sit back," he told Kline, whose face was still close to Halloran's shoulder. "And keep low, legs against the back of the front seat, as though you're resting. Cora, they'll be coming up on your side, so brace yourself. You'll be okay—they'd need a bazooka to dent this tub."

"Speed up," Kline urged. "Don't let them get alongside us!"

"Stay low," Halloran calmly repeated. "They may be no threat at all."

"Why take the chance? I don't like this, Halloran."

"Trust me."

Cora wasn't sure if Halloran's tone was mocking.

Monk had drawn his revolver by now. Halloran didn't even look his way but said, "Keep that bloody thing tucked into your lap and don't even think of using it unless I tell you."

They were rounding a bend, and the Peugeot was straddling the middle of the road ready to pass.

Halloran continued to instruct the bodyguard. "Put your elbow on the sill and keep your left hand in sight. You know how to act nonchalant?"

The American grunted something.

"Okay," said Halloran. "Here they come. See that church steeple in the distance? I want you all to keep your eyes on that. No watching our friends here."

The road had straightened, and a clear stretch lay ahead for at least half a mile. The Peugeot drew level with the Mercedes' rear wheel, and Halloran deliberately glanced over his shoulder and touched his brakes, a gentlemanly gesture to allow the other vehicle to pass by. His hand tightened on the steering wheel, holding it steady, as the Peugeot inched its way alongside. He could feel the occupants' eyes on him, and his senses sharpened to such a degree that he could smell new-cut grass under the gasoline fumes, even though all windows were closed, could hear the Mercedes' tires rumble over the road's hard surface, could feel the pounding of machinery beneath the hood of the car. The acuteness of danger overlaid all those sensings.

Halloran smiled at the other driver, nodding at the deserted road ahead, an indication that he was leaving the way clear.

The Peugeot suddenly accelerated even more, then was by them, tail rapidly receding into the distance.

"Hogshit," grumbled Monk.

"You scared us for nothing, Halloran," Kline complained. "Bastard, you scared us for—"

"Keep down," Halloran warned.

There was yet another bend ahead, and the blue car had disappeared around it.

Kline's mouth dropped. He snapped back into his seat and said, "You're right. They're there."

The Peugeot was parked across the road, blocking it completely. A fence lined one side of the road, trees the other. The occupants of the car were outside, crouched low behind the bodywork.

Halloran slammed on the Mercedes' brakes and the car screeched to a halt, rubber burning off into the concrete in straight black lines. He immediately shifted into reverse and stabbed down hard on the accelerator pedal, throwing his passengers forward, then back into their seats.

Monk's revolver had slid onto the floor and he doubled over, restrained by his seat belt, pudgy hands scrabbling at the floor to reach the weapon. Cora lurched forward again, propelled by the reverse motion of the car. Kline had already scrambled down into the well between backseat and front.

Halloran increased speed, looking over his shoulder through the back window, both hands still on the steering wheel. The bend in the road loomed up fast. He began the turn, hardly slowing down at all, the passengers hurled to one side, traveling around the curve and out of sight of their attackers. He straightened the car, increased speed.

Suddenly Halloran stamped on the footbrake, rapidly turning the steering wheel as far as it would go. The Mercedes responded beautifully, making a 180-degree turn so that it faced the direction in which it had been reversing.

Hard on the accelerator again, and they were away, scorching road, using its full width.

The backup Granada was hurtling toward them and Halloran swerved over to the left-hand side of the road, both cars screeching to a halt beside one another. He was already snapping orders before the electric window was fully down.

"Hostiles just around the bend. Stop them following."

"You want us to engage?" the other driver shouted back.

"Not if you can help it—I saw guns in their hands. I'll use another route to Home."

The cars took off at the same time, the exchange taking no more than seconds.

"Am I safe?" came Kline's querulous voice from the back.

"Not yet," Halloran replied, looking into the rearview mirror in time to see the Granada disappear around the curve. He returned his attention to the way ahead, on the alert for possible support for the "hostiles." A van was approaching, two more cars behind that. He pressed the button to raise his window and made ready to accelerate or slam on the brakes yet again, whichever course of action might prove necessary. The line of vehicles passed without incident and he checked the mirror once more. Still nothing coming up from behind, the van and cars continuing to travel away from the Mercedes. He felt some of the tension ease from him.

Kline was back by his shoulder. "Why didn't you tell your guys to shoot the bastards?" he demanded angrily.

"This is Surrey," Halloran told him, "not the Middle East. Gun wars are frowned upon here. Besides, they're not armed at present, a condition that'll have to be changed, I think."

"Listen to me, Halloran . . ." Kline began to say when the radio transmitter interrupted.

"Hector-Two."

Halloran reached for the handset. "Hector-One. Give me the news."

"They were gone before we rounded the bend. We drove on, but there was a junction not far ahead—they could've gone off in any direction. Our guess is that they'd spotted us earlier, so didn't hang around or try to follow when you got away."

"You made out the license?"

"Sure, when they passed the garage."

So had Halloran, but there was no need to repeat it to his operatives: they were too well trained to have made any mistakes. "Call Base, get them to use their influence to run a check."

"Will do. As it was a Peugeot, it's probably been stolen, not rented."

"I agree. Check it out though. Scout the area for a while, then make your way to Home. Out."

"Catch you later. Out."

Halloran drove on, moving briskly without breaking any speed limits, using the roadway to the full when he could, ever-watchful at side roads and bends, even though instinct told him they were now safe.

"Who were they, Felix?" he heard Cora ask from the back, nervousness still in her voice.

"How should I know?" was the reply. "Thugs, lunatics!"

"Take it easy," Halloran soothed. "It won't be long before we reach your place."

Kline peered out the windows. "Oh yeah? Well, this isn't the fuck the way."

"No, but it'll get us there eventually. I worked out various routes this morning before I picked you up. My team will use another way and meet us there. Monk, you can put the gun away, you won't be needing it."

The ponytailed bodyguard reluctantly obeyed.

"I told you, Cora," Kline said, his words rushed, his breathing excited. "I said I was in danger, I told you all." He was once again the Felix Kline Halloran had first met, nervous, arrogant, too many words spilling from his lips. "I sensed the danger, I damn well knew, didn't I? Bastards! Halloran, I need more of your men to protect me. I could've been hurt back there."

"Wasn't it your idea that we limit our forces?"

"Yeah, yeah, you're right. You'll do. You got us out of a tight spot. No more manpower required. Right. I don't feel too good."

Cora immediately reached for him.

"Leave me alone!" Kline snapped, sinking back into his seat. "I'm tired, I need to rest. You all want too much from me, you all expect too much. Let me rest, will you?"

Halloran heard a clasp being opened, a rattling of pills in a container.

"Felix," said Cora, "take them, they'll calm you."

"You think I want drugs at a time like this? You trying to make me weak?"

There was a slapping sound and the pills sprinkled onto the seat and floor.

"I've got to stay alert, you stupid bitch! Those bastards want to hurt me and you're trying to dope me up."

"They're only Valium, Felix, that's all. You need to calm down."

Monk's seat jerked as Kline kicked its back. The bodyguard continued to watch the passing countryside as if he hadn't noticed.

Kline's voice had risen to a high pitch. "You know what I oughta do with you, Cora? You know what? I oughta dump you right now, out of the car into the road. Leave you here. How would you like that, Cora, huh? How would you get by then? What fucking use are you to me?"

"Don't, Felix." There was a mixture of misery and low panic in her voice. "You've had a bad scare, you don't mean what you're saying."

"Don't I? Oh, don't I? You think I give a shit about you?"

Halloran heard the smack of flesh on flesh, heard the girl's small, startled cry. He brought the Mercedes to a smooth halt by the side of the road and turned around to face Kline, one arm resting casually on the back of the driver's seat. Cora was leaning her forehead against the window, eyes closed, a watery line slowly seeping onto her eyelashes; there were red marks on her cheek.

"Kline," he said evenly, "you're beginning to irritate. I can do my job better if you don't. I want you to sit quietly so I can think, observe, and get you to our destination unharmed. If by the time we arrive you're sick of me too, you can make a phone call and have me replaced. It's no skin off my nose, know what I mean? Do we have an arrangement?"

Kline stared openmouthed at him, and for the merest instant Halloran saw something in those liquid eyes that he couldn't recognize. He'd faced killers and fanatics before, and each had a distinctly similar and identifiable glint adrift in their gaze; he'd looked upon gunmen, abductors, and extortionists—child murderers even—and a certain mien linked them all, setting them apart from others of the human race. But there was a glimmer shining from deep inside this man that was like nothing else he'd witnessed before. Kline's stare was almost mesmeric—until whatever held him became dulled or, at least, was veiled by a creeping normality.

Kline laughed, and it was a full, rich sound, unexpected and unlike his usual cackling. "Whatever you say, Halloran," he said good-humoredly. "Yeah, whatever you say."

Halloran turned and shifted into drive. The Mercedes pulled away, heading into the winding country roads. And during the last part of that journey, Halloran frequently checked the rearview mirror. But this time he was mostly studying the man who was resting, with eyes now closed, in the backseat.

While Monk, from the corner of his eyes, watched Halloran.

MONK

A PILGRIM'S PROGRESS

It was a lousy name anyway. But none of the other kids ever added the *ey*. Monk*ey*. Nah, too easy. They called him Ape. Up until he hit fourteen, that is. That was when the ape pissed right back out of the cage.

Theo, or Theodore Albert, as his mama always called him, was never gutsy. Every day it was the same thing. "Theodore Albert you wuz baptized, and Theodore Albert you be called, honey mine," she'd say as she parted his hair right down the middle, slicking either side with a licked palm, every fuckin' morning before she pushed him out the door and along the path to where good ol' Uncle Mort waited in the pickup. "You'd look real purty, boy, if you wunt so porky," Uncle Mort often observed as they drove down to Coatesville Junior High where the boys bent their knees and dragged their knuckles along the ground behind him, lumbering from side to side in an ape waddle, imitating his high wheezy voice, another affliction which didn't help, until he finally flipped his lid and whirled around and *knocked them squat*. No, that was a lie: he cried, he always fuckin' cried, 'cos he was a mama's boy, he knew it and they knew it and they all knew he'd never raise a pudgy fist because he was too chickenshit to hit back, but . . . But he hadn't been chickenshit those few years later at West Chester High when he struck the fire under the assembly hall on prize-giving (no prizes coming to him anyway) morning, when all those turds had been up there nudging and sniggering and whispering, but soon wailing and screaming and punching, falling over each other to break out of that burning hell hall, where only three were really roasted by the fire, but fifteen (no teachers damaged—the parents hated *them* for that) kicked off from chokin' and crushed ribcages.

That day was the turning point for Theodore Albert Monk, "pissin'-out day," the day he discovered every person had a power. Anyone—big, small, fat, or skinny—could decide for someone else when their Pay-Off Time (POT) had arrived. You didn't need to be Einstein or Charles Atlas (or even Charlie fuckin' Brown) to choose their day for 'em. Point a stubby finger and raise a meaty thumb like a cocked gun and that was it. Bingo. Not right there and then, of course; but that was decision time, that was as good as. After that you waited for the right moment. Could take days, weeks, maybe months. Thing was, it always came. You got them when they and nobody else expected it. When *you* were safe.

He'd shown it to insects first, graduating to animals, mice, frogs (slice 'em, dice 'em), Grandma Kaley's old cross-eyed cat (weed killer in its milk bowl), a stray mutt (lured by half a salami sandwich into a rusted freezer left to rot on the town's rubbish dump. He'd opened it up two weeks later and the stink had made him throw up). Then on to the big time.

Four of 'em he'd wasted (he enjoyed the macho sound of *wasted*), two boys, two chicks. And nobody the wiser.

When he'd moved on to Philly, there'd been two more—three if you counted the spic. In LA almost—*almost*—one (the hooker had fought like a wildcat when, on the spur of the moment—maybe just to get himself excited—he'd decided to cancel her subscription, and the stiletto-heeled shoe she'd been treading him with for his pleasure had nearly taken out his left eye, hurting him so bad that he'd had to leave her there moaning and hollering in a way he didn't think possible with a snapped neck and a bellyfull of bruises).

Things had gotten a mite tricky after that. The pigs had a description, they knew who they were looking for. The hooker had seen him around before, that was the piss-puller, seen him hanging loose with Glass-Eye Spangler (an inch to the left with that stiletto heel and they'd have been calling *him* Glass-Eye, too). And good ol' boy Spangler knew his drinking buddy's name, where he was from. Turned out there was a small matter of an unsolved crime and a missing delinquent back there in Coatesville. Nah, not the two boys, two chicks —one drowning, one car burning (the lighted rag stuck into the gas filler had blown the tank right under the backseat that the boy and girl were using for a make-out pad at the time), and one rape with strangling as the dessert (or maybe the main course, it was hard to remember now), not those. There was the little mystery of Mama and Uncle Mort, brother and sister, found locked together in bed (joined at the loins, that is) with bedbugs buddying up with maggots on what must have been one sweltering, rotten feast week. Rosie Monk's sixteen-year-old, the one they figured was a semi-imbecile because he never talked much and lumbered around like . . . like . . . *say it* . . . like one of them fuckin' orangy-tans and just about as smart (this was in the days before Mr. Smith), had lit out, making him number-one suspect, since no one in his right mind would even *think* about kidnapping the big fucker (oh yeah, Theodore Albert aka Ape had filled his fat with muscle in the two years after POT power), after bludgeoning Mama and that groin-groping bastard Uncle Mort with his battered old Jim Fregosi baseball bat in the bed where they'd grunted and heaved and made the springs sing along.

So the pigs were on his tail again, years after the event, hot for his ass. And maybe now those cops were finally figuring the big ape had something to do with those other unexplained homicides, and if not, why not? Neatened up things to hang them on Monk too. Yeah, let's go for it, let's nail the mother-killer, the uncle-pounder, let's hand him the check for them all. They recalled nobody'd liked the fat creep anyway.

Escape. To Vegas. Some stuff on the way, most of it a blur now. Teaming up with Slimeball and Rivas in the glitz city, rolling drunks and mugging hookers for their purses nights, dealing crack days. Fine until the pimps ganged up (a pimp posse no less), sorely aggrieved that their take margin was down because three stooges from outa town hadn't yet learned their place in subsociety. This very point was explained to Monk one night by a big buck who had razor blades glued to the insides of the fingers of one hand so that when he slapped —palm or backhand, made no difference, the blade edges stuck out from either side—neat red lines would crisscross your cheeks until the cuts got closer and closer to eventually become one huge open wound, while five other hoods crushed Slimeball and Rivas's fingers and toes before chopping off an ear from each and making the boys chew on it (each other's ear, that is). They were saving him for something else because he was the muscle and he had badly altered one of the girls' features two months ago, turning her into an asset loss, no good to no muthuh.

But what the razor-toting buck hadn't counted on—he had a crazy grin to match his crazy eyes—was that pain hardly meant a pig's ass to Monk (it took extreme and prolonged agony to give Monk any pleasure, even in those days), so the slicing steel could have been chopping cheese for all he cared. Monk did what he had come to know best. POT—Pay-Off Time—had arrived for the nigguh and introduced itself in the form of Monk's hawked phlegm in his eyes (ol' Uncle Mort, in between feeling him up, had taught young Theodore Albert how to do that to dogs straight out of the pickup windows) and a grinding of the black's privates by Monk's raised knee. The buck's own razor-blade fingers were used to sever his own jugular.

This last upset had proved too much for the rest of the vigilante squad who, pissed enough already by the cash loss, decided that what they'd had in mind for the ape-walking creep (their girls' description had pinpointed Monk nicely) wasn't quite special enough. This bozo required something more permanent.

They came for him with open switchblades and surgeon's hatchets, that season's "in" weapon, and Monk would have been chopped ape if he hadn't used the still-gurgling black man as a battering ram.

Oh yeah, he'd gotten away, but had been damaged in the getting, although not as damaged as the two dead he'd left behind. A knife stuck firmly in his shoulder blade had proved uncomfortable as well as a bad feature for walking the streets. Fortunately, a shithead who knew him on a supplier/client basis and whom he ran into several blocks away obliged him by tugging the knife free after much jiggling and muttering "man-oh-man" and some giggling. Jiggle and giggle. The junkie had paid for the enjoyment with a windpipe so badly flattened that he talked like Popeye for the rest of his short years.

Once again, Monk was on the hoof, and this time both pigs *and* mob were after him. He robbed a drugstore for some traveling money (no gun necessary for a crude dude like Monk), leaving the druggist seriously splattered among his pills and potions.

The old flaky Dodge he stole only took him as far as the outskirts of town before coughing oil and chunking to a permanent demise.

Shoulder all fiery and already beginning to fester in the

heat, ragged oozy cheeks like fast-food counters for flies, Monk legged his way down U.S. 95, a fat thumb hoisted every time he heard an engine motoring up from behind. But who would stop for a hiker with a dark bubbly stain on his back and tomato-ketchup spread across his face? Right. No fucker. Nobody normal.

Except one car did stop.

The black car, its windows all tinted dark and mysterious, glided to a soundless halt beside him, the movement as easy as a vulture landing on a carcass.

Monk shifted his bulk so that he was facing the silent car (no grace in *his* movement, none at all), pain and fatigue stooping him by now, his clothes and ponytailed hair powdered with dust, his face, with its scarlet-rose cheeks, puckered up into a shit-eating grimace. For a few moments he wondered if the occupants were Big Guys who kept Small Guys down (to keep the law in your pocket you had to maintain a certain law yourself) and he waited for a snub-nose to poke through a lowered window like some black viper sliding from its hole.

But a window didn't sink down. And no gun was pointed toward him when the rear passenger door was opened wide.

He squinted to see into the big gloomy interior and could only just make out the dark shape sitting in there among the shadows.

Then a voice said in a persuasive way: "Need a lift, Theo?"

(That was the first and only time Kline had called him by his first name.)

12

NEATH

"Not far, Liam," said Cora, leaning forward slightly in her seat. "Look for the gates, just ahead on your left."

Kline, beside her, opened his eyes and for a moment that seemed no less than infinite, he and Halloran stared at each other in the rearview mirror. It was Halloran who averted his gaze, and he was surprised at the effort it took to do so.

Thick undergrowth and trees crowded either side of the road, the greenery even more dense beyond, the few gaps here and there almost subterranean in their gloom; these were woodlands of perpetual dusk. The high, old-stone wall that appeared on the left came as a surprise: it looked firmly rooted, as though having grown with the trees, a natural part of the forest itself, organic life smothering much of the rough stone and filling cracks. Twisted branches from trees on the other side loomed over, some reaching down like gnarled tentacles ready to snatch unwary ramblers.

He noticed the opening in the near distance, the forest withdrawing there, allowing the smallest of incursions into its territory. Halloran slowed the Mercedes, turning into the drive, the roadway here cracked and uneven. The rusted iron gates before them looked impregnable, like the forest itself. Letters worked into the wrought iron declared: NEATH.

"Wait for a moment," Kline instructed him.

Halloran waited, and studied.

Tall weathered columns hinged the gates, stone animals mounted on each, their blank eyes glaring down at the car, their lichen-filled mouths wide with soundless snarls. Griffins? he wondered, but they were too decayed to tell. The gates would be easy to scale, he noted, as would be the walls on either side. No barbed wire and, as far as he could tell, no electronic warning system. And all the cover between wall and road that any would-be intruder could desire. Security was going to be difficult.

Then he noticed, beyond the gates, the lodge house.

It was a two-story building with stone as seasoned as the walls and windows as black as the Devil's soul.

Halloran frowned when the thought sprang into his mind.

. . . as black as the Devil's soul.

A phrase remembered from early years in Ireland, only then it had been: *The Divil's owhn soul.* Father O'Connell, thrashing the living daylights out of him, had said it. Thrashing Liam because of the heinous wickedness into which he had led the two Scalley boys (the younger one had confessed, fearful of the mortal jeopardy in which his soul had been placed because of Halloran's leadership). Thrashing him because of the sacrilege against St. Joseph's, breaking into the church in the hush of night, leaving the dead cat—the boys had found it crushed at the roadside—inside the holy tabernacle, the animal's innards dripping out onto the soft white silk lining the vessel's walls, its eyes still gleaming dully when Father O'Connell had reached in for the chalice the next morning. Beyond redemption was Liam's soul, the priest had told the boy with every sweep of his huge, unpriestlike hand, beyond saving, his spirit as graceless and *as black as the Divil's owhn soul.* A creature spawned for Hell itself, and a rogue who would surely find his way there with no problem at all. His troublesome ways would . . .

Halloran blinked and the memory was gone; but the disquiet lingered. Why think of boyhood iniquity at that moment? There were worse sins to remember.

"The gates are locked?" The trace of Irish in his voice once more, the unexpected reverie tinting his speech.

"In a way," replied Kline.

Halloran glanced over his shoulder and the psychic smiled.

"Wait," Kline repeated.

Halloran turned back and looked through the bars of the gate. There was no movement from the lodge, no one leaving there to come to the entrance. But then his eyes narrowed when he saw—when he *thought* he saw—a shadow shift within a shadow inside one of the lodge's upper windows. His sharpened focus detected no further movement.

"Open up, Monk," Kline ordered his bodyguard.

With a low grunt, the heavyset American pushed open the passenger door and hefted himself out. He ambled toward the gate and indolently raised a hand to push one side open, taking it all the way back, its base grating over the road's uneven surface until foliage poked through the struts. He did the same with the other half, then stood to one side like an unkempt guardsman while Halloran drove on through. He closed the gates once more when the Mercedes drew to a halt inside the grounds.

Halloran had been irritated by a simple procedure that had been dramatized into a ritual. He could only assume that an electronic device in the gate's lock had been triggered by whoever was inside the lodge; yet when driving through, he hadn't noticed any such mechanism.

"I take it there's someone inside"—he nodded toward the lodge house—"capable of stopping any uninvited visitors from coming through?"

Kline merely grinned.

Halloran was about to put the question again, more pointedly this time, when he heard the sound of a vehicle braking sharply on the road outside the grounds. He turned swiftly to see the other Shield car reverse back to the opening, then turn in.

"Tell Monk to open the gate again," he said.

"I'm afraid not." Kline was shaking his head. "You know the rules, Halloran." There was a hint of glee in his voice, as though the psychic were enjoying the game now that he was safely home.

"Have it your way." Halloran left the Mercedes and walked back to the gate, Monk grudgingly opening it a fraction to allow him out. The two Shield operatives waited for him beside the Granada.

"Nearly missed this place," one of them said as he drew near.

Halloran nodded. "No bad thing. How about the Peugeot, Eddy?"

"Clean away. No sign at all."

Halloran wasn't surprised. "Response from Base?"

"As we figured. The car was stolen from Heathrow's short-term parking lot sometime last night. As usual, the owner had left his exit ticket inside."

"Should we inform the Blues?" asked the other man, who had been keeping a wary eye on the road.

"That's for Snaith to decide, but I don't think our client would want the police involved at this stage. If things get serious, we might have to insist."

Both operatives grinned, aware of how much it would take to render a situation "serious" as far as Halloran was concerned.

"D'you want us to check the grounds?" inquired Eddy, gesturing toward the gate.

Halloran shook his head. "Off limits for you two. Patrol the roads around here and keep an eye out for that Peugeot. You never know, they might chance their luck again later. I'll keep my radio transmitter with me at all times, so you can warn me if you spot anything suspicious. From what I've seen so far this place is high-risk, so stay sharp. Be back here by the main gate in three hours so the next team can take over."

"Body cover's a bit thin, isn't it?" the second operative remarked, never once allowing his observation of the main road to stray, "particularly now we're sure the contract's positive."

"We've no choice. It's how our target wants it. Maybe Snaith and Mather will convince him otherwise through the insurers, but till then, we do it as briefed. I'll be back here for changeover, so we'll compare notes then."

He turned away, and the two operatives shrugged at each other. Halloran was never forthcoming with finer details, but they trusted his judgment implicitly; if he wanted the operation to proceed in this way, then they wouldn't argue. They climbed back into the Granada and reversed from the drive.

Once he was inside, the gate closed behind Halloran with a solid *thunk*, leaving him with an absurd feeling that the estate had been sealed permanently. Monk glowered resentfully at him as he passed, and he knew there were going to be problems between them. That was unfortunate; if outsiders had to be involved in an operation, Halloran preferred them at least to be dependable. Ignoring the big man, he went to the Mercedes, gunning the engine as soon as he was inside. Monk's leisurely stride became more brisk when he realized he might be left behind.

"How much of the perimeter does the wall cover?" Halloran asked as the bodyguard lumbered in beside him.

It was Cora who answered. "Most of the estate's northerly border. Wire fencing and thick hedgerows protect the other aspects."

None of it was adequate, Halloran thought, but he said nothing. Before moving off, he looked past Monk toward the lodge once more, curious to catch a glimpse of whoever watched the gate from there. The windows could have been painted black, so darkly opaque were they.

The car rolled into motion, crunching stones beneath its tires, gathering moderate speed as it traveled along the winding road through the estate's woodland. The lodge house shrank into the distance, then was cut from view by the trees, and it was only at that point that Halloran was able to concentrate on the road ahead without constantly glancing into the rearview mirror.

He pressed a button and the window on his side slid down; the scent of trees wafted through as he inhaled deeply, relishing the air's sharpness, only then realizing how cloying the atmosphere inside the vehicle had become; fear, and excitement, left their own subtle odors, neither one particularly pleasant. The woodland itself was an untidy mix of oak, willow, beech, and spruce, no species more dominant than another. Here they canopied the roadway, creating a gloomy tunnel, the air inside cool, almost dank. Ferns stirred on either side, disturbed by the Mercedes' passage.

A sudden stab of color ahead startled him. It was instantly gone, the angle of vision through the trees changed by the moving car. Then again, a flash of redness among the green shades. The route was curving gently, winding downward into a small valley, and soon the house was in sight, a wide area of grass and then a placid blue lake spread before it, wooded slopes framing its other sides. Those hills disturbed Halloran, for he realized it would be easy for intruders to slip unseen down through the trees to the very boundaries of the house itself.

His attention was irresistibly drawn back to the building, which appeared to be a curious jumble of irregular shapes. Principally Tudor in period, the house had apparently been added onto during its history with no regard for symmetry. The two gables were of unequal height and pitch, and the twisted chimneys were scattered almost inconsequently over the various roofs. There were different levels of turrets, and a wing had been built onto the far side that stood higher than any other part of the building. Yet the overall image was not unpleasing, and much of that had to do with the rich coloring of its brickwork, for the walls fairly glowed in the sunlight, the aged stone mottled a warm red, that same redness even within the roof tiles; the gables were half-timbered and the many turrets fringed gray, serving to complement the ruddiness of the main walls.

Although the building as a whole was compact, Neath was nevertheless hugely impressive, its position alone, between the small hills and lake, supplying its own special grandeur. Halloran began to reassess Kline's worth in terms of personal wealth.

They were moving on level ground again, the expanse of water on their right, the entrance porch to the house looming up on their left; across the lake Halloran could see the muted hills of Surrey. He drew the car to a halt outside the stone entrance, and just behind a white Rover, the porch itself jutting from the building, wide and dented pavement inside leading up to the main door. Both sections of that door were already opening; two robed figures appeared together, dashing forward with heads bowed. They ran to the Mercedes' rear door, one of them eagerly pulling it open for Kline.

The two Arabs bowed even more deeply when Kline stepped out. *"Marhaba, Mouallem,"* they welcomed.

Halloran heard one of them mutter something further as he himself climbed from the Mercedes, and he saw Kline smile, the glitter of his dark eyes containing some kind of satisfaction but no warmth.

"Youssef meeneeh," Kline said quietly.

Halloran opened the other rear door for Cora, while Monk walked around to the back of the car. The bodyguard caught the keys tossed by Halloran against his chest and opened the trunk, reaching for the luggage inside. Cora seemed unsteady, and Halloran gripped her arm.

"You okay?" he asked. He thought there was apprehension in her expression when she looked toward the house, but it may only have been nervousness, a delayed reaction perhaps to their experience earlier.

"What? Oh yes. Yes, I'm fine." She stiffened, finding her strength, and he let go of her arm. "Thank you for what you did back there. You acted quickly."

"We'll discuss it inside. You look as though you could do with a stiff drink."

Kline was watching them across the roof of the car. "Cora needs no excuse for that, Halloran. I bet even you could use one after that nasty little business." He was smiling gleefully, his earlier panic obviously forgotten.

"Let's move inside as quickly as possible," said Halloran, scanning the road they had just traveled as well as the surrounding area.

"No need to worry," Kline assured him. "Not here, not inside the estate."

"I wouldn't be too sure of that," Halloran replied.

"Oh, but I am. Completely. Nothing can touch me here."

"Then humor me. Let's go in."

The Arabs and Monk followed behind with the luggage, although Halloran retrieved a black bag himself. They crossed the uneven pavement inside the porch and entered the house. Halloran found himself inside a large hall, a coolness rapidly descending upon him as if it had pounced; directly opposite the main door was a screen of linen-fold paneling, above that a minstrels' gallery, stout oak beams set in the walls and rising to the high, bowed ceiling. A broad stairway led to the floor above, from where diamond-paned windows provided inadequate light.

"Refreshments in the drawing room, Asil," Kline snapped, stone floor and walls creating a hollowness to his words. "Not for me, though. I've got things to do. Cora, you'll take care of our guest, show him around the place."

"We need to talk," Halloran said quickly to Kline.

"Later. We'll talk all you want later." He skipped up the stairway to their right, soft shoes almost silent against the wood. He turned back to them at the bend of the stairway and leaned over the balustrade.

"Can you feel Neath's welcome, Halloran?" he asked. "The house senses you, can you feel that? And it's confused. It doesn't know if you're friend or foe. But you don't really know that yourself yet, do you?" He sniggered. "Time will tell, Halloran. You'll be found out soon enough."

Kline continued his ascent, leaving Halloran to stare after him.

13

CONVERSATION WITH CORA

From this level Neath resembles a small monastery, thought Halloran. Except that there was nothing godly about the place. The day had become overcast, clouds hanging low and dark over the Surrey hills, so that now the redness of Neath's stonework had become subdued, the floridity deepening to a tone that was like ... the notion disturbed him ... like dull, dried blood. The house *looked* silent, as though it could never contain voices, footsteps, life itself. It might resemble a monastery, but it was hard to imagine invocations inside those walls.

He and Cora were on one of the slopes overlooking Kline's home, Halloran's brief reconnoiter of the estate confirming his doubts about its security. The two thousand acres were enclosed well enough to keep stray ramblers out, but there was no way any interloper of serious intent could be deterred. Kline's confidence in his own safety within the bounds of the estate was surprising, to say the least.

Immediately below them was what once must have been a splendid topiary garden. Now its bushes and hedges had become disarrayed, their sculptured shapes no longer maintained; where once there had been carved animals, cones, and spheres, there were protrusions and distortions, the vegetation neither natural nor engineered, but tortured and bizarre. At present these green deformities served only to provide random screening for anyone approaching the house.

"Can we sit for a while?"

Halloran turned to Cora again; the fragile anxiety behind her gaze puzzled him. She had changed into jacket and jeans for their tour of the grounds, the transformation from city lady into country girl both easy and pleasing. Even so, that slight darkness beneath her eyes seemed more pronounced, tainting some of her freshness.

"We've covered quite a distance in a short space of time," he said. "I'm a little breathless myself."

"It's not that. It's . . . just peaceful up here."

He caught the hesitation and wondered at it. He also caught her glance toward the house as she'd spoken. She sank to her knees and he followed suit, lounging back on one elbow while his search roved the grounds below. The lake had become leaden and gray, no breeze stirring its surface, no sunlight dappling its currents.

"Tell me about him, Cora."

She looked startled. "About Felix?"

He nodded. "Is he as mysterious as he pretends? Is he as crass as he pretends? I'll accept that he can do these wonderful things for Magma—why else would they insure his life for so much?—but what is his power exactly, where does it come from?"

Her laugh was brittle. "Perhaps even he doesn't know the answer to that last question."

"Why are you afraid of him?"

Her look was sharp, angry. Nevertheless she replied. "Felix commands respect."

"Fear and respect aren't the same thing. You don't have to tell me, but is he much more than an employer to you?"

"As you say, I don't have to tell you."

There was something moving from the trees on a slope at the far side of the house. Halloran watched without alerting the girl.

She mistook his silence for something else. "I'm sorry," she said. "I understand you're only doing your job. I suppose it's important that you know as much as possible about Felix."

The shape had slunk back into the trees. Too small, too low to the ground to be a deer. Too big and dark to be a fox. Why hadn't it been mentioned that there was a dog on the estate? Maybe it was a stray.

"It isn't quite that important, Cora," he said. "I think the reason I ask is that I want to know more about you, not Kline."

A subtle flaring of her pupils, the movement noticed by Halloran. His words had roused emotions in her. Those black spots within the brown quickly retreated. "I suppose that's part of your job too. You obviously think I could endanger Felix in some way."

"It's possible, but it isn't why I'm interested."

She gave a small shake of her head, her expression confused. "Then why...?"

He shrugged. "It's bothering me too. Let's say I don't feel we're strangers."

Cora stared at him. He wasn't smiling, but there was humor in his eyes. At first she thought he was mocking her, but then he did smile and its warmth was enveloping. That warmth spread through her, seeping into her body as if to purge the coldness there. Yet paradoxically she sensed a chilling danger in this man and she was afraid of how much he would discover about her, about Kline—about Neath itself—before this affair was through. She had sensed Kline's fascination with his newfound protector at their first meeting and it frightened her, for there might be unguarded moments they would all regret. There was a perceptiveness about Halloran, a *knowingness*, that was as intimidating as it was reassuring. There was the dichotomy of the man and perhaps that was part of his allure.

"I... I think we should return to the house," was all she could think of to say.

He caught her wrist as she began to rise, and the touching startled her. "I'm here to see that no harm comes to you," he said.

"To Felix you mean," she replied, staying there on the ground when he took his hand away.

"You're part of it. Your safety is just as important."

"Not as far as Magma is concerned." She managed to smile.

"You're part of it," he repeated, and Cora was unsure of his meaning. "You still haven't answered any of my questions," he persisted.

"I'm not sure that I can. I'm not sure that I know."

He watched her confusion and realized he had delved too soon. Cora could never accept him so quickly: an instinct told him she held secrets that bound her to Kline in some way.

"All right," he said. "For now."

He stood, then reached down to pull her to her feet.

At first Cora thought he was angry, so forceful was his grip; but he held her to his chest for a moment longer than necessary, looking down into her face, a quiet intensity to his gaze.

"Liam . . ." she said, but he had already released her and turned away. She watched him for a few moments before following, an unsteadiness to her movement that threatened to make her slip. She caught up with him, and Halloran noticed her awkwardness; this time he reached for her arm and held it gently, lending just enough support to help her walk more steadily. Cora's breathing was shallow, nervous, and she felt something had drained from her; not her strength, and not her resolution—Felix Kline had subjugated those a long time ago —but perhaps her fear of Halloran himself.

"Who are you?" she could only whisper.

"Nothing more than you can see," he replied.

But she felt that was not quite true.

14

ROOMS AND CORRIDORS

There were dark places in Neath, corners, niches, which sunlight could never touch, rooms gloomed in permanent dusk, corridors where dust motes seemed to clog the air, halls where footsteps echoed in emptiness. Yet there were also areas of dazzling light, the sun bursting through leaded windows with a force intensified by thick glass; these were cleansing places, where Neath's dank chill could be scoured from the body, although only briefly, as other rooms, other corridors were entered, brightness left behind like some sealed core.

Halloran explored and found many locked doors.

Tapestries adorned hallways. Fine portraits hung in main rooms and on stairways, meaningless to anyone other than direct descendants of the subjects themselves. Curved giltwood furniture displayed itself in arrangements that precluded comfortable use. Ornaments and sculptures were set around the house like museum pieces, there for admiration but perhaps not out of love—or so it seemed to Halloran. The house was a showcase only, full of history, but oddly devoid of spirit, Kline's attempt (presumably) at presenting an aesthetic side to his nature revealing nothing more than an indifference to such things (or at the most, pretensions toward them). The giveaway was the separateness of each item, the lack of relationship to those nearby, every piece of furniture, every sculpture or painting an isolated entity in itself, set pieces among other set pieces. Fine for a museum, but not for a home.

Yet spread among them, as if at random, were curios from a vastly different and more ancient culture: an encased necklace with thinly beaten gold pendants shaped like beech or willow leaves; stone statuettes of a bearded man and a woman, their hands clapsed over their chests as though in prayer, their eyes peculiarly enlarged so that they appeared to be staring in adoration; a board game of some kind, its squares decorated with shell and what appeared to be bone, two sets of stone counters of different color laid alongside; a silver cup with a robed figure in relief. Perhaps these, thought Halloran, along with other similar items, were a clue to where Kline's real interests in art lay, for they provided a consistent thread, a continuity that was missing in the other, later antique pieces. It would seem that his client had a penchant for the older civilizations.

The room allocated to Halloran was at the front of the house, overlooking the lawns and lake. Furnishings were functional rather than pleasing to the eye: wardrobe, chest of drawers, bedside cabinet—utility fare with no heritage to boast of. The wide bed, with its multicolored, lumpy quilt, looked comfortable enough; bedposts at each corner rose inches above the head- and footboards, the wood itself of dark oak.

He had unpacked his suitcase before exploring the rest of the building and placed the black case he'd also brought with him on a shelf inside the wardrobe.

His inspection had taken him to every section of the house —save where the locked doors had hindered him—even out onto the various turrets from where he had surveyed the surrounding slopes with considerable unease. The frontage, with its lawns and placid lake, provided the only point of clear view; the rear and side aspects were defense uncertainties. And worse: there was no alarm system installed at Neath. It was difficult to understand why a man who was evidently in fear for his own safety hadn't had his home wired against intrusion, particularly when his penthouse in the Magma building was a place of high, albeit flawed, security. Well, at least conditions here could soon be rectified. Halloran had wandered on through the house, examining window and door locks, eventually becoming satisfied that entry would prove difficult for the uninvited.

Another surprise was that Neath had been built around a central courtyard with a disused fountain, its stone lichen-coated and decaying, the focal point.

Halloran walked along the second-floor corridor overlooking the courtyard and made his way downstairs, quickly finding a door that led outside. The house was quiet and he realized he hadn't seen Cora nor any of the others for over an hour. He stepped out into the courtyard; the flagstones, protected on all sides from any cooling breeze, shimmered with stored warmth. Brown water stains streaked the lifeless fountain, fungus crusting much of the deteriorated stonework; the structure appeared fossilized, as if it were the aged and decomposed remains of something that had once breathed, something that had once moved in slow and tortuous fashion, had perhaps grown from the soil beneath the flagstones. He walked out into the middle of the courtyard, circling the centerpiece, but his interest no longer on it. Instead he peered around at the upper windows.

He had felt eyes watching him, an instinctive sensing he had come to rely on as much as seeing or hearing. From which window? No way of telling, for now they were all empty, as if the watcher had stepped back from view.

Halloran lowered his gaze. There were one or two doors at ground level other than the one he had just used. No risk these, though, for there was no direct entry into the courtyard from outside the house.

He crossed to the other side of the enclosure and tried a door there. It opened into a kitchen area, a large, tiled room he had come upon earlier. Closing the door again, he moved on to the next, looking into windows as he passed. The house might well have been empty for all the activity he saw in there. The second door opened into another corridor—Neath, he'd discovered, was a labyrinth of such—which was closed at one end by yet another door.

This was a passageway he hadn't discovered on his exploration of the interior and, curious, he stepped inside. To his left was a staircase leading upward, yet he could not recall finding it when he had circuited the first floor. Probably a staircase to one of the rooms he'd been unable to enter. He decided to investigate that possibility after he'd tried the door at the other end.

He walked down the passage, noting that the door looked somewhat more formidable than any others inside the house. The lock was of sturdy black iron and there was no key inserted. He reached for the handle.

And turned quickly, when he heard a creak on the stairway behind.

One of Kline's Arabs was smiling at him. But just before the smile, Halloran had glimpsed something else in the robed man's expression.

There had been anger there. And apprehension.

15

A STROLLING MAN

He walked along the pavement blank-faced, his eyes meeting no others, a plainly dressed man, suit as inconspicuous as his features. His hair was thin on top, several long loose strands tapering behind, indicating the slipstream of his passage. One hand was tucked into his trouser pocket, while the other held a rolled newspaper.

Occasionally he would glance into a doorway as he went by, no more than a fleeting look, as though taking care not to bump into anyone on his way out. Not once did he have to slow his already leisurely pace though, his journey along the street unimpeded. On he strolled, perhaps a clerk returning home after the day's work and, judging by his appearance, someone who lived in one of the older houses that hadn't yet succumbed to developers' mania for wharfside properties.

After he had passed one particular doorway he casually tucked the newspaper under his left arm, his pace even, still unhurried.

He walked on, and some way behind him two men in a parked car looked briefly at each other, one of them giving a sharp nod. The driver started the engine and gently steered the vehicle away from the curbside. It came to rest again only a hundred yards or so farther down the street.

The two men settled back to watch and wait.

16

A DIFFERENT KLINE

Dinner was obviously of little interest to Kline later that evening. To Halloran he seemed drained, listless, his sallow skin tight over his cheekbones, hollowed beneath them. His dark eyes had lost much of their luster, and his usual banter was less sharp, as though his thoughts were elsewhere. His youthfulness had unaccountably vanished, or so it appeared to Halloran, the man before him looking at least ten years older than the one he had first been introduced to at Magma.

Maybe the incident earlier in the day had taken more out of Kline than Halloran had realized. He'd witnessed delayed reaction many times in the past, had even suffered it himself — the abrupt recognition of what might have been, the leadening of spirit, the swift evaporation of energy followed inevitably by a further apathy. True, his client was unpredictable, but Halloran was surprised at the abrupt change.

Only three had sat for dinner, Cora, Kline, and himself, the two Jordanians serving, Monk off somewhere keeping watch or, more probably, reading his comic books. Kline had barely touched his food, which was solid English fare and not the exotic dishes Halloran had half-expected the Arabs to prepare (Khayed and Daoud ran the kitchen as well as the rest of the estate for their employer, with Monk and the Polish bodyguard, Palusinski, sharing the task of maintenance, both inside and outside Neath itself, with apparently no outsiders at all allowed within the boundaries).

Opposite him at the long and rough oak table that could easily have seated two dozen, Cora tried dutifully to engage both Halloran and Kline in conversation. But more than once she averted her eyes when Halloran spoke directly to her. He found her demeanor perplexing, yet so were many other aspects of this operation.

"You still haven't explained why there's no alarm system inside the house," he said to Kline, putting thoughts of Cora aside for the moment. "It's hard enough to understand why there's no system around the grounds, let alone inside."

Kline sipped wine and his tone was dulled when he replied. "I have locks, I have bodyguards. Why should I need anything more?"

Again that different manner of speech, an older man's intonation, the words themselves more considered.

"I think adequate alarm protection will have to be a condition of contract."

Lethargy gave way to irritability. "The contract has already been agreed and signed. You have to take my word for it that I'm quite safe here. Nothing can reach me within these walls, nothing at all."

"That isn't very sensible."

"Then consider me stupid. But remember who calls the tune."

Halloran shook his head. "Shield does that when we offer our services. I want you to understand that this place is too vulnerable."

The other man's laugh was dry. "I'll make a deal with you, Halloran. If you still feel this way about Neath when the weekend is through, we'll discuss your proposals some more. Perhaps you'll be able to persuade me then."

Halloran rested back in his chair, suspecting that Kline was too arrogant to be swayed by reason alone. He looked over at Cora for support, but again she gazed down at her plate to toy with her food.

"I think we'll need more men patrolling the perimeter," he said finally.

"That's entirely up to you," Kline replied. "As long as none of them stray into the grounds. That might prove unpleasant for them."

"You didn't tell me there were dogs roaming the estate."

Both Cora and Kline seemed surprised.

"I saw one of them earlier today," Halloran continued. "Just how many are there running around loose out there?"

"Enough to see off any intruders," answered Kline, his smile distracted.

"I hope you're right. Let's talk about these people who tried to stop us today: you must have some idea who they were."

"That's already been discussed. Jealous rivals of Magma, or hoodlums who want me for my ransom value."

"You knew you were in danger, that's why Magma is paying for my company's services. It follows that you're aware of where that danger's coming from."

Kline wearily shook his head. "If only that were true. I sense the threat, that's all. I sense many things, Halloran, but sensing is not the same as knowing."

"You can be pretty specific when you're locating minerals."

"A different matter entirely. Inert substances are nothing compared to the complexities of the mind."

"Aren't thought patterns easy to pick up by someone like you?"

"But difficult to decipher. Take your own thought waves—what am I to deduce from them?" Kline leaned forward, for the first time that evening his interest aroused. A slight gleaming even came back to his eyes.

Halloran drained his wine. One of the Arabs immediately stepped forward and refilled his glass.

"I look at Cora," Kline said without taking his eyes off Halloran, "and I feel her emotions, I can sense her fear."

A small sound from the girl, perhaps a protest.

"Her fear?" questioned Halloran.

"Of me. And of you."

"She has nothing to fear from me."

"As you say."

"Why should she be afraid of you?"

"Because I'm . . . her employer."

"That's reason enough?"

"Ask her."

"This is ridiculous, Felix," Cora said, her manner cold.

Kline leaned back in his chair, both hands stretched before him on the table. "You're quite right, of course. It's utterly ridiculous." He smiled at her, and there was something insidious in that smile.

For an instant, Halloran caught sight of the man's cruelty, a subtle and fleeting manifestation; it flitted across his face like some shadowy creature from its lair, revealing itself to the light momentarily, almost gleefully, before scurrying from sight again.

The moment was swiftly gone, but Halloran remained tense. He saw that Cora's hand was trembling around the stem of her wineglass.

Kline waved a hand toward the two manservants who stood facing one another on opposite sides of the room. "I can feel Asil and Youssef's devotion," he said, the smile less sly, weariness returning to weaken his expression. "I can sense Monk and Palusinski's loyalty. And of course I'm very aware of Sir Victor's avaricious need of me. But you, Halloran, from you there is nothing. No, a coldness that's worse than nothing. Yet perhaps that very quality—can it be called quality?—will protect my life when the moment comes. Your reaction today showed me your skill, and now I'm anxious to know your ruthlessness." He drew a thin finger along his lower lip as he pondered the Shield operative.

Halloran returned his gaze. "Let's hope it won't be necessary," he said.

A void seemed to open up in those somber eyes of Kline's. His breathing became shallow, and Halloran realized the man was somehow afraid.

"Unfortunately it will be," said Kline, his words no more than a murmur.

17

A DREAM OF ANOTHER TIME

Secure as Kline felt within his own grounds, Monk had the task of closing up the house completely each night when they stayed on the estate; Halloran, however, had little faith in the big man's diligence, and patrolled the house twice after dinner, on both occasions testing doors and windows. He arranged three-hour shifts with the bodyguard, taking the first until one in the morning himself.

Dinner had been cut short, Kline's evident fatigue finally overwhelming him. He had left the dining room without apology, the two manservants shuffling anxiously in his wake, leaving Cora and Halloran to themselves. Halloran had gently probed in an effort to discover more about her employer, about Neath itself, why certain rooms were inaccessible, who it was that guarded the gates by the lodge house, where the dogs were kept. But Cora had been unforthcoming, steering the conversation toward matters that had nothing to do with Kline or the estate. It was frustrating for Halloran, as well as puzzling, and he eventually excused himself so that he could phone Mather at home to report on the situation so far and to find out if there was any news on the would-be abductors. He learned that the Peugeot had been found abandoned by the police in a London suburb, and there were no clues as to who had stolen the vehicle. Naturally they had wondered at Shield's curiosity over the theft, but Dieter Stuhr, who had made the inquiry through a personal contact on the force, had promised that all would be revealed at some later date. That statement had, of course, aroused even more interest from the police, for they were all aware of the kind of activities Achilles' Shield was involved in. Mather had warned that total discretion might be difficult to maintain as far as the police were concerned.

At precisely one A.M., Halloran made his way up to the second floor and knocked on the door of Monk's room. The silence around him was occasionally disturbed by the creaking of aged timbers as they settled after the heat of the day. Corridors were poorly lit as though power was low. He waited and heard movement from inside the room, heavy but dulled footsteps—no shoes on those lumbering feet—approaching. The door opened only a few inches and a section of the bodyguard's face peered out, his eyelids drooping as if sleep was reluctant to lose its claim. The sour odor of sweat drifted out, and it was as unpleasant as Monk's stare.

"Your watch," Halloran informed him.

"Uh?" came the reply.

"Time to earn your keep. Check exterior doors and all windows first, then settle down in the main hallway. Take a walk round every half hour, more often if you get bored."

The door opened wider and he saw that Monk was dressed in undershirt and loosened trousers, his belly pushing outward so that the hem of his undershirt was stretched to its limit, the flesh between it and open belt buckle matted almost black. The hair on his head was no longer tied back, hanging loose around his broad flat face, strands curling inward to touch his stubbled chin, while the hair on his arms, thick and dark, reached up to his sloping shoulders and splayed there like pubics.

The day of the Neanderthal wasn't quite over, mused Halloran.

Monk moodily turned away, revealing the shambles of his room in the wedge of light from the open door. Magazines and comic books littered the floor, a tray filled with dirty plates and a beer can rested by the bed—a surprisingly small bed considering the man's bulk. Halloran had no desire to see further.

"Monk," he said quietly, and the bodyguard looked back. He stood there as if rooted, his shoulders hunched so that his neck seemed sunken into his chest. He glowered at Halloran, who told him, "Any disturbance at all you come straight to me. Is that understood?"

"You're shittin' me," was the response.

Halloran shook his head. "You come and get me. Not Kline. You warn me first."

"That ain't the way."

"You find me first or I'll break *your* arms when the fuss is over."

The bodyguard turned back all the way, squaring himself at Halloran. "I'm paid to watch out for Mr. Kline," he said, his piping voice as low as he could register.

"I'm being paid more to do the same. You want to discuss it, take it up with Kline in the morning. Tonight you do as I say."

Monk might well have rushed him there and then, and Halloran didn't think it was the memory of what had happened last time that prevented him from doing so: no, it had more to do with getting into trouble with his employer. Monk flicked his tongue across his lips, glistening them, his mind still not made up.

"I want you downstairs in two minutes," Halloran told him curtly. Then he walked away, hearing something shatter in the room behind. Monk's bedroom must have been even more of a shambles with his dinner things scattered across the floor. Halloran smiled, knowing that a score would have to be settled when this affair was over; he himself, was prepared to let it lie, but he knew the other man wouldn't share the same view. That was going to be Monk's misfortune.

He returned to his bedroom on the second floor, pausing to look out over the center courtyard on the way. The moon palely laminated the flagstones, the fountain throwing a misshapen shadow across the whiteness, an irregular stain on a pattern of rough squares. He searched to one side of the fountain, wondering about the sealed door he had found in the short corridor there. It had been Youssef Daoud who had disturbed him as he tried the door.

Halloran had asked where the door led to and why was it locked, but Daoud's comprehension of the English language (it was mentioned in their files that both Arabs spoke good English) had suddenly become very poor, and he could only grin at Halloran and shake his head. Halloran had gone back outside to the courtyard. Later Cora told him that the staircase the Arab had watched him from led to Kline's private quarters.

Darkness crept over the rooftops and down into the well

below, thick clouds claiming the moon for their own, dim lights from windows around the house asserting little influence over the blackness. He moved away, going to his room and quietly closing the door behind him, relieved to shut the rest of Neath away for a short while. He shrugged off his jacket, hanging it on one of the posts at the foot of the bed. Taking the Browning Hi-Power from its waist holster, he placed it on the bedside table, then set his soft-alarm clock for ten minutes to four. With one last scan of the grounds outside the window—there wasn't much to see save for the black humps of hills and an orange glow over a nearby town—he lay on the bed, undoing two more shirt buttons, but leaving his shoes on and laced. He put one pillow on top of its mate and rested back, his eyes closing immediately, the dim light from the bedside lamp no bother at all.

Sleep was not long in coming. And with its dream came a memory...

...He could hear the harsh breathing from behind the wood latticework, as though drawing in air was an uncomfortable process for the priest...Bless me, Father, for I have sinned...Liam wondered why he did not feel the shame he was supposed to. He recounted his "crimes" against the Holy Father in Heaven and smiled in the unlit confessional, feeling no resentment even in having to reveal secrets to a man whom he had no liking for, and worse, no respect for...I've lied, Father, I've stolen things...the bow of the priest's large head in the diamond holes of the struts, a nodded acceptance of the confessor's iniquity...I've abused my own body, Father— that's how the boys were taught to say it, "abused" instead of "pleasured"...and I've called God dirty names... movement stopping in the adjoining cubicle, the priest's breath momentarily held...Liam's smile widening...I've asked God why He's a wicked bastard, Father...The bulky head turning toward him, the priest's eyes, unseen but felt, burning through the latticework. He took him from Mam an' me...the boy's smile hard, his eyes staring ahead, seeing nothing...Liam, gunmen took your father's life, not God... why He...why He made me Mam...why He made her... the boy's eyes moistened, the smile still there...do things...mad things...why she's to go away...Liam—the priest again, gentle now...why...the boy's first sob, the hunching of his shoulders, hands reaching up, fingers sinking

through the black diamonds of the grille, curling around, clutching and pulling as if to wrench away a barrier against truth . . . the shadow beyond moving, light thrown to show emptiness there . . . the door beside Liam opening, Father O'Connell reaching in, touching the boy's shoulder . . . Liam pushing him away, shrinking down into the booth's corner, forcing his head hard against his raised knees, tears uncontrolled, thin body jerking with the outflow . . . the priest, a burly and dark silhouette, bending forward, arms outstretched . . .

. . . A tapping on the door.

Halloran's eyes opened immediately, consciousness returning almost as fast. The dream remained as an image, one that could be put aside for the moment. He was moving toward the door, gun tucked into holster, before the tapping resumed. He opened up, one foot rigid against the base of the door so that it couldn't be forced wider.

Outside stood Cora.

18

UNHOLY COMMUNION

There were candles all around him, tall thick-stemmed candles, candles that were black. They hardly lit the chamber, though his wretchedly thin naked body glistened highlights under their subdued glow; the two dark-skinned men had used oil on him, their excitement enhanced by the slippery smoothness of his skin.

And there were eyes watching him constantly. Large, unblinking eyes, grouped together at the far end of the room.

The youth moaned, twisted his head, movement weakened by the frequent injection of fluid into his veins. They kept him passive. But not all the time. Sometimes the Arabs liked to hear him screaming.

No sound could escape this room, they had said, grinning at him, holding each other's hand. This was a secret place, one of worship, where the walls were strengthened by the very earth itself. Scream, they had urged him. Shriek, for our delight, they had said as long needles pierced his flesh. Let us see you weep, they coaxed as sharp things were imbedded in his genitalia.

They had taken the hair from his body, even pulled free the eyelashes, plucked his nostrils clear, so that he remained only gleaming colorless flesh, a languid, loose-muscled object one moment, a fitful shivering creature the next. And sometimes, perhaps because of the drugs, the pain was exquisite.

They had removed his tongue when they grew tired of his words, suspending his body so that he would not suffocate on his own blood, sealing the wound with liquid that blazed more than the cutting. Then they had mocked his gibbering as they used his body with their own, thrusting into him with a force that tore and bloodied him inside.

The youth attempted to move his limbs, but they were restrained, not by drugs but by manacles. He lay on the hard flat surface, arms and legs stretched outward, body punctured by wounds, many needles still protruding, metal dull in the poor light, thin rivulets of blood, now dried and crusted, on his skin. Every part of him seared pain and, had his senses been more lucid, the agony might have checked his heart. While one channel of his mind struggled for reason, others closed down, refuting the hurt to his body, the degradation it had suffered, instinctively knowing that full acknowledgment could only mean insanity. The remaining dregs of morphia were an ally to their cause.

The low flames wavered, caressed by a breeze. He raised his head from the cold slab he was chained to, the motion sluggish, taking all his strength, and looked down along his own body. The slender spikes in his chest were huge to his fuddled brain, rising like crooked metal poles in a greasy snow field, and their undulation as he breathed became mesmerizing. But light from above was seeping into the chamber. He struggled to keep his head raised, but it was too heavy, the strain was too much. It fell back onto the stone with a sharp crack. He had seen the figures emerge from the passageway though, grouped together at the top of the stairs as if their bodies were joined. The youth moaned aloud, his dread even more acute.

He tried to call out when he heard their footsteps on the stairs, wanting to plead with them, and could only manage an incoherent wailing sound that became a whimper when his head lolled to the side and he saw them approach.

The two Arabs, as ever, were grinning down at him and between them stood—no, sagged, for the others were supporting him—a small man whose ravaged face was so old and so wicked that the youth tried to turn away. But it was impossible—the strength wasn't there; the side of his face could only rest against the stone and his eyes could only stare.

The dark-haired man, whose features were wizened and cruel, skin flaking away as though diseased, gazed on the youth, and his tongue flicked across dry, cracked lips. He extended a tremulous hand, index finger pointing, and trailed a yellow fingernail along the white stomach, bringing the nail up toward the sternum. As it traveled, the finger sank into the flesh, with no apparent effort, leaving a shallow rent behind.

Once more a syringe found a vein in the youth's spindly arm and fluid was pushed into him. The glow rapidly spread through him and he almost smiled his gratitude. Now he could turn his face toward the black, limitless ceiling above.

He was conscious of, but did not feel, the pulling apart of his skin, and the vapor that rose from his stomach into the cool air was no more to him than a light cloud rising from a warm dampness.

The dark-haired man shuffled away, aided by one of the Arabs, the other disappearing to a different part of the room.

The youth lay there on his blood-soaked slab, his body opened, and dreamily wondered why they had gone away. He didn't mind, not at all. It was pleasant lying there, watching steam gently curl upward from a source near him, but just out of sight. He wanted to drift away, to sleep, but for some reason his mind wouldn't allow him. It was nagging, trying to tell him something, something desperately urgent, but he didn't want to know, the peace after so much pain was too intoxicating. Now the needles were like birthday candles, their heads gleaming as tiny flames. Was it his birthday? He couldn't remember. Any celebration was nice though.

He heard nearby sounds and turned and craned his neck as far as it would go. Nerve ends twinged only a little. The dark-haired man was inside an alcove, opening something, a cabinet of some kind. No, not a cabinet. One of those . . . what were they called? The sort of thing they had in churches, a box-thing priests were always poking into. Funny, this place was like a church with all the candles, even though they were black. The stone he lay on was like an altar.

The youth giggled, although the noise he made was more like a gurgle.

The three men converged on the pale, supine body, the dark-haired man carrying a dish of black metal, a veil, black again, draped over its edges. Blood was spilling over from the long scission in the youth's body, spreading in pools on the stone's surface, beginning to trickle down the sides. The youth had scant life left in him.

The veil was drawn away, revealing the dish to be more like a wide-brimmed chalice, for it had a base that was clutched in one trembling hand. With his other hand, the dark-haired man removed the contents and placed it inside the youth's stomach, gently pressing down, soaking it in blood, smothering it in slithery organs.

Now the youth did scream, a piercing screech that echoed around the stone walls of the chamber, for no drugs could deaden the pain nor the horror.

He was alive, but barely, when the Arab on the other side of the stone raised the tool he had collected and began cutting into the youth's outstretched limbs.

And still those myriad eyes stared, never closing, never wavering.

19

CORA'S NEEDS

"I need company," she said simply. "I get . . . frightened when I'm alone in this house."

Halloran had opened the door wider and she'd hurried by him, glancing back over her shoulder as if someone had been stalking her along the corridor. He looked out to make sure there really was no one there.

He turned, and she was putting the bottle and glasses she'd brought with her on the bedside cabinet.

"I remembered you liked Scotch," Cora told him, and there was no confidence in her voice.

He shook his head. "I'm on watch again in"—he checked his wristwatch—"a couple of hours. You go ahead if you want."

She did. Cora poured herself a stiff measure, turning slightly away from him to avoid his eyes, and he wasn't sure if she felt guilty coming to him in the middle of the night or because she needed a drink. He closed the door.

Cora wore a white bathrobe against the night chill. "You must think me silly. Or . . . " She let the sentence trail away.

Halloran walked toward her, lifting the big automatic from its holster and laying it beside the bottle and empty glass. "We all have fears," he had said.

Halloran began to move into her, taking care, even though she dug her fingers into his naked back, urging him on. Her teeth nipped his neck, his shoulder, as she squirmed beneath him, thrusting herself upward. Cora still wore the bathrobe and he pushed it open so that he could caress her breasts. She moaned and there was a desperation to the sound. He lifted himself so that he could see her flesh, could kiss her breasts.

He bent to a raised nipple and softly drew on it with his lips, moistening the tip with his tongue. She caught her breath, then let it escape in an unsteady sigh. He pulled the robe from her and tossed it over a chair, then turned back to her welcoming naked body.

He let his fingertips trail away, touching her side, her hip, his hand moving inward so that it was between them, his palm smoothing her stomach, fingers reaching down into her hair. Her thighs rose around him and he was inside her, pushing inward, meeting only slight resistance. Cora's hands were low on his back and they pulled him tight so that he lost control of the movement. He was drawn into her sharply, causing her to give a little cry of pain.

Every part of her seemed stretched, her muscles stiffened as if she had been pierced rather than entered. Halloran's demand now matched hers as he felt the familiar floating sensation, the incredible tensing of his own muscles, the swift rise toward the breaking of that tension. He gasped air and the low moan came from him this time.

But it changed. Her clutching altered in intensity, became fraught rather than encouraging; her cries became those of frustration rather than passion. Halloran slowed his rhythm, aware that he was losing her.

Cora's legs straightened and her motion subsided, then became still. She turned her face away from him. Perplexed, Halloran raised himself and looked down on her. A tear gathered in the corner of her eye, welling there and finally spilling.

"Cora . . . ?"

"Please, Liam. Help me."

He frowned.

Her eyes closed. "In my robe," she said so softly he scarcely heard.

When Halloran left the bed and found the thin coils of leather inside the pockets of the bathrobe, he began to understand . . .

20

ABDUCTION

They had watched the man with the strange scar that looked like the continuation of a smile leave the building, and the observer in the passenger seat of the car nodded his head in affirmation. The man who had earlier ambled down that same street carrying a rolled-up newspaper leaned forward from the back, resting an arm on the top of the driver's seat, his face keen with interest.

The balding figure had turned in the other direction to where their vehicle was parked, and they allowed him to get some distance away before the backseat passenger reached for the door handle. The man in front stopped him with a motion of his hand. Their quarry was unlocking a car parked by the roadside.

The driver switched on the ignition and waited for the other car to pull out. When it did so, they followed.

They came for him before dawn, easily and quietly forcing the lock on the door to his basement apartment without causing damage. He awoke only when they were at his bedside, his cry of *"Wer ist da?"* quickly stifled by his own bedclothes. Several blows were dealt to his head, the first two stunning him (the second breaking his nose in the process), but the third, delivered with impatient strength, rendered him unconscious. The fourth blow was just for the satisfaction.

His limp body was removed from the bed and dressed, wallet placed in an inside pocket, watch strapped to his wrist. The bloodied sheet was then stripped from the bed and folded into a neat square. It would be taken with them. The bed was remade and, first checking that everything was in order, they carried Stuhr into the hallway, then up the short concrete stairway to the street where a car was waiting. The last man carefully closed the front door behind him. There was no wife, no lover, no one at all to witness the German's abduction.

21

BENEATH THE LAKE

Morning had brought with it a low-lying mist, the night's dampness evaporating as the earth slowly warmed again. Trees in the distance appeared suspended in the air; low bushes nearby were like spectral animals crouching in the whiteness, waiting for prey.

Halloran scanned the slopes above the mist as he walked through the neglected gardens, looking for any sign of movement on them, studying one spot for a while, going back to it seconds later to see if anything had altered. He also kept an eye out for the dogs that apparently roamed the estate, and even though Cora had told him they never came near the house itself he had little faith in that particular notion, wondering just how they could be trained to keep away. He thought of her as he walked, confused by the ambivalence of his feelings toward her. The bondage and the harshness of their lovemaking had helped satisfy Cora, but his own pleasure had been limited. True, his arousal had been enhanced to begin with, but the satisfaction afterward had not been so complete. Prudish guilt, Halloran? Was the Catholicism of his youth still intrinsic to his attitudes? With all he had been through, all he had done, he doubted it. Maybe he'd been mildly disappointed in her; and yet her inclination, her weakness had made Cora more vulnerable to him. After, when she had risen from the bed to find her robe, he had noticed marks across her back and buttocks. He made no comment, aware that they could only be faded whipmarks. But he couldn't help wondering what else there was to discover about her.

He rounded the corner of the house and saw the mist shrouding the lake, slowly rolling across its surface, shifted by a mild breeze. His feet crunched gravel as he approached the dew-stippled Mercedes. Halloran dropped flat to inspect underneath the car, searching with a penlight for any object that could have been attached during the night. He quickly checked all underside parts, then the wheel wells, shock absorbers, and brake lines. Satisfied, he walked around the vehicle looking for grease spots, pieces of wire, handprints, even disturbances on the gravel near the car doors. Before opening each door fully, Halloran ran a credit card around the tiny gaps to check for wires. This done, he sniffed the interior before entering, seeking the smell of bitter almonds or any other odd odor. Wary of pressure detonators, he checked the dashboard, glove compartment and ashtrays without putting any weight on the seats. He then looked under the seats. He examined the engine, using the credit-card check once more before lifting the hood completely; afterward he did the same with the trunk. Only when this ritual was complete did he start the engine and let it run for a few minutes, moving the car backward and forward a few feet. Sure that the Mercedes had not been tampered with during the night, Halloran cut the motor and climbed out, locking up again before leaving it.

"Was all that really necessary?" a voice asked from the porch.

He turned to find Felix Kline watching from just inside, his arms folded as he leaned one shoulder against the stonework. He was dressed casually once more—jeans and loose-fitting jacket, a sweater underneath. And he had a grin on his face that dismissed all the fatigue Halloran had noticed the night before.

"I'd have done the same even if the Merc had been locked away in a garage overnight," Halloran replied. "I'll check out the Rover if it's unlocked."

"So you really didn't believe me when I told you I was safe here."

Halloran shrugged. "It isn't Shield's policy to take chances."

"Nope, I suppose not." Kline emerged from the shade, stretching his limbs and looking up at the sky. "It's going to be a good day. You want to take a trip, Halloran? A little pre-breakfast exercise, huh? Something to keep you in trim."

"What've you got in mind?"

"Follow the leader and you'll find out."

He strode off in the direction of the lake, and Halloran was surprised at the briskness of his step. Only last night Kline had appeared overcome by exhaustion, his features haggard, all movement wearied; this morning the man exuded energy.

"C'mon, forget about the other car," Kline called back cheerfully.

Halloran walked after him at a more leisurely pace, although he was far from relaxed: all the while he kept an alert eye on their surroundings, looking for any sudden change in the landscape, any glints of light that might be sun reflecting off binoculars or a rifle barrel; he paid particular attention to the road leading from the estate's entrance.

Kline was well ahead, almost at the edge of the lake. Occasionally he would wind his arms in the air or skip full circle, and Halloran half-expected him to do a cartwheel at any moment. It was as if the small man had too much energy to spare.

The ground dipped slightly toward the water and Kline was stooping, only his head and shoulders in view. Halloran hurried his pace and found his client on a low jetty; moored to it was a rowboat.

"This'll set you up for the day," Kline said as he untied the mooring rope.

"No outboard?"

"I like the quietness of the lake, its stillness. I don't like engines upsetting that. Monk or Palusinski usually does the rowing for me, but you can have that privilege today." Kline hopped into the boat and settled at its stern. "Let's get going."

"There won't be much to see with this mist," Halloran remarked, stepping onto the jetty.

"Maybe," Kline replied, turning away to look across the cloud-canopied surface.

Halloran climbed aboard, using a foot to push the boat away from the landing stage. Sitting on the middle bench, he used one oar to set the boat further adrift before sliding both into their oarlocks. Turning about, he set course for the middle of the lake, soon finding an easy rhythm, their passage through the curling mists smooth and unhurried. His position gave Halloran an opportunity to study his companion at close range, and he realized Kline's change had little to do with any physical aspect but was linked with the man's volatile nature, his puzzling split personality, for nothing in his features had altered. There was just a brightness to him, a shining in those dark eyes, a sharpness in his tone. Not for the first time, Halloran wondered if his client was on drugs of some kind.

Kline, whose face had been in profile, suddenly swung around to confront him. "Still trying to figure me out, Halloran?" He gave a short laugh. "Not easy, is it? Nigh on impossible, I'd say. Even for me." His laughter was longer this time. "Thing of it is, I'm unlike anyone you've ever met before. Am I right?"

Halloran continued rowing. "I'm only interested in your safety."

"Is that what your bosses at Shield instruct you to tell your clients? Is that in the handbook? You can't deny you're curious though. Wouldn't you really like to know more about me, how I got so rich, about this power of mine? You would, wouldn't you? Yeah, I know you would."

"I admit I'm interested."

Kline slapped his own knee. "That's reasonable." He leaned forward conspiratorially. "I can tell you I wasn't born this way. Oh no, not *quite* like this. Let's call it a late gift." His smile was suddenly gone, and although his eyes bore into Halloran's, Kline seemed to be looking beyond.

"You make it sound as if your psychic ability was handed to you." An oar had dredged up some rotted weeds, and Halloran paused to free the paddle end. The tendrils were slick under his touch, and he had to tug several times to clear the wood. When he dipped the oar back into the water he found Kline was smiling at him, no longer preoccupied with distant thoughts.

"Did you sleep soundly last night?" the dark-haired man inquired.

Was his smile really a leer? And why the abrupt change in topic? "Well enough for the time I had," Halloran replied.

"You weren't disturbed at all?"

"Only by Neath's lack of security. You're taking unnecessary risks here."

"Yeah, yeah, we'll discuss that later. Cora's an interesting lady, don't you think? I mean, she's not quite what she seems. Have you realized that?"

"I don't know much about her."

"No, of course not. Has she told you how she came to be working directly for me? I decided I wanted Cora the first time I laid eyes on her in old Sir Vic's office about three years ago. Recognized her potential, y'see, knew she had . . . hidden depths. Know what I mean, Halloran?"

Halloran ignored the insinuations but had to hold his rising anger in check. "She obviously makes a good PA."

"You're right, she does. Aren't you curious though?"

Halloran stopped rowing, resting the oars in the water, letting the boat drift. "About what?" he said evenly.

"Hah! You are. Me and Cora, what goes on between us. Does she do more for me than just arrange schedules, type letters? Maybe you want to know if she and I are lovers."

"That's none of my business."

Kline's smile was sly. "Oh no? I'm an extremely aware person, Halloran, and it isn't hard for me to sniff out something going on under my nose. I don't mind you having your fun as long as you remember who Cora belongs to."

"Belongs to? You're talking as if you own her, body and soul."

Kline turned away, still smiling. He squinted into the low white mist, as if to pierce it. The trees and slopes were faded along the edge of the lake, the haziness of the sky belying the sharpness of the early-morning air.

"Can you feel the weight of the water beneath us?" Kline suddenly asked, still looking away from the other man. "Can't you feel the pressure underneath these thin wooden boards, as if all that liquid down there, all the slime and murkiness that lies on the bottom of the lake, wants to break through and suck us down? Can you sense that, Halloran?"

He almost said no, a total rejection of the notion. But then Halloran began to feel the potency beneath his feet, as if the water there really could exert itself upward, could creep through those tight cracks between the boards like some glutinous absorbing substance. Kline's suggestion had somehow turned the lake into something less passive. Halloran shifted uncomfortably on the rowing bench.

A ripple in the lake caused the boat to sway.

Kline's attention was on him once more and his voice was low in pitch, less excitable, when he spoke. "Look over the side, look into the lake. Notice how silky is its skin beneath this mist, and how clear. But how far can you see into the denseness below? Come on, Halloran, take a peek."

Although reluctant, Halloran did so. No big deal, he told

himself, no reason to be churlish. He saw his own shadow on the lake.

"Keep watching the water," came Kline's quiet voice. "Watch how it swells and falls, as soft as anything you could ever wish to touch. Look into your own shadow; how dark it makes the water. Yet somehow the darkness allows you to see more. And what if the whole lake was shadowed? What depths could you perceive then?"

Halloran was only aware of the blackness of his own reflection. But the blackness was spreading, widening in tranquil undulations, forcing away the mist as it grew. Kline's voice coaxed him to keep his eyes fixed on the lapping water, not even to blink lest that merest of movements disturb the placid surface, to stare into the darkness until his thoughts could be absorbed . . . absorbed . . . *absorbed* by the lake itself, drawn in so that what was hidden before could now be viewed . . .

"*. . . There are monsters beneath us, Halloran . . .*"

He could see the shapes moving around, sluggish, lumbering patches of greater darkness, and it seemed to him—it was *insinuated* to him—that these were grotesques who knew nothing of light, nothing of sun, creatures who slumbered in the depths, close to the earth's core. Among them were sleeker denizens, whose very tissue-like structures prevented pulverization under such pressure; they glided between their cumbersome companions, two opposite natures coexisting in a nocturnal underworld. There were others with them, but these were less than fleeting shadows.

Halloran sensed their yearning, the desire to ascend and make themselves known to the world above, weary of perpetual gloom but imprisoned by their own form. Yet if they could not rise, perhaps something of what they sought could be lured down to them . . .

The boat tilted as Halloran leaned further over the side.

"*Touch the water,*" he was softly urged. "*Feel its coldness . . .*"

Halloran stretched his hand toward the lake that had become a huge liquid umbra, and there was a stirring below at his approach, a kind of quivering expectancy.

"*. . . sink your fingers into it . . .*"

He felt the wetness and its chill numbed more than his flesh.

"... *deeper, let it taste you* ..."

The water was up to his wrist, soaking his shirtsleeve.

"... *reach down, Halloran, reach down and* ..."

He heard laughter.

"... *touch the nether region* ..."

Halloran saw the shapes rising toward him, mutations that should only exist in the depths, mouths—were they mouths? They were openings, but were they *mouths?*—gaping, ready to swallow him in . . . to *absorb* him . . .

The laughter was sharper, startling him to his senses. Halloran pulled his hand clear, standing in the boat as if to push himself as far away from those rearing, avaricious gullets as possible.

Still they surged upward, climbing as a single gusher, an almost solid stream of misshapen beings, terrible, unearthly things without eyes but which had limbs that were stunted and as solid as their bodies, while others were only tenuous substances housed around jagged needle-teeth . . . coming closer, rushing as if to shoot above the surface itself . . .

. . . Until they began to disintegrate, to shatter, to implode, for they were never meant for the fine atmosphere of the upper reaches.

He heard their anguished screams though there were no sounds—their torment was in his mind only. All around the boat the water was bubbling, white foam spouting upward as if the lake were boiling. Here and there geysers appeared, jetting into the air and carrying with them—or so Halloran imagined—remnants of flesh, all that was left of the abyssal creatures.

The boat pitched in the ferment and Halloran quickly sat, both hands gripping the sides for support, staying that way until the turbulence began to subside, the lake becoming peaceful once more.

The two men were in an area of clarity, for the mist had been driven back to form a wide circle around the boat. Everything was still within that clear area, the boat now barely drifting.

The only sound was Kline's low chuckling.

22

FOOD FOR DOGS

Charles Mather was kneeling among his shrubs when his wife called him from the terrace steps. Always used to rising early, he had found the habit hard to break after leaving military service. So nowadays, rather than disturb Agnes, who did not share his fondness for early-morning activity, he would creep from their bedroom, dress in the bathroom, take tea in the kitchen, then wander out into the garden, which had become his second love (Agnes would always be his first). Whatever the season, there was always work to be done out there, and for him there was no better way to start the day than with lungs full of sharp—and at that time of the morning, reasonably untainted—air. The only negative factor was that the chill (always a chill first thing, be it winter, spring *or* summer) upset the metal in his leg.

He looked up from the bed he had been turning over with a short fork. "What's that, m'dear?"

"The telephone, Charles. Mr. Halloran is on the telephone. He says it's important that he speaks to you."

Agnes was a trifle irritated because she'd had to climb from a bath to answer the phone, knowing that her husband would never hear its ringing in the garden. Here she stood shivering with the morning freshness and catching pneumonia by the second.

Mather pushed himself up from the padded kneeler, the tip of his cane sinking into the soft earth as he hobbled toward the terrace.

"I should get back inside if I were you, Aggie," he said as he awkwardly climbed the steps. "You'll catch your death of cold standing around like that."

"Thank you for your concern, Charles, but I'm sure poking

around in the damp grass for a couple of hours hasn't done much for your leg either," she replied more tartly than she felt. "I think you'd better take a bath right after me."

"Mother knows best," he agreed with a smile. "Now you get yourself back indoors before I whip off your dressing gown and chase you naked around the garden."

She quickly turned to hide her own smile and walked to the patio doors. "That might give the neighbors a breakfast thrill," she said over her shoulder.

"Y'know," he murmured, limping after her and admiring her rear with almost as much enthusiasm as when they were younger, "I really believe it would."

He took the call in his study, settling down into an easy-chair first and waiting for the click that signaled Agnes had replaced the upstairs receiver. "Liam, Charles here. I hadn't expected to hear from you today."

There was no urgency in Halloran's voice. "I've been trying to contact Dieter Stuhr since eight this morning, but had no luck."

"As we have an ongoing operation he'll be at Shield all weekend," said Mather. "I assume you've already tried to reach him there though."

"I thought I'd probably catch him at home earlier, then I rang the office. No answer from there either."

Mather checked his wristwatch. "Hmm, just after nine. He'd have one other coordinator with him today, and she should have arrived by now."

"Only Stuhr would have a key."

"Then she might be waiting outside at this moment. It's not like Dieter to be late, but perhaps he's on his way. That could be why you missed him."

"I rang his apartment over an hour ago."

"Well, he could have been delayed. Look, I'll get on to Snaith—don't see why his Saturday shouldn't be disrupted and between us we'll see what we can find out. No doubt it'll prove to be something trivial—his car's probably had an upset." With his free hand, Mather rubbed his aching knee. "D'you have a problem there at Neath, Liam?"

"I wanted to arrange for extra patrols outside, that's all. And I think our men should be armed. Security here is virtually nil."

There was a pause, but Mather sensed that Halloran wanted

to say more. When no further words came, the older man spoke up: "Anything else bothering you, Liam?" The question was put mildly, but Mather knew his operative well enough to understand something was wrong.

More silence, then, "No, nothing else. Our client is unusual, but he can be handled."

"If there's a problem between you two, we can switch. No need for added complications, y'know."

"Uh, no. Leave things as they are. Let me know what's happened to the Organizer, will you?"

"Surely. Soon as we know something ourselves. Perhaps Stuhr stayed somewhere else overnight—I understand it frequently happens to single men. Could be whoever he's with has found ways to detain him."

"It's not like him to be out of touch."

"I agree, particularly when there's an operation in progress." Mather was frowning now. "We'll keep you informed, Liam, and in the meanwhile we'll organize some extra cover for you. I assume last night went without incident?"

"It was quiet. Anything more on the stolen Peugeot?"

"Still drawn a blank there, I'm afraid. Police can't help. You're sure our client doesn't know more than he's telling?"

"I'm not sure of anything."

Mather stopped soothing the ache in his knee. Again he waited for Halloran to continue, but all that came through were atmospherics on the line. "It might be an idea if I paid Neath a visit myself," he suggested.

"We'll be back in London on Monday. Let's you and I meet then."

"If you say so. Look, I'll get back to you as soon as I've got some news."

"Fine."

He heard the click as Halloran hung up and he held his own phone close to his ear for several seconds before putting it down. Mather was thoughtful for several more moments before he lifted the receiver again.

Halloran stood by the telephone in the large open hallway, his hand still resting on the receiver. He was concerned about Dieter Stuhr's absence, well aware that it was out of character for the German to be missing during a major assignment (or even a minor one, for that matter). Maybe, as Mather had suggested, he was having problems getting into the office that morning. Less likely was that he'd been detained at some other address; the Organizer didn't run his life that way—he'd have at least let Shield know where he could be contacted no matter how impromptu the situation. Halloran ran his fingers across his as yet unshaven chin. Maybe Kline—and Neath itself—were getting to him. He was beginning to feel uneasy about everything.

There were footsteps on the staircase behind him. He turned to find Cora approaching, her descent faltering momentarily when he looked into her eyes, her hand touching the wide balustrade for balance.

"Good morning, Liam." Her greeting was subdued, as if she were not sure how he would react toward her.

"Cora," he responded. He moved to the foot of the stairs and waited. Neither one smiled at the other, and both were conscious that this was not the usual way for lovers to say hello after a night of intimacy.

"Have you had breakfast?" she asked, the question put to break the awkwardness between them rather than out of any real interest.

"I'm on my way in," Halloran replied. He touched her arm to stop her from walking on. She looked up at him, startled. "Cora, why didn't you warn me about Kline?"

She could not conceal the tiny flicker of alarm that showed in her eyes.

"Why didn't you tell me he had the—I suppose you'd call it power—to hypnotize? We took a little trip this morning, out on the lake. He made me see things there, things I never thought possible. Creatures, Cora, monsters that seemed to be living in the slime beneath that water. I don't know whose imagination he dredged them from—his or mine—but they scared the hell out of me even though common sense told me they couldn't really exist. He froze me, and it's been a long time since anyone did that."

"He was playing games with you." She had moved closer and her voice was quiet, almost mournful. "It was Felix's way of showing you how manipulative his mind is, how sometimes he can direct images into the minds of others."

Halloran shook his head. "Thought transference—it's the same as hypnosis."

"No. No, it isn't. He can't make you *do* things, control

your actions. He can only suggest images, make you *feel* something is happening."

Halloran thought back to the white room at the Magma building, remembering his first encounter with Kline, the finger prodding him in the darkness when no one was near, reaching out and touching withered skin when only he and Kline were in the room . . . "At least it makes a kind of sense," he said aloud, although it was more a rationale for himself.

Her laugh was brittle. "Don't look for sense in any of this," she said. Cora slipped from his grip and made her way toward the dining room.

A creak from the balcony above. He looked up sharply and was just in time to see the bulky shape of Monk stepping back out of sight. Halloran was sure the big man had been grinning.

"Well, I can see your appetite hasn't been spoiled by this morning's little upset." Kline waved away the Arab who had been pouring him more coffee.

Halloran glanced up from his plate and returned his client's smile. "It takes a lot to do that."

"Oh yeah? For a moment there in the boat I thought you were going to puke. Couldn't figure it—there was hardly a ripple in the lake. Unless all that mist out there disoriented you. It can often make you giddy, y'know, that and the drifting sensation. You had me worried." He sipped from his cup. "Youssef, give Miss Redmile some more coffee. She looks as if she needs it. Make it strong, leave the cream. Cora, you've got to eat more than you do, you're going to waste away otherwise. Don't you think she looks kinda drawn, Halloran? You not sleeping well, Cora?"

Halloran had to agree: she looked pale, the dark smudges under her eyes even more pronounced.

"I think that business yesterday is having some effect on me," Cora said. "Delayed reaction, I suppose."

"The attempted kidnapping?" The incident sounded pleasurable to Kline. "There was no problem, not with our hero along to protect us. Those bastards didn't stand a chance. Am I right, Halloran? Not with you around. I bet they couldn't believe their eyes when they saw our car reversing away like a bat outa . . ." He didn't complete the sentence, gulping coffee instead.

"Hopefully your own driver, Palusinski, will have learned

the technique by now. That and a few others to get away from a roadblock fast." Halloran continued eating, a surprisingly good English breakfast provided by the two Jordanians. He noticed that Kline, for all his jibes at the girl, hadn't eaten much either. Monk probably made up for the pair of them in the kitchen.

"Were you an army man, Halloran?"

The question from Kline was unexpected.

"Most of your outfit are ex-military, aren't they?" Kline went on. "You ever killed anybody? Shot them dead, knifed them? You ever done anything like that?"

Cora was watching him, along with her employer. Halloran leaned back from the table. "What makes you ask?" he said.

"Oh, curiosity. Wondered if you had the capability. Can't be an easy thing taking someone else's life away. No, got to be the hardest thing in the world to do. Or is it? Maybe it's easy once you have the know-how, the experience. Have you had the experience? Could you do it?"

"It would depend on the situation."

"Hah! Let me give you a situation then. Suppose those creeps yesterday had managed to stop our car. Suppose they came at me with guns—which, presumably, given the chance they would have. Would you have used your own weapon?"

"That's why I'm here, Kline."

"Okay. Let's change the scenario a little. Say they held a gun at Cora's head and threatened to blow it off if you made a move toward them. You got your own gun in your hand and it's pointed in their direction. They're dragging me into their car and the guy with Cora is blocking your way. What would you do in that situation? Would you risk her life to protect me? I'd be interested to know." He smiled at Cora. "I'm sure she'd like to also."

Halloran looked from one to the other, Kline grinning, enjoying the moment, Cora uncertain, as though the question was more than academic.

"I'd let them take you," he replied.

Kline's grin faded.

"Then I'd negotiate the ransom for your release."

His client's fist hit the table. "That's the wrong fucking answer! You're being paid to look after me, Halloran, nobody else! Not her, nobody!"

Halloran kept his tone level. "By shooting the one who

held Cora—and I could probably do it without her being harmed—I'd be endangering your life. Everyone would get gun-happy, and undoubtedly you'd be the second target after me. It'd make sense to keep things peaceful, bargain for your release later."

Kline was noticeably quivering. "Bargain for my release? You crazy fuck. They could take the money and then kill me."

"It doesn't work that way. These people are normally professional in what they do. To break a negotiated contract would mean they'd lose credibility next time."

"You talk as if the whole thing is nothing more than a business."

"That's just what it is, a multimillion-pound business. Kidnap and ransom has become one of the world's few growth industries. Sure, every once in a while you get amateurs trying their hand, but they're few and far between, and generally frowned upon by their own but more competent kind—their bungling makes successful transactions more difficult for the professionals. It doesn't take organizations like mine, or the police, to discover which type we're dealing with, and I have to admit I prefer to be up against professionals—they're more predictable."

"And that bunch yesterday? How would you classify them, Halloran?" Kline's fists were clenched on the tabletop, and his lips were drawn tight.

"I'd say they knew what they were doing. The car they used wasn't traceable, they were patient and waited for exactly the right moment. Fortunately for us we had them spotted before they made their move."

"They weren't that good. They failed, didn't they?"

"Only because we were better. And the fact that they managed to get clean away confirms my belief that they were competent. Once the first attempt failed they didn't compound their mistake by giving chase. That could have been too messy. My guess is they'll be patient awhile longer, wait for the right opportunity to come along. Or, at least, engineer that opportunity themselves. Now they know we're on the alert they'll be even more cautious."

"They'll try again?" It was Cora who had asked the question.

Halloran looked at her in surprise. "Of course. But at least we have the slight advantage of knowing our client is a definite target."

"I already told you that!" Kline was glaring at him, but although his words were spoken angrily, the shrillness had gone from them. "Why d'you think Magma hired your company in the first place? You think I'm on some kind of ego trip? Or suffering from paranoia? This is a *real* situation, Halloran, I told you that from the start."

"Okay, so let's go back to an earlier question: who or what organization do you think is behind it? I still can't accept that you've no idea."

"Have any of your previous so-called targets known just who was out to get them? Why d'you expect me to?"

"Because you were aware before an attempt was ever made."

Kline's sigh transmuted into a groan. "After all I've shown you, you still don't believe."

"It's precisely because of what I know about you that I don't understand why you can't sense who your enemies are."

For the first time Kline looked unsure. His eyes went to Cora, then back to Halloran. "There's the mystery, Halloran," he said. And then, as if to himself, he repeated, "Yeah, there's the mystery."

Once more Halloran was checking through the house, prowling the corridors, ensuring that no outside door or window had been left unlocked. Even in daytime he wanted Neath shut tight. It was when he was passing along the second-floor hallway overlooking the inner courtyard that he paused. A door was opening on the other side of the decayed fountain.

He waited by the window and watched, curious, as Khayed came through. The Arab was carrying a round metal container with handles on either side, and by the way Khayed's body leaned backward the burden had some weight. He scuttled across the yard, calling out to someone behind. Youssef Daoud appeared at the same doorway and he, dressed in the robes of his country as was his companion, carried a similar metal container. Both men were laughing and apparently joking as they went through another door leading to the front of the house.

On impulse, Halloran hurried downstairs and went out into the courtyard. He quickly crossed over and went through the door the two Arabs had emerged from. He was in the short passageway he had entered the night before, at one end the stairway, at the other the sturdy closed door. He walked to the latter and tested the handle. It was still locked. Or, if the two men had brought the containers from there, locked again.

Halloran stooped to examine the lock and immediately felt cold dank air from the keyhole on his cheek. He touched the stone floor at the base of the door, and the chill draft was even more noticeable. It had to lead to a cellar of some kind, perhaps where Kline kept his best wines.

Noises outside. The Arabs returning. Halloran straightened, taking one last look at the lock as he did so. It was old and strong, with a large keyhole needing a long key. Shouldn't prove too difficult to open. But he wondered at his own curiosity. And why not ask Kline or Cora what was down there? He also wondered why he was reluctant to do just that.

The voices outside were louder, approaching.

He quickly went down the short length of the passage and stepped through the open doorway. The two Arabs stopped when they saw him. The one called Khayed was the quickest to regain his composure, his friend's look of hostility dissolving a fraction later.

Khayed gave a small bow and regarded Halloran questioningly. *"Assayed?"*

"I found it open," Halloran said, indicating the doorway behind.

"Ah," said Khayed, then spoke to his companion in their own language. *"Sadi koona hashoor."* Daoud smiled at Halloran, who offered no more explanation than he'd already given.

A smell of spices drifted toward him from the two men. They waited there and he guessed they'd stay all day without saying another word until he went on his way. It was in his mind to ask them again what was beyond the locked door, but he doubted he'd receive a reply. He noticed Khayed held a long key by his side.

Halloran waved them through, but they remained where they were, politely indicating that he should pass them. *"Min fadlak, assayed,"* said Khayed.

With a shrug, he cut back across the yard, this time making for the corridor leading to the main hall and the front of the house.

Coolness and gloom after the brightness of the yard struck him as soon as he entered, and his footsteps were hollow on the stone flooring. He frowned when he saw that the double-doors of the entrance were open wide and guessed that Khayed and Daoud were the culprits. He went to the door and passed through into the porch area.

Outside he saw that the Rover's tailgate was up and inside were the two metal containers. He walked over to examine them more closely, tapping them both at first, the sound heavy, indicating they were full. The tops were tightly sealed.

He was prizing at one with his fingertips when he heard the crunch of gravel behind him. Now there was no quick disguising of the alarm in Khayed's expression. He was alone, obviously having followed Halloran out while his companion went on about his business.

"Kala, assayed," the Arab said, recovering well enough to smile.

Halloran raised his eyebrows. He indicated the containers. "What's in them?" he asked.

"Nothing to concern the good sir," came the reply.

"I'd like to take a look."

"Oh no, sir, there is nothing of interest for you in them. It is food, you see."

"What?"

"I said it is food inside the bins."

His companion appeared on the porch and was holding yet another container. He halted to look at both men, then hurried over to the back of the car, politely edging past Halloran to place his load inside with the other two. He straightened and grinned at Halloran, his eyes full of amusement.

"For the dogs," he said. *"Akel llkaleb.* They will eat well tonight."

His snigger became laughter. Khayed joined in that laughter.

23

THE LODGE HOUSE

Dusk was aided by a clouded sky, the fine day having changed its mind mid-afternoon, becoming overcast and broody, yet shedding no rain, as if sulking without tantrum, leaving the air warm and muggy. Halloran took off his jacket as he strolled away from Neath's front gate, no longer having to worry about exposing his waist holster now he was away from the public road.

He had just completed briefing the two sets of Shield operatives, keeping them no more than ten minutes so that the roads around the estate would not be left unpatrolled for longer than was necessary. He realized even double the number of observer cars would still be inadequate because it would be easy enough for intruders to enter the grounds during surveillance "gaps"; nevertheless, even two cars could usually spot potential trouble—parked vehicles, loiterers, anything out of place or suspicious—and two were better than one, one better than none. Halloran wasn't happy with the situation but knew that only a small army would really be adequate under the circumstances, and at least the operatives were now discreetly armed; he could only hope that Kline's faith in his guard dogs was justified.

It had been an odd day (no reason it shouldn't have been, Halloran told himself, considering the whole affair was odd), beginning with his hallucination on the lake that morning. But that had amounted to no more than Kline flexing his psychic muscles, showing Halloran his psyche's strength, a mild "frightener" to let him know he was dealing with a man who had a genuine ability, one that could be used in any direction Kline chose. Fine. The experience had been unnerving, but at least had given his client some satisfaction, and that in turn might make him more amenable to following Halloran's strictures on security.

Kline's outburst at breakfast had left the operative unperturbed: he already knew the man was an egomaniac, as well as being somewhat eccentric, so it wasn't surprising that he was concerned solely for his own safety. How Cora tolerated her employer's boorishness Halloran couldn't understand at all. The question had been in his mind most of the day: why was she so dependent on Kline?

Halloran had wanted to talk with her alone, but she had avoided his company, disappearing to her room immediately after breakfast. He had gone to her, and she had opened her bedroom door only slightly, her eyes downcast, almost as if she were ashamed of what had happened the night before. Cora had told him she was suffering from a migraine headache, that she needed to lie down for a few hours, curtains drawn, if it were to pass. He'd left her, disappointed in her lack of response to him, for even though her sexual preference had surprised him (and, if he were to be totally honest with himself, dismayed him a little) a tenderness between them had followed the lovemaking. Cora had wept when he untied her, and had clung to him, body trembling, tears dampening his chest, for a long time before falling into a troubled sleep.

Somewhere in the distance he heard the faint sound of church bells, evensong in some nearby parish, and his thoughts drifted back to the country of his childhood. The small town in Kilkenny, where the priest's authority was irrefutable, his word law, his temple the court, his judgment final ... Halloran checked himself. It wasn't the time for such reflection—he needed to be alert, aware of what was going on around him at the present moment, not having his thoughts wandering around the past. That was happening too much of late.

Adding further to the day's discord was the news that Dieter Stuhr had disappeared. Mather had called Halloran before lunch to inform him that Shield's Organizer couldn't be located, but everything at his apartment appeared to be in order. Key members of Shield had been recalled to the office to try to track him down, and Gerald Snaith had decided it was far too soon to involve the police. Besides, out of keeping though it might be for the German, there might just be a rational explanation for his absence. Mather would call Halloran the moment he had more information.

He was before the lodge, a building of similar but darker stone to Neath itself, its gray-slated roof full of holes, windows dulled by grime. It looked unlived in. Yet someone inside had somehow allowed him to open the front gates (he'd had a better chance to examine the lock and still hadn't detected any electronic device installed within), for on first try the gates wouldn't budge. He studied the lodge awhile longer before leaving the road and walking the short track up to the front door. The best he got when he stretched a hand to the rusted bell was a dull clunk. He rapped on the wood.

There were no sounds from inside the house. No one came to open the door.

He knocked louder, then tried the handle; it was as though the door were solid to the stone itself, for it did not even jar in its frame. Halloran stepped back to look up at the second-floor windows and saw nothing through the smeared glass. He walked back to the edge of the rutted road for a better view, but the angle merely rendered the windows an opaque black. He took one more backward step.

Halloran was suddenly cold, as if he'd stepped into a pocket of wintry air. He was being observed.

Such an awareness was not unusual for him—experience in his particular profession brought with it a certain sensitivity toward prying, unseen eyes—yet never before had the sensing been so acute for him. The coldness, he realized, was from the crawling sensation of his own skin, as if it were undulating in small ridges. He shifted his jacket to his other arm so that his gun hand was free.

Nothing stirred inside the lodge. At least, not as far as he could tell. But the urge to run from there, to put as much distance between himself and that uninviting abode, was immense. A whisper whose source was somewhere deep in his own mind cautioned him against further investigation. Irrational, he told himself. Are you sure? his subconscious taunted.

He raised a hand to his forehead as if to dispel further insinuations that had gathered, warnings that something nasty, something unclean, was waiting for him inside the lodge house, and that contained within its walls were secrets that should remain secrets; but physical action was useless against the tenacity of the psyche. The thoughts continued.

Halloran almost sagged under their force. He willed their dispersion, and it was only gradually that his mind became calmer, that his own consciousness became dominant.

For those other thoughts had not been his. He was certain they had not originated from some sublevel of his own mind, but had been implanted by another. He turned his head, searching the woods behind the roadway leading to Neath. *Kline.* Those thoughts had been Kline's. He had the gift: Kline had shown him that very morning. But the psychic was still at the main house. Or should have been. Again Halloran scanned the area around him. Did distance bother someone like Kline, could ideas be directed no matter how far away the recipient? *Or was Felix Kline inside the lodge?*

The coldness was still with him, and Halloran slipped his jacket back on. He took a step toward the building.

And the thoughts intruded once more, stabbing at him, bringing with them not only fear but a curious reluctance to discover what was inside the old house. He remained where he was.

Halloran could see no one at the windows, but he sensed a presence beyond those walls. He had lost the inclination to enter the house, though, no longer wanting to find out who the occupant was. Not at the moment. He'd return when he was . . . prepared.

Halloran backed away.

With a last lingering look, he turned from the lodge and began the long trek to the main house where earlier he had decided to leave the Mercedes, preferring to make the journey to the entrance of the estate on foot. Too much could be missed when viewed from a moving car and Halloran had wanted to get the *feel* of the area surrounding the house, with particular regard to the private roadway that was a natural place for an ambush, safe from public gaze, out of sight from anyone in Neath itself. Now, with the evening gloom taking a firmer hold and the unease left by the uninvited thoughts, Halloran regretted his decision. At once he berated himself, a little astonished by his own trepidation. But then, as he'd already acknowledged, it had been an odd day.

In the stillness around him his footsteps seemed louder than normal. Ahead the road narrowed, trees on opposite sides linking leafy arms to form a tunnel. It was twilight inside that tunnel.

He was too warm suddenly, the air almost too heavy to breathe. The clouds were swollen and dark, and he relished the idea of rain, or even a storm. But it was as though the dampness was sealed into the masses above. He walked on, at irregular intervals glancing from left to right, occasionally checking the road behind. All was quiet. The lodge house was a distant image, rendered small and impotent. The road in front of him had begun to curve, no exit visible inside the tunnel.

A stirring of ferns by the roadside, no more than a transient breeze. A faint crash farther within, merely a dead or broken branch shed from a tree.

Light faded as he passed beneath the canopy of leaves. It was cooler, although not much, and Halloran quickened his pace. The more he progressed, the dimmer became the light. Soon it was as though night had fallen prematurely. His senses sharpened and he allowed his vision to wander, never focusing on any particular section of forest for too long, constantly shifting his attention from one dark area to another.

At first he thought he had imagined the snuffling, for it had been barely audible over the sound of his own footsteps, but then it came again. He stopped to listen. Nothing now. And that in itself was unusual, for the woods were always full of noises of some kind, small scufflings, the flapping of wings, an owl settling in for the night's vigil. Over many years he had learned to discern nature's disturbances from those that might originate from stealthy humans, the difference being that animal or natural noises generally continued even if for no more than a second or two, whereas those caused by humans—be they hiding or stalking prey—had a tendency to cease immediately.

He resumed his journey, the tension in his stride indicating an extra alertness. Keeping his steps as quiet as possible, Halloran moved into the curve of the tunnel. A rustling to his right, a definite movement. He carried on walking, a hand reaching under his jacket to the butt of the Browning. More movement, something keeping pace with him. He began to suspect what that something might be.

He had assumed that the dogs were controlled during the daytime and allowed to run free at night. Perhaps it was at dusk that their keeper set them loose on their own.

Snuffling noises again, and then a louder rustling through

the undergrowth as though the animals were hurrying to get ahead of him. Initially the sounds had come from some distance inside the woodland, but now they were drawing close, as if the dogs were cutting in at an angle. Halloran deliberately maintained his own steady pace.

For one brief moment he caught sight of a shadow loping through the trees, low to the ground. It was followed by another, then another . . . he watched a stream of shadows slinking through the undergrowth.

Strange that they didn't come straight at him, but maybe that was part of their training, to cut off and intimidate rather than attack. He sincerely hoped so. Could be that they'd also been trained to keep silent while they tracked their quarry. Halloran resisted the urge to break into a run, knowing he would never outpace them: there was no point in turning back either—they'd only follow. He slid the gun from its holster and held it down by his side.

It could have been midnight, so dark had it become under the trees. The disturbance to his right had settled, as though the procession of dim shapes had passed on its way, having had no real interest in the solitary walker. Halloran did not relax his guard.

Something moved out into the open ahead. He could hardly make out the dog's form, so mantled was the roadway, but he could hear the soft panting. The animal loitered there, making no other sound. Waiting for him. Soon others joined it, slinking from the undergrowth to create an undefined obstacle across the roadway. Their combined breathing seemed to take on a rhythm.

Halloran aimed the weapon in their direction. He moved forward again, his step slow and steady, his body erect, offering the beasts no fear.

He heard their base, scratchy snarling. Drawing near he sensed rather than saw those closest tensing themselves to pounce. He was within seven or eight feet of the nearest shadow. His steps did not falter.

Until there was a different sound, and this from behind, growing louder by the moment. He stopped, but dared not look away from those looming shapes lest they take advantage of a brief second's distraction. The trees and the road were becoming brighter as lights approached, rounding the bend. Illuminating what lay ahead of Halloran.

He drew in a breath, his grip tightening on the automatic. Eyes, yellow-white in the glare from the car's headlights, were watching him. The rest of their lean bodies became brighter.

They were indeed dogs, but of a special loathsome breed.

They stole back into the woods, soon swallowed by its inkiness, and he listened to their quiet retreat until the sounds had faded completely.

The car drew up behind him, and he slid the gun back into the holster. He turned around to face the vehicle, shielding his eyes with an arm and, save for the dazzling lights and the soft purr of its engine, the car might never have been there, for its blackness blended perfectly with the darkness of the forest. As he walked around to the driver's side he heard a window descending. A broad face appeared, barely recognizable in the dimness.

"It is better that I drive you back to the house, *mój kolega*," said Palusinski. "The jackal can be a ferocious beast, particularly against the defenseless."

JANUSZ PALUSINSKI

A PEASANT'S SURVIVAL

His father, Henryk Palusinski, had been a hero of the people, a peasant farmer who had joined the march to Zamosc to do battle with the much-feared General Semyon Budenny of Russia's First Cavalry.

So fiercely did the tiny ragbag army of Polish cavalry, peasants, and gentry fight there, sheer desperation their driving force, that General Budenny had no other choice but to order a retreat and flee back to Russia with his defeated and humiliated troops.

The year was 1920, and Janusz Palusinski had not yet been born.

Henryk returned to his village wearied but triumphant, the saber slash wound in his side never to heal completely, weeping small amounts of blood mixed with foul-smelling poison for years to come. The villagers were proud of their man and, still mourning for those who had not come back from battle, pledged their help to Kazimiera, their hero's devoted wife, in running the small farm until Henryk was well enough to cope for himself. Unfortunately it was two years before he was able to plow his field again, and then only with his faithful Kazimiera by his side to lend support. Still his neighbors offered assistance, but less so than before; hero worship is difficult to sustain when danger has long since passed. Besides, Henryk was no longer the solid and pleasant individual they had once respected and liked: his disability and reliance on others had soured him considerably.

So by the time little Janusz was born some three years later, conditions in the Palusinski household (which had always been less than comfortable anyway) had somewhat deteriorated. Nevertheless the couple was happy to have been blessed with a son; he would grow broad and strong as his father had once been, and in time would work the farm, rebuild it to its former (modest) glory. Providing they didn't all starve before he came of working age.

Due to Kazimiera's fortitude and the continuing kindness of others—albeit a dwindled kindness—the Palusinski family survived. But the father became more morose as the son grew older, for Janusz was not the kind of boy Henryk had in mind when he had dreamed of the offspring he would eventually raise. The boy was sturdy enough, no disappointment there, but there was a sly laziness to him, a reluctance to offer more than was required of him. Janusz's mother despaired, and she herself often did extra work her husband had ordered the boy to do, always taking the greatest care that Henryk would not find out. They ate poorly, selling what they could of their meager produce and, because theirs was a farm without livestock, turnips, beetroots, and potatoes became their staple diet. The boy craved something more.

Then one night his father, out of desperation and perhaps even bitterness, stole a neighbor's pig. It was a young pig, not yet plump, but one that could be dealt with quickly and easily in the dead of night. Henryk felled the animal with one sharp blow of a *mlotek*, not even its sleeping mother rousing to the short squeal of pain. He yanked the pig from its pen, concealing it beneath his coat even though there was no one around to see, then scurried back to his own home.

The family did not wait for morning to cook their prize, for their stomachs groaned at the sight of the pink flesh. The small animal was quickly gutted and set over the fire to roast, liver and kidneys set aside for later consumption. Henryk's wife chopped vegetables, adding to them dried mushrooms picked from the forest weeks earlier. Some would be cooked for the feast they could not deny themselves that night, while what was left would be used for the soup they would make from the pig's bones and trotters. Any guilt Kazimiera felt over her husband's dishonesty vanished as soon as the first aromas from the roasting meat wafted toward her.

Young Janusz was impatient. And there was something about the pink nakedness of the uncooked pig that had its own allure. His father brought out a bottle of the cheap wine he had taken to consoling himself with of late, filling tin mugs for himself and Kazimiera, even allowing his son one or two sips.

It had been a long time since Henryk had felt in such hearty mood, and his wife enjoyed his suddenly restored robustness. While they toasted each other, Kazimiera almost coy under the leering looks she received from her man, Janusz's gaze kept wandering toward the liver and kidneys that lay neglected on the table.

The harsh wine on empty stomachs took no time at all to lighten heads, and Henryk, after warning his son to watch the roasting pig as if his life depended on it—the slightest charring would mean the severest beating for the boy—pulled his not-unwilling *kochanie* into the bedroom.

Janusz obeyed, turning the pig on its spit every few minutes. His mouth was wet with juices as the meat cooked. Yet his eyes kept returning to the raw meat glistening on the table at the center of the room.

Making sure that the bedroom door was closed, he approached the table as stealthily as his father had approached their neighbor's farmyard. With trembling fingers he picked up the liver, finding its clammy softness not at all unpleasant. He sniffed the meat like a nervous mongrel. The smell wasn't strong, yet somehow it prevailed over the roasting pork. He bit into it.

He discovered that devouring raw meat was not so simple. It stretched and stretched, its shininess preventing a firm grip. He laid it down once more and lifted the kitchen knife. Janusz carefully cut off a thin sliver of meat (some enjoyment there, cutting into the moist softness, blood staining the blade), then pushed it into his mouth. To begin with the taste was repugnant, but the more he chewed the more he became used to it. And soon he began to appreciate the raw freshness.

Janusz, aged just nine years, swallowed the meat and cut off another sliver.

The whole family feasted in the early hours of the morning, eating the pork and vegetables in enraptured silence, Henryk swilling wine until the bottle was empty, occasionally winking at Kazimiera and grinning lewdly. The very fact that the meat was so clandestine added its own special flavor.

It was a feast that the young Janusz would never forget. Indeed the memory would taunt his tastebuds many, many times in the years to come.

Neither of his parents mentioned the missing liver the following day. Perhaps Henryk's improbity toward his good neighbor subdued any anger he felt against his own son for stealing the meat, and Kazimiera could only feel shame that circumstances had driven her little Janusz to such a hungry state. Conditions did not improve when suspicion for the loss of the pig fell on the Palusinski family, although no accusations were made. Help from others came less and less.

Janusz grew, his frame sturdy enough, but his flesh lean and undernourished. He was disliked by the other boys of the village for Janusz could best be described as shifty, always on the edge of any group, constantly seeking ways to better his own lot (he was hungry most of the time, a discomfort that can easily shape a person's character). As the years passed and the boy was able to take on more man's work, albeit unenthusiastically, conditions for the Palusinskis improved. They were still impoverished, true, but then so were many of their neighbors, and Henryk's old wound continued to make prolonged labor difficult: yet food for the table slowly became less of a problem, and occasionally there were *zlotys* enough to spend on other things, usually new farming equipment. Poland itself was establishing a more benevolent governance, initiating land reforms that were beneficial to the small farmholder, creating a social security system and organizing health care for its population. Janusz Palusinski might well have grown into a relatively normal young man had not yet another unfortunate chapter in Poland's history begun.

On September 1, 1939 Germany invaded, bringing a reign of terror that would eventually lead to the total subjugation of the Polish people. Important officials, potential troublemakers, men of learning were to be eliminated under the new order of the General Government. The Polish workers were to be intimidated into submission: the murder of countless numbers saw to this. Failure to obey the edicts of the Third Reich meant immediate execution or being sent to a concentration camp (which usually resulted in a more lingering death). All Jews were to be exterminated.

For Poland it was a return to the bad old days of rule by fear. For Janusz Palusinski, then sixteen years old, it meant a return to the bad old days of permanent hunger.

The Nazis had set the Polish farmers working for the sustenance of the German people, each district commander ensuring that no produce was withheld, only the most meager amount left for the farmer and his family so that they had the strength to work the fields. To hide food from the occupying forces meant punishment by death.

The people of Janusz's village, both men and women, young and old, were decimated during the terrible years that followed, for the Polish people are a proud and defiant race and the village was no more, and certainly no less, than an encapsulation of the country as a whole. Many of the younger men became partisans, hiding in the surrounding forests by day, venturing forth to sabotage where they could by night.

Henryk Palusinski saw this as a time to redeem his former glory. Age and his old wound prevented any active part in resistance operations, but he endeavored to supply the hiding groups with what little food he and the other villagers could spare. He also fed them any information on German troop activities that came his way. He urged his son to join the partisans many times, but Janusz was even more reluctant to do that than he was to plow the field, and Kazimiera, when her son complained to her, forbade Henryk to persist with such suggestions. The risk in providing food for the cause was enough, she scolded, without exposing their one and only son to more danger than already existed for them all. Besides, who would work the farm if anything happened to the boy? Although disappointed in his son's lack of spirit, Henryk was forced to listen to reason.

Events took their own course when the older Palusinski fell ill in the winter months with a severe respiratory condition. In the early hours of one morning when he lay wheezing in his sickbed, there came an urgent rapping on the front door. Kazimiera feared it was German soldiers making a spot check on the farms around the village, a frequent occurrence in those dark days, searching for hidden food stores, perhaps hoping they might discover a partisan or two skulking on the premises. She opened the door with much trepidation, and it was with relief that Kazimiera recognized the woman standing outside, hair dampened by drizzling rain: she was from the village, her husband a member of the resistance. The woman held a small bundle in her arms.

"Food, *pani* Palusinska," she told Kazimiera, "for my husband. The Germans watch me, they suspect my Mikołaj is with the resistance. But our men are starving in the forest. *Pan* Palusinski must take this to them." Kazimiera explained that Henryk was too ill for such a journey. "You have a strong son," she was reminded, the woman's tone cold.

Henryk had heard the conversation through the open door of his room and he called out for his wife to bring the woman inside lest by chance she were seen by their enemy. The villager rushed to Henryk's door and pleaded with him to send Janusz into the forest with the food. The older Palusinski began to rise, prepared to undertake the mission himself despite his poor health, and Kazimiera pushed him back again, agreeing that their son should go, afraid that such an effort would surely kill her husband.

Janusz had no other choice. If he refused he would be pilloried by the villagers and neighbors, branded a coward, and his own father would make his life even more unbearable for him than it was already. Besides, the risk should be minimal at that hour of the morning.

His father gave him detailed instructions on where to find the partisans' forest hideaway, and the youth set out, pulling his coat tight around his neck against the chill rain. It was one of those few occasions when Henryk Palusinski felt truly proud of his son. Unfortunately that pride was to be short-lived.

Janusz was captured in the forest by German soldiers who had always been aware that there was a supply line between the partisans and the villagers and farmers. As fate would have it—and as perversely ironic as fate often is—a patrol had chosen that morning to watch a particular section of woodland in which the young Palusinski crept. He was caught within ten minutes of leaving his home.

To his credit, Janusz did not instantly break under the Nazi threats and beatings that followed. However, it took less than a day at the dreaded Lublin interrogation center for that to happen.

He gave the names of partisans, revealed where their encampment in the forest was hidden, mentioned which villages assisted them (much of this was guesswork on his part and he strove to make it sound convincing to his tormentors), and who among the farmers supplied the underground movement with food. It was not until they took him to another room and completely immersed his body in water, pulling him up just before he lost consciousness, repeating the process several times, that he admitted his own parents were involved with the partisans. Only when lighted cigarettes were pressed against his testicles and no more information babbled from his broken lips was the Gestapo sure there was nothing left for him to tell.

The next day Janusz was driven to Zamek Lublin, a hillside castle that served as both prison and courthouse. There, in an old chapel that had been transformed into a courtroom, the dazed youth was sentenced to imprisonment. He was lucky: others with him found guilty were dispatched to a room next door and instantly shot.

From Zamek Lublin he was taken to Majdanek, a notorious internment center just east of the city where many thousands of Poles, Hungarians, and Czechoslovaks were being held, and it was here that Janusz received the tattooed number on his wrist that forever would identify him as the unfortunate victim of a Nazi concentration camp.

Once he had recovered from his injuries, he began to realize he had certain advantages over many of the other inmates that might possibly help him survive: he was young and had learned to exist on a limited amount of food for a number of years (on this point he was soon to discover that at Majdanek "limited" meant hardly any at all); he was cunning, already a natural scrounger; he held scant remorse for any personal misdeeds (the thought of what had befallen those he had betrayed —including the fate of his parents—hardly disturbed him); he was not Jewish.

And there was one particular aberration of character that would eventually ensure his survival under the worst of circumstances, but that was not to be appreciated until much later.

His clothes were of a black-and-white striped material, thin and coarse and loose-fitting; his bed was a plank of wood on damp ground. His companions were the starving.

Janusz became used to raving hunger once more. He dreamed of great plates of sauerkraut, sausages, boiled pork and pickles with coriander seeds mixed in. And often he dreamed of when he was nine years old, of the night his father had stolen the tiny pig, how his family had feasted, the pork lasting for days, thin soup made from the bones lasting even longer. He would wake from the dream in the darkness of the night, his sunken eyes wide and staring, the succulent memory vanquishing the moans and smells around him in the rough hut. He would remember other details of that clandestine night, and juices would run from his open mouth.

Time passed and Janusz mentally sank into himself just as his flesh physically sank into his bones. Yet there was ever one bright, although tormenting, light for him. Unlike many of his fellow internees for whom food had become almost an abstract thing—they still craved it, still licked their bowls that had often contained only watery, meatless soup, a piece of black bread, and sawdust; but the less they were fed, the more unreal to them became true sustenance—he never relinquished that one glorious memory of his family's night feast all those years ago. It became an obsession with him. And oddly, a driving force. Where others slowly drifted down into their own private abysses of despair, Janusz's thoughts constantly stretched toward his vision, perhaps as a drowning man might reach for a swooping seagull.

He worked as hard for his jailers as his enfeebled body would allow (and with considerably more eagerness than on his father's farm) and was never averse to mentioning any subversive talk he might hear in the barrack huts during the night, always willing to point out potential troublemakers to the German guards. He became a pariah among the prisoners for, although they could only guess he was an informer, it was for his readiness to serve the Third Reich beasts that he was hated. Fortunately for him, there was too much dread in their hearts and too much passion sapped from their souls for them to take vengeance.

Then one day, Janusz and two dozen or so others were marched from the camp to a hillside that was used for mass executions. They were instructed to wait beside several open pits.

The number of *Unerwünschte*—"undesirables," as the Nazis referred to Jews—was too many to count (years after the nightmare Janusz could not remember if there had been hundreds or if there had been thousands), as they were lined up before the pits in groups. There they were machine-gunned, most of the bodies toppling into the open graves. It was the task of the working party to throw in those who had fallen the wrong way, then arrange the bodies so that the next batch could be heaped in on top. When the pile reached a certain level, they were to cover the pit with lime and soil. Before that was done though, there was a special job to perform for a chosen few. Janusz was one of the chosen.

An SS captain provided Janusz and three companions with pliers and short, blunted knives; their orders were to pull any gold teeth they could find among the corpses and to cut off any rings that had not already been confiscated.

This was no shock for Janusz because his mind had long since decided to protect him from such traumas. He crawled among the still warm corpses, giving them no more regard than if they were freshly slaughtered livestock. Dead meat. That's all this great tumble of arms and legs was. White carcasses. Some still pink-colored. Like the little pig . . .

No one was watching as he lifted the hand of the plump woman, the flesh of her finger swollen over the rim of her gold ring. The Gestapo had been merciful: they hadn't cut the jewelry from her while she was still alive. He sawed at the finger. No one was paying any attention. He slid the ring off. And drew meat from the fingerbone with his teeth. He swallowed. The woman's eyes opened. She looked at him, and he fought to keep the bloodied morsel down. It lodged in his throat as life went from the woman's eyes. He swallowed again, once, twice. The meat was accepted.

That was the real beginning of Janusz Palusinski's survival. He had found a food supply. He was filled neither with joy nor shame, merely relief that he had a means to exist.

Exist he did, even though he was violently ill for days after that first eating of human flesh; his stomach was not accustomed to such richness. He was lucky to recover, for his general weakness might have allowed permanent damage. But Janusz was resilient, if nothing else. From then on he was more cautious about how much he cut from the piled corpses, often concealing small segments in his loose clothing to be consumed late at night beneath his thin blanket. The amount he was able to eat was never enough to have any marked effect on his physique, and that was fortunate, for such a change would have been easily noticed amid the walking skeletons of the Majdanek concentration camp. But it was sufficient to strengthen him and thus renew his desire to survive.

Disaster, for him, came months later when for no apparent reason he was taken off the burial detail. Perhaps the German soldiers themselves had grown sick of his eagerness to crawl among the dead, or perhaps they felt he had become too privileged. Whatever the reason, Janusz's specialist services were no longer required. His condition deteriorated rapidly with no regular sustenance.

He became as the others of the camp, a shuffling corpse, eyes enlarged as his skin shriveled, his bones jutting with deep hollows between. He began to have fits of coughing that drained him of any strength he had left, and blood spots speckled his palm when he took his hand away from his mouth. Delirium soon followed. Finally he was moved to a hut where those who were dying were left without food or care, their passing hastened by lack of both.

He had no idea of how long he had lain there; it could have been days, it might only have been hours. But something had drawn his senses toward one focal point. It was a smell. Familiar. From the past. He stared into the grayness above and his tongue ran across dry, cracked lips, failing to moisten them. He drew up his knees as hunger cramped his stomach, and his head lolled listlessly when the pain passed. That faint smell, what was it? So familiar. He was a boy again, and he stood in the center of the room watching a door. *Mamusia* and *Tatuś* had shut him out. They always did when they did things to each other, unless they thought he was sleeping. He could hear them laughing, and then he could hear them moaning as if they were hurting each other. But one night, when they thought he was asleep, he had watched them across the bedroom . . . and hadn't liked what he saw . . . but had wanted to be part of it . . . to enjoy the game with them, to be hurt in the same way . . . but he knew it was forbidden . . . The faint smell. The boy looked toward the table, toward the source. The meat was dark red, blood seeping onto the rough wooden surface. He moved closer.

Janusz recognized the odor of raw liver. But it wasn't possible. He was no longer a child and this place was not his home. No, this was the death hut. The smell though. It was here. There was raw liver somewhere nearby. His smile made his lips bleed.

For the first time he heard the dull moans, and they were around him, not from behind a closed door. And the smell was with the moans.

He let his head fall to one side, and in the predawn light saw the shapeless bundle next to him. There was hardly anything left of the man, and he barely moved. But the smell was from him and it was mouthwatering. Janusz's arm trembled when he reached toward the figure.

The man was not sleeping, nor was he really conscious. He was near death, and that proximity was comforting for him. Most of the pain had gone to some distant point, so far away it could scarcely be felt. He sunk further within himself and realized that the journey inward was the way to final peace. Yet something was moving him, interrupting his floating descent. Something was caressing his stomach. Pain was coming close once more, and the man did not want that. He tried to protest, but a murmur that was only a sigh was all the sound he managed. Sharp agony now. And something hard covering his mouth and nose, stopping any more sighs, any more breathing. The agony increased as something gnawed into his belly, and he was too feeble to protest further. But the pain was becoming dulled, bliss was washing through him, for his senses were leaving and he, at long last, was leaving with them and it was good, so ultimately good.

No one went near the hut that day, nor the next. No corpses were taken away, no more of the dying were dumped inside. It was to be five days before the door of the Majdanek death hut was opened again, and then by Russian soldiers, for this was the summer of 1944 and the German invaders were being driven from Poland.

The Russians, already hardened by their own suffering in the terrible war and by the atrocities they had witnessed during the march across their neighboring country, were sickened by what they found inside the hut. Only one man was still alive and he, understandably, was demented by what had happened around him. He lay on a floor that was filled with corpses. Many had been mutilated, for it seemed rats had found their way inside and fed off his dead and dying compatriots.

Unfortunately for the Polish people, once the Russians had occupied their country they felt no compunction to leave. Poland came under Communist control, and oppression, although never as severe as under Nazi rule, remained the norm. Again farmers and factory workers found themselves working for the State rather than for themselves, with the government dictating at what rates produce should be sold.

Janusz Palusinski, who bore the indelible mark of German brutality on his wrist and never failed to let the tattoo show on any occasion that sympathy might help better his cause, came to thrive under the system, for scrounging and self-interest was the ideal apprenticeship for a black marketeer. It took him a full year to recover from his treatment by the Nazis (although a whole lifetime would never erase the damage to his psyche) but his will to survive at all costs had been enhanced rather than depleted. He did not return to his father's farm for two reasons: he was not sure of the reception he would get from the villagers who must have known that it was he who had betrayed the partisans and those who helped them; and he had no desire to become a farmer once more. During the year of recuperation, most of which took place in a small hospital just outside Lukow, he read through the published crimes of the Nazi regime, always searching for mention of his own village, and one day he came across what he had been looking for. Listed were the names of locals and villagers who had been shot for giving aid to the underground movement. A hundred and thirty-two people were on the list, his parents among them. Even now, when concern for his own well-being was no longer acute, he felt no remorse, not even for the fate of his own mother. Such emotion, never strong within him anyway, had been entirely eradicated over the last few years.

As time passed, life began to flourish for Janusz, who took to the illegal trade he dealt in as if born to it. He supplied goods-hungry farmers and food-hungry manufacturers with what they desired, trade between the two factions being lucrative for the middleman. But he always operated in a small way in those early years, never wishing to rise in fortune so much that he became visible to the authorities.

Janusz could have survived very comfortably under the Communist system, except that the older he grew the more he prospered, and the more he prospered the greedier he became. He bought a four-story house in the suburbs of Lodz and, as a front that legitimately enabled him to visit farmers around the country, he maintained a small farm equipment spare-parts workshop. Middle age had softened his caution though, and he went against his own basic rule. He had gained too much and was no longer invisible.

The authorities began to take an interest in the activities of Janusz Palusinski. His spare-parts business was discreetly investigated and it was found that the profits derived from it by no means accounted for the relative luxury in which the owner appeared to be living. His movements were watched. Party officials came to his house to question him. His answers were not entirely satisfactory. They took away all documents found in his home, warning him that they would return as soon as the papers had been thoroughly studied and that he was to keep himself available until such time. Janusz stole away that same night, taking with him what little cash he had and leaving behind his automobile, knowing how easy it was for the authorities to trace any vehicle on the roads of Poland. He left the city on foot, sleeping in cheap lodging houses at night, traveling by bus during the day, too afraid even to take trains. His journey led him toward the north, in the direction of the great forests. He had no idea why, panic and self-preservation driving him onward without calculation, only instinct telling him that the dark forests were a place to lose oneself and be lost to others. He was aware of the severe punishment dealt to those caught trading on the black market and was sure that his mind would never stand another term of imprisonment—too many dreadful memories would have been rekindled. There was no grand plan to his escape, no considered scheme for invisibility once more. Janusz fled merely because he had no other choice.

Because of the furtive manner in which his journey progressed, it took him several weeks to reach the medieval town of Grudziadz, and by then his money had nearly run out. A basic plan had formed though, an idea that took no details into account. He would make for the Baltic seaport of Gdynia, avoiding nearby Gdansk, where too many merchants knew him. There he would bribe his way onto a boat. He didn't care where his passage took him, just so long as it was far away from this accursed country and its oppressively authoritarian government that constantly hindered entrepreneurs such as he. The problem now was money. He had barely fifty *zlotys* left, and such a secret voyage would prove expensive.

Late at night Janusz went to the home of Wiktor Svandova, in Grudziadz, a particular businessman with whom he'd had many dealings in the past.

But Janusz had not reckoned on Svandova's respect for (or fear of) the State. The business associate ordered Janusz from his home, threatening to call in the police if he didn't leave at once. The fugitive reasoned with Svandova, cajoled, pleaded, even wept before him; he only produced the short metal bar he carried inside his greatcoat when Svandova strode to his desk and reached for the telephone. The first blow struck the businessman across the left temple, but amazingly he was able to stagger to the door, with Janusz following and beating at the back of his head and shoulders as he went. He threw open the door and even managed to scream out his wife's name before collapsing to his knees while his assailant continued to rain blows on him. At last, and to Janusz's great relief, Svandova pitched forward onto his face, blood from his broken head instantly flooding the hallway. Janusz ran from the house when the dead man's wife began screeching from the top of the stairway. He knew she had recognized him and he had it in mind to climb the stairs and silence her forever too; but other figures had appeared behind her, presumably Svandova's sons, and Janusz had no desire to battle it out with them.

He left the city, heading north once again, cursing his bad luck and his business associate's foolishness. He was now a fugitive for a far more serious crime, and every endeavor would be made by the police to capture him.

For nearly three months Janusz eluded them, the northern forests swallowing him up completely, bestowing upon him the invisibility he craved. But autumn was turning to winter, and even the extra clothing he had stolen to wear under his greatcoat could not prevent the chill reaching his bones. Food —the roots and nuts he found, the turnips, beetroots, and potatoes he dug from farmers' fields late at night, the small animals he occasionally was able to trap and kill—already scarce, was becoming even more so. Yet again Janusz became intimately acquainted with terrible hunger. When stealing from farms—odd items of clothing came from outside washing lines—he yearned to come across a pigpen, dreamed of reaching in and pulling out a piglet, just as his father had all those years ago. When he slept he dreamed of his family's feast, when he had watched the roasting pig, making sure the meat wasn't burned black. He awoke many times with the delicious smell still in his nostrils, and before reality edged it away, a more subtle aroma would become dominant . . .

His heavy beard was matted and dirty, and Janusz may have appeared plump, but only layers of clothing created the illusion, for beneath them his flesh was hollowed between the bones, just as it had been in the years when Germans had occupied his country. He had plodded for two days through the snow-laden forest, sheltering where he could, cramming any foliage he could find into his mouth and chomping until it was mulched enough for him to digest. He even pulled pieces of bark from trees to gnaw on.

The *policja* had been waiting for him at the last farmhouse he had attempted to rob; he had remained in one area for too long, the stealing becoming more than just an annoyance to the locals. A trap had been set for him, and only blind panic had lent him the strength to outrun his pursuers. Now it was only stomach pains that drove him on.

Janusz saw the column of smoke rising above the treetops and stumbled off in that direction. He came upon a small, log house in a clearing. His weary legs barely got him to the front door. His fist made the faintest of sounds when he pounded on the wood.

The woodsman caught him as he fell inside and dragged him over to the fire. He called for his wife to warm some *sok* and bring it to the half-frozen man while he loosened the unfortunate's clothing. They were kind to this wretched wayfarer, even though suspicious, and they did their utmost to revive him. After a while, when he was able to sit at the table and sip more of the warm brew, they tried to question him, but his replies were incoherent, his voice rambling. They soon realized the man was crazed with hunger and exhaustion. And the wife was uneasy at the way he kept staring at their twelve-year-old daughter who sat quietly in the corner watching everything with a wide-eyed expression on her plump little face, her skin pink and unblemished in the glow from the fire.

Janusz repaid their kindness by killing them all. He used his trusty metal bar to batter the man unconscious as he stooped to put another log on the fire, and a breadknife quickly grabbed from the table to cut all their throats.

When the two *policjants* who had been following his tracks through the forest burst in less than an hour later, he had already started to eat the woodsman's daughter.

In one respect Janusz was lucky. The officers were fresh enough in their careers not yet to have witnessed the worst of criminal brutality, nor were they old enough to comprehend the true barbarism of the Nazi occupation during the last World War. When they saw what had become of the woodsman and his wife, when they *realized* that what their quarry was stuffing into his mouth was from the child's open belly, they were too shocked—too *revolted*—to move.

The madness in Janusz, further incited by the excitement of his deed, overcame the fatigue that was still with him; he threw the breadknife at one uniformed intruder and rushed screaming at the other. The vision of this wild man, his body puffed up by the layers of clothing he wore, mouth and beard daubed with blood, eyes huge and crazed, would have frozen the bravest of men, and the two *policjants* had thus far won no service awards for gallantry. Neither of them could help but cringe away.

One was pushed back against the wall while the other scrambled to retrieve his rifle, dropped when he had dodged the thrown knife. The thief they had tracked so many miles was through the door and out in the snow again, scurrying back into the trees as a single shot was fired at him. The bullet chipped the top of his right collarbone but, despite the agonizing jolt, he did not stop running. Nightfall helped cloak his escape.

Soon the gunshots behind him grew fainter, and Janusz was both laughing and weeping as he scrambled up a slope. He toppled over the ridge and rolled down the other side, giggling and crying out as he went. He came to rest at the bottom of the hill, spread-eagled on his back, half-buried in snow and his chest heaving with exertion.

He stayed that way for some time, his breathing gradually slowing as he listened for his pursuers. Their voices came from high above him and soon drifted away again, the darkness now concealing the trail of disturbed snow he had left behind. He had lost them. He had got away. He giggled once more and licked his lips, the taste still strong on his tongue.

Janusz waited a little while longer before rising to his knees.

He was instantly blinded by dazzling white light.

Russian tanks were strategically positioned in many sectors of Poland, never obtrusively, but usually in areas where their threat could be felt rather than continually observed. The soldiers who manned them were highly disciplined and never mingled with the community; but they were always on standby, ready to move against insurgence at a moment's notice. Perpetually bored by their low-profile assignment, the tank crews were eager for any distraction that might come

their way. They had observed the dark figure tumbling down
the hillside and patiently waited for it to move again once it
reached the bottom. When it did, they switched on their tank
lights as one.

Janusz screamed in terror. He stumbled away, not caring in
which direction he ran, his only thought to be out of that
intense glare as quickly as possible. The two *policjants*,
alerted by the abrupt flaring of light, turned back.

Never had Janusz felt so naked, so visible. There was
nothing he could see, nothing but blinding light, and he felt
like a specimen exposed on a scientist's slab. He crashed into
a tree, tasted his own blood rushing into his mouth. He staggered away, hands to his face. Then onward, refusing to allow
pain to stop him, too afraid to let it.

He was hurtling downward again, over and over, this slope
much steeper than the previous one. He shrieked when his
damaged shoulder struck something solid. He was no longer
falling, the surface flat and hard beneath him.

Janusz sobbed with self-pity. He was lost now. He no
longer had the strength to run. They had him and they would
punish him for the wicked things he had done.

He raised his head. The lights had found him. They were
coming close, exposing him in the roadway as if he were
some helpless animal, broken-limbed and prey to anything
that should come along. Janusz tried to shield his eyes against
the blaze, but there was no strength left in his arms.

The light was almost upon him. He waited in despair.

But now the bright beams were passing him, shining
beyond. He blinked and it took an eternity for his eyes to
discern the big black car that had drawn up alongside his
prone body. The engine was still quietly running and nothing
happened for a while. Then a rear door opened.

"Mogę cię zrobić niewidzialnym, Janusz," a soft voice
said from within. "I can make you invisible."

(And in a way, Kline did make him invisible.)

24

CORA'S ANGUISH

"Why jackals, for God's sake? There are plenty of other breeds that make better guard dogs." Halloran had craned his neck around to look through the black limousine's rear window, half-expecting to see shadowy shapes back on the roadway.

Palusinski shrugged, then gave a short laugh, his eyes becoming small behind the wire-rimmed glasses he wore. "Perhaps Felix cares for the underdog." He laughed again, enjoying his joke.

Halloran faced the front. "I've never heard of trained jackals before."

"All animals can be trained, *mój kolega*. As can all men."

"I thought they were nocturnal, yet I saw one roaming in daylight yesterday."

"They prefer night hunting, but even inherent habits can be changed. The dogs obey their master."

"Kline?"

"Ah no." Palusinski's foot gently touched the brake pedal as they gathered speed on the hill. The lights of Neath were like a beacon against the leaden slopes behind. "Even an old dog such as I has learned some new tricks over the past two days. Your driving instructor teaches well."

"Let's hope you never have to use those techniques."

The older man nodded. "I am informed that you yourself had to do so yesterday."

Halloran made no comment. "How long have you been employed by Felix Kline, Mr. Palusinski?" he asked instead.

"Please, you may call me Janusz. Rest assured, I bear you no ill will for your rough treatment of me two nights ago. I appreciate that you were merely pointing out the weakness of our defense. And there was no pain at the time, only an aching of the neck muscles afterward. A skillful blow, sir, if I may say so."

"Pity your partner can't forgive as easily."

"Monk? An animal. A beast. It would be prudent to watch yourself with that one. Now, as to your question, I'm sure your company has access to the files on all of us. You must know how long I have been in Felix's employ."

"Those files are pretty vague. They give no account of length of service."

"I see. And you are curious, naturally." The car pulled up behind the silver Mercedes at the front of the house. "Felix brought me from Poland some years ago," Palusinski said as he switched off the engine. "Fourteen or fifteen years ago, I think."

Halloran was startled and about to question the Pole further, but Palusinski was already getting out of the car. "Wait," he said, and the bald-headed man bent down to look back inside. "How old is Kline?" Halloran asked.

Palusinski smiled, his eyes narrowing behind the spectacles. "Felix is older than you would imagine, sir." Then he was gone, walking around the front of the car toward the house.

Halloran quietly tapped on the door and waited. He was tired, and that was from more than just the lateness of the hour. There was a tension about this house that had little to do with any kidnap threat. Yet the day before there had been a stillness in Neath, a brooding heaviness that dragged at the spirit. That had now given way to a peculiar atmosphere of instability, and he could almost feel a charge in the air, as if the building itself had been roused by the visitors like some slumbering monolith disturbed into a tensed wariness. He pushed the fanciful idea aside. A house was a house, bricks and mortar, timber and glass. The events of the day and the unpredictability of his client were having an adverse effect on him. That Dieter Stuhr was still missing—Mather had phoned Halloran an hour before to inform him of this—added to his general unease for, as the Shield Organizer, the German was at the hub of an ongoing operation. Nothing seemed right about this particular assignment.

He raised a hand to tap on the door again but stopped when

he heard the lock click from the inside. Cora looked out at him.

"I wondered if you were okay," he said, then added: "You weren't at dinner."

Her hair was damp around her face as if she'd just stepped from the bath or shower. "I wasn't hungry," she told him.

"Nor was anyone else. I ate alone." He was silent for a moment, waiting for some response from her. When none came, he said, "Can we talk?"

Hesitation, then: "I'm sorry, I'm acting like a stranger to you." She opened the door wide and stood aside so that he could enter, their roles reversed from the previous night.

He rested a hand against the door frame. "I didn't know..."

"Come in, Liam. Please."

He entered the room and saw that it was bigger and more comfortable than his own. One half contained a small sofa and armchair, a coffee table in between, an antique writing bureau by the wall; the other side was occupied by a four-poster bed, bedside cabinet, and dressing table, and a wardrobe of cavernous proportions. An open door led off and he assumed this was to an *en suite* bathroom. The curtains at the windows were drawn closed, which seemed unnecessary considering Neath's remote location.

Cora shut the door behind him and went to a table. "Can I offer you a drink?" she asked, adjusting the belt of the white bathrobe she wore. "Oh no, I forgot. You're always on duty, aren't you? I suppose you won't be surprised if I have one." She poured herself some wine from a bottle on the table and settled back in the sofa, drawing her legs up under her.

"Why the antagonism, Cora? After last night—" He stopped when she bowed her head as if the words had stung her.

"Have I disillusioned you?" There was scorn in her voice. "I drink too much, I make love in an odd fashion, I'm subservient to a man who's half-mad, half-genius. I can imagine what you think of me."

Halloran sat next to her, their bodies touching. "The only thing I can't figure out is what you really drink."

Cora had to smile. "Whatever happens to be on offer," she replied with only a hint of sullenness. She sipped the wine and he noticed the bottle level was down to the last quarter. "Did I shock you last night?" Cora asked, looking into her glass.

"Sure," he answered.

She looked up sharply.

"I'd be a liar if I said I didn't enjoy it, though," Halloran added.

"He made me do it."

"What?"

"He made me go to your room." She reached for the bottle and topped up her wineglass, even though it was still half-full. "Felix told me to go to you last night."

Halloran was stunned. "I don't understand."

"He ordered me to seduce you. I don't know why. Perhaps he was testing you in some way. Or testing me. Perhaps he got some kind of kick out of it, finding another way to degrade me, turn me into a whore."

"Why should he want to do that?"

"Felix enjoys corrupting people. But it's too soon for you to have realized that."

"Cora, this doesn't make sense."

"You already know there's no sense to any of this, Liam. Why persist in looking for it? I'm sorry if I've bruised your ego, but the truth is I was merely obeying instructions last night." Her hand was shaking and she quickly drank to prevent the wine spilling over. She glanced at him and was surprised to find him smiling still, but this time that coldness was there, the glint of cruelness that somehow was constantly lurking beneath his surface manner.

"Maybe Kline wanted me kept busy," he said.

She caught her breath. He was right. For reasons of her own—reasons that were unclear even to herself—Cora had wanted to hurt Liam, to break through that aura of sureness. But there was more to it than that. She had wanted him, had wanted him to make love to her, had gone to him willingly as if . . . Cora struggled to crystallize the thought . . . as if he might be her . . . savior? Redeemer? Oh God, what a fool she was. Even then, when he had been inside her, it wasn't enough. She'd needed something more, much more. And they'd had to make love a different way so that she could achieve her own satisfaction. Felix had reduced her to that, made her a creature of sensations rather than emotions. And she'd despised Liam for this also, for she had allowed him to see her for what she was. Tonight she had tried to hurt him, but he had turned it around. It was she who had been humiliated further.

"Please go, Liam," she said, her voice brittle.

"Oh no, not yet. Not yet, Cora."

That faint Irishness to his voice again. How strange that it should make him sound so dangerous.

"I want you to leave."

Instead he took the glass from her hand.

"I don't know what game it is you all think you're playing," he said quietly, "and honestly, I don't much care. But at least there's something more to you, Cora, something that megalomaniac hasn't touched yet. I don't know how he's managed to bring you to this point, but I do know you've kept a part of yourself away from him. You were different the first time I saw you, and I think it was because I was seeing you the way you used to be, the way you can still be."

"There's nothing left for—"

He touched his fingers to her lips. "You're wrong." His own lips replaced his hand and she tried to turn away. He held her firm and kissed her, hurting her.

Cora sank into the sofa and pushed at his chest. She didn't want this. He wasn't the man to take her from Felix. They were alike, Felix and Liam. Cruel men. Vicious men. That was why Felix was fascinated by him. They were akin.

He was hurting her, and there was pleasure in that. But she mustn't let him, she couldn't let him . . .

Halloran grabbed her wrist and pulled it aside. She was lying on the sofa now, the robe open beneath the belt, exposing her thighs. He continued to kiss her, his mouth hard against hers, and when she finally wrenched her head away, his lips sank to her neck and he bit, but used no strength. Cora moaned, partly out of self-pity and partly out of self-disgust, for feelings were being aroused in her.

"Please don't," she tried to say, but Halloran had pulled the robe away from her breasts. He lowered his head to them. "I don't want this!" she hissed, but his hand was on her thigh, pressing firmly, then gliding down to her knee, reaching behind, touching delicate nerve-points. His weight was on her, pinning her, and he used his body to part her legs. Still she protested, squirming against him, her fingers clenched on his shoulders. She could have clawed him, or pulled his hair, or bit him. But she didn't.

He sank to the floor, kneeling before her, keeping his body between her legs. Her robe had fallen open completely, the belt loose around her waist, and Halloran deftly undid his own clothing. He entered her, the movement hard and quick, causing her to cry out even though she was moist, ready for him despite her resistance. His lips found hers once more and this time she did not refuse him; the force of her kiss matched his.

Her arms reached around him, drawing him tight, and now Halloran groaned, a soft murmur that excited her. Cora's legs were rigid against his hips and she thrust herself forward, letting him fill her, wanting more, crying for more, her breathing tight and her arms trembling. Cora's cries turned into gasps, and Halloran's hands went under and around her shoulders so that he could pull her down onto him, his own thrusts controlled and rhythmic. But that restraint was soon overwhelmed and he twisted his face into Cora's wet hair and she arched her neck, pushing her head back into the cushions, her hips almost rising off the sofa, clutching at him as their juices surged to mix inside her body. Her cry was sharp, trailing to a whimper, their bodies shuddering together, slowly calming to a trembling, eventually relaxing to a stillness. They lay there, neither one willing to separate.

Halloran felt the wetness on his cheek and lifted his head to look at Cora. She was weeping, and when he tried to speak she pulled him down against her. His arm slid beneath her neck and he held her tightly.

They stayed that way until her weeping stopped, neither one saying anything, feeling no need to, content to rest with each other. Cora loved the feel of him inside her, even though he was soft now, and she ran her fingers beneath his shirt, caressing his spine. Halloran raised himself without withdrawing and lifted her legs onto the sofa. He lay on top, brushing his mouth across her face, kissing her eyes, her temples, her cheeks, passion subdued, replaced by tenderness.

"You don't know what he's done to me," she said.

"None of that matters," he soothed.

She sighed, a sweet sound, when she felt him becoming hard again. They made love slowly this time, their movement sensuous, almost languid, sensing each other in a different, more perfect way. Their passion grew but was unleashed easily, a flowing, then gently ebbing release.

As before, they remained locked together for some time and, when at last Halloran withdrew, it was with reluctance. He adjusted his clothing, then sat on the floor, an elbow resting on the sofa where Cora was still stretched. He leaned forward to kiss her lips, his hand smoothing away the damp hair from her face.

"Liam..." she began to say, but he shook his head and smiled.

"No need, Cora. We'll talk tomorrow. Tonight just think about what's happened between us." He stroked her body, fingertips tracing a line over her breasts down to her stomach, running into the cleft between her thighs.

Her arms went around his shoulders and she studied his eyes, her expression grave. "I need to know more about you, can't you see that?"

"In time," he said.

"Is it possible for me to trust you? There's something"— she frowned, struggling to find the word—"*dark* about you, Liam, and I can't understand what it is. There's a remoteness in you that's frightening. I felt it the first time we met."

He began to rise, but Cora held on to him.

"I told you yesterday," he said. "I'm what you see, no more than that."

"It's what I *feel* in you that scares me."

"I often deal with violent people, Cora. It can't help but have an effect on me."

"You've become the same as them? Is that what you're saying?"

He shook his head. "It isn't that simple."

"Then try to explain." There was exasperation in her demand.

He began to rise again, and this time her arms dropped away. "In my trade violence usually has to be met with violence," he said, looking down at her. "It's sometimes the only way."

"Doesn't that corrupt you? Doesn't that make you the same as them?"

"Maybe," he replied.

She pulled at her robe, covering her nakedness.

Halloran walked to the door and paused there. "It's when you start to enjoy the corruption that you know you're in trouble." He went out, quietly closing the door after him.

Leaving Cora to weep alone.

Halloran washed himself in a bathroom along the hall before returning to his room. Once there, he hung his jacket over a bedpost and took the gun from its holster, placing it on the bedside cabinet. He removed his shoes this time, set the small alarm clock, and lay on the bed. The curtains were apart, but moonlight was feeble again that night and barely lit the room. Despite the fact that there was an extra bodyguard on duty inside the house, Halloran would only allow himself four hours' rest, intending to check on Monk and Palusinski during their individual watches, scouting Neath and the immediate outside area in between. Cora had taken up nearly an hour of his rest period. And a lot of energy.

He shut his eyes and remembered the hurt on her face as he'd left the room.

A brightness flashed beyond his eyelids.

Halloran opened his eyes again. The room was in darkness. Had he imagined the sudden flare?

It came once more, filling the room like a lightning flash. Yet no rumble of thunder followed.

He quickly moved from the bed, going to the window. He peered out into the night. A muted white glow marked the moon's presence behind a bank of clouds, the ragged-edged, mountainous shapes barely moving, the landscape below blurred and ill-defined. The lake was a huge flat grayness that appeared solid, as if its depths were concrete.

Halloran blinked as the light flared again. The source was the lake itself, an emanation from its surface. And in that brief light he had seen forms on the water, black silhouettes that were human. Or so he assumed.

He rolled back over the bed, pulled on his shoes, and grabbed his gun. Halloran headed for the stairs.

25

LAKE LIGHT

Monk should have been on guard duty. But the main hall was empty.

Halloran wasted no time searching for him; he switched off the hall lights, then opened one side of the front doors just enough to slip through. He was disturbed that the door had been left unlocked. His steps were barely audible as he hurried through the stone-floored porch, and he stopped only briefly once out in the open.

The lake was nothing more than a broad expanse, slightly lighter than the area surrounding it.

Halloran holstered the Browning and moved off, quickly edging along the frontage of the house, using it as a dark backdrop against which it would be difficult to be seen, his intention being to approach the lake from an angle rather than in a direct line from the main door. Once at the corner he made a crouching dash toward the lawn. Instinctively he dropped to the ground when light flared from the lake again. He blinked his eyes rapidly, feeling conspicuous and vulnerable lying there on the damp grass. But imprinted on his mind was the image the sudden brightness had exposed.

There was a boat out there, three or four figures huddled together in its confined space. They were watching something that was outside the boat, on the lake itself. Something that was not in the water but *on* the surface.

The vision dissolved as his eyes adjusted to the darkness once more. He stiffened when a howling came from the shore-line to his right, an eerie, desolate cry in the night. It was followed by a collective ululation, the baying of wolves—or *jackals*—a fearful sound wending across the water. He narrowed his eyes, hoping to see them among the indistinct shapes of trees and shrubbery that edged the side of the lake.

He thought he could make out the jackals, although it might only have been a clump of low foliage, for there was no movement. Halloran rose to one knee.

And again was temporarily blinded by a fulguration from the lake.

It had come from below the water, a silvery white luminance swiftly expanding across the flat surface, its extremities shading to indigo and the deepest mauve. The illumination lasted only a second or so but there was time for Halloran to observe the jackals gathered there at the edge of the water. The glare had frozen them. Their heads, with long pointed muzzles and erect ears, stood high from their shoulders, cocked in alertness and perhaps puzzlement. At least a dozen pairs of glowing orbs, set in irregular pattern, reflected the light.

Darkness, total after the glare. But again an impression lingering. Halloran had seen someone standing among the beasts. A bent figure, a cowl concealing its features. Whoever it was had been watching the lake.

Halloran heard a voice—no, laughter—and his attention was diverted to the boat. He had recognized the dry cackle of Felix Kline, the sound amplified across the water. Halloran rose to his feet and moved forward at speed, keeping low, taking the gun from its holster as he went.

He could make out the landing jetty ahead and noted that the boat he and Kline had used that morning was no longer moored there. Did Kline enjoy a nighttime boat ride as well as an early-morning one? Or had he been forced into a trip not of his choosing, the lake making an obvious route to avoid the guard dogs? But he had heard Kline laughing, hardly the attitude of someone being kidnapped. Nevertheless, Halloran did not relax. If they moved any farther away he would get to a car and be ready to meet them on the opposite bank at the border of the estate. He would also have a chance to call in backup on the journey.

There was no cover this close to the shoreline, so Halloran moved back a ways, then spread-eagled himself on the ground, his gun pointing toward the dull shape on the lake. He waited and yet again was dazzled by another vast spasm of light. The intervals between had not been regular in length, so there was no way of preparing himself for each surge. The light vanished instantly, neither fading nor receding, snuffed like a candle flame. He rubbed at his eyelids, disbelieving what he had seen, telling himself there had to be a simple explanation, that he hadn't been able to take in everything during that short burst of light. Reason reassured him, but the afterimage refused to compromise.

Halloran had seen four men in the boat—Palusinski, Monk, and the two Jordanians. Kline had not been with them.

He was several yards away. He had been standing on the calm surface of the water.

Halloran shook his head, resisting the urge to laugh at the absurdity. There had to be something else out there just below the water level, a sandbank, a submerged platform, perhaps even a large rock. There was a logical explanation. Had to be. It was in Kline's nature to play such childish games. But surely they would have come across such an obstruction when he himself had rowed out there that very morning?

In the distance the jackals howled, the sound farther away this time, as though they were leaving the shoreline to slink back into the wooded slopes. He heard oars swishing on water. Voices. Drawing close to the jetty. He waited for them all to disembark before getting to his feet and going toward them.

Moonlight squeezed through the merest rent in the clouds, and the group came to a halt when they caught sight of Halloran.

"No need for weapons," Kline said, humor in his voice. "No enemies among us tonight, Halloran."

"What the hell were you doing out there?" The question was quietly put, Halloran's anger suppressed.

"I'm not a prisoner in my own home," Kline replied jovially. "I do as I please."

"Not if you expect me to protect you."

"There's no danger tonight."

Moonlight broke through with greater force, and he saw that Kline was grinning at him.

"The light from the water . . . ?"

Khayed and Daoud, dressed in the robes of their country, grinned as broadly as their master, while Palusinski glanced anxiously at Kline. Monk remained expressionless.

Kline's eyebrows arched uncomprehendingly. Then: "Ah, the lightning flashes. Yes, there seems to be quite an electrical storm raging above us tonight. With thunder soon to follow, no doubt. And then, of course, a deluge. Best not to linger out here, don't you agree?"

Once again his manner had changed. Kline's disposition had become that of an older, more reasoning man, the insidious mocking still in his voice, but his tone softer, less strident. His persona was vibrant, as if brimming with energy, though not of the nervous and neurotic kind that Halloran had become used to.

"You weren't in the boat," Halloran said almost cautiously.

There was elation in Kline's laughter. "I'm not one for moonlight dips, I can assure you."

Palusinski snickered.

"I saw you . . . on the water."

"*On* the water?" Kline asked incredulously, continuing to smile. "You mean *walking* on the water? Like Jesus Christ?"

Halloran did not reply.

"I see you've been hallucinating again, Halloran. Something in this lake obviously doesn't agree with your mental processes."

The Arabs chuckled behind their hands.

"I really think you should be resting," Kline went on in mock sympathy. "The strain of the last couple of days is apparently affecting your judgment. Or should I say your perception? I can't say I'm not surprised, Halloran. After all, you did come highly recommended as a bodyguard. I wonder if your employers realize that stress is getting the better of you."

At last even Monk smiled.

The clouds resumed their dominance and the landscape darkened once more.

"I think we should talk," Halloran said evenly, ignoring the stifled sounds of mirth coming from Kline's followers. For that was what they were, he had decided, not just employees, but in some way disciples of this strange man.

"But you should be sleeping. Isn't this your off-duty period? That's why we chose not to disturb you—we are perfectly aware that someone under your kind of pressure needs his rest."

"Monk and Palusinski had instructions to alert me to any activity, no matter what time it was."

"A late-night excursion on the lake was hardly worth rousing you for."

"I gave them orders."

"And I countermanded those orders."

"My company can't function under those conditions. Tomorrow I'll recommend the contract is canceled, or at least that I'm taken off the assignment. There's too much going on here that I don't like."

"No." At least the mood had been broken; Kline's tone was sharp, urgent. "You mustn't do that. I need you with me."

"You might need Shield, but you don't need me. There are other operatives equally as good." He tucked the automatic back into its holster and turned to walk away.

"Wait." Kline had taken a step after him, and Halloran paused. "I suppose I'm being a little unfair," the smaller man said, and immediately something of his "other" self was in evidence, almost as though it were another guise. "You're right, we should have let you know we were coming out here, should've brought you along for safety. But it was a spur-of-the-moment thing, y'know, something I felt like doing. I didn't see any need to worry you."

"That doesn't explain why you went on the lake. Nor does it explain the light. Or what I saw."

"Look at those clouds. Just study them for a while."

"That isn't nec—" A flash of light stopped him. He gazed skyward. Another, fainter discharge of energy, but enough to throw the tumbled cloud into relief. "That isn't what happened before. The light came from the lake."

"Reflections, that's all. It bounced off the water's surface. The lake's calm tonight, just like a big mirror."

A stuttered glare from above lit the group of men standing before him, hardening them into statues, bleaching their faces white. In the distance, as if to confirm Kline's explanation, came a deep rumbling of thunder.

"Let's get inside before the rain comes," Kline suggested.

"I saw—"

"You were mistaken." There was a firmness to the statement. "We'll go back to the house, Halloran, and I'll tell you a few things about myself, about this place. You'll find it interesting, I promise you that."

Halloran was tempted to advise his client to go to hell, but part of him was intrigued. The man was an enigma and unlike any person he'd had to protect before. "One condition," he said.

Kline lifted his hands, palms toward Halloran. "Whatever."

"You answer all my questions."

"Can't promise you that."

Light blazed the land again.

"I'll answer as many as I can, though," Kline added, and the thunder was nearer this time.

"Tell your Arab friends to go on ahead." Halloran indicated Monk and Palusinski. "You two follow behind. And don't watch us—keep your eyes on those slopes and the road."

"Ain't nothin' here to worry us," Monk protested.

"Just do as I say," Halloran snapped.

Palusinski slapped a hand on the American's shoulder as if to warn him not to argue. "You go," the Pole said to Halloran. "We'll follow. Everything is fine."

As the group started walking toward the house, fanning out so that Kline and Halloran were at the center of a square formation, the first raindrops spattered the grass. Kline grinned at his protector. "I told you it was about to rain," he said.

The deluge broke as though by command, and within seconds the men were soaked through. That didn't appear to worry Kline at all. He laughed and suddenly ran free of the formation, twisting his body around in the air, raising his arms high, fingers stretched outward. He came to a stop facing the hurrying group, his face turned up toward the sky, mouth open wide to receive the pelting raindrops. He slowly lowered his head and arms and something in his gleeful expression brought the others to a halt.

Kline pointed behind them. "Look at the lake!" he shouted over the downpour.

They turned to look back.

The broad expanse of water, suddenly lit by another flickering of lightning, was a churning mass, the rainfall exploding into the surface and creating millions of tiny geysers.

After the light was spent, Halloran was left with the unnerving impression of a million fingers pushing through the surface from the other side.

26

AN ANCIENT CULTURE

They sat opposite each other in the drawing room, Kline furiously rubbing at his dark curly hair, grinning across at Halloran as he did so.

"Refreshing, huh?" he said. "I love the rain. It purges the flesh. Pure and fresh, uncontaminated by human effluence. You ought to get dry. Don't want my bodyguard coming down with pneumonia."

"I'll take a bath before I turn in." He realized ruefully there would be scant time for sleeping if he were to keep to his own schedule.

The room was like most others at Neath—sparsely furnished and cold in atmosphere, even the roaring fire Kline had ordered to be lit infusing little spiritual warmth to the surroundings. Save for the fire glow there was no other light source in the room, for Kline had switched it off moments before. On a pedestal in one corner, its face animated by dancing shadows, stood the stone figure of a robed woman; the eyes were wide and staring, her hair swept back in almost medieval style. Above the mantel over the fireplace was a frieze depicting chariots and soldiers on the march; its colors, almost lost in the shadows, were of blue and white with the palest of reds for contrast.

"Made of shell and limestone," Kline said when he noticed Halloran studying the frieze while Khayed tended the fire and Daoud went off to fetch a towel. "Part of the Royal Standard of Ur. See one of the enemy being crushed by a chariot? There was plenty of gore in art and literature even in those distant days. People's taste doesn't change much, does it? You know anything at all about the Sumerians, Halloran?"

With the feeling he was about to find out, Halloran shook

his head. "History was never one of my strong points."

"Not even ancient history? I think you'd have found it fascinating."

"I'm more concerned with what's going on right now. You agreed to answer some questions."

"Sure. Just relax. Let me tell you something about these Sumerians first, okay? Never too late to learn, right?"

Daoud returned with a towel at that moment, which he handed to his employer.

"You can go ahead and feed Palusinski," Kline told him. "Our Polish friend has been drooling all evening."

The Arab grinned. "I have kept for him some tasty morsels," he replied, and beside him, having completed his task at the fireplace, Khayed chuckled. Halloran noted that, unlike yesterday, Daoud had not bothered to disguise his understanding of the English language. Both Arabs gave a slight bow and left the room.

Kline dried his hair with the towel, his rain-soaked jeans and sweater apparently not bothering him. Halloran watched his client, tiny orange glows fluttering in Kline's dark eyes, his features sharp, as if he were eager for conversation, with no thought for the lateness of the hour. One side of the psychic's body was in shadow, the side close to the fire warmly lit, shades of yellow dancing on his skin. His chair and body cast one corner of the room into deep, wavering gloom, but from its midst Halloran could see and feel those enlarged eyes of the stone woman staring at him.

Kline draped the towel over his head like a shawl so that only the tip of his nose and chin caught the glow from the fire. "Did you know they invented the written word?" At Halloran's quizzical expression he added, "The Sumerians."

"No, I didn't know that," Halloran answered tonelessly.

"Yep. And they were the first to count in units of ten and sixties. That's how we got sixty minutes to an hour and sixty seconds in a minute. They applied it to time, y'see. It's why we divide a circle into three hundred and sixty degrees, too. Not only that, but those old boys invented the wheel. How about that?"

"Kline, I'm not really—"

"*You might be.*" The retort was sharp, but a hand was immediately raised, palm outward, to indicate no offense was meant. "They knew about algebra and geometry, even had some idea of anatomy and surgery. I'm talking about *3000 B.C.*, Halloran, 3000 B.C. and earlier. Can you beat that? Shit, the rest of the world was barely past Neolithic!"

"You haven't told me why you went out on the lake tonight."

"Huh? I thought I had."

"No."

"Okay, okay. Look, would you believe me if I told you that the lake acts as some kind of conductor to my psychic power? That my psyche draws strength from certain physical sources. You know how a divining rod in the hands of special people is attracted towards an underground spring or subterranean lake, how it vibrates with energy and bends towards the source? My mind does the same thing, only it also absorbs psychic energy from these places."

"That's impossible. You're mixing the physical with the psychical."

"And you naturally assume there's no connection between the two. Never heard of kinetic energy, Halloran? How d'you imagine certain gifted people can move inanimate objects through the power of their own minds? It's that very connection I'm talking about, the link between the physical and the psychical. There's energy in everything around us, but energy itself has no form, no substance—it's an incorporeal thing, just like our own mind-wave patterns. Is it getting through to you, or are you the type that never wants to understand?"

Kline was leaning forward so that his whole face was in the shadow of the cowl. Halloran did not respond to the last question.

"It's the reason I bought Neath," Kline went on. "In these grounds I have my own psychic generator—the lake itself, one huge receptacle for spiritual force. You saw for yourself tonight how the lightning was drawn to it, and how those mysterious properties of the waters reacted. There are hundreds, maybe thousands, of such fields on our earth, places that different races have worshiped from, built their shrines on, paid homage to, since man first became aware of the other side of his nature. They still do to this day. And very few really understand why."

He sat back and the towel swung away from his jaw. He was smiling.

"In some locations, metaphysical and physical deposits be-

come almost one, and that's because both kinds of energy are
related. The moon affects the minds of men—ask any psychi-
atrist or psychologist—as well as influencing the earth's tides.
Vast mineral deposits—ores, oil, gas, or whatever—have that
potential because they're all sources of energy. How d'you
think I locate them for Magma? My mind's attracted to them
because it's from these sources that it draws sustenance, the
same way an animal can sniff food from great distances, a
shark can sense blood in the water from miles away. Instinct
or mind power? Or is it all the same thing?"

Halloran understood what he was being told, could even
appreciate that there was some kind of weird logic to it, but
Kline's dissertation was difficult to accept. "Are you saying
the lake has particular properties, minerals that—"

"I don't know what the fuck it has, Halloran. Nor do I
care. Maybe there's something underneath the lake itself, or in
the sludge swilling on the bottom. None of that matters to me,
I'm just happy to have my own private supply." Kline rubbed
at his hair again with the towel. "I still have to search out
sources in other parts, though. Like the Bedouins have their
secret water holes all over the desert, always handy when one
dries up, I have my own wells. It involves some traveling, but
like they say, travel broadens the mind. Right?"

"Is that how you picked up your bodyguards, passing
through various countries?" Halloran asked, keen to lead the
conversation away from such "mystical" overtones.

Kline was reflective. "Yeah. Yeah, I did a lot of traveling.
Found suitable people along the way."

"People and animals. How did you get the jackals back
into the country?"

Kline shook his head. "They were bred for me here. Unusual pets, huh?"

"You could say. I can't help wondering why you chose
such a breed."

"Because they're despicable, Halloran. I like that." Kline
chuckled as he gazed into the fire. "And they're scavengers.
But an underestimated species, all the same. Scavengers, yes,
but not cowardly as popular belief would have it. Oh no,
they'd fight off eagles and hyenas for food. And they'd snatch
a morsel from under a lion's nose."

He shook his head as if in wonder. "Cunning, too. You
know, one will distract a mother antelope while another grabs

the baby. They'll tear off pieces of a kill and bury them in different places for another day to foil rival scavengers. They'll even swallow food and regurgitate it later to avoid the risk of it being stolen by swooping eagles on the journey back to their young. Wonderful survivors, these creatures, Halloran."

"As you say, they're scavengers."

"True, their main diet is carrion, but they appreciate other delights. The jackal is very partial to the afterbirth of the wildebeest, for instance. They'll follow a herd for miles sniffing after the pregnant cows."

"There was someone with them tonight. He was standing by the lakeside."

Kline turned back to Halloran. "So?"

"I assume it was the person who controls the gates."

The other man nodded.

"Someone else you picked up abroad?"

Kline ignored the question. "I haven't finished telling you about the Sumerians. Did I say they were the first astrologers? No, I don't think I did. They built ziggurats, massive square towers, as temple observatories. That was the start of astronomy, just in case you're unimpressed by zodiac predictions."

He draped the towel over his head again and rested back in his chair, watching Halloran from the shadows.

"Their nation sprang up between the rivers Tigris and Euphrates in what these days is called Iraq. A green, lush area, desert all around. It's the traditional site of the Garden of Eden, where that bad old angel called Serpent got Adam and Eve into deep trouble and had his wings clipped—his legs too—for the rift he'd caused. Serpent was forced to spend the rest of his existence crawling on his belly, and when you're immortal, as all angels are, that's a long time. Anyway, the Sumerians knew how to govern themselves, with laws and organization of labor forces and rates and taxes and coalitions between the different cities. The smaller towns and villages even had their own mayors and municipal councils. Thing is, they took their farming seriously, and because whole communities could be fed by a few, others were left to get on with developing new skills and professions. The beginning of real civilization, Halloran. For better or worse, the start of the whole cultural shebang."

"Look, right now there are more relevant matters to discuss. Like the lack of security on this estate, for instance."

It was as if Kline hadn't heard him. "They even had their own surefire method of dealing with crime. On an eye-for-an-eye basis, y'know? A son who raised his hand against his father would have that hand cut off, same with a doctor who fouled up an operation. An unfaithful wife would have a breast cut off. A man who set fire to a house, or maybe looted a burning home, would be roasted alive." Kline sniggered. "Rough justice, but effective. And oh boy, their death penalty. As well as roasting, there was beating, strangulation, and being thrown from their highest temples. Oh yeah—and mutilation. Anyone who really pissed them off was mutilated, had their arms and legs chopped off. The idea was to make sure that particular evil would never rise up against them again. Literally. So they turned these sinners into limbless creatures, snakes—like the Serpent of old, you see—only fit to crawl on their bellies in the dirt. Nasty way to die, left all alone, unable to move, the only hope being that death didn't take too long." Kline visibly shuddered.

"You said they were civilized."

"They found a way to make their system work. A cruel regime in many respects, but they taught the rest of the world something. Strange thing is that, as a race, they vanished from the face of the earth. Can you beat that? Just died out, absorbed into other cultures. You have to wonder why, don't you, considering all their achievements."

"Yeah," Halloran replied wearily, "you have to wonder."

"Even their language died with them."

A burning coal cracked, a gunshot sound that made both men glance toward the fireplace.

After a moment, Halloran said: "I want to ask you about Cora."

Kline settled back in his chair and slowly pulled the towel from his head. There was a curious mixture of innocence and wickedness in his expression, perhaps because while his smile was ingenuous, there was a glint of maliciousness in his eyes.

"This on a personal basis, Halloran, or to do with my protection?"

"Maybe both. Why is she so"—an apt word was difficult—"dependent on you?"

The other man giggled, a childish outburst. Halloran waited patiently.

"She isn't," came the reply. "Nobody's ever truly dependent on another person, didn't you know that? It's only their own weaknesses that they're servile to. An indulgence on their part. Self-inflicted. The tendency is to use someone else as a focus for their own deficiencies, maybe even as a patron to them. Surprised you haven't figured that out for yourself." Kline leaned forward as if to make the point. "We all have total governance over our own will, Halloran. Ultimately, no one can interfere with that."

"People can be corrupted."

The reply was swift. "Only if that's what they secretly want."

Halloran realized that he was now reluctant to pursue the matter. "We, uh, have to make arrangements for tighter security around the estate."

Amused, Kline studied his protector for several seconds. "Why so interested in Cora? You haven't become involved in anything that might be construed as unprofessional, I hope. After all, you've been contracted to take an interest in my well being, no one else's."

He knew his client was mocking him and wondered, not for the first time, why Kline had sent Cora to him the night before. "There's a difference between loyalty and dependence."

Kline looked genuinely surprised. "You suggesting Cora would betray me?"

"Not at all. I just need to know the full picture."

"Well, let's talk about her some more." Kline interlaced his fingers over his stomach, his elbows resting on the arms of the chair, eyes closed as if picturing Cora in his mind. "She's intelligent, works hard, is superefficient at her job. She's also some looker, wouldn't you agree? A little jaded nowadays, though, like she's got deep-rooted troubles. D'you feel that? Yeah, it's pretty obvious. What do you suppppose those troubles are?"

He was being taunted, but Halloran refused to take the bait. "Let's get on to other things."

"I think she's agonizing over some terrible moral dilemma, don't you? You can see she's losing sleep over it. Can't be anything to do with the job, otherwise she'd leave, wouldn't she? No, it's got to be something in her personal life. She's a sensual woman, so maybe sex is involved, huh? What d'you think, Halloran? Stupid of me—how would you know?"

The urge to wipe the leering grin from Kline's face was almost overwhelming. "We need chain-link fences topped by barbed wire erected at all access points to the grounds," Halloran said calmly, "with vibration sensors attached. Intruders can always cut their way through hedges, but at least we'll slow them down and make it easier for patrols to spot them."

"Maybe Cora likes things she's been taught not to. She had a strong moral upbringing, you know. I understand her parents were pillars of society, so maybe they wouldn't have approved of her little ways. You think that's what's bothering her? Parental disapproval, even though they're dead and gone? Guilty conscience on her part? Destructive thing, guilt."

"I'm not in favor of moving searchlights—they're too easy to dodge—but a good lighting system close to the house and pointing outwards would be useful. That and low-frequency audio scanners or magnetic fields would provide a good cover. You need intrusion-detection sensors between the house and the lake, too, with sonar equipment directed onto the lake itself."

"Still, none of us are infallible, are we, Halloran? We all have our weaknesses and foibles that make us vulnerable. We wouldn't be human without them. Can't help wondering what yours are."

"Along the inside road you could do with one or two access-control points where vehicles can undergo thorough checks. Closed-circuit television is essential for the main gates, incidentally, with a guardhouse by the side. That'll have to be built with hardened walls and glass, and will require a telephone line direct to the house. Reliance on your man at the lodge isn't good enough."

"What makes you so inscrutable, Halloran? What goes on behind that mask of yours?"

"As well as closed-circuit TV points on entrances to Neath, you ought to have bars mounted on all windows that provide easy access. It goes without saying that intrusion alarms will have to be installed on all windows and doors, too."

"Do you believe in God, Halloran?"

He stared back at Kline. "I'll draw up a list of firm recommendations and submit copies to the Magma Corporation and Achilles' Shield," he said evenly. "If we don't receive your or

Magma's consent to carry out these precautions, there's not much my company can do for you."

"My question rattle you? You should see your face. I thought all the Irish were God-fearing, no matter what particular brand of religion they followed."

"I'm not Irish."

"Your old man was. And you may not have been born there, but you were raised in the ol' country."

"How did you know that?" He realized immediately that Cora must have told Kline.

"You still haven't answered *my* question."

"Information about myself isn't part of the contract. All you need to know is that I'm capable of doing a good job."

"Just curious, that's all. You suddenly look even more dangerous, d'you know that?"

There was an abrupt vision between Kline and himself. Father O'Connell's big, ruddy face was contorted with anguish, his tear-soaked cheeks catching the flames from the fire. Only these reflections were of flames from another time. Halloran cleared the image from his mind. But the sounds of the priest's wailing as he ran into the burning church were more difficult to erase.

"You still with me, Halloran? You look as if you've seen a ghost."

The Shield operative blinked. Kline was watching him intently, and the slyness of his smile somehow suggested he had shared Halloran's vision.

"The Sumerians had lots of gods—lots of goddesses, too," Kline went on as if nothing unusual had occurred. "A whole team of 'em. Anu, god of the heavens, Su'en, the moon god, Enlil, god of the storm, Marduk, god of Babylon, Ea, one of the good guys, and the goddess, Inin, later known as Ishtar—now she was something else. She was a whore. Then there was Bel-Marduk, the one they came to despise." His smile had become venomous. "They misunderstood his cruelty, you see. But there was always someone—excuse me, some *deity* —to pray to for any cause, or to blame for any wrong. Delegation was the idea, spreading the load. Don't put too much pressure on the one god or goddess in case they get vexed and turn nasty. Or was it because they didn't believe in putting all their trust in one master? Maybe a lesson learned from their past. And that's the weird thing about these people, Halloran:

we know hardly anything at all about their origins. Now, like I said before, that's odd, considering the Sumerians invented the written word."

Halloran scarcely heard, for he was still numbed by the strength of the vision of moments before. And tiredness also was beginning to weigh heavily upon him.

"It seems," Kline continued, his enthusiasm not curbed by lack of interest from his audience, "that kings, princes— maybe even the high priests—hid or destroyed all records of Sumerian early history. Yet they'd been setting things down as cuneiform writing on clay tablets since 3000 B.C.! What d'you suppose they needed to hide? I mean, to wipe out centuries of their past like that, they must have had some terrible dark secret they wanted to keep from the rest of the world, don't you think?" He was leaning forward again, hands resting on his knees, his face bright in the glow from the fire.

Halloran struggled to rouse himself, the warmth of the room and Kline's almost mesmeric tone abetting the weariness. "There's something more I need to ask you," he said, and then had to concentrate to remember what it was. In the gloom of the far corner, the stone woman's eyes seemed larger.

"Even one of the greatest archaeological finds ever failed to turn up any evidence of what went on in Sumerian society much before 2500 B.C.," said Kline, ignoring the pending question. "That was when Sir Leonard Woolley discovered a gigantic grave site near the city wall of Ur in the 1920s. Thousands of the graves had been plundered, but something spurred on the old boy to dig deeper, and what he found *underneath* that cemetery staggered historians all around the world."

Halloran pinched the corners of his eyes with thumb and forefinger. What the hell was Kline rambling on about?

"Know what was there?" Kline gripped the arms of the chair as if unable to contain his excitement. "Stone tombs. Sepulchres! Can you believe it? Woolley's team got to them by ramps leading into deep shafts. Inside those chambers they found intact skeletons of Sumerian kings, queens, princes, princesses, and members of the high priesthood, all decked out in full regalia of gold and semiprecious stones—and that's why it came to be known as the Royal Cemetery. Around them were golden cups, stelae and statues, beautiful vases, silver ornaments—all kinds of valuable stuff." Kline gave an excited laugh. "And know what else, Halloran? All their servants and attendants were buried right there with them. Court officials, soldiers, priests—even oxen with their wagons. No signs of violence, though. Those people had accepted their fate without argument. They'd taken poison and allowed themselves to be sealed in with their masters and mistresses." He grinned. "How's that for loyalty?"

Halloran experienced a peculiar sense of relief when the other man turned away from him to gaze at the fire, as though Kline's intensity was a parasitical thing. Some of his tiredness lifted and he remembered the question he had meant to ask.

But Kline was speaking once more. "For twelve years Sir Leonard worked that site, delving, dusting, probing, digging, yet nowhere did he find anything that told him of the early Sumerians. Some historians surmise that everything was destroyed at the time of the Great Flood—*if* there ever was such an event. No one's ever been sure whether or not that was only a myth, and one borrowed by another religion, incidentally. For Noah, read Utnapishtim, a hero of Sumerian legend. Anyway, no matter, flood or not, something should have survived from that catastrophe—unless those old boys didn't want it to. But what could be so bad, so *diabolically* awful, that they'd want the knowledge of it obliterated from their history? Answer me that."

His head slowly came around so that he was facing Halloran again, and there was a meanness to his smile. The flames of the fire had died down, the room considerably darker. Halloran felt oppressed by the shadows, as though they were drapes closing around him. And the weariness had returned, resting on his eyelids so that they were difficult to keep open.

The question. Not Kline's but his own. What was the question? Kline had reminded him. *Underneath* the cemetery. Under. Neath. Kline had even emphasized the word. He thought of the sturdy oak door that led to the cellar.

But Halloran hadn't voiced the question. His head sagged with tiredness.

"Not falling asleep on me, are you?" said Kline. "Ah well, it's been a long day, so go ahead, close your eyes."

He didn't want them to, but his eyes closed. Halloran

stirred in the chair, his limbs leaden. Sleep was approaching and it was irresistible.

"Not just a cellar," he heard Kline say from a great distance. "Something more than that. Down there is where I have my very own sepulchre. Did you hear me, Halloran?"

Barely. Kline must be a long way away by now...

"...*My sepulchre, Halloran*..."

...yet the words were suddenly near, a whisper inside Halloran's mind.

27

A DREAM AND BETRAYAL

"*Liam*. Wake up."

He felt a hand shaking his shoulder, and consciousness quickly drew him away from the unreality of his dream. Halloran's body was tensed and ready before his eyes opened, his fingers instinctively curling around the butt of his gun. Cora was leaning over him, her face anxious.

"Liam, we have to go back to London immediately."

He looked past her at the empty chair opposite. Only gray ashes were in the fireplace, and daylight did its best to penetrate the heavy curtains over the windows. Stone eyes still watched him from the corner of the room.

"Liam," Cora urged.

"It's all right." He stood, all drowsiness gone, his senses fully alert. He was angry with himself when he glanced at his wristwatch and saw that it was nearly 8:40. Why the hell had he allowed himself to fall asleep in this room, and why hadn't one of the bodyguards woken him at the proper time? "What's the problem, Cora?" he quickly asked.

"Felix has just had a call from Sir Victor. He has to return to Magma right away."

"On a Sunday?"

She nodded. "It's serious."

He made toward the door, but her hand on his arm stopped him.

"Last night . . ." she said.

So much had happened the night before that it took him a second or two to understand what Cora meant. Her expression was so solemn, her eyes so grave, that he couldn't help smiling.

"We'll talk later," he told her, then kissed her cheek. They left the room together.

The streets of the city were empty, save for the few tourists who took the occasion of such quietness to view London's financial sector. Light drizzle soaked the pavements and road-ways, freshening them for the onslaught they would take dur-ing the rest of the week. Glass towers glistened as though newly varnished, while older buildings hued darker as they soaked up the dampness.

A convoy of three cars, a black limousine, a Mercedes, and a Granada, sped through the deserted streets, the drivers of each checking their surroundings and rearview mirrors each time they were halted by traffic lights.

Halloran was in the back of the second car, the silver-gray Mercedes, sitting next to Felix Kline, prepared to cover his client with his own body should anything untoward occur. Janusz Palusinski was driving the armored vehicle, and Cora sat beside him in the passenger seat. Monk was the driver of the car ahead, Khayed and Daoud, who never ceased looking back to satisfy themselves that their master was not far be-hind, were his companions. In the Granada, the last in the procession, were two Shield men who had been taken off pa-trol duty around the estate.

Kline had been unusually silent throughout the journey, mentioning neither the events of the previous night nor the reason for the summons to the Magma building that morning. Halloran realized he was witnessing yet another facet of this strange man's nature, a quiet, brooding stillness that was in sharp contrast to Kline's irritatingly animated and talkative side. This mood was more akin to the soft-spoken, cultured role that Kline sometimes adopted, although again it was dif-ferent, for there was no mocking in his gaze and no air of secret knowledge. The small man was withdrawn, thoughtful, seemingly unaware of any danger he might be in, with no agitation in his movements, no nervousness in his scrutiny. Yet Halloran could sense a deep anger burning inside him.

The Shield operative remembered the dream Cora had roused him from, for Kline had been part of it. They had walked together, he and Kline, Halloran allowing himself to be led by the other man through a great blackness, his hand in Kline's as though they were lovers. Although nothing could be seen, he had felt a frightening vastness of space around and above them, as if they were inside a cathedral or a huge subterranean cave. Now and then something light would waft across his face so that he recoiled, fearing there were long, trailing cobwebs on all sides. Kline's whispered voice assured him that there was nothing to be afraid of, they were merely passing through thin, unseen veils. There was something in the distance, a tenuous mass that was blacker than the blackness around them, and Halloran could hear the sound of his own heartbeat as they drew nearer to that ultimate darkness, the thudding growing louder, joined by the beating of another's—Kline's—their life-surge keeping time, becoming as one. And then, all about the darkness, eyelids were opening in slow, drawn-out movements, so that a multitude of stone eyes stared as the two men drew closer to the void, the nucleus of the blackness itself. Kline had released his hand and was stretching his arms toward the core, creating an opening within its shell, their combined heartbeats becoming thunderous, joining—or so it seemed—with yet another whose loudness grew so that soon, very soon, it smothered their own, and although the rising sound appeared to emanate from the void before them, it was everywhere, filling the infinite space, deafening the two men. Kline was reaching inside that pitchy nothingness, arms trembling, his mouth gaping in a silent ecstatic scream, and Halloran had moved close to see what it was that the other man grasped, but he was blind in such blackness; he could feel a terrible heat, sense something there, something he was glad he could not see. Yet still he reached out with Kline, the two men joined in an unholy alliance, compelled by the mystery. . .

"*Liam.*"

And Cora's voice had recalled him from the dream.

"Liam."

The Mercedes was passing the Mansion House, the Magma building not far away, towering above others around it. Cora had turned in her seat and was looking directly at him.

Halloran blinked. He'd been completely lost in his own thoughts and once again was angry at himself for his negligence.

"Should we drive straight down into Magma's underground carpark," Cora said, "or do you want us to be dropped by the front entrance?"

"The carpark," he replied. "I arranged for it to be checked out by Shield before we left Neath. If there were problems they'd have contacted us."

"Was there any news of those people who tried to stop us on Friday?" she asked.

Cora's face was still pale, her actions skittish, the weekend in the country apparently having had little calming effect, Halloran thought wryly. "Nothing's turned up so far. Something'll break soon though, it usually does. We'll be okay so long as we're prepared." He had addressed the last remarks to Kline, but the psychic's attention was averted; he was watching the streets, though Halloran had the feeling his client's vision was directed inward.

The Magma Corporation's headquarters came into full view, and Halloran was once again impressed by its grandeur. The rain had intensified the luster of its bronze surfaces, the deep shade of the windows defining and enhancing the metal sections so that the building's complicated structure was drawn in bold and deliberately simple lines. The curved buttresses and various levels added to the forcefulness of design, a formidable edifice amid staid and less aggressive architecture.

The limousine ahead pulled into the curb outside the main entrance, and Halloran instructed Palusinski to keep moving until they reached the garage entrance around the corner on a narrow side street. A member of the Shield team saw their approach and signaled for the entrance barrier inside the building to be lifted. The Granada followed the Mercedes down the ramp, the limousine now in the rear of the convoy. The Pole reversed their vehicle into a bay, and Halloran stepped out as soon as it came to a halt. He quickly went around to Kline's side, right hand inside his jacket. A figure was already limping toward them as Palusinski opened the passenger door for Kline, and Halloran raised a hand in greeting. Mather's countenance was unusually grim.

"A word, Liam," he said as he drew near.

"Go on ahead to the elevator," Halloran told the others. "I'll join you there." He went toward Mather, who ushered him a short distance away so that they would not be overheard.

"How have things been at your end?" the Planner said, stopping by a concrete pillar. At the top of the ramp the Shield operative who had signaled the approach of the car stood with his back to them, observing the street outside.

"Not good as far as security's concerned," answered Halloran. "Neath is wide open."

"But you've had no more trouble?"

He hesitated before giving a shake of his head. "What's wrong, Charles?"

"It's Dieter, I'm afraid." Mather looked down at his cane, unconsciously tapping it twice on the ground. "His body was recovered not more than an hour ago."

Halloran saw the others were walking toward the elevators, Monk and the two Arabs following close behind. The two operatives from the Granada were standing by their car, waiting for further instructions. "What happened?" he said to Mather.

"Shot through the back of the head. Gerald is with the police finding out a bit more at this very moment. What we do know is that Dieter was tortured before being killed."

"Jesus, Mary..." breathed Halloran. "Who?"

Mather shrugged. "I haven't a clue, Liam. No trademarks that we're aware of as yet."

"Where was he found?"

"Floating in theThames. Whoever did it didn't even bother to weigh down the body."

"Anything to do with this operation?"

"We can't discount that factor. If there *is* any logical reason for his murder, and providing it isn't the work of some outraged husband, then torture obviously suggests information was being sought. Nevertheless, it's somewhat drastic to go to such lengths just to gain details of our plans for Felix Kline. It's reasonable to assume that any would-be kidnappers have sufficient knowledge of their target without resorting to that kind of violence. Another theory is that someone with a grudge from Dieter's past hated him enough to inflict such injuries before ending his life."

"There's another possibility," suggested Halloran. Kline and his entourage were at the elevators and looking over to see what was delaying him. "It could be a way of warning us off."

"From protecting Felix Kline?"

He nodded. "It's our only major assignment at the moment."

"Hmm, it's a thought, I suppose," voiced Mather. "Unlikely, though. In the event of a successful snatch, kidnappers would rather negotiate with K & R people than the authorities, who're invariably against payment of ransom money."

The elevator doors were opening. "We'd better join the others," said Halloran. "I assume we keep this to ourselves."

Mather limped alongside him, the group ahead beginning to enter the elevator. "No need to cause undue anxiety as far as our client is concerned. We may have to issue some kind of public statement once the press gets hold of the story, but even then there's no reason why Dieter's death should be linked with the Magma contract."

Halloran signaled the two Shield bodyguards to wait in the parking lot and stepped ahead of Monk and the Arabs before they could follow their employer into the elevator. "Take the other one," he ordered, and before they could protest, Kline nodded his head in a gesture of assent.

Mather endeavored to promote conversation during the swift journey to the eighteenth floor, but the psychic refused to be drawn from his brooding silence, and Cora's replies were perfunctory although polite.

Sir Victor Penlock himself was waiting to greet them when the elevator doors opened again. He wore a navy-blue double-breasted blazer over a fawn turtleneck pullover, sharply pressed beige slacks adding to the casual elegance. Halloran realized that Magma's security guard in the booth by the entrance to the parking lot must have reported Kline's arrival. It seemed unusual, though, that the chairman of such a vast corporation should be waiting so anxiously for one of his own employees.

"Sorry to have dragged you back to town, Felix," Sir Victor apologized, "but as I explained over the phone, the situation is serious."

Apparently a day for bad tidings, mused Halloran as Kline swept by Sir Victor with barely a glance. The tall chairman nodded toward the two Shield men before walking after the psychic. "Henry is waiting for us in my office," they heard him tell Kline as they, too, followed behind along the mauve-carpeted corridor. As they passed the display cabinets set in the walls on either side, Halloran rubbed a hand across his stubbled chin and wondered what the fuss was about. Kline had not been forthcoming on the drive up to London, and Cora appeared to know no more than he himself. Judging by the gravity of Sir Victor's tone and by the fact that the matter could not be fully discussed over the telephone, the cause for concern was not only serious but extremely confidential, too. The corridor widened into the broad hallways and whereas previously he had heard normal office hubbub from the offices to his left and right, now there was only silence. The big double-door opposite was already open, and the chairman ushered them through. Once inside, however, he asked Mather and Halloran to wait in the outer office.

Then Kline spoke up. "No. Halloran can listen in on this. But not Cora." Without another word he disappeared into Sir Victor's office.

The chairman raised his eyebrows at the girl, then indicated that Halloran should follow him. He went after Kline.

"Seems you're to be privileged," Mather remarked lightly. "Well, Miss Redmile, shall we see if we can brew up some tea for ourselves? Perhaps you'll remain on guard here, Mr., er, Palusinski?"

The Pole sat at one of the two secretaries' desks. "I will keep good watch," he assured them, and frowned, his eyes narrowing behind his spectacles as he regarded the computer screen on the desk top. "Such knowledge inside this tiny window," he said distractedly.

Before Halloran went through to the main office, he caught Cora's surprised expression; she was obviously bewildered by her employer's blunt dismissal. He closed the door behind him, curious himself about Kline's motive.

Quinn-Reece glanced up briefly from the papers neatly spread on a low table in front of him but gave no sign of welcome. Kline was standing with his back to the room, staring out of the huge floor-to-ceiling window, the rain outside stippling the glass. Sir Victor vaguely waved toward a chair, and Halloran lowered himself into it. Kline then did something quite unexpected: he whirled around, walked across to the chairman's broad, oak desk and took the seat behind it. He looked directly at Quinn-Reece and asked, "How is it possible?"

The deputy chairman cleared his throat before answering. "Obviously we have a leak within the corporation."

Sir Victor sat in a chair close to his own desk and tugged at the crease in his trouser leg. "But who? How could such information be divulged so quickly unless its source was from a very high level?"

Halloran shifted in his seat, puzzled by the conversation.

"That isn't necessarily so," said Quinn-Reece. "Someone in the field team could be selling us out."

"You mean that every single time that Consolidated Ores has negotiated exploration rights before us one of our agents in that particular area has gone over to them?" Kline spoke as though the notion were not feasible.

"It's hardly likely, is it?" Sir Victor agreed. "The betrayal must be from these offices."

Halloran interrupted. "Does what you're discussing have any bearing on my company's assignment for Magma?" As Kline himself had insisted that he "listen in," it was a reasonable assumption to make.

Quinn-Reece's reply was brusque. "This matter doesn't concern Achilles' Shield in any way. As a matter of fact, I don't understand why your presence is required in this room."

"I invited him," Kline said quietly. He was staring at the deputy chairman, his dark eyes unblinking, and Quinn-Reece appeared uncomfortable under his gaze. "Halloran has been hired to protect me, and this morning I feel in particular need of that protection. Strange how betrayal can leave you feeling so vulnerable."

"You can't seriously imagine that Consolidated would be behind an attempted kidnapping?" the astonished Sir Victor protested. "They may be formidable business rivals, and admittedly we've fought some fierce battles with them in the past, but it's always been purely on a competitive business basis. I can't honestly believe that they would resort to any kind of physical violence."

"Someone has," Kline snapped back.

"It might help if I know what's happened," Halloran suggested.

"What's happened, my friend," said Kline, "is that over recent months, practically every new source of mineral deposits I've discovered has been laid claim to by Consolidated Ores before our field agents have had a chance to make tests. It doesn't take an Einstein to figure out someone from within our own organization is tipping them off."

"If that's the case and they're getting their information anyway, why bother to kidnap you?" Halloran commented.

"Wouldn't that in effect be killing the golden goose? Besides, industrial espionage may be illegal, but it's nowhere as serious as abduction."

"That's a fair argument, Felix," put in Sir Victor. "Why should any rival company take that risk when it doesn't appear to be necessary?"

"Because sooner or later the informer will be exposed." Kline's reply was calm, his demeanor having changed yet again, his normal (normal? Halloran had to wonder at the term) excitability subdued.

"But what good would kidnapping you do?" queried Quinn-Reece.

"Maybe the idea's to eliminate me permanently."

Sir Victor and his deputy chairman exchanged astonished glances.

"I think that would be too extreme, particularly if Consolidated really is involved. I know the chairman personally, and although he's something of a scoundrel, I cannot believe he'd sanction murder. No, no, Felix, that really is beyond the bounds of reason."

"Then why do I feel so threatened?" Kline coolly retorted.

"Uh, perhaps, Felix, perhaps you're overwrought," Sir Victor suggested cautiously. "After all, so much reliance on your psychic ability must eventually take its toll. You know, you haven't had a proper break for quite some time now."

Kline smiled. And Halloran's eyes narrowed. Despite everything that had happened over the past few days, he hadn't realized until that moment that there was so much danger in the man.

"Yes," the psychic admitted, "I do feel in need of some rest. A few more days at Neath, maybe. And then some traveling. Yes, it's time I ventured abroad again." His smile withered. "But that doesn't resolve our current crisis."

"How often has this other company managed to beat you to these new locations?" asked Halloran, genuinely interested in Magma's problem.

Quinn-Reece provided the answer. "Three times in a period of five months."

Halloran raised his eyebrows. "That doesn't seem an awful lot."

"I can assure you," Sir Victor said, "that in a world of diminishing natural resources, it is."

"Couldn't it be coincidence?"

"We were prepared to accept that on the first two occasions," replied the chairman. "But Felix indicated to us only last Thursday that an as yet untapped source of copper could be found in a certain region of Papua New Guinea. By the time our agent had arranged to see the appropriate authority dealing with land-exploration rights, negotiations were already well under way with Consolidated Ores. These matters are usually dealt with on a first-come, first-served basis—provided contracts are favorable to the country of origin, naturally. But no, Mr. Halloran, this time we're certain that confidential information is being disclosed outside almost as soon as we ourselves learn of new deposits."

"Could be they use a psychic of their own."

Sir Victor received the suggestion gravely. "There is no other person on this earth who can match the sensory ability of Felix Kline." It was a statement not meant to be argued with, and Halloran saw no point in doing so.

"How many Magma personnel knew of this recent find?" he asked.

"Not many," replied Quinn-Reece, leaning forward and shuffling the papers before him. "Myself, the chairman, and of course Felix and Miss Redmile. At the other end, only the agent whom I contacted. The news hasn't even been announced to our board of directors, and only one or two of our executives have become involved since, although we now know that wasn't until after Consolidated made their move."

"Don't forget me," said Halloran. "It was mentioned to me on the first day I visited Magma."

Sir Victor turned inquiringly to Kline, who nodded. "As you've only been associated with the Corporation for less than a week, I think we can sensibly discount you as a mole," the chairman reasoned.

"Well, your range of suspects is mercifully limited," said Halloran. "But before you point a finger at anyone, I suggest you investigate these offices for electronic listening devices and make sure your phones aren't being tapped. You ought to check that your computer codes haven't been cracked also. Shield can make a thorough sweep, if you like."

"Antibugging searches are carried out every week by our own security," Quinn-Reece assured him.

"In an irregular pattern? I'd hate to hear, for instance, that you search the offices every Monday morning at nine o'clock."

"Our security people aren't that naïve, Mr. Halloran."

"Let's hope they aren't disloyal, either. And your computer codes?"

"We've no reason to suspect they've been broken."

"Might be an idea to find out if there have been any recorded but unauthorized admissions over the past few months."

"That wouldn't have any bearing on our immediate problem," Sir Victor remarked.

"No, but locating a hacker might help direct those accusing fingers." Halloran stared across the room at Kline, who seemed almost dwarfish behind the broad desk, the high, rain-spattered window at his back increasing the effect. "Aside from that," he said, "you're the psychic: don't you have an idea who's giving away company secrets?"

Kline returned the Shield man's stare. "Oh yeah, Halloran," he said, "I'm sure I know who's the traitor in our midst." He looked at each person in the room, and his face was expressionless when he spoke.

"It's Cora," he told them.

28

HALLORAN

"If I may say so, m'dear, you don't look at all well."

Cora had taken Shield's Planner to one of Magma's smaller conference rooms on the eighteenth floor, a place used for private meetings with business associates rather than full-scale executive gatherings or board meetings. Cora had disappeared for a few minutes, returning with tea for them both. Rather than sit at the long table, they had relaxed in easy chairs that were spaced around the walls of the room. As Cora sipped her tea, Mather noticed a slight tremble in her grip.

"I sincerely hope this kidnapping business isn't upsetting you too much," he said soothingly. "We have you well guarded, you know. And I promise you, Liam is the best operative we have in this kind of situation. He has an uncanny instinct for striking before being struck." He caught her sudden glance at him with the mention of Halloran's name. Ah, he thought, our man is having an effect on her.

"I suppose it's made us all nervous," Cora said.

But you look as though you haven't slept properly for several weeks, Mather thought to himself. "Yes, I can appreciate that. Perhaps the blackguards will be flushed out soon and then we can all get some rest. Our job isn't only physically to protect the target; we spend a great deal of time searching out those who are the threat." He deliberately refrained from saying "or assassins," unwilling to worry the girl any more than was necessary. "We've been working on that since we agreed to the assignment."

"But without any success."

"True, but it's early days. We'll find out who's causing these problems soon enough, never fear." He placed the empty teacup in the saucer by his feet.

"Would you like some more?" she asked.

"No, thank you, one's enough. Of course, these villains might well have cried off after their unsuccessful attempt the other day. Nothing like a show of strength to make such thugs turn tail and run." He smiled, doing his best to reassure her.

Cora merely stared blankly into her teacup. Her question was tentative. "Liam would kill anyone he considered to be a danger, wouldn't he?"

Mather was slightly taken aback. "Why, yes, if that was the only way. However, he isn't a murderer, Miss Redmile. He'll only take what measures are necessary to retrieve a situation. I can assure you that Achilles' Shield is a law-abiding organization which doesn't employ reckless hit men. All right, it must be confessed, we sometimes bend the rules here and there, but our operatives are trained to control a situation rather than be pressured by it."

"He . . ." Cora looked up and Mather saw the anxiety there. ". . . he frightens me."

Mather's short laugh was meant to be encouraging. "There's nothing *you* need fear from Liam," he told her.

"What makes such a person deal in violence? He can be so gentle, and yet . . ."

Oh dear, mused Mather, it's gone deeper than I'd imagined. "Liam is essentially employed to deter violence," he said.

"You know it's there inside him, a terrible coldness. Sometimes, when he smiles, you can see it in his eyes. I could easily believe he has no conscience."

"Perhaps you've mistaken that coldness for an immunity against . . . well, it's difficult to put a word on it, but you might consider it as an immunity against . . . forgiveness. Liam is unremitting, relentless even, when he, or others in his charge, are threatened. I don't believe he's a man who would ever seek vengeance, but nor is he one to turn the other cheek."

Mather tapped his cane against the shoe on his outstretched foot. "Let me tell you something of his background, then perhaps you'll understand him a little more."

She appeared apprehensive, as though uncertain that she really wanted to know too much about the man.

"Liam's father, Pat Halloran, was a captain in the British Army, who met Siobhan, his future wife, while on leave in

Southern Ireland—apparently he was a keen walker and angler, so what better place to spend his free time? He was also of Irish descent himself, so felt a natural affinity to the country. He returned some months later, proposed to the girl, was promptly accepted, and both came back to London where they were married. Within a year, Liam was born."

Mather reached down and retrieved his cup from the floor. "Perhaps I will have more tea, m'dear." He watched her as she walked to the table and refilled his cup. She's confused about Halloran, he thought, and could hardly be blamed for that. Even to Mather, who knew him better than most, Halloran was still something of an enigma. But it was Felix Kline and his strange cohorts that the Planner had misgivings about, doubts which he could not explain rationally; the girl could be an ally to his operative, an insider who could give warning of any odd business going on that might affect Halloran's course of action. The Planner had voiced his growing unease concerning the Magma assignment to Gerald Snaith that very morning, after the discovery of Dieter Stuhr's mutilated corpse. Naturally, the Controller of Achilles' Shield, a pragmatic individual to say the least, had demanded evidence of any link between the two matters, which Mather could not provide.

He thanked Cora when she handed him the fresh tea, and waited for her to sit before proceeding.

"His father's army career involved a fair bit of traveling that did not, unfortunately, require any long-term overseas duty whereby the family could stay with him. He took them when he could, but more often than not, Siobhan and the boy were left at home. Eventually it was decided that they might be better off living with Liam's grandfather back in Ireland."

The girl had remembered that Mather favored Earl Grey, and he sipped gratefully before continuing. "I mention these early details, Miss Redmile, because I believe they, for good or bad, helped shape the man."

He received no response.

"The captain spent as much time as possible with his wife and son, but their marriage had created a rift between Siobhan and other members of her family. You see she had cousins who had links—strong links, as it turned out—with the IRA, and they suspected that her husband was no more than a British plant, put there to seek out information on rebel activities in the area. It was sheer nonsense, of course, but fanatics can rarely be bound by commonsense. And who knows? Perhaps over the years, Captain Halloran did innocently hear of certain nefarious goings-on that he felt duty-bound to report to his superiors. Whatever, suspicion alone was enough for the terrorists.

"Liam, just eight years old, had gone fishing with his father, who had been home on leave for only a few days while serving in that bloody, if discreet, war in South Arabia. God knows, the man needed the rest."

Cora regarded Mather curiously.

"They were both standing in the middle of a shallow stream, father and son, no doubt enjoying each other's company after so many months apart, when the gunmen struck. Liam saw his father shot dead before him. He told the Garda later that his father had struggled to the bank and had tried to crawl from the water. The boy was frozen with fear and could only watch when one of the masked gunmen kicked his father down into the stream again, then stood with one foot on the dying man's back holding him beneath the water. The boy said the stream had already turned crimson with blood when the man pointed his revolver into the water and shot Captain Halloran in the back of the head."

Cora closed her eyes, but the ghastly image became sharper in her mind. She quickly opened them again.

"Siobhan knew her cousins had been involved, otherwise Liam would have been murdered, too, as a witness. That's why the assassins had taken the trouble to wear masks, so the boy wouldn't recognize any of them. But there was nothing she could do. If she were to voice her suspicions, not only would she be at risk, but so too would her son, and possibly the grandfather. It's my opinion that her silence partly contributed to her eventual breakdown. Grief did the rest."

The girl was staring at him. "How . . . how do you know all this? Did Liam tell you?"

"Pieces," he replied. "Even as a youth, Liam was never one to reveal his inner feelings. I made inquiries, I talked to his grandfather. You see, I was Captain Halloran's commanding officer in Aden. He was an excellent soldier, one I had a high regard for, and his death was a great loss for my unit so early in the campaign. I took a personal interest in the family he'd left behind, and that's how I learned of the boy."

Mather finished the tea and again placed the cup on the floor. When he straightened, his hand began to soothe the ache in his knee. Talk of the war in Aden somehow always revived that pain.

"As Liam grew older, it seemed he was always in some kind of trouble, as though a wildness in him had been unleashed. Perhaps that was his way of smothering the sorrow, disguising it with anger. I've no idea, to be honest. The wildness grew out of hand when his mother, unhappy and unstable for all those years, finally committed suicide. I'd kept track of them both since the death of Captain Halloran, made sure the widow received full financial compensation from the British Army, but lost touch for some time when I had difficulties of my own." He tapped his aching knee to indicate the precise nature of those "difficulties." "Thought I was going to lose it, but managed to convince the medics the leg would come good again after a little tinkering with their scalpels. Nowadays, I wonder if I did the right thing," he added as if to himself. "Anyway, I received a letter from the grandfather informing me of Siobhan's death, and when I was well enough, I traveled to Ireland myself to see what could be done for the boy." He smiled wryly. "I believe I arrived just in time."

It was difficult for Cora to picture Liam as a boy, angry, probably frightened, grief-stricken again with the loss of his mother, her death a direct consequence of his father's murder. How could she equate that image with the man who had come to her room the night before, had taken her against her will, that very act of ravishment stirring the familiar pleasure such defilement had for her, so that she could not help responding? But then the quieter passion afterward, the lovemaking that was gentle, so tender, arousing purer emotions that eclipsed mere desire. It had left her stunned, unsure, as though he had deliberately enacted both sides of passion with her, the cold harshness lacking any caring, and then the simple joy that came without abuse or pain, a fulfillment she'd almost forgotten. But then Cora had to wonder if Halloran was someone on whose actions others put their own interpretations. Was she presuming too much of him? Was he really only a man of violence?

Mather's voice broke into her thoughts. "Liam had been getting into scrapes. No, more than that—his mischievousness went beyond the bounds of natural boyhood hooliganism.

From what I heard on my arrival, he was in serious danger of being taken into youth custody. Several incidents around the small town where he lived with his grandfather had been attributed to him, although on the worst occasions no damning evidence of his involvement could be laid absolutely on his doorstep. There were particular problems with the local priest. Whether or not it was because the Church represented the nearest authority against which he could rebel, I've no way of knowing. One particular incident... but no, as I say, there was no definite proof, it would be wrong for me to speculate."

The Shield Planner interlocked his fingers, his elbows resting on the arms of the chair. He pressed his forefingers against his lip, momentarily lost in thought. "I felt it was time to take Liam away from that environment; Ireland held too many tragic memories for him. So I arranged for him to board at a school in England, the least I could do in honor of his late father. The school had close connections with the army, turned out many fine cadets. I'm afraid I was rather preoccupied with my own career, which was starting afresh after my leg injury, but I tried to keep an eye on things as much as I could. The boy appeared to settle down—perhaps a strict regime was what he needed all along. I suppose because of what his father had been, the type of school that had educated him, and the fact that his grandfather had passed away and that there really was no other place to go, Liam eventually decided that soldiering was the profession for him."

Mather's face wrinkled with pleasure. "Damn good at it, too, by all accounts. Oh, he was still somewhat reckless, never quite losing that touch of Irish wildness; but the army has ways of channeling that kind of spirit. Liam took to that way of life as if ordained for it, and was good enough to make the SAS.

"Unfortunately, he was involved in an incident in 1972 that I believe was the root cause of Liam's later cynicism. Still not into his twenties, he was stationed with a small British Army training team at Mirbat in Oman—about ten of 'em in all. A civil war was going on between the monarchy of Oman and its left-wing opponents, and the SAS unit had spent three months in that dreary little town of Mirbat attempting to drill some kind of order into the loyalists. They held two forts, thirty Askaris in one, around twenty-five Dhofar Gendarmerie in the other, with an unruly bunch of counterguerrilla irregulars billeted in the town itself. The only artillery of any real weight they had was a Second World War twenty-five-pounder, a .50-inch Browning, and an eighty-one-millimeter mortar.

"One morning, just after dawn, they were attacked by nearly three hundred rebels armed with machine guns, mortars, antitank rifles, and a Russian rocket launcher. It should have been an outright massacre, but the SAS commanding officer, an absolutely fearless individual, and only a few years older than Liam himself, organized his own men and their Arab allies into a fighting force to be reckoned with.

"I won't bore you with all the battle details, m'dear, but the officer, a captain, was here, there, and everywhere, screaming orders, directing what meager artillery they had, shaping his defense so that the attackers couldn't take a hold. Under enemy fire, he crossed four hundred yards of open ground with a medical orderly to reach the fort where the Gendarmerie was holed up. He'd already radioed his HQ for a helicopter to evacuate casualties, but enemy firepower was so fierce the damn thing couldn't even land. The captain took over the second fort's gun position, the guerrillas no more than thirty yards away, and nearly had his head chopped off by machine-gun fire. Men were being cut down around him, but not for one moment did the captain consider giving the order for surrender. No, no chance of that. From his position, he was able to site targets for two Strikemaster jets that had arrived to lend support, but still the battle raged.

"At last, a relief squadron flew in from Salalah to assist, and the rebels, already stopped in their tracks and their numbers considerably depleted, gave up the ghost and fled. A quite remarkable resistance by the commanding officer and his men, and the rebel forces never really recovered from the defeat, although it took another four years for the war to end.

"I believe that battle affected Liam in two ways, the first being that he was involved in a carnage of mindless ferocity, and he himself had dealt out much of it; and the second was that he was shown an example of outstanding courage by his commanding officer—a captain, don't forget—which I'm sure he imagined his own father had been capable of. Yet the battle was never officially recognized by his own government, even though he was awarded a Military Medal for his actions, and the captain a Distinguished Service Order. That and the fact that he was unclear in his own mind as to whether he was on the side of the goodies or the baddies made him rather cynical about war itself. Worse was to follow.

"Seven years later, that same captain, a man he had come to admire and respect, by then promoted to major, died from exposure during an SAS exercise on the Brecon Beacons. A totally wasteful death which so filled Liam with disgust that he resigned from the army shortly after.

"He became a mercenary, using conflict for his own ends, which were purely financial, rather than allowing it to use him. I observed from a great distance, learning of his activities through contacts I had in various countries and, it must be confessed, I was saddened, appalled even, by what I heard. Although it was never said that he killed indiscriminately, or ever used violence when it could be avoided, he had a reputation for being utterly ruthless as far as his enemies were concerned—and enemies were defined as those being on the side of those *not* paying his wages."

Mather noticed that Cora did not appear shocked, nor even surprised; it was as though he had merely confirmed her own suspicions about Halloran.

"A few years ago I began recruiting for Achilles' Shield," he went on. "Ex-SAS officers make extremely good operatives, so they were my prime targets. I'd lost all contact with Liam by then—it may be that I was afraid of what he'd become—but something inside urged me to seek him out, a niggling guilt perhaps, a feeling that it was *I* who had let him down. It may possibly have been nothing more than a nagging curiosity.

"I eventually located him in Moshupa, a small township in Botswana, very close to the border of South Africa. He was training ANC guerrillas for incursions into their homeland, where they would wreak as much destruction as possible before stealing back across the border to the neighboring state. But Liam was a far different person from the young man I had come to know. He seemed . . . empty. As though what he was doing, the killers and saboteurs he was training, the awful conditions he was living in, meant nothing at all to him. He didn't even register surprise when I turned up, only a chilly kind of amusement. When I spoke with Liam it was like talking to someone drained of emotion; but gradually I began to realize he possessed an inner seething that frightened me more than anything else about him. God knows what he'd been involved in after resigning from the British Army, but its mark had been left. No, he hadn't been brutalized; it was as though he'd become immunized against outrage, wickedness, against *caring*. As I said, that was on the surface: inside, emotions were being stifled, held so firmly in check that I suspect even he was unaware they were there. Or perhaps he glimpsed them now and again, yet refused to let them rise, refused to be influenced by them. I was sure I'd come at exactly the right time, couldn't help but feel I'd been nudged by some inner instinct of my own, because I could tell that Liam had had enough, he was ready to break. Those suppressed emotions—his own self-hatred—were about to erupt.

"He wouldn't admit it, not even to himself, but I think he saw me as some kind of lifeline, a means of dragging himself from that moral squalor he'd sunk into. As for me, I was only too happy to throw down the rope.

"Liam told me he had discovered there were no absolutes. No absolute right or wrong, no absolute good or evil. There were degrees of everything. Once you accepted that—truly accepted it, he insisted—you were able to set your own balance, you understood the bounds within which you could function without guilt clawing at you, tainting your thoughts and so hindering your actions. And he said that virtue, righteousness, whatever you like to call it, often held little sway over evil, because its own rules inhibited. Sometimes only evil could defeat another evil. Degrees, he kept repeating, the lesser against the greater.

"None of it made much sense to me, but it indicated the slough of despair he was wallowing in. No, perhaps despair suggests self-pity, and the man I spoke to was too hardened for that. Pessimism might be a more appropriate word, cynicism even better. Anyway, he agreed to return to England with me and work for Achilles' Shield, protecting lives instead of the opposite. In my opinion, that change was vital for Liam, because it pulled him back from the brink."

Cora, who had been listening quietly throughout, finally spoke. "He was that close . . . ?"

"In my opinion," Mather reasserted. "It may be an old-fashioned notion on my part, but when all probity is lost, total degradation is swift to follow. It seemed to me at the time that Liam had almost lost all reasonable values."

The girl looked down at her hands, and Mather wondered

if he had embarrassed her. Were his ideas too rigid, or too "quaint" for these racy times? Probably, but no less valid for that, he reassured himself.

"And has he changed?" Cora asked softly.

"Well, he's been with Shield for over six years now, and in many ways he's the best operative we have. Yes, he has changed." Mather smiled. "But just how much, I really can't say."

29

RECONNOITER

They drove past the gates, all three occupants of the car peering around, looking along the uneven drive to see where it led. Unfortunately it curved into woodland that obscured any further view.

With a nod of his head, the front passenger indicated the old lodge house set to one side of the big iron gates. The car did not slow down.

They studied the high wall as the car picked up a steady speed once more, and then the dense trees and undergrowth when the weathered brickwork ran out. They traveled a long way before a narrow lane came up on the left. The driver steered into it, the other two occupants continuing to study the hedges that bordered the left-hand side of the lane. Presently they were able to catch brief glimpses of downward slopes, woodland, a lake. The man in the backseat told the driver to stop the car.

Although their view was restricted by the trees closest to the lane, they could just make out what appeared to be a red-stoned building on the far shore of the lake, nestled beneath low hills. Reluctant to linger too long, the back passenger instructed the driver to move on.

The lane joined a wider road and again the car turned left, maintaining a casual speed, neither fast nor slow. There were bends and dips along the route, but the observers' attention rarely wavered from the heavily wooded countryside on their left. Through his rearview mirror, the driver noticed another vehicle approaching from behind. It was a Granada, and he mentioned the fact to his companions. It slowed down, keeping a distance of forty or fifty yards away, following without pressuring the lead car into hurrying.

The driver of the first vehicle watched for a road to come up on his right. One did, and he drove on by. Soon another appeared, again to his right, and this one he took.

In his mirror he saw the Granada pass along the road they had left, its two occupants staring after them. It quickly vanished from view, but the driver of the first car kept on going, picking up speed.

Only when they had traveled a mile or so further did he pull in by the side of the road and turn to look at his companions.

The passenger in the back nodded. From what they'd seen so far, the scar-faced man (when they had finally broken him) had been quite correct: the estate was large, very large indeed.

30

RETRIBUTION IN DARKNESS

Quinn-Reece was alone in his office on the eighteenth floor of the Magma Corporation.

The tiniest smile of satisfaction twitched his lips as he completed the last paragraph of the report concerning the Papua New Guinea copper situation—a report that Felix Kline had requested he provide before leaving the building so that the chairman could call a forward planning meeting after he had broken the news to the board of directors on Monday morning.

Did they really hope to retrieve the situation? Exploration rights for that particular area of land had already been granted to Consolidated Ores, and not even if Magma's bribe to the government officials involved outmatched their rival company's could the agreement be rescinded.

He gathered the papers together on his desk. They would be ready for his secretary to type first thing in the morning. Rarely a happy man, Quinn-Reece allowed his smile to broaden. He was pleased with the wording, for it emphasized, in all due modesty, of course, his strenuous efforts to secure those rights before anyone else got wind of the find, continuously trying to contact their agent on the island by telephone, telex, and even personal messenger to his hotel. Unfortunately, the man could not be located (or so Quinn-Reece indicated in his report) and in the meanwhile, Magma's biggest rival had learned of the "find."

He allowed himself to chuckle.

Time to go home, he decided. Enough is enough. The report could indeed be more full, but why the hell should he put in any more hours on a Sunday? It was late afternoon and the skies were already darkened by clouds and drizzle. Before he went, though, a stiff gin and tonic to celebrate yet another successful deception.

He left his desk and went to a wall cabinet, opening it to reveal his private liquor stock, there for entertaining business associates or, more often than not, for the frequent "nips" that got him through the day. The small ice bucket was empty, but who needed ice? He poured a good measure of gin into a glass tumbler and added an equal amount of tonic. He raised the glass to his lips when the noise outside his office door stopped him.

He shrugged. Security on their rounds, checking all offices. Your excellent health! he silently toasted himself, and took a large swallow of the drink. The mixture warmed him, lightening his mood even further. Just a few more months' subservience to that obnoxious, stunted oaf, then set up for life, working for a company who would appreciate his business acumen and who would be extremely grateful for past services. The risk had been worth it. And what could the corporation do anyway, even if they had discovered he was the source of the leaks? Take him to court? Oh no, he knew too much for that. The shareholders would be unhappy if they were to learn of Kline's true position at Magma, and the financial press would have a ball. Even Consolidated was unaware of the psychic's presence within Magma—they merely assumed that the corporation's field agents were more astute than their own. No, the worst that Magma could do would be to dismiss him. And pay him off for keeping his mouth shut, of course. Instead they were firing the girl, Cora.

He was smiling again.

Quinn-Reece turned his head. Was someone still outside? He was sure he'd heard movement in the outer office. Leaving the glass on the corner of his desk, the deputy chairman walked to the half-open door.

He pulled it open all the way and looked through. "Anyone there?" he called out, feeling rather foolish.

There was no response.

He stepped forward and caught a whiff of spices just before something soft fell over his head and blocked out the light.

Hands shoved him from behind and he staggered forward, fell, lay sprawled on a hard floor, his head still covered.

Quinn-Reece remained prone for a few seconds, regathering his senses, terribly afraid to move. He heard the click of a door closing. He was trembling badly.

The brief, stumbling journey had been one of the worst experiences of his life (so far), for it was a brutally rushed trip toward a fate unknown. He now knew how murderers must have felt in the old days when they were taken hooded from their cell and hurried to the gallows, giving them precious little time to consider the eternity waiting for them at the end of the corridor (except there was *always* time to consider that prospect, no matter how fast they took you, no matter how roughly they treated you, because part of your mind was quiet, entirely remote from the rest of your feverish thoughts, numbingly and so fearfully aware...). He had been held down, and even though no words were spoken, no one answered his demands, nor his pleas, he was sure there were two of them—yet he had felt himself rising. The elevator. They must have bundled him into the elevator. But why? Where were they taking him? Oh God, was it true then? Were these people after Felix Kline? Had they made a mistake, thinking that he was the psychic? That had to be it! So perhaps it was safe to look up, to show them, convince them they'd got the wrong man. He had no allegiance to Kline, far from it: he could tell them all they wanted to know. No need to harm him, he wasn't the one they were after.

Quinn-Reece hesitantly raised his head and saw the whiteness of the floor below the edges of the cloth. Tentatively, expecting to have his hand knocked away at any moment, he lifted the hem. He could see the room now. Slowly he pulled the fluffy material away (it was a large towel, he realized, probably from one of the executive bathrooms) and looked around.

He was in the white room. Kline's white room.

And he was alone.

He pushed himself to his knees, his eyes half-closed against the brilliant glare. What was happening, what the hell were they playing at? Was the idea only to keep him out of the way for a while? The notion came as a relief. It emboldened him enough to rise to his feet.

Quinn-Reece went to the double-door and listened with his ear flat against the glossy surface. No sounds without. He tried one of the door handles. Locked.

Stepping back, he surveyed the entrance for a while, gradually becoming used to the assailing brightness. He turned and began walking toward the smaller door on the opposite side of the room, his footsteps loud because of uninterrupted acoustics. He had reached the low central dais when the harsh whiteness around him collapsed into utter darkness.

Quinn-Reece cried out, as if the abrupt change had come as a physical blow.

There was nothing to see, absolutely nothing to focus on. Even the floor beneath his feet had somehow lost substance. His hands— unseen—waved in the air before him, as though grasping for light itself.

"What are you doing?" he shouted, a feeble entreaty to the blackness.

Naturally there was no reply.

So disoriented was Quinn-Reece that he had to will one foot to go forward. The thought that he might be stepping over the brink into an abyss was difficult to dismiss. He moved his other foot, arms still outstretched like a blind man's (which, in effect, he was), even though he knew there were no obstacles in his way.

Another step.

His breathing was fluttery.

Another step.

He could not see them, but he was aware that his fingers twitched like insect antennae.

Another step.

And he touched flesh.

So unexpected was the sensation, and so tense had Quinn-Reece become, that he shrieked like a woman. He fell away, a leg coming into sharp contact with the dais. He slumped across it and lay shaking.

Wondering why the fingertips of the hand that had touched whatever—no, he meant *who*ever—stood in his way were tingling, he brought them closer to his face, disregarding the fact that he was unable to see. He felt something clinging to them.

He rubbed his fingers together, and whatever had been there flaked away. It had been tissue-thin.

"Who's there?" he managed to say, and was uncomfortable with the sound of his own voice.

The silence was more frightening than any reply.

A warm breath brushed his cheek. He spun around on the

platform, scurrying to its farthest edge, away from whoever
had leaned over him.

But a sigh close to his ear sent him scuttling back.

The men who had dragged him into this room must have
slipped inside somehow after the lights had gone out! Yet he
hadn't heard the opening and closing of a door, there had been
no sudden shaft of light. How *could* they be in there with him?
He remembered the spicy smell before he had been hooded.
The smell was familiar. From where, from when?

A low chuckle. From someone close by. And then a hand
caressing his cheek.

Quinn-Reece flinched violently and quickly squirmed
away. The touch against his cheek had been roughened as
though the other's skin was crispy with age. When he tried to
wipe off the mark he felt had been left there, he discovered
flaky tissue hanging to his own skin. He slapped it off in
revulsion.

He twisted his head, this way and that, sightless but attempting to perceive. His whole body was quivering uncon-
trollably now. He sniffed, for there was a peculiar aroma in
the air. Nothing to do with spices, this. Something different,
vaguely unpleasant. Like a faint molding dampness. Decay.

Light lashed out at him.

He cringed, covering his face with his hands. Peeped
through open fingers at the rectangle of vivid colors high on
the wall. One of the screens was lit.

It depicted a relief map of an island. A recognizably irregular shape. New Guinea. The colors merged, became a muddy
blur. Faded to white. Became black.

A new map lit up. He forced himself to look. Was it?—
yes, it was. Brazil. There had been a recent find, a low-grade
gold deposit. Not by Magma, though. No, by Consolidated.

As the colors merged, Quinn-Reece looked around the
room. The brightness from the screen should have revealed
anyone else present. But he was the only occupant.

Blackness again.

Another screen came alive, and this time he could guess
the location without recognizing it. Namibia. Yes, there had
been a new discovery of uranium there. Again, not by
Magma. He began to understand some of what was going on.

"Felix?" he ventured.

Total blackness. Still no reply.

"Felix, you're making a mistake. The girl, you said yourself..." His words trailed away. Kline wasn't in the room. Why was he talking as if he were?

Quinn-Reece began to slide his legs off the dais. He stopped when he heard a soft chuckle.

This time not only three screens lit up: they all did. And the colors ran together, from one screen to the next, frames no longer divisive, blues and greens and browns beginning to streak, to flow around the room, a swift-moving stream, faster and faster, a kaleidoscope of color, dazzling him, mesmerizing him, melting together, faster now, merging, gradually becoming white, an absence of color, a broad pale strip circumscribing the room.

Things began to break through that white band. Creeping things. Black and shiny like giant cockroaches, although their limbs, three on either side of their glossy shells, were like human arms—but scaly, and dark.

They hatched from the whiteness, wriggling through, dropping to the floor and into the shadows where only muted reflections on their curved backs could be observed. They scuttled across the floor toward him.

Quinn-Reece moved to the center of the platform, drawing up his legs, denying to himself that this was happening, certain it was a nightmare, wondering why he could not wake.

The cracked band of white vanished.

Terrible blackness around him once more.

Nothing at all to be seen.

But he could hear those things tapping toward him.

"Felix, please!" he implored, for he knew that Kline was responsible, that Kline was punishing him for his betrayal. But he didn't understand how *this* could happen, for he realized it was no nightmare, the pain in his lower lip, where his teeth had clamped down, too sharp to be a dream. He shrieked this time. *"Please!"*

A chuckle from somewhere behind.

And a clicking close by as the first of those creatures scrambled over the edge of the dais.

Sometime later, the doors to the white room opened and Khayed and Daoud slipped in. They went straight to the dead but unmarked body spread across the low dais, lifted it between them, and carried it out.

When the doors closed behind them, the room swiftly regressed to black.

KHAYED AND DAOUD

DISPLACED AND FOUND

They were not truly Jordanians. Asil Khayed and Youssef Daoud were, in fact, displaced persons, their families having fled Palestine when the independent State of Israel was declared in May 1948. Their parents were of the same clan and came from the same village, which was close to Jerusalem. They had been led to believe by those who had their own political motives that the Zionist forces would destroy their homes and meager crops, would slaughter their children and livestock, would rape their women, would torture and murder the men. Flight to the River Jordan was their only hope.

They came to the refugee camp at Ein es Sultan, one of many such sites scattered around the city of Jericho and along the West Bank. The two Arab boys had been born within weeks of each other, and were now to be raised in the squalor of a vast tent city containing tens of thousands of grieving migrants, where there were no toilets, kitchens, or medical facilities, and where most days were spent awaiting the arrival of water trucks and supply convoys from Damascus and Amman. The tents provided by the International Red Cross were of thin canvas that, unlike the tough Bedouin tents of animal skins and furs, were virtually useless against the rains and sandstorms. Their beds were nothing more than light sleeping mats. Running, open sewers and hills of rotting garbage were everywhere, attracting flies and mosquitoes by the millions. Severe dysentery was rife. Cholera, typhoid, and other diseases claimed thousands of lives. Fierce rainfalls and then intolerable heat brought in by khamsin winds from the desert weakened all.

The *mukhtar* of their old village, whom the clans gathered around, could offer no comfort, for his spirit had been broken by the ignoble flight of his people and the hopelessness he saw all around. Hate with all your heart, he could only tell them, despise the Zionist dogs who have brought you to this. Nurture the hatred, live for revenge against the Jews.

Typhoid took Youssef's father, along with his two older brothers and a sister. That the youngster and his mother survived was no miracle, for death was indiscriminate. The widow and her child came under the protection of Asil's father, there being no energy for jealousy among the women. And the Koran, which spoke severely against adultery and fornication, also preached the blessedness of caring for cripples, idiots, blind men, and widows. The boys grew up together and became closer than natural brothers.

Although rough hovels of mud bricks gradually replaced the tents, a form of rough villages taking shape along the Jordan, the rule of *kaif*—a passivity that might be described as idleness—prevailed. Few businesses were set up, no industries were started. There were no schools for the younger exiles, no games or activities organized for them. The demoralized Palestinians relied on the charity of others, as if content to wallow in their own hatred for the Jews and the foreign powers that had betrayed them. The Moslem Brotherhood was eager to exploit the persecution and never tired of stoking the fires of vengeance against these infamous "invaders," while at the same time extolling the virtues of martyrdom for the great Arab cause of repatriation.

Asil and Youssef were children of a rubbled ghetto, existing on whatever was sparingly given, thriving on bitterness that was generously supplied. When Asil's father was killed in a riot against the reviled Arab Legion of Jordan's King Abdullah, who, along with certain leaders of other Arab states, saw the political advantages in keeping the Palestinians a nation in exile rather than welcoming and absorbing them as true brothers (acceptance of the State of Israel would be a threat to his own power in the Middle East), the boys took on the responsibility for their family. By then the United Nations had taken charge over the welfare of the refugee camps and at least some progress was taking place in these humble villages. In Ein es Sultan there were mosques, a ritual slaughterhouse, stores, warehouses, and food distribution centers. The boys were lucky enough to find jobs as coffee vendors, passing from shop to kiosk with their trays bearing coffee finjans, cups, and sticky sweets, often trekking out to the lines of trucks awaiting customs clearance at the Allenby Bridge.

For pleasure they hung around the cafés and listened to the elders reminiscing about the old life in their villages, of the main square always awash with the aromas of pungent spices, cardamom in coffee, incense, and camel, donkey, sheep, and goat dung. They spoke of important feasts, sighing over the exotic foods once served, while the boys would drool at their mention.

The elders' conversation would turn to memories of the houses they once dwelled in, solidly built with mud bricks and dung, brightly whitewashed to deflect the sun's rays, with a single color outlining doors and windows, the roofs flat for collecting water during the rainy season. They spoke of village tradesmen, the potter, the carpenter, the sandal maker, the basket and cloth weavers. Their eyes brimmed with tears as they remembered what had been lost to them. How life once centered around the village square with its well and ovens, the store and café where they could listen to the radio all day while they watched the passing activity, the cameleers, the peddlers on their loaded donkey carts, the knife and scissors grinders—the veiled women going about their daily tasks.

Eventually, when nostalgia held them in its soft-edged grip, they would boast of their feats in battle, their bravery, their cunning. And they would dismiss the Arab defeat by the Jews as a misconception, for they had been tricked by the agents of the devil, *jinn*—evil spirits—in human form. The Jews were not a worthy enemy. The Jews had an alliance with unholy forces. Mohammed himself had declared that the Jews had been led away from the edicts of Allah, and for that their punishment would be burning.

Asil and Youssef listened and absorbed. They wept for their homeland and for the life they had never known but missed dearly. They seethed with hatred for these people who called themselves Israelis.

The boys grew and became wise in the ways of survival. Schooling, even under the auspices of the UNRWA, was little more than a revolutionary training ground, the Arab tutors organizing their students into cells, each with its own aggressive title, incitement against the so-called State of Israel and its treacherous allies the main lesson of every day. Physical education included weapons training, knife fighting, tracking, and the negotiation of assault courses.

Black-marketeering became the most profitable occupation, stealing and intimidation the second best. Asil and Youssef became the runners for dealers in hashish, then lookouts for raids on supply depots.

Crude and boastful chatter between the two boys of the sexual delights they would bestow upon females soon faded when awareness took on physical actuality and they discovered their true yearning was for each other, their experiments resolving in glorious consummation. Asil and Youssef could imagine no other form of lovemaking surpassing the pleasure they had given one another. Although males were allowed to hold hands and kiss in public, homosexuality was frowned upon generally in the Arab world; Asil and Youssef kept the intimate side of their relationship to themselves, the illicitness adding to its deliciousness.

As with other Palestinian youths, they were pressured into joining the fedayeen when they were old enough, its members' violence and unruliness directed toward the *jihad*, the holy war, and against the oppressor. The Jordanians encouraged guerrilla raids into Jewish territory, the killing and maiming perpetrated in the name of Allah, and the more youths lost in such expeditions, the more martyrs the Arabs had to hold up to the world. A mark of manhood for the fedayeen recruits was to bite off the heads of live chickens and snakes, or to strangle puppies and cats.

Although they had never been considered outstandingly bright by their superiors, Asil and Youssef's performance in the field and their cunning in fighting was impressive. And the elders were suitably struck by the youths' cruelty.

Their missions into enemy territory became more frequent —and more hazardous. It was on one such expedition that they discovered for themselves the extent—and the true nature—of their own barbarity.

Avoiding Israeli patrols, they had slipped across the border, their venture more of a test than a serious assault (the fedayeen were considering the two youths for important work in the revolutionary movement), their destination a kibbutz some miles from Bira. Dunams of marsh and swampland there, as at countless other settlements in this relatively new state, had been skillfully irrigated and cultivated, so that what was once barren land had become areas of rich soil suitable for vines, orchards, and grain. The fields were protected against incursion with nothing more than fences of cactus and thorny jujube, although the living quarters themselves were behind a tall stockade. Asil and Youssef's intention had been to blow up one of the water towers located outside the compound with explosives readily supplied by their Jordanian hosts. But as they broke through the crude boundary under the cover of darkness, they came upon a young Israeli couple, a youth and a girl, who had found a remote spot where they could make love without being disturbed.

The couple was lying beneath a eucalyptus, and it was their murmurings that caught the attention of the two Arab intruders. Asil and Youssef looked at each other in surprise, their eyes wide and clear in the starlit night, then crept closer to the source of the breathed sounds. The things they saw the youth doing to the girl sent shivers of excitement running through them, for never in their lives had they witnessed such wantonness, and never before had a female's hidden flesh been exposed thus. Because of the urgency of their lovemaking, the young couple did not hear the Arabs' approach.

Asil quickly disposed of the girl who, apart from curiosity over her secret places, held little interest for them. He slit her throat while Youssef rendered her lover unconscious with a hefty stone picked up from the ground. Between them they dragged him back through the opening they had made in the rough perimeter fence. Once they were a safe distance away they tore strips from the Israeli's clothing to tie and gag him. Then they enjoyed themselves with his body.

But they did far more to him than they had ever done to each other.

Their sadism was spoiled only by his abrupt finish, a lesson well learned by them, for in later years they practiced curbing their extremes so that the exquisite pleasure would last for hours, if not days. The corpse was barely recognizable as human when they had done, and their *coup de grâce* was to cut off their victim's private parts and bring them back in a goatskin pouch to their masters in the fedayeen (who, although irritated that their orders to destroy the water tower had not been carried out, realized the dismemberment and castration of a Jew held true significance).

Asil and Youssef had proved they were worthy soldiers of

the *jihad,* as well as revealing their skill in passing through
well-guarded enemy lines without detection. It wasn't long
before they were sent to a terrorist training camp in the Bekaa
Valley of Lebanon. There they lived in a cement shack and
were taught how to use Russian firearms, rocket launchers,
and mortars, how to make bombs and use them with altime-
tric, movement, and time detonators, assassination techniques, how to enter locked buildings quietly, stalk their prey
through the streets, and methods of escaping pursuit. They ran
six miles every morning, then did four hours of physical training. All this was followed by daily indoctrination classes.

They were taught that their destiny (not merely their duty)
was not only to kill Zionists and their close allies, but
members of any nation showing friendliness toward the non-
State of Israel. Within a year or two, Asil and Youssef were
traveling to other countries as an efficient and respected assassination team. However, they had a weakness they strove to
keep from their associates (although not as cleverly as they
thought; fortunately their masters allowed certain indulgences
as long as operations were never jeopardized). That ecstatic
thrill of their first sadistic murder of the Israeli youth at the
kibbutz near Bira had never been forgotten. They sought to
relive and refine that excitement time and time again in the
foreign capitals they visited. There are many hundreds of
missing persons reported in cities all over the world every
year, and most of them never appear again. At least not alive.
It was relatively easy for Asil and Youssef to pick up men or
boys, or sometimes even girls (for the two terrorists, the latter
was a perversion of a perversion), and lure them to some quiet
place where they could abuse, torture, and finally kill their
prey. And sexual crimes, where there is no other motive involved and no previous connection between victim and murderer, are perhaps the most difficult to solve.

The bomb had gone off prematurely.

Asil and Youssef had left the package with its quietly tick-
ing contents beneath a bench at the Gare du Nord, leisurely
strolling away from it through noisy and earnest-looking travelers toward the arches that led out to the streets of Paris. The
explosion from behind stunned everyone into an eerie three-
second silence (or perhaps the roar had deafened ears to the
screams). Pandemonium broke loose, commuters and tourists

curling up against walls, running out into the streets—incredibly, some going toward the source of the explosion—or clutching at each other and waiting for the worst to happen.

The two terrorists knew that the European clothes they wore and the fact that they were among a cosmopolitan crowd would not help if they panicked and rushed from the scene, even though others around them were doing precisely that. At that particular time, Parisians were regarding any Arab or Algerian "type" with suspicion, for the French authorities had arrested a known PLO activist a few weeks before under a charge of conspiracy; an ultimatum had been delivered by Al Fatah that unless the "hostage" was released and allowed to leave the country, then France could consider itself at peril. The French authorities had a reputation in those days for "going soft" under such pressure, and the bomb planted at the Gare du Nord was meant to show how serious the terrorists were.

Asil and Youssef forced themselves to walk calmly away from the train station. Unfortunately it was their apparent coolness that gained the attention of an astute gendarme who was making his way into the station. The police, including the CRS and CSP, had been put on special alert since the arrest of the terrorist, and this particular gendarme had taken note of his preduty briefing on exactly what to look out for before and after an outrage such as this. He hurried after the two smartly dressed Arabs, stopping them with a sharp, *"Alors, messieurs!"* when he was close.

The mistimed blast had considerably shaken Asil and Youssef, for if the bomb had exploded just a few moments earlier, it would have been their own bodies spread across the station concourse. Now they were being apprehended by the police! Without even waiting to be questioned, Asil drew a knife from a hidden sheath in his jacket and stepped toward the uniformed man. He was expert with the blade, as Youssef had become expert with the garrote, and knew that the policeman's belt and buttoned tunic might prevent a clean thrust into the stomach. The heart was equally as difficult, because their pursuer had raised his left arm across his chest, intentionally or unintentionally blocking a lunge. Asil went for the next best target, aware that it would take his victim a minute or so longer to die, but at least he would drop instantly and lose consciousness within fourteen seconds. The knife slashed across the gendarme's upper left arm, the thrust outward and deep, severing the brachial artery. The wounded man stared in disbelief, then fell to the pavement.

A woman screamed, but in the hubbub of similar cries and the blaring of sirens, no one took much notice. The Arabs fled, no longer concerned whether or not they were more noticeable. They ducked into the Métro, hastily purchasing tickets and anxiously waiting on the *quai* for a train—any train—to come in, expecting shouts from the barrier at any moment. When one arrived, Youssef shuffled along beside it, pulling at the latch which opened the compartment door before the train had fully stopped. They collapsed into seats, praying to Allah that the doors would shut and the train move off before any blue-uniformed men tumbled in after them. They changed at the next station, Gare de l'Est, going on to Chaussée d'Antin and from there to Montmartre. They had journeyed no great distance, but enough to throw off any pursuers and not long enough for the police to set up checks at Métro exits (even if that were possible with so many stations). They emerged into the soft glow of evening and the distant sounds of sirens.

They strolled down the wide, tree-lined boulevard toward the river, mingling with tourists, their hearts still beating wildly, although outwardly they managed to appear nonchalant. They passed streetside restaurants, sniffed at roasting meat and spicy sauces, politely declined when approached by smiling prostitutes, not stopping until they reached the Seine, where they watched the passing *bateaux-mouches* crammed with sightseers.

Only then did they look slyly at each other and giggle.

They had a "safe house" to go to, an apartment in one of the small courtyards in the Rue Mouffetard area close to the outdoor market across the river. But there was no need to make their way back yet; indeed, training had taught them it was often better to stay lost in the crowd for as long as possible.

They wandered along the riverbank for a short while, then headed back into the streets toward St. Denis, taking their time and watching the street entertainers—singers, dancers, jugglers, even fire-eaters. They felt frightened but exhilarated. They felt alive. The operation had been successful, and there was the bonus of one dead gendarme. Their clothes were too nondescript for easy identification, even if witnesses to the stabbing had come forward; and at the height of the tourist season, with students of all races gathered in this city of culture and romance, two young Arabs of murderous natures would be almost impossible to weed out.

The only disappointment came when they were seated at a streetside café drinking white wine (so wonderful to be away from the strictures of a Moslem society) and learned from the conversations around them that nobody appeared to have been killed in the bomb blast that day at the Gare du Nord, although five people, a child among them, were seriously injured.

Asil and Youssef drifted on, soon finding a crêperie where they took delight in decadent European cooking. As they consumed the food and wine, it was with each other they flirted. The bustle and the festive atmosphere (despite the bombing) around them heightened their excitement; the killing and maiming served as a stimulus for their passion.

Eventually they crossed the river at the Île de la Cité, going toward the market quarter and their apartment, but stopping once again to take more wine at one of the cafés on the Place de la Contrescarpe. After two more glasses they decided that the night still held further adventures for them. The crowds had dwindled, most of the tourists having tottered back to their hotels and pensions, leaving the streets mostly to students and winos, the *clochards*. Asil and Youssef finally went in search of yet another victim, one who would fulfill a certain need in them.

They rejected the first two male prostitutes because they looked too old—in their twenties at least—and too tough. The third was an effeminate boy who looked no more than seventeen. He led them into a dark cul-de-sac where he assured them they would not be disturbed. Youssef did not have his beloved garrote with him, but the tie he wore would do; prolonged torture would not be possible here, but Asil would have fun with his blade while the boy's skin turned purple and his tongue swelled from his mouth.

Unluckily for them, the "boy" was neither as young as he appeared nor what he claimed to be (and certainly not effeminate).

Light from a distant lamp glinted on the pistol he produced from beneath his jacket. "Police," he informed them, holding up an ID in his left hand.

The bullet scraped along the bone of Asil's lower arm as he lunged with the knife, this time his victim's stomach exposed and an easy target. The fake prostitute dropped like a stone, the gun firing into the pavement before falling from his grasp.

Asil screamed with the pain in his arm, the knife slipping away, lodged in the policeman. Somewhere not too far away a whistle blew, for the *gendarmerie* was out in force that night because of the bomb outrage, and the gunshots had been heard. Youssef dragged his friend away, hurrying him through the narrow streets in the direction of their apartment. A car screeched around a corner ahead of them, its lights blazing.

The two terrorists ducked into an alleyway, breaking into an awkward run, convinced they had been spotted. They had. The police car came to a halt at the alleyway entrance; doors flew open, uniformed men jumped out. They shouted, *"Arrêtez!"* before aiming their weapons and firing.

Bullets smacked into the walls around the fleeing Arabs and one ricocheted off cobblestones to tear through the outer edge of Youssef's calf. Both men were handicapped, although they were able to keep on the move. Youssef was weeping as he limped along, the whole of his leg numbed with the shock, pain not yet registering.

They emerged into a wider street and saw other uniformed men coming toward them. There were still a few pedestrians around, one or two cars crawling close to the curbs. All came to a standstill as the shouting gendarmes weaved through them. Asil and Youssef started in the opposite direction, running as fast as their wounds would allow, cursing themselves for their foolishness, knowing how angry their masters would be at the risk they had exposed themselves and the organization to. They silently implored Allah to lend them wings.

Rounding another corner, they stumbled over the bodies of three *clochards* huddled on a Métro vent (these raggedy men relished the underground warmth whatever the season). Asil struck his head against the pavement, stunning himself. The complaining winos kicked out and Youssef rolled into the gutter. He quickly sat up and was horrified when he saw the inert body of his friend. Running footsteps drawing near, headlights and blaring sirens approaching fast. He scrambled to his feet and pulled up his dazed companion, urging him to run.

Into an alleyway opposite they went, the smell of an underground river that had been turned into a sewer strong in the confines of the narrow space. A saxophone played bluesily overhead, the musician uninterested in the commotion below. Garbage was piled up in heaps against walls near the back doors of restaurants. Run, Asil, run, Youssef! But to where? Paris was not familiar, and now they were disoriented. They would never find their way to the apartment that night.

The numbness had left Youssef's leg. It felt as though it was on fire. Asil's head had not yet cleared, and all he was really conscious of was the searing pain in his arm. He had to rely on his lover to lead him onward.

Out into another street, this one wider than the last, but with little cruising traffic. Across the road, into a courtyard, shouts and footsteps behind. Both men were near to exhaustion, their wounds draining strength. They knew they could not go much further.

Akhoo sharmoota! No way out! The courtyard was a closed trap! Beloved Allah, show mercy to loyal soldiers of the *jihad!*

Shouted commands outside. Whistles blowing. Tires screeching to a halt. Doors slamming.

But Asil was pointing, and Youssef could not understand how his dazed companion had seen the tiny opening between the buildings, a dark cleft as if the houses had been eased apart.

Yatamajad ism al rab! The way had been shown!

They staggered across the courtyard, where lights from windows were coming on to throw reflections like searchlights down on them, and entered the pitch-black opening, where there was just enough room inside for them to lope along helping each other. A dim glow seemed to rise from the ground ahead, and they soon found themselves at the top of a steep flight of stone steps. A single street lamp lit the exit a short distance away.

Voices in the courtyard behind. No time to linger. Down they went. But blinding pain gnashed through the muscles of Youssef's calf and he slipped, grabbed for Asil as he fell, taking him along, over and over, the edges of the worn steps scraping skin, jarring bones as they plunged then slid, slowing to a tumbling roll as they neared the bottom.

They lay there, tangled together, sobbing and moaning, with no strength to carry on, and no will either.

The exit was not far away. Yet it was too far.

Echoing footsteps from above. The policemen would punish them severely for killing one of their own. And when they realized they had killed yet another earlier in the day, that they were responsible for the bombing at the station, what then? Asil and Youssef shuddered, the thought shared. They reached for each other's hand and waited, shivering with hurt and fear.

But something was moving across the opening in front of them. A shiny blackness. Sleekly slow. They thought it would pass by, but the vehicle stopped when the rear door was level with the passageway.

The door opened. A voice whispered to them down the close walls of the alley.

"Ta al maee wa sa ta eesh lee taktol mara sani ya—come with me and you'll live to kill again," it said.

The promise gave them enough strength to crawl into the black limousine.

(And it was a promise that Kline certainly kept.)

31

RETURN TO NEATH

Kline stirred, shifting in the seat so that his face was away from Halloran.

The Shield operative watched him, his attention momentarily away from the passing countryside. The psychic had hardly moved since the Mercedes had left the Magma building an hour or so before, yet he had seemed too still to be sleeping. No rhythmic breathing, no total limpness; it was almost as if he had gone into some kind of self-induced trance. Maybe he had, Halloran considered. Wasn't that what psychics did?

Not for the first time during the journey, Halloran looked over his shoulder through the rear window. A couple of cars behind but, as far as he could tell, nothing to worry about: they weren't being followed. The Granada containing his own men came into view, keeping well back, ready to accelerate into action should a problem arise. He checked ahead before settling back into the seat, remaining alert, but reasonably sure there were no immediate worries. Although Monk and the Jordanians had been left back at Magma, evidently to collect some items for Kline from his penthouse, he considered it no great loss of manpower. If the Mercedes were to come under attack, then he could rely on himself and the two Shield men without the blunderings of untrained bodyguards to hinder his own countertactics. The fact that his own men were armed now added to his confidence.

Halloran ran a hand over his eyes and across his rough chin. He was tired, the dream last night obviously having disturbed what little rest he'd had in the armchair. A shower, a shave, and something to eat wouldn't be amiss. An inspection of the house and grounds and then, with luck, a couple of hours' sleep. There was an unsettled feeling in the pit of his stomach that had nothing to do with hunger, but which told him he would need all the rest he could get if he were to cope with the next day or two. An instinct he had come to depend on through the years made him aware that something was imminent. It was a feeling he couldn't explain even to himself, but there was a familiar tension building inside him, honing his senses, sharpening his reactions, preparing him for what was to come. Fear had always mingled with that sensing, and that was natural; but this time a deep foreboding was involved, a disquieting dread, and that was new to him.

A muffled sound from Kline. The psychic's shoulders rose and slumped. His breathing became regular. Now he was sleeping.

Cora, next to Palusinski in the front of the car, turned to look at her employer. Her eyes caught Halloran's, and her smile was tentative. A moment went by before he returned the smile.

She faced the front again, and Halloran, on the opposite corner of the Mercedes, was able to study her profile. He wondered if she really had it in her to give away company secrets. Unlikely. She was too closely linked to Kline and, Halloran was sure, too much afraid of her employer to betray him. Yet Kline had had no doubts. He'd denounced her before Magma's chairman and deputy-chairman. Surely there had to be good reason for that?

Halloran checked the windows again. All clear, with only the Granada behind them. He realized they would soon be at Neath.

So what plans *did* Kline have for Cora? Would she be accused once they arrived at Neath, or would he set a trap for her, catch her in the act of betrayal? Kline's paranoia suggested the former, his sly vindictiveness the latter. Halloran made up his mind that he would get to her first, warn her of what was to happen. To hell with Kline and the Magma Corporation. To hell with the assignment. He'd continue to guard the target, but he would also keep the girl from any harm. Halloran had already suspected that Kline's four bodyguards were more than just that; he was sure they were well used to meting out punishment—particularly Monk, in this respect—whenever their employer pointed a finger. It was an unnecessary complication to the situation, but guilty or not, Cora wasn't going to suffer in their hands. He intended to keep a good watch on her.

As the car rounded a bend, Kline's hand flopped down by his side, its fingers curled into a claw. Halloran noticed that small sections of skin were whitish, as if about to peel off.

"It is good to be away from the city," came Palusinski's voice from the front. "The air is cleaner here. My father was a farmer, Mr. Halloran, *rolnik*, so countryside is my love. Cities are a bad place for me."

"Where in Poland d'you come from?" Halloran asked with no real interest.

"Ah, it is of no importance." Palusinski tapped the steering wheel. "I am here now is all that matters. He"—the Pole inclined his head toward the sleeping man, and Halloran was surprised to catch the hint of a sneer in his tone—"brought me here many years ago, took me from my beloved country."

"You could always go back," Halloran suggested, watching the road, which was becoming familiar, as they neared the estate.

"Back?" Palusinski uttered a bitter chuckle. "To what go back? To Russians who bleed Poland dry? I will stay here, I think. Yes, I will stay here where everyone is friendly, and the food is good!" He laughed aloud and thumped the steering wheel.

The gates to the estate were not far away, and Halloran checked the front and rear windows yet again. Only the Shield vehicle was bringing up their rear. The Mercedes swung in toward the iron gates and stopped no more than a foot away from them. Kline stirred but did not awaken.

Halloran opened his door and stepped out, walking to the edge of the road, and waited for the Granada to pull up beside him. He leaned forward, one hand on the roof, as the passenger lowered the window.

"Contact the patrol and make sure everything's okay. I'll meet you back here"—he lifted his wristwatch—"in three hours."

"Anything extra we should do?" the driver called across his passenger.

Halloran shook his head. "Just patrol, the full tour. Don't come into the grounds."

"What if we spot someone?" the man nearest said, plainly irritated.

"Use the RT to let me know. Don't come in."

"Why the hell not?"

"You wouldn't like it."

Halloran straightened, examined the roadway in both directions, then walked to the gates. He heard the Granada speed away as he reached out and grasped one of the thick iron struts. There came a dull, heavy click, and he pushed against the metal. The gate swung open, a grating of rusted hinges accompanying the sluggish movement. Halloran took it all the way back, then did the same with the other half, feeling observed from the lodge house as he did so.

Another resolution for Halloran: he was going to confront whoever it was inside that place, the person who guarded the gate, who was master of the dogs. He would visit the lodge later, and this time he would find a way inside. Before leaving Magma, he had discussed the vulnerability of the Neath estate with Charles Mather, and the Planner had promised to raise the matter with Gerald Snaith, after which an ultimatum would be delivered to Sir Victor Penlock: either adequate defenses were installed around the house and grounds, or Shield would be forced to relinquish the contract. The enormous sums of insurance money involved would ensure the alliance of the Lloyd's underwriters. Mather had been horrified to learn there were jackals roaming the estate and perplexed when Halloran had told him that he had not yet met the lodge keeper to discuss any emergency measures. A queer business altogether, Mather had voiced in his dry manner. Time to lay down stricter ground rules.

Halloran waved the Mercedes through, then closed the gates. There was a solid permanence about the thudded clunk as they locked together.

He climbed back into the car, and as it pulled away Palusinski said cheerfully: "No dogs to bite you today."

Halloran frowned. "Where are they kept?"

"Kept?" came the reply. "You mean caged? Hah! These beasts wander freely, they go where they please."

"They're not much in evidence."

"We are not hostile."

"Yesterday . . . ?"

"You were alone. And perhaps they sensed . . ."

Halloran wondered why the Pole did not complete the sentence.

"They tend to keep under cover in the daytime," said Cora, twisting in her seat. "They dislike people, they keep away from them. But at night they prowl."

"And search out intruders," Palusinski finished.

"Have there been any?" asked Halloran. "Intruders?"

Palusinski giggled. Cora said, "There have been one or two trespassers, but they've always been frightened off."

"They were lucky they weren't savaged," Halloran commented.

"No, the jackals didn't touch them. They were frightened off by . . . other things."

"I don't understand. What things?"

Palusinski giggled again. "Wood devils, *Pan* Halloran. You have not heard of the wood devils?"

The house, its walls a deeper and duller red under the overcast day, came into view. Cora turned away from Halloran, as if unwilling to continue the conversation, but he leaned forward and grasped her shoulder.

"What does he mean, wood devils? What's he talking about?"

"It's nothing, Liam. Really it's nothing."

"But explain to him," said Palusinski, his tone bantering. He snatched a quick look at Halloran, eyes small and squinted behind his wire-framed spectacles.

"They're only images, no more than that," Cora said quickly. "Felix can project mental images, make a person see what isn't really there."

Oh yes, Halloran knew that. He had seen such visions for himself in the lake.

"Felix senses when the dogs are alerted. I don't know how —it's as if there's some kind of telepathic link between himself and the animals. He doesn't even have to hear the jackals to know there are trespassers in the grounds."

Halloran started to understand why Kline felt so secure within his own territory. The man had his own inbuilt alarm system, according to Cora, and his own defense weapon. With such power, no wonder his subordinates feared him.

The car drew up outside the house, and Cora leaned over the back of her seat to rouse Kline. "Felix," she said, quietly at first, then again, louder, when there was no response.

"Felix, we're here." Cora reached down and tapped his knee. The dark-haired man, curled up into the corner of the

Mercedes, twitched but did not awaken. She shook his leg this time and repeated his name more sharply.

Kline stirred, his legs stretched. He mumbled something and began to push himself up in the seat.

"We're home?" he asked, voice slurred with tiredness.

"Yes, Felix, we're at Neath," Cora told him.

"Good," he said, "good." He turned, sitting upright, one hand touching the door lever.

Cora's gasp stopped him. Her eyes were wide as she stared.

Halloran had become still.

Puzzled, Kline looked from one to the other, and, as he did so, flakes of skin shed from his face. A face that was bubbled and broken, thin tissue hanging loose in layered scales.

As he frowned, more pieces fell away, falling lightly onto his chest and lap. He began to tremble.

32

A SHEDDING OF SKIN

The gun was in Halloran's hand before the bedroom door was fully open.

Cora stood in the doorway, frightened by the weapon. "I'm sorry," she said. "I should have knocked."

He waved her in, swinging his legs over the edge of the bed and sitting up. He put the Browning back on the bedside cabinet.

"How's Kline?" he asked.

Cora closed the door and leaned against it, her hands behind her. "He hasn't left his room since we got back."

"Have you sent for a doctor?"

She shook her head. "Felix won't allow that. He told me he suffers from psoriasis, a rare type of skin complaint that recurs every few years, but it's nothing to become alarmed about."

"Some complaint. And he wasn't too relaxed about it when Palusinski helped him into the house. Have you seen him like this before?"

"No."

"We really ought to get a doctor to take a look at him."

"He insists that we shouldn't. His orders are that we let him rest and send Khayed and Daoud to him as soon as they return from London. They have special lotions that can help." She seemed uncertain. "I didn't want to disturb you. You must be very tired."

"A cleanup and a change of clothes helped. I even managed to grab a sandwich." He extended a hand. "Cora, I need to talk to you. Please come over."

For a moment he thought she might leave. But then she walked to the bed. "Sit by me," he said.

She obeyed, and immediately leaned into him, her head

against his chest. He held on to her, surprised, but glad her reserve had broken.

"Liam," she whispered, "I have such strange feelings, such a sense of dread . . ."

"I can understand why. I get the same feeling about this place."

She looked up at him. "You too?"

"Maybe it's a neurosis we're catching from Kline. You know he's mad, don't you?"

"In a way I wish that were true—insanity would be easier to deal with. Felix is unstable and, as you say, neurotic; but not mad, Liam, not totally mad."

"He thinks you've been giving away company secrets." Halloran had been deliberately blunt, the unexpectedness of the remark meant to throw her off balance so that he could judge her reaction.

"You're not serious," she said incredulously.

He took her hand, now having no doubts about her loyalty to Kline. "I'm afraid so. That's why all the fuss at Magma this morning. New locations of untapped resources have been leaked to one of your rival companies."

"It's happened again?"

He nodded. "Kline put the finger on you."

"But why? I wouldn't—"

Halloran shrugged. "You're closest to him."

She seemed to shrink within herself. "How could he even think that? Liam, I—"

He pulled her to him again. "I know it isn't true, and maybe Kline will see reason. Who can tell with someone so unpredictable?"

"I still don't understand why he should accuse me."

"*I* don't understand what makes you so loyal to such a bastard."

She didn't answer right away. Then she said, almost sorrowfully: "I depend on him. He . . . he's like a drug to me. I need him, Liam."

"Then you're as crazy as he is."

"No, don't say that, you don't know . . ."

"What is there to know, Cora?" he said angrily. "Just what the hell goes on between you and Kline?"

She began to weep. "Help me, Liam," she said quietly. "Please help me."

"How can I when you won't tell me what's wrong?"

Cora began to fumble with the buttons of her blouse. "Make love to me. Hold me and make love to me, but gently, like last night, after you . . . Let me feel how good it can be again."

Baffled, Halloran stood up and crossed to the door. He locked it.

The thick curtains of the room were drawn against outside light, so that scattered artifacts of another age stood as dark shapes in the gloom. The smell of burning incense came from one corner, filling the air with a heavy and faintly acrid musk. Zodiac signs and symbols, drawings of horned beasts, of winged creatures, of single eyes, were roughly etched into walls and woodwork, obscure and patternless in the poor light. Books lay scattered around the floor. A canopied bed dominated the room, its four stout carved posts supporting layers of sheer drapes, the material hanging in loose folds.

A dry, rasping breathing came from within.

Kline lay on the bed, the skin of his naked body broken and ravaged, creating new fissures, causing paper-thin tissue to dislodge and fall away.

He feebly lifted an arm, but the darkness was even greater inside the shroud, and all he could see was a myriad of interjoining cracks. His arm fell back to his side and a sob escaped him.

It couldn't be, it wasn't time. The ritual had been enacted, the psyche strengthened. The sacrifice made. This shedding of the outer layer had come too soon, and with it there was pain. But why, what did it mean?

His unsightly body spasmed as another sob burst from him, and he felt the breaking of delicate tissue with the violence of the movement.

Must lie still. Must not move until Asil and Youssef arrive with their salves. It was too soon, too soon! He was not prepared! And the pain had never been like this before. Hurry, my friends, bring me your soothing oils! Spare me from this wretchedness!

Kline tried to steady his breathing, for even the rising and lowering of his chest was loosening the dead skin. He moaned, a self-pitying sound, and salt from his tears stung the sensitive grooves around his eyes.

And as he lay there, his mind absorbed in his own suffering, something inside the sepulchre that was hidden away in the blackest depths of Neath throbbed once.

33

INSIDE THE LODGE

From his position by the main entrance, Monk watched the Shield operative descend the broad staircase and wondered what was inside the black case he was carrying. The bodyguard's thick lips set in a sneer, his heavyset body tensing as Halloran approached.

"I'm taking a look around the grounds," Halloran told him.

"You'll get your ass bit off."

The hope in Monk's high-pitched voice did not go unnoticed by the other man. "I intend to stay in the car," Halloran replied. "Did the Arabs let you know how Kline is?" Khayed and Daoud had returned some hours earlier, rushing up to their master's room as soon as they learned of his condition.

"They ain't been down," said Monk, shaking his large head.

"All right, let's assume it's nothing drastic. Lock the door behind me when I go out and don't open it for anybody until I return. I'm taking a spare key, but I'll let you know it's me before I come in just so you don't get overexcited. If I knock a regular three times it means there's trouble and I'm not alone. I'll repeat that knock after a pause so you'll know it's for real. You got that?"

Monk smirked rather than replying.

"Check around the house every fifteen minutes, test windows and doors each time. And I mean test them—try them, make sure they're properly locked."

"What the fuck for?" Outrage accompanied the bodyguard's hostility now.

"Just do it. I'll be back in about an hour. Any calls for me and you write down the message. Don't try to remember."

"You think I'm stupid, Halloran?"

"We both know it."

Monk's shoulders visibly straightened and he almost took a step forward. Only Halloran's hard-eyed smile stopped him.

The Shield operative went by the American and unlocked one side of the double-doors. A breeze of cold air from the lake made him shiver as he stepped outside. It was like the first chill of winter out there instead of the coming of summer. He called back to Monk: "Lock it and take out the key." Then he walked through the porch to the outside.

Although cold, the night had temporarily cleared, the moon, an edge sliced off, still low in the sky. There were thunderous clouds on the horizon. The slopes around the house and lake were of deep-toned grays, trees and shrubbery the darkest patches. The lake itself appeared smooth and unbroken, even though a wind ruffled the grass before it.

Halloran climbed into the Mercedes, placing the black bag on the passenger seat beside him. He switched on the engine and lights and pulled away, gravel crunching beneath the tires, bringing the car around in an arc. As he did so, he glimpsed the neglected topiary garden at the side of the house, the tortured shapes resembling surrealistic figures, misshapen limbs twisted toward Neath like a frozen tableau of anguished souls.

He left the house behind, heading uphill toward the main gates, the woods soon closing around him, the beams of the car seeming to cut a swath through the trees. Halloran kept a vigilant eye on either side of the road, searching for low shapes slinking through undergrowth, but saw nothing that moved. A sharp *crack* on his left startled him. A thin branch had snapped against the side window. Halloran eased over the center of the road, realizing he had drifted too close to the edge.

The Mercedes rounded a curve and from there the roadway became a straight line running up to the gates. Halloran let up on the accelerator, approaching the beginning of the drive at a cautious speed. The headlights picked out the iron gates, and he dipped the beams to reduce the glare. His foot touched the brake pedal, slowing the car even more, so that he came to the lodge house at a smooth glide.

Halloran pulled over onto the rough shoulder in front of the old building, switched off the lights, and cut the engine.

The lodge was in darkness, not even a glimmer showing from the grimed windows. Halloran sat there for several minutes, watching for any sign of life. There was none. But that didn't mean the house was empty.

Without using the interior light, Halloran unzipped the black bag by his side. He lifted out the stubby weapon an inch or so, loosening it, making sure it wasn't snagged on the inner lining. He carefully lowered the submachine gun again, then reached for the door handle.

A breeze ruffled his hair as he stood outside the vehicle studying the upper windows of the lodge. The moon was rising behind the building so that its frontage was an unlit void, the windows merely black shapes, barely distinct against the brickwork.

Again he had the unshakable feeling of being observed. Carrying the gun bag in his left hand, Halloran walked into the shadow of the house.

The ringing of the telephone came almost as a relief. Mather laid the newspaper on the pile of Sunday papers, foreign as well as English, by his feet, exhausted with reading of yet more terrorist outrages and despairing of various governments' weakness in dealing with them despite the vowed joint intention to do so over the past decade. Unfortunately it was the price paid for a world without major conflicts, the major evil giving ground to the lesser evil, a fact recognized by those same governments. Nevertheless, the atrocities committed in the name of so-called freedom or religious beliefs were hard to stomach, and the time was coming when "official" war would have to be declared on those countries and states who overtly supported and encouraged the multifarious terrorist groups. And even then the problem would never be eradicated.

He stood up from the dining table on which more journals were spread and limped out into the hall.

"I'm here," he called out to Agnes, who was in the sitting room, no doubt indulging herself in the current television trivia with her evening sherry.

"Mather," he announced into the phone, first removing his pipe from his mouth.

"I'm sorry to disturb you. It's Sir Victor Penlock here."

"Sir Victor?" Mather's brain stepped up a gear, alerted by the gravity in the Magma chairman's voice.

"I'd like you to meet me at my office once again. My

apologies for calling on you twice in one day, particularly as it's a Sunday, but I'm afraid I had no other choice."

"That's perfectly all right. Do I take it Mr. Kline and my operative will also be there?"

A pause first. "No. No, this will be strictly between you and me. It's rather serious, so do you think you could come immediately?"

"Shouldn't take much more than twenty minutes this time of evening."

"It's very much appreciated. I'll let security know you're on your way. One other thing: no one else must know about this. Can I have your word on that?"

"Naturally, although I don't understand why."

"I'll explain when you get here."

When Mather replaced the receiver he went into his study and, as a precaution, wrote a note of his destination and whom he was to see, then sealed it in an envelope on which he scribbled his wife's name. He left the envelope propped up on his desk.

The stench at the back of the lodge house caused Halloran to catch his breath. No doubt this was where the jackals were kept when they were not prowling the grounds. He shone the thin beam of the penlight around the yard, expecting to find kennels or a stockade of some kind. There was none, and no animals either. But the light reflected on something shiny.

With a twist of the head of the flashlight, the beam was broadened to take in more. Halloran recognized the three metal containers Khayed and Daoud had carried from the house the day before. All were lying on their sides, the lids close by, as though the contents had been spilled out. He moved closer, using the light to guide himself through the mounds of excrement scattered around the yard. Drawing near to one of the bins he bent low to shine the light inside. His foot crunched something beneath him. He shifted to see shattered bone where he had been standing and realized that there were many more pieces around him, clean and meatless. At the bottom of the container there were clogs of maggot-infested meat, the jackals obviously having been unable to reach them. Much of the yard's putrid stink came from these containers.

Halloran straightened, relieved at least that the beasts

themselves were nowhere in evidence. He flashed the beam up at the windows, heedless of giving anyone inside warning of his presence; he had, in fact, already pounded on the front door, knowing that his approach in the Mercedes would not have gone unnoticed by anyone supposedly guarding the entrance to the estate. The lodgekeeper might have been roaming the grounds with his pack, of course, but Halloran could not rid himself of the notion that there was someone inside. Even now he sensed he was being watched.

He lowered the flashlight, finding the back door, then maneuvered his way through the feces and bones toward it. As expected, this door, like the front, was firmly locked. He moved along the wall to a window and, although also locked, this was less of a problem. Placing the bag on the windowsill, Halloran slid a knife blade up alongside the catch, then forced it aside, its movement stiff but yielding. He closed the blade into its handle, dropped it into his jacket pocket, then heaved at the lower frame. The window resisted at first before, with a groan followed by a squeal, it opened upward.

Halloran lifted the bag, switched off the light, swung a leg over the sill. Once inside he quickly stepped away from the window, where moonlight had silhouetted his shape. He leaned back against the wall and waited, holding his breath, listening for sounds.

The room smelled musty, damp, unlived in. Light from outside revealed sparse furniture: an armchair, its cushions lumpy, arms threadbare; a nondescript cabinet, neither antique nor modern, against one wall; a curled rug; and nothing else. Apart from the small rug, the floorboards were bare. Halloran flicked on the penlight once more, the beam still broad, and waved it around the room. Wallpaper hung away in strips, and black fungus grew in the corners and near the ceiling. There were ashes in the ancient iron fireplace, but they looked solid, as though they had set many years ago. There was an open door to the right.

Halloran listened for a while longer before allowing himself to breathe normally. He swept the light across the floor to make sure there were no obstacles in his path, then crossed the room to the door, unconcerned with the creaking of floorboards. Narrowing the beam, he peered out into the hallway, shining the light along its length. Moonlight glowed through the grime of the tiny windows above the back door. The hallway had a turn in it, and he surmised that it straightened again and led toward the main door to the lodge. The stairway would be in that direction too.

He eased himself from the room, holding the flashlight away from his body. Keeping close to the wall opposite the door he had just left, Halloran slowly walked toward the front of the building. He passed another door on his right but did not try the handle, guessing it would lead to a cellar.

He reached the point where the hallway turned, and hesitated, listening intently for a few seconds. Only silence. But the smell of oldness was even stronger here.

Halloran noticed a light switch close to where he stood and he reached out, pushing it down with one extended finger, the thin penlight gripped with the others. Nothing happened, and he was not surprised. Whoever lived in the lodge house enjoyed the darkness.

He went on, rounding the bend, and pointed the beam at the front door. There were large bolts, top and bottom, rusted fixtures that looked as if they hadn't been shifted for decades. Another door was on his left, the staircase rising above him on his right. Halloran made his way toward the door.

Slipping the straps of the bag over his left shoulder and changing the penlight to that hand, he used an elbow to push open the door. Its creaking was explosive in the silence of the house.

Before entering, he shone the light through the crack by the hinges, satisfying himself that nobody lurked behind the door, and only then did he step into the room. It was empty, devoid of any furniture, its curtains colorless with age and filth. The mustiness prevailed, and here the mold festered in thick clusters. Ceiling struts could be clearly seen where plaster had fallen away. Halloran left the room, leaving the door open wide.

The staircase loomed up before him.

And it was from there that the worst of the smell wafted down.

Halloran began to climb.

Mather parked directly outside Magma's main entrance, disregarding the NO PARKING signs. As he limped around the hood of his car, he could not help gazing up at the towering building, its glass and bronze façade brooding under a sky that was quickly filling with leaden clouds from the east. He felt a charge in the atmosphere, the coming of an electrical storm.

The two security men inside had noticed his arrival, and one was crossing the concourse toward the closed entrance while his companion at the circular reception desk lifted a phone. Mather started forward again, an urgency in his stride.

The security guard had come to a smaller door beside the main entrance and had already opened it a fraction by the time the Shield Planner was outside.

"Mr. Mather?" the guard inquired, and Mather opened his wallet to display his Shield identity. "Sir Victor's waiting for you. I'll take you right up."

The guard said nothing as the elevator swiftly ascended to the eighteenth floor, but he appeared tense, as much on edge as Mather himself. They trudged the thick-carpeted corridor to the chairman's outer office, passing through, waiting when the guard rapped on the inner door. The guard opened the door after a voice on the other side responded, then stood aside to allow the older man entry, still not uttering a single word. Mather heard the door close behind him.

Sir Victor did not rise from his seat. In front of him was a tumbler half-filled with Scotch.

"Good of you to get here so quickly," the Magma chairman said, waving Mather forward.

Although on first glance Sir Victor appeared his usual immaculate self, there was an indefinable dishevelment about him. Perhaps it was the weariness in his eyes, the slight sagging of his jowls, the few loose strands of silver hair hanging over his forehead that gave the impression, the Shield Planner mused. As well as the unexpected laxity in manners, for Mather had not been offered a seat, nor had Sir Victor risen when he had entered the office. Hardly a return to Stone Age etiquette but surely an indication of the stress this usually most civilized of men was under.

Now the chairman did rise, but not in deference to the other man. "I want to show you something," he said, "after which we must discuss our course of action."

Curious, Mather followed the tall man back into the corridor, and then into another office which, like Sir Victor's, bore no title on its door. They walked through an outer room, where the chairman unlocked a further door into the main office itself.

Mather drew in a sharp breath when he saw the figure slumped forward across the glass and chrome desk. He hurriedly crossed the room to examine the body.

"Quinn-Reece?" he asked, already sure that it was.

"Security discovered the body earlier this evening," the chairman replied grimly.

Mather moved around the desk and leaned close to the prone man's face. He was prepared to feel for a pulse in Quinn-Reece's neck, but realized it was pointless. The blueness of the deputy chairman's lips, the yellowish tinge to his skin, his very stillness, told him all he needed to know.

"Heart failure?" he ventured.

"I believe so. But lift him into his seat, look at his face."

Even more puzzled, Mather slid an arm beneath Quinn-Reece's chest and pulled him backward. He was stunned at what he saw.

"My God, he looks as if he . . ."

"Died of fright?" Sir Victor finished for him. "He was sitting upright like that when he was found. I ordered security to lay him on the desk. I couldn't bear the thought of him staring that way, his mouth locked open . . ."

Mather frowned. "I think you'd better tell me what's going on. I assume your people haven't yet called for a doctor or an ambulance?"

The chairman's guilt was barely apparent. "Our security guards are under strict instructions never to bring outsiders onto the premises unless someone in authority sanctions it. We regard anything that happens within the walls of Magma as company business, and only I or my executive officers may deem otherwise."

"Good Lord, man, this has nothing to do with your business. It's possible that medical attention might have saved him."

Sir Victor was adamant. "No, I can assure you he was quite dead. Nothing could have helped him, nothing at all."

"Well, I suggest you call for an ambulance now."

"Yes, of course. But first we must talk. Please allow me a few minutes."

"Is there good reason?"

The chairman looked away from the corpse. "I believe so," he said quietly.

The stairs groaned under his weight. He thought one or two might break altogether and quickly shifted his footing. It seemed a long climb to the bend in the stairs, as if time itself were being stretched, and at any second he expected someone to appear above him, so strong was the feeling of another's presence inside the lodge house.

He stopped for a few minutes when his head came level with the landing, and listened again, depending on hearing rather than seeing in such poor light. There were three doors along the upstairs hallway, one to the left of the staircase, one directly in front, the last farther down. The latter would have a view overlooking the entrance gates, but it was not for that reason alone Halloran chose to inspect it first: he knew, as surely as if someone were calling him, that he would find what he was searching for inside there.

As with the rest of the house, bare boards were the only flooring along the landing, and he saw no reason to avoid making noise as he walked its length—it was too late for that. Nevertheless, his movement was stealthy and his right hand was kept free, ready to snatch the gun from its holster at the slightest provocation, even though he was there in his role as Kline's protector, not as an enemy.

The smell of rotting was nauseating as he drew close to the door, and he swallowed the wetness rising in his throat.

Halloran went on by the door, going to the window at the far end of the hallway. He pushed aside half-drawn curtains, the coarse material stiffened with dust, and rubbed a palm against the dirt on the glass, clearing a section to see out. Moonlight glimmered from the roof and hood of the Mercedes below; the iron bars of the entrance gates looked blackly solid; the undergrowth opposite seemed impenetrable. Light withered as a cloud rolled over the moon.

Halloran returned to the door, his penlight haloing the handle. He pressed his ear close to the wood but heard no sounds from the other side. Hitching the bag so that it was secure on his shoulder, he reached for the door handle.

He was sure the door would be locked. It wasn't.

He expected to use force to push the door open. It opened smoothly.

He thought he would confront the lodge keeper, the guardian of the gates.

Instead he met his past.

34

INTO THE PIT

Kline moaned as Khayed ministered the lotion to his ruptured skin. The burning would soon pass, the Arab assured him, and Kline knew the truth of what he said; his loyal servants had soothed him with their oils many times before. But that was when the sloughing of his skin had been expected, had become a ritual, a ceremony to be indulged in, to be celebrated, for it was the outward sign of spiritual rejuvenation. And a continuance of his own servitude.

He uttered a cry, more in fear than in pain. Asil misunderstood and hurried forward with the syringe. *"Mouallem?"*

Kline saw the needle and raised a hand to deny the morphine, for the drug would dim his thoughts, euphoria would blunt the danger that was so close. Yet his senses were already hindered, for dread gnawed at them like some avaricious parasite. The killing that day of the enemy within had not calmed his unease, as he thought it would; instead the mental effort had further drained his psyche and weakened him physically. The death of Quinn-Reece had not resolved his own anguish but had merely contributed to his present condition.

He beckoned Asil forward again, speaking to the Arab in his native tongue. "A moderate amount, Youssef. Enough only to soften my"—he almost said *fear*—"my pain."

The needle was like a blade heated by fire, but Kline's scream swiftly relaxed to a sigh as his senses began to float. Soon he dreamed, but in truth, it was a memory...

...he lowered himself into the pit, terribly afraid. It was so deep, so black. But for that reason, it would yield even greater treasures. Why else should it be so skillfully concealed from the other sepulchres? The reward for his courage would indeed be great! The Jewish merchant in Jerusalem had prom-

ised him that. "Journey to Ur, find employment with the English archaeologist. He needs men of education, people who can direct the lazy and treacherous laborers, and who will appreciate and understand the cultural value of his great discovery. The Arabs will obey because the Englishman will put his trust in you and they will have little choice. You are clever, you are cunning. Bring back to me what small treasures you can easily steal and I will make you a rich man, for I have collectors who will pay kings' ransoms for the most meager of items from the fabulous and glorious era! These Arabs are plunderers, destroyers, scum of the earth, and care nothing for their heritage. They will allow their own history to be taken from them by foreigners. But we will profit by their stupidity, my young friend. And we will bring great joy to those who honor such relics."

The journey to the Royal Cemetery of Ur had been long and wearisome and he had worried that the dig would be over by the time he arrived there; but no, there was still much to be done, many more tombs that lay at the bottom of deep shafts beneath thousands of surface graves to be revealed. And the merchant had been correct: the team of foreigners needed several of his ilk to organize the transient labor force, arrange permits and payroll, maintain supplies and medicines, as well as to secure the site against thieving infiltrators. He had worked diligently, never becoming too greedy with his own finds, taking only those objects small enough to be smuggled safely from the camp to the single room he had rented inside the city, a place where he could hide his private cache and where, every so often, the merchant from Jerusalem would arrive to relieve him of the treasures. The system worked well, and when all was complete, the merchant assured him, the profits would be admirable.

He had not come upon the secret tunnel leading to the pit by accident, for he had always had the gift, the seeing in the mind, the ability to predict a death before it was claimed, a birth before conception, to judge beforehand good fortune for some, tragedy for others. Even when he was a child, should his mother lose a needle, it was he whom she urged to find it; should his father misplace an article, it was the boy who sought out its hiding place. Later, when his gift became known to others, it was he who was taken into arid territories to locate a source of water beneath the soil so that new settle-

ments could be built around it. Rewards for that rare inner knowledge had paid for his welfare and education after his entire family had been taken by disease (strangely a tragedy he had not been able to predict). So it was that the merchant realized the young man's potential when the great find outside the distant city of Ur in the land where the ancient Sumerians had once reigned became world news. Who better then to seek out those exquisite but concealed antiquities that would end up as mere exhibits in some stuffy London museum unless redirected elsewhere?

On his very first day inside that vast labyrinth of shafts and corridors, hidden rooms, and sepulchres, he had become confused and almost overwhelmed by mourning voices of the dead, whose spirits were locked beneath the earth, for their human vessels had taken their own lives to be with their deceased kings and queens and their high priests. Over the weeks that followed he had learned to shut out those incorporeal murmurings from his mind; yet one sensing persisted throughout, something that was not a spiritual utterance, but a kind of pulse, a split-second shifting of atmosphere, as if time itself had hiccuped. He would feel it but once or twice a day, never more than that. At first he had believed it was a physical phenomenon, a faraway subsidence, but no one else ever noticed the brief disturbance. The deeper he worked his way into the complex layers of tombs, the louder—or more sensed—the unheard "sound" became. Then one evening, when the day's labor was done, after the workmen returned to their tents or hovels outside the city walls and the foreigners retired to their lodgings, he had wandered alone through the lowest chambers, drawn by h knew not what, but compelled toward a destiny he had never dreamed of.

The secret tunnel was behind an empty room at the furthermost extremity of the Royal Cemetery, a square space that had puzzled the learned archaeologists for it seemed to have no purpose: its walls were bare and there were no casks or ornaments within. It was merely an isolated chamber, one that was reached by crouching low along a lengthy corridor that had many turns and dips.

The pulse had come as he had stood in that soulless room, and this time it was as though he had really heard the sound. The walls themselves had seemed to tremble. Startled, he had swung his lamp around and the light had caused a shadow on one wall. He moved closer to inspect the shadow and found a mud brick jutting out a fraction from its neighbors. He had used the trowel he carried, standard equipment along with brushes for the diggers, to cut around the brick and ease it from the wall. The stench of released gases sent him reeling backward.

He approached again more cautiously, and the smell was still strong but less of a shock. Other mud bricks easily came loose, and soon a passageway was exposed. A dreadful fear had overcome him then and he had almost run from that place. But a curious fascination stayed him.

He crawled into the narrow passage, holding the lamp before his face.

The passage led downward, so steeply at certain points that he had to use his strength to prevent himself tumbling forward.

Before long it opened out into a wide circular chamber at the center of which was a gaping hole, an open pit. Around the opening lay human bones, their rotting robes those of high priests and priestesses. Resting against the walls were clay tablets of cuneiform writing, wedge-shaped signs that represented words or syllables. He trod carefully to the edge of the pit and stared down at the blackness. That was when his fear became too much to bear, for something was urging him to descend, an inner compulsion inviting him to leap.

And the mind-sound was a sound, disgorging from the pit.

THUD-UP

He had fled.

Despite his terror, he had resealed the opening to the secret passageway, using dirt from the floor to cover the cracks (not that the room was of any interest to Sir Leonard and his team of archaeologists, who had treasures in abundance to drool over without bothering with empty chambers). This discovery would be his alone.

Four days went by before he gained enough courage to venture down to that pit again, four days of nagging agitation and four nights of feverish nightmares. He knew he would go back; the difficulty was finding the will to do so.

He waited until evening once more when all digging had stopped, only a few guards that he himself had helped organ-

ize left on duty above ground. This time he returned to the pit with rope and stanchion . . .

. . . Kline wailed as he slept, and Khayed and Daoud leaned over him anxiously. . .

. . . and fearfully, his limbs trembling so badly that he almost lost his grip, lowered himself over the edge of the pit. He descended slowly, drawn by an allure he could not comprehend, his lamp dangling below him, attached to his waist by thick string. He was aware that something evil awaited him, something ancient and cruel, for his dreams over the past few nights had revealed that at least to him, although no images, no visions of what it was, were presented. For in his sleep he had tasted the joys of carnality, had been seduced by the delights of depravity, had been pleasured by the thrill of vileness. The dreams had promised that those glories would be his if . . . if . . . if . . . he would but claim them. And to claim them, he would have to descend the pit.

THUD-UP!

The pulse was thunderous, reverberating around the shaft, causing a tremor, dislodging dust. His grip on the rope slipped and he plunged.

But not far.

For the pit was not deep at all. Its very blackness had created that illusion.

His legs buckled and he crashed onto his back, the lamp toppling over, fortunately still burning. Without pause to regather his breath, he reached out and righted the lamp lest he be cast into complete darkness. Only then did he suck in the foul air and feel the pain of his jarred body.

He pushed himself into a sitting position, his back against the crumbling wall, his chest heaving, his eyes wide and frightened.

Opposite was a niche. A square hole that was no more than two feet high, cleverly concealed in shadow so that no one above would ever realize it was there.

It was some time before he was able to crawl toward the niche.

The lamp revealed a closed receptacle of some kind inside, its surface dulled by centuries of dust. He brushed shivery

*fingers across the front and felt metal; bumps and ridges that
might have been symbols were embossed on what must have
been a door, for set in one side was a small projection that
served as a handle.*

*He stared. He did not want to open it. He knew he was
going to.*

*His hand shook so violently he could barely grasp the han-
dle. Squeezing his fingers tight around it, he tugged.*

The door opened easily.

*And his scream threatened to bring the walls of the pit
down on him . . .*

. . . Kline's scream caused Khayed and Daoud to leap away
from the bed in surprise. They quickly ran forward again and
babbled soothing words to their master, assuring him it was
only a nightmare, that he was safe under their watchful protection, nothing would harm him while they lived and
breathed.

He looked from one to the other, his face a cracked mask
of seams and ruptures. Suddenly he understood.

"*He's dying,*" Kline rasped.

35

THE WAITING GAME

He watched the Granada cruise by, its headlights brightening both sides of the narrow road. Keeping low and pulling aside minimum foliage so that he could observe but not be seen, he checked that there were still only two occupants in the patrol car. When it was gone, he stood and held up his wristwatch, waiting a moment or two for the moon to reappear from behind rolling clouds. Just under twenty minutes this time. The driver varied his speed during the circuit around the estate so that there was never a regular time interval between certain points. The driver of the second patrol car did the same.

The man sank into the undergrowth, making his way back through the thick woods, only bringing out a flashlight when he was well clear of the road. Soon he arrived at a lane, one that eventually joined the route he had been watching; he continued his journey away from the estate.

Two vehicles were waiting in a picnickers' clearing a few hundred yards on, their occupants sitting in darkness. He flashed his light twice, then switched off before climbing into the backseat of the first car.

"Well?" the passenger in the front said.

"Two patrols. Professionals, as you'd expect. We could easy take them out, though."

"Shouldn't be any need."

"No. It'll be no problem to get into the place. We only have to wait for them to pass, then make our move when they're out of sight. The fence'll be easy."

"We'll wait awhile, give them time to settle in for the night."

"It's been a time coming, Danny."

His expression couldn't be seen, but the man in the front was smiling. "It has that," he said, the softness of his accent hardened by the intent of his words. "But all the sweeter for it."

36

A ROOM OF MEMORIES

Halloran's senses reeled.

It wasn't a room he was standing in but a kaleidoscope of memories. They spun before him, some merging so that yesterday mixed with yesteryear, experiences of childhood confused with those of later times, scenes superimposed upon others. It was as if screens or veils fluttered in front of him—he thought of the veils he and Kline had passed through together in the dream of last night—thin, transparent layers, older images on those new.

He turned, ready to run from there, but the doorway was no longer behind him. Instead there were more visions, closing around him, the colors vivid and fresh, the details perfectly defined, as though they were being lived at that moment.

Slowly some began to dominate the others, dispersing weaker memories—less *significant* memories—to the peripheries of his mind.

He saw himself slicing the tendons behind the black tracker's knee, the man a volunteer of South Africa's Special Service brigade who would have followed Halloran and his small raiding band of ANCs back across the border to their camp, later to lead his own forces there, had he not been put out of action. Fading in over this was the church, moonlight through the high stained-glass windows revealing the three boys creeping along the center aisle, Liam hugging the dead cat wrapped in old rags to his chest, its body mangled, opened by the wheels of a speeding car, the other two boys giggling nervously as he approached the altar and reached up to the tabernacle, opening its gilt door, pushing the bloodied corpse inside, running for their lives, laughing and piss-scared of the consequences. *He whirled.* Now he was with the girl, Cora, taking her forcibly, ignoring her struggles, her protests, thrusting into her until she submitted, wanted him, her lust as intense as his, the rape no longer so, becoming a mutual desire which had to be satiated. And here he was with his father, and Dadda was being torn apart by bullets, his eyes bulging with disbelief while his son, Liam, urinated unknowingly into the stream, the father falling, then looking up at the boy, pleading—or was it warning?—telling him to run, to get away from there before the gunmen turned their weapons on him too, only unable to speak, his own blood choking his words. His father crawling to the bank, collapsing there, the masked Irishmen stepping on him, drowning him, shooting Dadda again. *Halloran blinked, long and hard, but the visions would not disappear.* Scenes from his military service, the killings, the terrible battle at Mirbat, the disillusionment with it all, the women who had drifted in and out of his life, the mother he had come to revile because of the craziness inside her head, the beatings he had dealt to others of his age who dared mock her affliction, and who dared spit the word *Britisher* as a curse at mention of his father, even though Dadda's birthplace was County Cork—and the beatings Liam received when his anger and frustration were no use against the gangs who taunted him. *Halloran staggered with the intensity of it all.* A blurred figure appeared, walking toward him through the hallucinations, the recognitions, arms out to him, calling his name beseechingly, and he could feel his Mam weeping, although she was but a specter, not yet clear in his vision. She drifted through the eidetic imagery, coming closer, her voice faint, begging for his embrace. And as she drew near, dissolving in and out of projections of his past, her head was distorting, becoming bent and twisted, as were her hands, pulping and spurting blood, as they had when she'd deliberately walked into the threshing machine on a neighbor's farm, her arms and upper body churned by the machinery, her head smashed and almost lopped off . . . as it was now, tilting, collapsing, hanging by bloody threads on her chest. *Halloran screamed.* But the memories were relentless. There was the big priest, Father O'Connell, warning Liam that the wildness had to stop, that the Good Lord Jesus would punish the boy for his wickedness, that his cankered soul would be damned eternally into Hell. The priest came at him, unbuckling the thick strap he wore around his waist, winding the buckle end around his fist, raising his arm to flail the boy, *the man*, pity as well as fury raging in his eyes. Then gone, before the black-robed priest could bring down the leather scourge. Replaced by the cousin of Liam's mother, one of the gunmen who had murdered his father. A man she had accused all those years ago, her accusations laughed off, sneered at. And here he was, sneering at Halloran again, a ghost not exorcised, even though the man had blown himself up along with a companion, a few years after the killing, the homemade bomb they had been carrying in the back of their car toward the border too delicate—or too faulty—for the rough, pitted lanes they had chosen to travel, the jigging and jogging causing wires to touch or to dislodge so that the boyos were blown sky-high, and the only person to celebrate the occasion was Liam, who could not understand how the assassin of his father could be venerated as a hero by the local townspeople, blessed by the Holy Roman Catholic Church when his bits and pieces had been returned for burial on consecrated ground, Father O'Connell himself pleading God's bountiful mercy for this poor unfortunate's soul, speaking of him as a martyr to the Cause, this killer who had robbed Liam of Dadda, who had laughed and sneered Mam to her death, who sneered at him now in this very room. *Halloran yelled his outrage at the apparition, shaking with the emotion, every muscle and cord in his body stiffened rigid*. Then it all began to darken and fade, the memories slipping away, fresh ones barely glimpsed until one bright spot remained; it seemed a great distance away, too far to be within the walls of the house itself. It grew in size, coming forward, the movement steady, a gliding, the object soon recognizable, its surroundings slowly filtering through, misty at first, but gaining substance. The tabernacle was on an altar, the altar itself raised above three broad steps, before the steps a Communion rail, the kneeling cushions and then the pews on either side of the center aisle. Liam, a youth, creeping toward the front of the church, in one hand a metal can from his grandfather's workshed, in the other a lit devotional candle. He swung over the low rail, leaving the candle on top, and mounted the steps. Doubt, guilt—fear—urged him to open the tabernacle, to save the chalice containing the

Communion wafers he knew Father O'Connell always prepared the night before early Sunday mass; but he didn't, too afraid to do so, for it would be like opening the door to God Himself, inviting Him to witness the sacrilege Liam was about to commit, and perhaps God—*if* any such creature really existed—might take away the hatred, the one emotion Liam did not want to lose, because it gave him his life objective, it overcame grief and insecurity, if only for a short while. He tipped the can and poured gasoline over altar and steps, retrieving the candle and holding it aloft, well away from the inflammable liquid he splashed along the aisle. Eyes almost blinded with tears, Liam dropped the candle into the puddle near his feet. The fire sped away from him and now he was outside, face bathed in a warm glow, gazing in stupefied awe with the other townspeople as their beloved church perished in flames that might have been sent from Hell itself. And Father O'Connell could not be held back. He broke away from his flock and ran into the church, was gone for long minutes, an eternity, while the men outside moaned, the women wailed, and then he was bursting through the doors, the Holy Chalice clasped in his seared hands, but he was alight, his clothes, his hair, his skin on fire. He staggered on the church steps, and the people—*his* people—were afraid to go near, as if they would be contaminated, the flames would engulf them too. The priest screamed and he shrieked and he raised his arms up to the night, the chalice falling to the concrete, spilling its contents. The crowd moaned as one when Father O'Connell slumped to his knees. They cried aloud when he pitched forward onto his face. His body flared, a fireball without shape, and Liam's scream Noooooooo *became Halloran's as he stood in the center of the room, hands striking the air as if to erase the memories, to banish the dreams*.

He stumbled back against the wall, the open doorway beside him. The worst of the stench came to him then, a smell so malodorous it was almost choking. He cupped a hand to his mouth and nose, blinking away wetness in his eyes. His whole body was damp, his clothes clinging, and it was only with considerable effort that he kept his legs straight. The urge to sink to the floor had to be fought against, for he was overcome with weariness and confusion; he resisted, acutely aware that there was danger all around him in this room, in this house.

The penlight was lying several feet away, its thin beam pointed at the wall opposite, revealing only a strip of torn wallpaper. He could just make out the shape of the black bag he'd also dropped lying close by.

In a crouch, his senses still not recovered from the onslaught they had received, Halloran moved forward and grabbed both items, then scrambled backward so that he leaned against the wall once more. He broadened the light beam to take in a bigger area.

The floor was littered with rubbish and filth, a threadbare carpet, corners curled, covering a minimal section of bare boards. The walls were stained, the faded paper hanging in tatters; to one side were cupboards, the wood cracked and dull. A small table and chair were to his left; a few paces away, on the tabletop lay a plate on which remains of a meal had furred green. He noticed that the ceiling light socket had no bulb, the ceiling itself bulging in places, and pockmarked with dark fungi. Mustiness from that fungi contributed to the pungency of the room; the rest was a mixture of urine, stale feces, and . . . and something else. A sickly sweetness.

The wide beam lingered around the single window in the room, the curtains of which were rendered gray by dust. A high-backed armchair faced the window. Wiry stuffing, like internal organs, spilled from holes in its upholstery. He knew that it was from here that the lodge keeper watched the gates to the estate. But Halloran could not see if the chair was occupied. Several seconds went by before he determined to find out.

He edged past the doorway, keeping to the wall, moving to a position from where he could shine the beam directly into the chair. Shadows shifted also, stirred by the changing light. The angle improved as he drew closer, yet somehow he was reluctant to discover who sat there, his mind scarcely coping with the hallucinations it had already been bombarded with; he knew, though, that he could not leave the room without confronting the lodge keeper.

He reached the corner, his shoulder brushing mold and dust from the mildewed wall, and raised the penlight so that it shone directly into the seat. Both relief and disappointment swept through him when he found it empty.

But a faint disturbance was coming from elsewhere in the room. A sighing of air. A breathing.

Halloran slowly swung the beam into the farthest corner, from where the sound came, the light passing an iron fireplace, this one too filled with hardened ashes, before coming to rest on a misshapen bundle of rags lying on the floor.

As he watched, the bundle began to move.

37

JOURNEY AROUND THE LAKE

There were five of them in all, lying low in the undergrowth, faces pressed into the earth as the car lights drew near. Only one of the men looked up when the brightest moment had passed, and he waited until the rear lights had become pinpoints in the distance before speaking.

"That was it, all right. The Granada. Ten minutes at least till the other one comes along."

Next to him, the man named Danny grunted. "Across the road, quick as you like, and as little noise as possible. There might just be a foot patrol inside the grounds."

They rose as one, brushing through the foliage and around trees, sprinting across tarmac to reach the wire fence on the other side of the road. They were trained men, and one immediately turned his back and rested against the mesh, cupping his hands between his thighs as a stirrup. He hoisted his companions over, then threw the two rifles left lying in the grass to them. The weapons were deftly caught, and he scrambled over after them.

The men melted into the shadows of the trees, then regrouped when they were well out of sight from the road.

The leader whispered loud enough for them all to hear. "Round the lake, boys, an' no talking on the way. We'll keep to its edge in case there's an alarm setup in the woods. Eyes sharp, lads, an' single file. Make your mothers proud."

He went forward, the others following down a slope that led to the edge of the water. They crept along the shoreline until the moon emerged from clouds like an all-encompassing searchlight; the group dropped to the ground. They crawled back into the undergrowth and waited to find out if they had been observed. Their leader eventually gave the order, and they rose as one to move silently through the trees.

"Look out," one exclaimed.

The others stopped, crouching low, hands reaching for weapons. Hammers clicked on revolvers.

"What was it?" the leader demanded when there was no movement nor sound for several seconds.

"I saw something ahead," the subordinate replied. "A shape."

"What the hell are you talking about? Was it man or dog?"

"Neither," came the nervous response. "Just a shape. I swear it disappeared in front of me."

"You're going soft in the head, McGuire. Let's get the job done."

They moved off again, but soon it was the leader himself who brought them to a halt. His scalp prickled as he watched the wavery mist that drifted in and out of the trees a few yards away. A cry close by distracted him.

One of his men had raised his Armalite and was about to fire.

"No," he ordered urgently, grabbing for the barrel. "What the hell are you playing at?"

"Jesus, God, I saw them there." He pointed into the grass a short distance away. "A goddamn nest of 'em. Snakes. They just faded away."

The leader shook his head in disgust. His men were behaving like old folk, frightened of their own shadows. He returned his attention to the spot where the mist had curled through the trees almost like arms reaching toward them. No mist now. God Almighty, he was as bad as the others.

"Danny, will you look over there."

"Keep it down," he growled, but turned to where the man was pointing. Through the woods he could see the lake. The water was choppy, stirred by a breeze that grew stronger by the moment, the moonlight tossed by undulations. But it was the far bank to which his man was directing him. There was movement there, a flowing stream that had nothing to do with water.

"What is it?" someone whispered.

"Can't you tell?" said the leader. "It's dogs, man."

"Coming for us?"

He could feel his men's panic.

"Not at all. They'd be across the water at a sniff of us. No, they're on their way somewhere else, an' thank God for that."

He watched the tiny, ghostly forms skirt around the lake, their low bodies catching the light so that in parts they looked silver. Clouds consumed the moon once more, and he could follow their journey no longer.

He frowned, wondering where they were heading with such haste.

38

THE KEEPER

The breathing became louder, a hissing that each time ended in a thick, muciferous sigh.

It faded again, became almost a whisper, and Halloran strained to listen. The heaped bundle of rags was still, having moved only once.

His own breathing was unsteady and Halloran realized that never before had he felt such debilitating trepidation, for a peculiar virulence seemed to poison the very air in the room. His inclination was to flee, to bolt through that doorway and get out into the night where the breeze was pure. But the curiosity that had led him to this place had become something more: an obsession, perhaps even a quest. Revelations from his own life had spun before him here, things that were bad, his worst sins re-created, and there had to be a reason why. He felt shame, a guilt he had always suppressed rising inside; yet it was his fascination that was stronger. It was that which prevented him from taking flight, for it prevailed over the fear, subjugated the exposed guilt.

Halloran tentatively made his way toward the tangled rags.

He saw the edges of a thin mattress, dried stains overlapping its sides, spreading where fluid had once seeped into the wood of the floor. The mound on top could have been anything—blankets, piled clothing, assorted pieces of material. That there was someone beneath there was no doubt, for the whispered breathing came from here and the jumbled covering quivered slightly with the exhalation. Halloran leaned forward and gripped the rags. He pulled them away.

A face, partially concealed by a cowl, turned toward him.

Halloran released the covering and stepped back, horrified at the countenance that stared up at him.

The skin was withered and deeply rutted, like wrinkled leather left in the sun; and its coloring, too, was of old leather, except where there were festering scabs that glinted under the flashlight. Most alarming of all were the eyes. They were huge, lidless, bulging from the skull as if barely contained within their sockets; the pupils were cloudy, a fine membrane coating them, and the area around them that should have been white was yellow and patchworked with tiny veins.

From this thing came the sickly sweet smell of death's corruption that dominated all the other scents of the room.

Something seemed to shrink within those globular eyeballs when they came to rest on the shadowy form of Halloran, and the figure tried to rise, its scrawny neck arching backward as if the weight of its head was too much to bear. The hood fell away from a hairless skull whose surface was mottled with deep brown blemishes; incredibly, the skin there, which should have been smooth, was also wrinkled and ridged, as though the bone beneath had no firmness, no substance.

Repulsed, Halloran took another step away. The impression of gazing down at an enormous lizardlike creature was enhanced when the figure's mouth opened and a tongue, so darkly red it seemed black, protruded and rolled across cracked, lipless flesh. The lidless eyes refuted the reptilian image.

The figure attempted to speak, but no more than a gasped sigh escaped. The head sank back into the rough bedding with a finality that suggested the body itself had expired. Only then, and with reluctance, did Halloran advance again. Those bulbous eyes were fixed on him, and he shone the light directly into them. They did not blink, nor did the pupils, behind their mist, retract.

"It's you," came the sibilant whisper.

Halloran froze.

The figure gasped in air, as though the effort of speaking had caused pain. Even deeper rents furrowed its skin, and the mouth puckered inward.

Halloran struggled to find his own voice. "Who are you?"

The slightest inclination of the withered head, a gesture that the question was of no importance. And then the whisper: "Death comes." Its grimace might have been a smile.

Halloran leaned close, ignoring the fetid air that rose from the rumpled head. "I can get help," he said, and the thought of touching this person almost made him retch.

Again that toothless, puckered expression that could have been a grin. "Too late for me," came the whisper. "Come closer."

Halloran shuddered inwardly and made no effort to comply.

"I must speak . . ." it said, ". . . with you."

He knelt, but still could not find it in himself to bend near the hideous face. "Tell me who you are," he repeated.

This time there was an answer, perhaps an inducement to draw him in. "The . . . Keeper." The voice was stronger, and that, he thought, of a man.

"The gate keeper?" Halloran said. Surely it wasn't possible. The person before him was too ancient and too infirm to bear the responsibility.

The man's laugh was a choking sound, and his head shook with the exertion. "The Keeper," he said again, the last syllable an exhaled breath. A silence between them, then: "And you . . . you are Kline's guardian." The dark tongue flicked out, the movement quicker this time as it swept across his mouth. The skin was hardly moistened. "I understand now," he murmured so softly that Halloran wasn't sure if he had heard correctly.

Those staring eyes with their veiled pupils were disconcerting, and he wondered how much the old man could really see. "I'm going to bring a doctor to you," he said, questions racing through his mind.

"Too late, too late." The words were drawn out as a sigh. "At long last . . . it's too late." His head lolled to one side.

Not anxious, but curious, Halloran reached out to feel the pulse between the still man's neck and chin. He jerked his fingers away when the face turned back to him.

"Do you understand why you're here?" he was asked.

"Felix Kline is a client," Halloran answered.

"Do you know why you came to this house?"

"Here, the lodge house?"

There was no reply.

"I came to check it out, to find out who was inside, who handled the . . . the dogs."

"Now you've seen me."

He nodded.

"But it seems you understand nothing." The wrinkled face creased even more. "I wonder what you sense." There was an accent in the soft-spoken words.

"What did you see when you entered . . . this room?" the old man whispered.

How could he know? Unless he had caused them, just as Kline had caused hallucinations out on the lake.

"Things past, but never quite forgotten?" A catching in the throat, perhaps a snigger. "Your account has been brought up to date. I wonder why."

"Is Kline still playing stupid games with me, putting thoughts into my mind?" Halloran felt anger overwhelming his abhorrence.

The shaking of the old man's head was feeble. "No . . . no . . . the thoughts came from you. They are yours alone. Memories. You brought yourself . . . to this point." Those disturbing, milky eyes watched him; the ragged gash of a mouth curled in what could have been a grin.

"Tell me about Kline," Halloran said at last.

A sighed whisper, a slow releasing of breath. "Ahhhh." The ravaged head shifted slightly so that his eyes looked into the blackness of the ceiling.

Halloran waited, uneasy in the stillness, wary of this person whose decomposition seemed to precede his death. Halloran was wary, too, of the lodge house itself: there was movement in its shadows, as if spectral shapes weaved and danced there. Things perceived not with the naked eye but through the mind. Halloran checked himself, tried to throw off such crazy notions. Yet still they asserted themselves.

The old man was murmuring and, despite his repugnance, Halloran edged closer, wanting to catch every hushed word.

"A cunning boy. With powers—powers valuable to us . . . us Jews. But he was . . . foolish, too. He imagined . . . he had claimed his deity, not realizing that he was the one . . . to be claimed." He groaned and clutched at himself.

Halloran held out a hand to steady him, but could not find it in himself to touch the thing lying there, even though it was covered by rags.

When the worst of the pain had subsided, the aged and crumpled man spoke again. "Almost three thousand years of waiting before the . . . the Christ . . . two thousand years after . . ."

He was rambling, and when he coughed, there was a pinkishness to the spittle dampening the corners of his mouth. He gasped, as though anxious to tell. "We searched the world for disciples . . . our kind. And we found them. It wasn't difficult. And Kline caused havoc wherever we went. All for the glory of Bel-Marduk . . ." He drifted away once more.

Kline had spoken that name before. Halloran shivered, for the air was very cold. He looked around at the shadows; the beam from the penlight was frail.

A stirring of the makeshift bedclothes, then a shriveled hand, more like a claw, fingernails long and curled, stained brown with age, appeared. It reached for Halloran's arm, and the operative shuddered when it came to rest on him.

"He . . . Felix . . . used me . . ."

He was drifting away. The trembling hand flopped from Halloran's arm. "No longer afraid . . ." came the hushed words. "No worse Hell than . . . here . . . ahhhh . . ." Life seemed to flow out from him.

Overcoming his revulsion, Halloran shook the covering over the old man's chest. "Tell me who you are," he demanded, both angry and frustrated. "How can you guard this estate, control the dogs? How do you keep the gates locked? You're old, you're sick . . ."

A dry, reedy chuckle. The remnants of life flickered. "I have . . . power, too. Kline . . . working through me. My mind holds the . . . gates. My . . . mind controls . . . the beasts, the demons . . . But no more . . . too weak. He needs another . . . Someone corrupted to his ways . . ."

"Who are you?"

"I am nothing."

"Tell me!"

"Nothing. Although once . . . I was a merchant." He drew in a grating breath. "He . . . he is vulnerable." Again he clasped Halloran's arm. "Is it you? Are you the one?"

"To take your place? Is that what you mean?" A different kind of fear came over Halloran now.

The slightest inclination of the wizened head. "No . . . no . . . something more . . . than that . . ."

There were noises from downstairs. A soft rushing. Halloran remembered he had left the window open.

He felt a tightening of the clawed hand on his arm. Then the fingers uncurled and the hand fell away.

A scuffling in the hallway below.

There was a liquid rattling in the old man's throat as a long exhalation of air escaped him.

Pattering on the staircase.

Halloran scooped up the black bag as he rose and leapt for the door in a desperate bid to close it before the jackals came through.

But he was too late.

39

A TERROR UNLEASHED

The first of the beasts burst into the room, a glistening on its jaws caught by the beam of light.

To Halloran's surprise, the jackal bounded past him. He quickly stepped behind the door, using it as a shield as others, snarling and yelping, their fur bristling, streamed through. They made straight for the bundle of rags in the corner of the room.

Halloran drew in a sharp breath as the first jackal reached the lifeless figure and tore into the bedding, its jaws snapping and rending material. He heard a feeble cry above the frenzied yapping and realized that the disfigured old man was not yet dead. The puckered skull suddenly emerged from the rags, its mouth a toothless, jagged hole, the eyes now totally white. The second jackal buried its teeth into the scrawny throat.

And still more poured through the doorway.

Halloran reached into the bag and pulled out the MP5K, not bothering to yank out its retractable stock as he aimed at the welter of shoving and tumbling bodies. Blood suddenly gushed upward to drench the agitated backs of the jackals, its smell, its taste, driving the animals into even greater frenzy. They ripped into their broken victim, shaking him in feverish rage.

Halloran loosed fifteen rounds of nine-millimeter bullets into the pack, aware that the old man would also be hit and knowing it really didn't matter anymore.

The jackals screeched, some leaping into the air, others thrown against the wall by the impact. In little more than a second, the room was a carnage of convulsing bodies, a redness coating the floor and running down into the cracks. But not all the beasts had been killed outright. Several had just been wounded. Others had only been frightened.

These turned toward their attacker.

Halloran quickly switched the weapon to single-shot, unwilling to waste the rest of the magazine on one short burst.

The howling subsided to an agonized whimpering, the sound piteous but invoking no pity from Halloran. He pointed the gun at the nearest advancing jackal. The animal leapt, carnassials bared and already stained. The bullet entered its neck and exploded from the other side, taking fragments of flesh and spine with it into the ceiling.

Halloran was pushed back against the wall, the penlight he had kept locked against the weapon falling from his grasp as the contorting body struck him. The dead animal dropped away, head loose from its shoulders, and Halloran, crouched now, heard rather than saw the rush of another jackal. He raised the weapon and fired blindly.

The first bullet did not stop the animal, merely creasing its flank, and teeth sank into the operative's wrist. He scarcely felt the pain.

The next bullet, the weapon itself directed downward by the jackal's weight, scythed along the creature's underbelly. The piercing yelp set off a renewed howling from its injured companions, and Halloran cringed under the cacophony. He tugged his arm free, the brute's teeth scraping across the skin of his wrist as it slid to the floor. He reached for the light, swiftly turning the beam into the mass of quivering scavengers. Those that were still able were crawling toward him, some limping badly, others squirming on their stomachs. The mattress and bedrags behind them were sodden with dark, seeping liquid.

Submachine gun held in one hand against his hip, Halloran stooped to retrieve the bag, which contained extra magazines, never once letting the light beam waver away from the creeping bodies. The howling had died, to be replaced by a low, menacing growling. He edged around the door.

A limping jackal suddenly made a dash at him. Its legs gave way and it slumped at Halloran's feet, jaws weakly snapping the air, a low snarl coming from deep within its throat. He backed out the door as the others gathered their strength and staggered forward. Halloran pulled the door shut with a jarring thud and heard the jackals scratching at the wood on the other side.

He leaned against the frame, forehead resting on a raised arm, breathing slowly, giving himself time to recover from the horror.

But a scuffling on the stairs would not allow that.

He stiffened, then moved to the rail overlooking the stairway. More jackals were bounding up the steps, their backs to him. Halloran leaned over and took them one by one, shooting at the base of their skulls, shattering the bone there. The first jackal stopped dead, as if stunned, then toppled downstairs, the one close behind becoming entangled with the falling body. The third, startled by the gunfire and trying to avoid its companions, dodged to the side and received a bullet in its shoulder. The jackal howled and tumbled out of sight.

Halloran swiftly walked along the landing and paused at the top of the stairs, shining the light down. Only two corpses lay at the bottom.

He descended cautiously, anxious to get away from the charnel house but wary of what might still be waiting below, hoping these were the last of the stragglers. From above came the continued scratching against the door and a kind of mewling whimpering.

Halloran stepped over the dead bodies at the foot of the stairs and backed away to the front door, keeping his eyes on the corridor leading to the rear of the lodge house. Slipping the bag over his shoulder and gripping the penlight firmly between his teeth, he tried the door handle. It resisted his pressure at first, the mechanism obviously rusted, then grudgingly turned. But the bolts, top and bottom, were rusted solid and would not budge.

He guessed the entrance hadn't been used for many years, but was reluctant to leave through the back way. Instead he went into the room on his right.

Halloran was halfway across the floor heading for one of the windows when something dripped onto his extended arm. He stopped, curious. Liquid spattered against his cheek. He pointed the beam upward and saw the blood dripping through the ceiling. That was when he heard the throaty snarling from behind the door.

The jackal was on him before he had time to aim his weapon. He went down, dust rising in great clouds as he hit the boards. The flashlight flew from his grasp, striking the wall and blinking off when it fell to the floor.

The slathering animal was only a dim form above as Halloran clenched its fur and tried to keep the snapping jaws away from his face. He was forced to release the submachine gun so that he could fend off the attack with both hands. Its long legs were sturdy, much more powerful than they appeared, and they raked his clothes, scratching the skin beneath. Halloran felt blood trickling down his wrist, but realized it was from his attacker's own wound. Using one hand again to hold the jackal off, with his other he reached for the blood-soaked shoulder and squeezed hard. With a sharp, high-pitched yelp, the jackal sprang away, but Halloran went with it, keeping the pressure on the wound. Because of their skeletal structure, he knew dogs or wolves were virtually armour-plated, their vulnerable points few; but a sharp blow to the jackal's neck, just in front of the shoulders, numbed it into immobility. Halloran followed through before it had a chance to recover by slipping both arms beneath its shoulder, joining hands behind the creature's neck, and bringing up his elbows while pressing down his hands in one fast, vigorous action. The jackal's breastbone split with a sharp crack, the shock killing it immediately.

He let the limp body fall away, and without taking time to recover his breath, Halloran searched around the floor for the weapon. When he had it in his hands, as well as the black bag carrying the extra ammunition, he returned to the door and closed it, a barrier against any other jackals not dealt with. He went to the window, felt for the catch and, with some difficulty, forced it open. When he attempted to lift the window, however, he discovered it was stuck solid.

Wasting no further time, he covered his eyes with one hand and used the stubby butt of the submachine gun to smash the glass. Halloran squeezed through the opening and dropped to the ground outside. The Mercedes waited in the gloom a short distance away.

He had taken only a few paces toward it when a window above shattered and screeching shapes rained down on him.

He stumbled when one landed on his shoulder, tripped when another jackal fell at his feet. There was no way of telling how many there were around him and he knew there was little chance of recovering the weapon in the darkness. He pushed an animal away, its resistance weak because of its wounds, kicked out at another when he had risen, sending the beast tottering backward on legs that were already unstable. Something tugged at his ankle and he lifted the jackal off the ground, hurling it away from himself. He ran for the car drawing the Browning from its holster, just as a section of moon appeared. Throwing open the door, he leapt inside. He changed gun hands to close the car door, pulling at the handle as another jackal launched itself at him. The animal became wedged, and Halloran leaned away to avoid its gnashing teeth. With his left hand he touched the automatic to the jackal's head and squeezed the trigger. The beast jerked once, then slumped lifeless. Halloran pushed the body away from the car and pulled the door shut.

He sat there, chest heaving, his arms and forehead against the steering wheel. When he raised his head again to stare back at the lodge, the moonlight revealed a macabre scene: the wolflike creatures were staggering around in circles, shocked by their wounds as well as in pain, baying at the moon, their stumblings almost a ritual dance.

Halloran reached for the RT, intending to alert the patrol cars of the estate's loss of inner security. It had been unfortunate that neither car had been passing the gates a minute or two earlier when gunfire from the house would have brought them in to assist, but that was always a problem if manpower was stretched; not for the first time he cursed Kline for his faith in his own security. Static blared out at him when he pressed the transmit button. He switched off, then on again, hoping that interference would clear. It didn't. He spoke into the mouthpiece anyway, but the static became even worse as he waited for a reply. Glancing up at the sky, he saw that the clouds were big and thunderous, the atmosphere itself muggy-close, charge-filled. With a muttered curse, he returned the RT, holstered the gun, and switched on the Mercedes' ignition.

Something was calling him back to Neath, a certainty that there was trouble there, that not only was Kline in danger, but so, too, was Cora. And it was her safety he cared about most. After what had happened inside the lodge house, reason or logic was of minor importance. Sensing—intuition—was all.

He flicked on his high beams and swung the car toward the gates, turning in a tight circle that threw up earth and gravel, cutting through undergrowth on the far side of the road. Instead of setting a straight course for the main house, Halloran veered to the left, bumping across the rough piece of ground, in front of the lodge. He plowed into the dazed and dying jackals, crushing them beneath the wheels of the Mercedes, smashing into those that tried to run so that they hurtled into the air. Only then did he make his way toward Neath.

The car tore down the road, headlights throwing back the darkness, dust curling in its wake. He saw the first flash of light silver the clouds, a strobe effect that reminded him of the fulguration on the lake the previous night. Into the tunnel of trees and around the curve he sped, the low-hanging branches never more threatening than now, tires screeching as they gripped. The road somehow seemed narrower, as if the trees on either side conspired to join together, only the searing lights forcing them to retreat. Yet the feeling that the path behind him had closed up was uncanny.

The road began to dip and the car burst clear of the woods. He could not help wondering if the trees behind had finally linked.

In the distance was the brooding shape of Neath, only a few of its windows lit. Halloran eased up on the accelerator, training taking over from impulse. So wary was he that he switched off the lights completely, trusting his judgment until his eyes had adapted to the night, following the blurred strip of road down to the house.

Lightning brightened the sky again, and a jagged but almost perpendicular streak shot from the clouds to strike the lake.

Halloran jammed on the brakes, the Mercedes slewing to one side before coming to a halt. He stared at the water in astonishment as flashes stammered in the clouds for a second or two longer. The afterimage was clear in his mind as he sat in the darkness, the engine of the car running. The lake was a turbulent storm of waves and erupting geysers, its foam as white as any ocean's.

The car reverberated with the sound of thunder directly overhead.

40

A TERRIBLE DISCOVERY

The deluge struck as he entered the porch, a torrent of rain so fierce it seemed unnatural. He turned briefly and saw bits of gravel tossed into the air with the pounding. The mass of rainwater looked almost solid, cutting off the view of the lake. Halloran ran along the flagstones toward the entrance of the house itself, reaching for the key in his pocket as he went.

At the double-door he knocked twice and called out his name. He inserted the long key into the lock, the dull porch light lending little assistance, and swung one side of the door open.

The hall was empty.

He moved to the center of the stone floor, looking up at the minstrels' gallery, the landing, searching the shadows, turning around full circle to study every door on ground level. Lightning outside frosted the windows. Thunder followed almost immediately, and it was as though Neath itself trembled.

Halloran drew the gun from its holster once again.

He took the downstairs first, swiftly going through every room, opening each door suddenly but quietly, the automatic held out before him. He switched on lights wherever he went, hating Neath for its darkness. The library, drawing room, sitting room—all were empty save for sparse furniture and ornaments. The dining room, kitchen, corridors, other rooms—all lifeless and feeling as if they had been that way for many years. He trod cautiously, even though rain drumming against the windows covered the sound of his footsteps; but he felt a rising desperation.

Halloran paused to listen, leaning back against a corridor wall opposite a leaded window overlooking the courtyard. Lightning flooded the air.

He drew in a sharp breath when he saw the defunct fountain at the center of the yard now bubbling dirty, viscid water clotted with black slime.

The piercing light stuttered away and thunder rattled the windowpanes. Halloran moved on, finding his way back to the main hall.

He took the stairs two at a time, his step agile despite the draining ordeal he had already been through. He hurried from room to room, pushing open doors and peering in, gun always at chest level, safety off. He even looked into his own bedroom.

He thought he heard a cry from somewhere in the house, but thunder cracked deafeningly a moment after so that he couldn't be sure. Halloran headed for Kline's quarters, his stride fast and light. This time he was certain he heard a cry. A woman's. Cora's. He broke into a run.

The door leading to Kline's rooms was open. Halloran went through, slowing to a walk; a glow spread from a doorway near the end of the corridor. He heard a whimper, its source from inside that doorway. A smell of incense tainted the air.

He crept forward, knowing it was Cora who had uttered the small moan of pain. Halloran forced himself to remain emotionless. He neared the door, stopped, waited a moment.

A sharp, slapping sound. Against flesh. Cora's gasp, then her whimper.

Halloran gently pushed back the half-open door.

It was a large room, the walls covered in symbols and rough drawings. He did not take time to study them. Scattered around the floor were untidy piles of books, maps, and folios of some kind. He did not pay them much attention. In front of him was a four-poster bed, the posts knotted with carvings, curtains of sheer lace draped between them. He hardly noticed the fine work. Halloran could only stare at what was on the bed.

The drapes were gathered and tied to the posts, revealing a crouched, naked figure, head hanging low between the shoulders so that the back was arched. The flesh was red and wealed. Cora's face was half-turned toward Halloran, but she did not see him, for her eyes were closed, her hair falling over her forehead. Her mouth was open in a slight smile.

Monk had his broad, sloping back to the door, his gaze too

intent on the girl to notice anyone in the doorway. The body-guard was naked too, a mountain of obese, loose flab covered in wiry hair that was thick around his lower arms and legs and splaying over his shoulders so that the skin was merely a dull-ness beneath.

The short, multithonged whip he held dropped to the floor as he pushed the girl over on the bed. He grabbed her ankles and yanked them toward him so that Cora was flat on her stomach. Halloran caught a glimpse of her manacled wrists.

Her groan was of pleasure, not of fear.

All calmness, all self-imposed remoteness, left Halloran in a gushing of rage. The anguish he felt was as deep and as painful as on the day he had witnessed the gunning down of his father so many years before. Or when he had learned of his mother's terrible death. It seared him and blinded all other senses.

He roared as he rushed forward and reached for the body-guard's hair, which had been loosened from the band Monk usually wore. He wrenched hard, hauling the gross man away from the girl, bringing the butt of the Browning down hard against the side of Monk's head, his anger, unleashed like rarely before, spoiling the accuracy of the blow.

Monk cried out and toppled over the footboard onto the floor.

Cora turned, drawing her legs up. Her glazed eyes looked into Halloran's uncomprehendingly. He raised the gun toward her, his hand shaking, wanting to kill her, wanting to punish her for breaking through to him, for making him care again, then for mocking those feelings. He cursed himself for allow-ing it to happen.

Cora smiled at him, an idiot's welcome. Then fear finally melted through her drug-induced haze.

Halloran lowered the pistol and closed his eyes against the sight of her.

A meaty arm closed around his neck from behind, a hand reaching around and grabbing his wrist. He was lifted off his feet as Monk heaved.

His windpipe was being crushed by the pressure, and Hal-loran knew it would only be a matter of seconds before he blacked out. The automatic was of no use to him in a situation like this, so he opened his fingers and let it fall, Monk's grip on his wrist still not slackening. The bodyguard was gurgling close to his ear, an animal sound. With his free hand, Halloran reached down behind him and found the fleshy part of Monk's inner thigh. He pinched with thumb and bent knuckle, squeezing with all his strength so that his assailant screamed, a high-pitched woman's cry. The hold on Halloran loosened and he wrenched the arm away.

He whirled and grabbed for the other man's throat, both of them going down slowly as he exerted pressure. Monk tried to pull the hands away, but Halloran's rage could not be opposed. Monk's small eyes began to bulge. The two men's faces were inches away as they sank to their knees, Monk making snorting noises as his face reddened. His thick lips curled back, the tip of his tongue quivered over his teeth. He spat mucus into Halloran's eyes.

Surprised and blinded, the operative loosened his grip fractionally. A blow to his stomach doubled him over, his fingers raking down Monk's chest. A swipe to his head sent Halloran scudding across the floor.

The other man rose and lumbered toward him, hurling himself forward the last few feet, intending to crush Halloran's chest with his bent knees. Halloran sensed the move as he wiped the stickiness from his eyes and rolled backward, scattering books. His naked opponent landed heavily on empty space. They rose together, but Halloran was faster. His toe cap smashed into Monk's groin. The bodyguard collapsed to his knees again and Halloran moved behind him. Again Halloran pulled Monk back by his long hair, holding him upright. Lightning flared outside, freezing their bodies momentarily. The operative's other fist clenched, middle knuckle raised slightly. His aim was straight and powerful as the fist cracked into a certain vertebra at the back of the kneeling man's neck.

Thunder drowned the cracking of bone.

Halloran reached out to a bedpost for support as the stiffened figure below him swayed, then slumped to the floor. He drew in deep lungfuls of incense-filled air, anger still raging inside, revulsion at Kline and the corruption around him heaving at his stomach.

In that distraction—his rage, his disgust—he failed to notice the figure that had watched everything from behind the door. He heard, or perhaps he sensed, a footstep though, but it was too late.

As he began to turn, Janusz Palusinski brought a short metal bar down against his temple. The oblivion was almost a relief.

41

THINGS FROM THE LAKE

They could hardly believe the power of the rain.

It pounded, weighing heavily on their shoulders and backs, making progress slippery and slow. At least the downpour rendered them less visible, their commander thought as he urged them along.

"What the hell is this, Danny?" McGuire yelled close to his ear. *"I've never known the likes!"*

A truer word never spoken. The man called Danny looked out at the lake and shivered, not from the cold. The water was as fierce as St. George's Channel in the worst winter months, a crossing he had made with loathing many times in the past. God in Heaven, it was eerie what was happening out there.

From the bank they had watched lightning strike the water more than once, sheening its tossed surface a silvery green, the froth on the shoreline luminous in the dark. The thunderclaps that followed had made their ears ring, caused them to throw themselves against the soaked earth as if mortar shells had dropped among them. His men were frightened, wanted to turn back. But that was not to be, and greater fear of their commander held them steady, kept them mindful of their duty.

They had been caught by the downpour on a steep embankment, the drenched soil slithery beneath their feet, the only handholds a few tree roots here and there. Two of the men walked along in the water itself, arms stretched out to the bank for support when the going got particularly tricky. Danny cursed the freak storm, wondering at it at the same time.

They had come this far and there was no turning back. Their man, their bastard target, was in the grand manor house they had glimpsed from afar, now but a few minutes away, and he was going to pay dearly for what he'd done. He was going to suffer for the suffering he had caused others. No doubting that, no turning tail now.

An alarmed shout from nearby. One of his men was sliding deeper into the churning water, his Armalite raised high. His companion, who had been wading behind, reached out to pull him up.

A jagged lightning streak pierced the lake, a startling irradiation instantly spreading outward. The crack of thunder overhead cowed the group, and in the white glare the leader saw the terrified expression of the two in the water, as if they had both received a shock.

They began to go under.

He slid down the embankment, shouting to the others to help their companions. But when he reached the edge of the water, his boots enveloped, parka smeared by mud, he stared in horror across the lake.

There were shapes out there.

Canescent, hazy, almost lost in the sheeting rain, but nevertheless discernible rearing shapes that were part of the storm itself.

It was impossible. He wiped wetness from his eyes, doubtful of what he saw. But they were there, growing like gray amorphous monsters out of the waves.

Something bumped into him and he turned with a start. McGuire—he *thought* it was McGuire in the dismal light— was also watching the lake, his mouth working loosely as though he had lost the power of speech.

A scream, and they saw their two companions were in the water up to their shoulders.

"Help them!" Danny yelled, scrabbling forward. He noticed that the Armalite was gone and swore at the frightened subordinate who had dropped it. Another of his men was closer and was leaning over, stretching an arm out to the two in the water.

But everyone stopped when whiteness flooded the sky and another discharge channeled itself to the lake, the shifted air booming. It was what they suddenly saw beneath the surface that had frozen them.

Vague, nebulous forms filled the water below, massing together, squirming spasmodically, tendril-like appendages waving in the currents, occupying the lake as though it were filled not with water but moving, liquid beings.

A waterspout erupted, then swooped down, like a tentacle, curling around the two men who clawed at the bank. It drew them into the lake and their screams became a bubbling froth. It seemed, although it was too dark to be certain, that other smaller tendrils of fluid pulled at them too.

The leader shuddered incredulously, then gasped when something tightened around his own ankle. With a frightened cry, he jerked his leg clear, and perhaps it was merely overwrought imagination that caused him to think a watery claw had risen with his leg to plop shapeless back into the choppy lake.

The two men were gone, he knew that. There was no helping them at all. He scrambled up the embankment, digging toes and hands into the slimy soil, afraid he would slide back into the water to lie among those things stirring there. His two remaining men were following suit, scrambling away from the foamy lake where waterspouts resembling misshapen creatures burst upward into the stormy night.

Waves hurled themselves at the climbing men as if to drag them back, but they plunged their fingers into the mud, using tree roots whenever their fumbling hands chanced upon them, grateful for every inch they could gain.

They collapsed on the grass at the top of the embankment, rolling over and over into the bushes, putting as much distance between themselves and the edge of the water as possible. At last they settled among the trees, trembling and panting, the force of the rain tempered by the leafy canopy above them.

"For God's sake, let's get away from here!"

Danny recognized McGuire's voice, distorted by terror though it was.

"No," he said, loud enough to be heard over the storm. "Whatever it was back there can't harm us now." He was shocked, stunned by what had happened and the loss of two good men. But Danny Shay was a determined man. An executioner who had already tortured and killed one person to locate his intended victim.

He rose and grabbed the shoulders of his exhausted companions, hauling them to their feet.

"Get yourselves moving," he told them. "The house isn't far, and there's a bastard there deservin' to die."

42

SEPULCHRE

As in the dream, there were large, staring eyes watching him. Unnatural eyes. Stone eyes.

Halloran held his breath as pain ached through his head. He raised a leaden hand to his forehead and held his temples, exerting soft pressure with fingers and thumb. The ache eased only slightly. He blinked, taking in the statues, a gathering of them, thirty at least, standing a few yards away. Observing. A few were in groups, man, woman, and child. Some were at least five feet high. Their fixed gaze was inescapable.

Among them in a high-backed ornate chair was a figure, this of flesh and blood, for it shifted slightly when Halloran pushed himself up onto an elbow. The figure settled back, a formless shadow amid the sculptures.

The floor was wet where Halloran lay, grimy water seeping through the cracks in the flagstones. The dampness brought with it a putrid smell, a different odor underlying that. Melting wax. The chamber was lit by hosts of black candles, their glow soft and unsteady.

"Help him to his knees," a voice said. It might have been Kline's except its rasping quality reminded Halloran of the lodgekeeper.

Hands pulled at him roughly, and his mind was too dulled for him to resist. As he knelt, something passed around his throat, and a sudden sharpness there jerked him erect. He tried to twist away and the pressure increased. His hands went to the cause, but there was nothing they could grip.

"Struggle and the wire will bite deeper," the same voice warned.

Halloran couldn't see the person behind him, but he could

feel whoever it was leaning into his back. A spiciness wafted down among the other smells.

"Youssef is master of the garrote," came the voice again, and this time he was sure it was Kline sitting there in the shadows, even though the tones were roughened. "Try to resist and you'll find out for yourself." There was a weariness to his words that made Kline seem very old.

When Halloran took his hands away they were smeared with his own blood.

"Let him see, Youssef. Let him see where he is."

The pressure slackened and Halloran was able to look around, although his view was restricted. The room was long and high-ceilinged, and the walls glinted in the candlelight as if water were trickling through the brickwork. A solid stairway led upward, and Halloran saw there was a passage but no door in the darkness at the top. There were archways around the sides of the chamber, as though the place might once have been used as a wine cellar; there was no way of knowing what was inside those cavities now, for they were cast into the deepest shadows. In addition to the candles, there were oil lamps here and there helping to light the place, these close to pedestals on which stood delicately worked statues and effigies in shiny metals. On one near to where Halloran knelt there was what appeared to be a goat rearing up on hind legs against a tree of gold, the animal's fleece of deep blue stone and white shell. The small statue was exquisite, but Halloran's eyes did not linger on it for long.

At one end of the room was a large rectangular slab of stone that rose from the floor, its surface a mat black. A parody of an altar. Spread across it, and lying perfectly still, was an obese, naked figure, thick curling hair covering its body. Halloran wondered if Monk were dead.

The rasping voice broke through his thoughts. "Impressive, Halloran. You paralyzed him; he can't move, can't raise a finger. Useless to me as a bodyguard, but valuable in another way..."

From outside came a belly rumble of thunder, the sound muted, a long way away.

The shadow stirred again, shifting in the seat. "A bad night up there," Kline said, something of his old, excitable self in the remark despite the distortion in his voice. "Hope your knees aren't getting too wet, Halloran. So many underground streams running through the estate, you see, with all these hills around. When the lake swells, so do they—"

"What is this place, Kline?" The question was quietly put, but Halloran's tone stopped the other man.

Kline studied the operative for a while before giving an answer. When he drew in a breath the sound was wheezy, as though his throat were constricted. "A hiding place," he said finally. "A sepulchre, Halloran, my very own sepulchre. A room no one would ever find unless they knew of it, and even then they'd have problems. Oh, it's always been here at Neath, I didn't have to *create* it. I had to disguise its existence, though. This place is a subcellar, you see. A passageway extends to the real one, but I had it bricked off so no one'd ever know." His giggle was dry, a scratchy sound. "Ingenious, huh? Just like the old Sumerian tombs. Impossible to get in, and impossible to get out unless you know how. You could rot in here, Halloran, and no one would ever find you."

Halloran tried to rise, but the wire around his neck tightened instantly.

"Two, maybe three seconds is all it'd take for Youssef to kill you, so don't be bloody stupid."

"For God's sake, why, Kline? I'm here to protect you." Still Halloran did not raise his voice. A coldness was in him, one he knew so well. A deadness of emotion.

"God? God has nothing to do with this. Not your God. Only mine." The wheezing breath, a movement in the shadows. Then he said: "You killed the Keeper."

"The gate keeper? He was dying, he'd lost control of the dogs—the jackals. They tore him to pieces. But how did you know he was dead . . . ?"

"You still doubt my abilities?" Kline was shaking his head. "More than just our minds were linked, Halloran. He was surrogate for my ills, my weaknesses. He took my years. Through him I was allowed to live without blemish, without aging, free to use my faculties without hindrance."

"The old man said you'd used him."

"I was allowed that gift."

"Allowed?"

"The power to discharge those physical things we all dread, the disadvantages that come with the years and with debility, was bestowed upon me. Now that power is waning.

Something has happened and nothing is right anymore. You killed my Keeper, you broke the link."

"I told you he was dying before the jackals got to him. The strange thing is he seemed glad to be dying."

"He was a fool."

"Listen, Kline, I want you to tell this idiot to take the wire away from my neck."

"After what you did to Monk?"

"I'm going to hurt him if he doesn't."

"I don't think so, Halloran. I don't think you're *that* good. Besides, you want your curiosity satisfied, don't you? You want to learn some more history. Last night I only meant to whet your appetite."

"Kline . . ." Halloran warned.

"Be quiet!" Kline's hands clenched over the chair arms. He shuddered, as if it had hurt to raise his voice. "You're going to pay for what you've done. You're going to help stop what . . . what's . . . happening to me." He slumped back, and Halloran could see the rise and fall of his narrow shoulders, could hear the squeezing of his breath.

When he spoke, Kline's voice was low again, the sudden verve gone. He sounded ancient, like the old man in the lodge house. "Be patient and listen, Halloran, because I want you to understand. You deserve that at least. Let me tell you about the god who walked this earth three thousand years *before* the Christ God. I'm sure you're no devotee of the Scriptures, but no doubt you had them drummed into you by your Catholic priests when you were a boy in Ireland. Let me make some sense of their fairy tales, allow me that."

"Do I have a choice?"

"Yes. Youssef could kill you now."

Halloran said nothing.

A dry snigger from Kline. "How precious time becomes when there's little of it left, even for those who have lived so long . . ."

The candle flames swayed as though a draft had swept in.

"The man-god was called Marduk by his chosen people, the Sumerians," Kline began, while Halloran wondered how long the Arab could keep the garrote tensed. "He civilized the Sumerians, advanced them, taught them the written word, revealed to them the secret of the stars, instilled order into their society. It was from him that they learned to cure by cutting into the human body, how to forge metals dug from rock, to make tools and instruments, to use vehicles for carrying. Was that evil? How could it be? It was knowledge. But for those mortals who ruled, such learning was regarded as a threat because it usurped their power. That was the fear of the Sumerian kings and certain high priests. And hasn't that always been the fear of your Christian God?"

The question was put slyly, Kline's tenor changing constantly, a shifting of character that Halloran had become used to, but the change never before as abrupt as this. It was as if Kline had little control over himself.

"But perhaps it was the other knowledge that these rulers feared most, because that *gave* power. I mean the knowledge of magic, the ways of alchemy, the understanding of the Cabala, the art of witchcraft.

"For more than a thousand years he influenced them, and how the Sumerian people enjoyed his control. All he asked in return was their worship, their veneration of his ways. Burnt offerings pleased him, the roasting of men, women, and children. Defilement of the other gods he demanded. The torture of innocents was an appeasement to him, for they also feared Marduk as much as their rulers did. The kings and princes, the other high priests, were powerless to act against him. Until King Hammurabi, that is, who united all the state leaders against Marduk, whom he declared was an evil god who should be known forevermore as *Bel*-Marduk."

Halloran glanced up at the stairway. He thought he had heard movement in the passage.

"The king denounced Bel-Marduk as a fallen god," Kline went on in a voice that lurched with anger. "Much later the Jews referred to him as the Fallen Angel."

Halloran frowned.

"Ah, I see a glimmer of understanding," Kline remarked. "Yes, I do mean the Fallen Angel of the Bible, later to become known as the Devil."

The lilt of Irish was in Halloran's mild comment. "You're crazy, Kline."

A silence.

Then a low chuckle.

"One of us might be," said Kline. "But listen on, there's more to tell."

The staring eyes of the stone effigies around the shaded

figure seemed threatening. Halloran tried to close them from his mind.

"Bel-Marduk was destroyed for preaching the 'perverted message.' His limbs were torn from him, his tongue cut out, so that his immortal soul would be trapped inside a body that could only lie in the dirt. The priests rendered him as a snake, and they called him Serpent."

The dark figure leaned forward. "Does it sound familiar to you, Halloran? Didn't your Catholic priests teach you of Lucifer, the Fallen Angel, who was cursed to crawl in the dust as a snake for his corruption of the innocents, for revealing the secrets of the Tree of Knowledge of Good and Evil to the unworthy? Don't you see where those stories of the Bible come from? I told you last night that the traditional site of the Garden of Eden was the land between the rivers Tigris and Euphrates in Sumeria from where, according to tablets found in Mesopotamia, the Jewish race originated. It was from Ur of the Chaldees that Abraham led his tribe into Syria, then through Canaan into Egypt. They took with them stories that later became the myths of their Bible. The Great Flood, the baby Moses found among bulrushes—borrowed history! The Hebrew account of the Creation and the first chapters of Genesis—they were based on old Sumerian legends. Legends because the old kings had ordered all records of their early history to be destroyed, their way of ensuring Bel-Marduk's corruption would not be passed on to other generations. But they didn't understand how evil can be inherited, not learned from the written word."

There were figures at the top of the stairs, but Kline appeared not to notice.

"We Jews even adopted the Cabala as our own, claiming it was passed on from Noah to Abraham, from Abraham to Moses, who initiated seventy elders into the mysteries during their years of wandering in the wilderness. Bel-Marduk's teachings were never discontinued, nor was his revenge on mankind! Even the other man-god, Jesus Christ, who chose the Jews as his people, couldn't stem the flow! He came to undo the Serpent's work, the only way of redeeming earth's people. And look what happened, Halloran. He was executed, just like his predecessor, Bel-Marduk! Makes you wonder why he bothered, doesn't it? Look around you today, Halloran, and you'll see the conflict still goes on. You're part of it, I'm part of it."

Kline leaned forward once more. "The question is," he said craftily, "on which side of the struggle are *you?*"

Halloran could give no answer.

Kline pushed himself back into the chair. *"Bring her down!"* he called out.

There was movement from above and Halloran raised his eyes to see Cora, flanked by Palusinski and the other Arab, descending the stairway. She wore her bathrobe, its belt tied loosely at the front, and her step was unsteady. When she reached the bottom and looked around, the soft bewilderment in her eyes was obvious. He wondered if the drug had been forced upon her.

"Liam . . ." she began to say on seeing him.

"Concerned for your lover, Cora dear?" came Kline's voice from the shadows. Now there was fear as she looked toward the source.

"What are you going to do with her, Kline?" Halloran demanded.

"Nothing at all. Cora won't be harmed. I haven't groomed her for that. But I need a new ally, you see, someone who'll watch for me. I always knew a replacement would be necessary one day; I just didn't realize how imminent that day was."

"You can't make her take *his* place."

"Oh, I can. She's filth, Halloran, degenerate. You must understand that by now. She's become—no, she's *almost* become—what I've always wanted her to be. The final depravity is about to happen."

"You made her like this?"

"Of course. Cora was a sweet little thing when she first came to my attention, much too good for the likes of you and me. An English Rose, you might say. It was an interesting exercise turning her into something else."

"With drugs?"

"At the beginning. She never even realized. A few drops of something mixed with her food or her drink, enough only to soften her inhibitions. A gradual process, an extremely slow journey into degradation. Eventually the drugs were hardly necessary—I'd helped Cora develop certain 'tastes.' There was more to be achieved before she became mine completely, but now time is too precious, the process has to be hastened if she's to fulfill her role."

The wire was cruel against his throat as Halloran tensed. "You can't make her into something like that."

"Like my Keeper? Why not? Who would know, who would care? She'll merely leave the employ of the Magma Corporation to become my private assistant. These kinds of relationships develop all the time in business, surely you know that?"

"This is insane."

"That's a stupid assertion you keep making, Halloran. You don't believe anything I've told you."

Despite his anger, Halloran smiled.

"You confuse me," Kline said, weariness heavy in his voice. "For a while I thought you could be of use to me, like the others. I searched the world for men such as Palusinski and Monk, Khayed and Daoud, seeking out wickedness wherever it might lurk. They're indebted to me, these men, because I gave them a channel for their evil—and such a fine evil it is. There are more, many more, as these four, and I use them on my journeys. You could have joined us because you're not unlike them. Yet I can't know you, and that makes me wary. You saved me from assassination—my dreams and my senses have told me the threat is near—but still I can't bring myself to trust you. You're an enigma, and while that may have its fascination for me, I see no reason to have an unknown quantity so close, particularly at a time when things are not as they should be. No, you'll have to be disposed of."

The wire bit deeper as the Arab behind Halloran giggled.

"Aren't you forgetting something?" the operative managed to say despite the constriction of his throat. The wire loosened once more, and he swallowed hard.

"Tell me." It came as a sneer.

"My organization knows where I am, who I'm working for. I can't just disappear."

"Tut, tut," Kline said flatly. "What a fool I am for overlooking that." The mocking ceased just as abruptly. "Don't you see? You put up a valiant fight against intruders, but they murdered you before my own bodyguards drove them off. How's that? Convincing? Who can prove otherwise? And incidentally, Monk was one of them, a traitor in our midst. He went with them after we fought them off. In fact, he was the swine who murdered you."

Halloran ignored the laughter. "Cora—"

"She won't be saying anything against me after tonight!" Kline snapped. His hands thumped the side of the chair. "Time to press on. All this talk is wearying. Help me, Asil."

The Arab brushed past Cora and Palusinski and hurried to where his master sat among the effigies.

"Let Halloran stand, Youssef, but watch him, keep him harnessed."

The wire brought Halloran to his feet, and he had to concentrate to keep himself steady, for his head was still groggy. Cora took a step toward him, and Palusinski grabbed her to hold her back. She looked dumbly at the Pole's hand as though wondering what it was doing on her arm.

Kline, assisted by Khayed, was rising from the shadows. He came forward, movement slow, an old man's shuffle, his servant close by his side. Part of the darkness came with him, for he was wearing a black robe whose hem swept along the floor. He left the statues.

He came into the light.

"Jesus, Mary. . ." Halloran breathed.

43

THE OPEN GATES

Rain lashed the windshield, the wipers barely able to keep the glass clear. Charles Mather peered over the steering wheel, his whole body tensed, the aching in his leg bad.

He was close, he was sure of that. The entrance to Neath had to be nearby. Unfortunately, the rain made it impossible to see too far ahead. Damned incredible night, he mused irritably. The storm was as fierce now as when it had first begun nearly an hour ago, with no sign of abating. The clouds were black and ragged with inner strife, the thunder they threw out rattling his very bones.

Lightning lit the way, whitewashing the landscape. The earth threatened to split under the explosive *crack* that accompanied the light.

It would have been safer—and more sensible—to have pulled over by the roadside and wait out the storm, but Mather would not consider doing that. He was too concerned for Liam Halloran. Something had been wrong with this assignment all along, and the revelation by Magma's chairman earlier that evening had furthered Mather's disquiet. Snaith himself had given the go-ahead to bring out their operative, although he had not personally felt Halloran was at risk. No, the Controller was more unhappy with the Magma Corporation's unreliable conduct, for deceit could easily jeopardize an operation of this sort. "Negative factor" was the term used by Achilles' Shield when carefully laid plans could be put at risk by deliberate misinformation. Under such circumstances, a commission could be resigned at once, and every Shield contract contained a get-out clause covering this particular area. As Magma had been quite prepared to withhold certain vital information, they could not be regarded as a trustworthy client.

Mather had agreed with his Controller on that score, but it was Sir Victor Penlock's insinuation that bothered him more.

Felix Kline was not an employee of the Magma Corporation. Far from it. He *was* Magma. Many years before, Mather had learned, he had taken over an existing mineral and energy research-and-development company, acquiring fifty-two percent of the stock through various other worldwide companies that had no connection with Magma. The secret of ownership had been kept because of "credibility" in the all-important city market—no financial adviser would recommend investment in a company whose major shareholder was a so-called "mystic." The world of high finance was not known for its sense of humor.

If Shield had been made aware of Kline's true role within the organization, then a much more comprehensive plan of action would have been undertaken and a larger protection force, with even more stringent restrictions, employed. As it was, Magma had used a blindfold on the agency.

But what concerned Mather most, though, was Sir Victor's suggestion that Kline might have been responsible for Quinn-Reece's death in some way. The deputy chairman had succumbed to heart failure, surely. But there had been others in conflict with the psychic in the past who had also died of sudden and, in two cases at least, inexplicable cardiac arrests. Three others, to be precise. One inside the corporation, a board member who had constantly opposed plans for development put forward (albeit surreptitiously) by Kline; another had been from a rival company, whose persistent investigations were slowly unraveling Kline's real worth to Magma; the third had been a communications magnate who had instigated a takeover bid for the corporation. This man had a known heart condition, but when he had been found dead from a massive coronary in his bed one morning, a look of sheer horror had been frozen into his features. It was concluded that a nightmare had aggravated his diseased heart to the point of killing him. But both Sir Victor and Mather had seen the horror-struck look also on Quinn-Reece's face.

There had been other incidents through the years, and the chairman had confessed to Mather that he himself had begun to live in fear of Kline's strange powers. Although nothing could be proved, Sir Victor realized there had been too many mysterious "happenings" to be ignored.

Why Quinn-Reece? Mather had demanded. What on earth could Kline have against his own deputy chairman?

Sir Victor had explained that for some time Kline had suspected Quinn-Reece of leaking news of possible mineral sites for development to another company. Indeed, he and the chairman had discussed those suspicions on more than one occasion. However, this time Kline had accused his personal assistant, Cora Redmile. But the chairman was accustomed to the psychic's deviousness, and Quinn-Reece's subsequent death was too much of a coincidence to be taken lightly. Yet there was no proof, none at all. Only misgivings.

That was enough for Mather. He already had doubts about the assignment, a gut feeling that things weren't quite right. The torture of Dieter Stuhr had added to his concern, for torture, unless perversion was involved, usually meant information was being sought of the victim. That information might well have been to do with Shield's security arrangements for Felix Kline. Somewhat drastic perhaps, but when huge sums of ransom money were involved kidnappers had few scruples. And then there was always the possibility that more than just abduction was in mind. Kline might well be a target for assassination—God only knew what enemies the man had.

Mather had left the Magma building and had gone straight to the home of Gerald Snaith with the recommendation that the contract be declared null and void. That had been over two hours ago, but he felt he had been driving for much longer.

Mather used the booster fan to clear vapor from the windshield, his own breath, because he was so close to the glass, contributing to the mist. For a few moments he was driving blind, and he slowed the car almost to a halt. He pushed another button and the driver's window slid down. Raindrops pounded at his face when he looked at the road ahead. There was a wall to his left, set back, undergrowth thick before it; on the opposite side of the road was forest. He ducked his head back inside and wiped a handkerchief across his face.

A light behind, dazzling in the rearview mirror, was coming up slowly. A car's headlights.

They blinked once, twice. He grunted with satisfaction when they blinked a third time.

Mather touched his brakes twice in acknowledgment, then

pulled over to the side of the road, bringing the car to a halt. He waited for one of the two men in the vehicle behind to come to him.

"Didn't expect you, sir," the operative said loudly enough to be heard over the storm. He crouched at the open window, collar up against the rain. "Gave us a surprise, seeing your license plate."

"I've been trying to reach you on the radio," Mather complained.

"The storm's fouled up communications. Never known one like this before. We've kept in touch with the other patrol by stopping each time we meet en route. What's up, Mr. Mather, what brings you here?"

"We're pulling out."

"Shit, you're joking."

"I'm afraid not. Anything occurred tonight that you're not happy about?"

"Only this bloody weather. Visibility's down to twenty yards."

"Where's the entrance to the estate?"

"Gates are up ahead, on the left. You're nearly there."

"Follow me down, I'll brief you off the road."

The operative shrugged, then ran back to the Granada. Mather set his car in motion, going slowly, looking for the gates. An open area swept back from the roadway, and he turned into it, driving right up to the tall gates. There should be . . . yes, there it was. A dark, bulky shape that had to be the lodge house. No lights on. Well, you'll have to get out of bed, chum, if that's where you are.

Mather flashed his headlights, beeping the horn at the same time.

Lightning blazed the sky, thunder rent the air, and the lodge house appeared as a bright, flickering image. Mather's eyes narrowed. Had there been something moving in front of it?

The patrol car came to a halt beside his, and Mather reached for his cane before stepping out. Both men joined him at the gates.

"Is there anyone inside?" he asked, pointing at the building with his cane.

"There's supposed to be someone there all the time to

operate the gates," one of the men replied. "Never seen the bugger, though."

Mather reached and pushed at an iron strut. That half of the gates swung open a few inches.

The three men exchanged glances.

"Something's wrong," Mather said.

"Could be an oversight."

The Planner shook his head. "I'm going in. I want you to find the other patrol and follow."

"We're not allowed in—"

"Forget about that. You just come after me as fast as you can. Phil, you'll come with me."

"Right, sir."

"Why not wait for the other patrol?" the second man asked, suddenly anxious.

Mather had no adequate answer, only a sense of urgency pressing him. "Just get on with it!" he barked. "Open them up, Phil."

He limped back to his car as the operative swung the gates wide. The other man climbed into the Granada and reversed into the road.

Mather settled uncomfortably into the driver's seat, his clothes soaked. He dreaded to think of the agony his leg would give him tomorrow. He took the car through the entrance, pausing just long enough for his operative to jump in beside him.

"Christ, what's that over by the house?"

Mather looked toward where the other man was pointing. Blurred shapes were moving slowly in the rain.

"Dogs," the operative said. "Must be the guard dogs. Funny, it's the first time I've laid eyes on them."

"Can you see how many?"

"Difficult in this rain. I can only make out a couple. Oh shit, there's others lying on the ground."

Mather wasted no more time. He pushed down hard on the accelerator and the car sped down the drive. Soon it entered a tunnel of trees.

44

A SACRIFICE

Halloran was stunned by the change in Felix Kline.

This was an old and bent man emerging from the shadows, one whose skin was cracked and scaly, ruffles of tissue hanging loose, pieces flaking away as he shuffled forward. Oil glistened over fissures in his flesh, dulling the rawness beneath. His hair trailed flatly over his skull and forehead, whitish seams crosshatching under the blackness, and his hands were mostly vivid pink, their outer layer all but entirely shed. Kline's breathing was husky with the effort of moving.

He came to an unsteady halt before Halloran, and even his grin seemed corroded.

"Scary, huh?" Kline said, none of his mocking arrogance lost. "It isn't irreversible, though. It isn't too late, Halloran. Maybe it's worse than ever before, but at least now I understand why."

The hideous face was close, eyes red-rimmed and bloodshot. With Daoud behind him, Halloran could not pull away. Kline had the same smell of decay as the old man in the lodge house.

"You took my surrogate," Kline hissed. "You killed him and upset the balance. I should only slough my skin once a year, that's part of the deal, my price for immortality. Like a serpent, you see, Halloran. Bel-Marduk made me like a serpent."

He gasped, a pain reaching him somewhere inside. Blood squeezed from a crack in his disfigured face to mix with the oily gel.

"There's a way to stop this deterioration. You'll see, Halloran, you'll see. You'll be part of it."

He turned away and with Khayed's help hobbled through

the puddles on the floor, passing by Palusinski and Cora, the Pole stepping back as if the shambling figure were a leper. The girl seemed mesmerized. Candlelight reflected from the glistening on Kline's head.

It took a long time for him to get to the slab of stone near the end of the room, and he reached out for it, staggering the last few feet despite Khayed's help. Kline eased himself around the stone so that he faced the others. An impatient hand beckoned them to him.

Palusinski led the girl, and it took only slight pressure from the wire to make Halloran follow. His eyes darted left and right as he and the Arab passed the archways, searching for possibilities, a weapon perhaps, should he manage to break free of the stranglehold. All he could make out in the shadows were stone tables, scored with symbols similar to those he had seen around the house itself.

Then he found himself looking down at the bloated body lying on the slab. And Monk's small, inset eyes stared back at him, his fat fingers twitching as if he were trying to move his body. Those eyes showed no pain, only hatred.

Halloran was surprised that the man was still conscious. He glanced over at Cora, who was frowning, at last some sensibility returning to her gaze.

"Do you see him, Monk?" Kline's voice was all the more insidious for its guttural roughness. "He did this to you, made you nothing. How you'd like to kill him. But no, my friend, that's impossible for you now. But I have a use for you."

Fear replaced the hate in the bodyguard's eyes as they darted toward Kline.

"Another injection, Asil," Kline told the Arab. "I don't want the pain to kill him. The cutting will do that."

The Arab ghosted away.

"The correct dosage is important," said Kline, touching his skinless hands to Monk's body. "Enough so that he doesn't feel the shock of the blade, but not enough to allow dreams to take him from us. Fortunately Asil has become something of a specialist over the years."

Anger surged in Halloran, but he held it in check, biding his time. "You turned Cora into an addict," he said.

"Oh no, not an addict, not in the true sense. Not yet. She'd be useless to me if she were. I told you, Asil is expert in such matters. Cora is dependent on me, not on any drug."

The Arab had returned to Kline's side, in his hand a syringe filled with liquid. He smoothed away hair on Monk's arm and pierced a vein with the needle. He emptied half of the liquid into the bodyguard.

Within moments, the bodyguard's eyes took on a dull glaze and the corners of his mouth flickered.

"What are you going to do with him?" Halloran asked sharply.

Kline drew in a long, gravelly breath and gripped the stone to support himself. Still he managed to grin at Halloran, his peeled lips blood red against the yellow decay of his teeth. "I'm going to feed off him," he replied simply.

In a night of gross horrors, when nightmares were living, Halloran was further repulsed.

Although delighted with the obvious discomfort his words had caused the operative, Kline shook his head. "Not his flesh, Palusinski can fill himself with that afterwards. I need something more, Halloran, something that has no substance, no materiality. The part of him that will be set free at his moment of death." A luminescence glittered in the darkness of Kline's eyes. "The ethereal energy that's the source of our existence. The psyche, Halloran, the soul. Can you understand that?"

Again Halloran felt a loosening of the pressure around his neck. Daoud's concentration was wavering. "If I understood, I'd be crazy like you," the operative replied.

Kline straightened, his look fixed on the operative. The bodyguard lying on the stone between them moaned either with pleasure or trepidation; the emotion was not clear.

"You're still a mystery to me," Kline said to the operative. "My psychic faculties are dimmed where you're concerned. Why is that, Halloran? What is it about you . . . ?"

"I'm just a hired bodyguard, nothing more than that."

Kline's stare did not shift. "But you're a danger to me."

"No, I'm here to prevent any harm coming to you." Halloran tensed the muscles of his arms, preparing himself to strike, concentrating his strength. "Tell me, Kline, tell me what this is all about."

"I've already explained."

"I'd like to know more. How can you . . . ?" He couldn't find the words; it felt too ridiculous to try.

"Tap into someone's soul?" the psychic finished for him.

"Absorb its vitality?" He laughed, a choking in his throat. "The secret was left for me." His eyes closed, the lids hideously raw, but his smile was rapturous. "I learned from the ancient cuneiform writings of the Master himself. They were hidden away with his remains, spread around him to give sustenance during his long wait. He drew me to them, so many years ago, a time of ignorance for me, when I was a shell waiting to be filled. I found his works in a chamber, a sepulchre beneath the Royal Cemetery of Ur, and piece by piece I smuggled them out, and piece by piece I had them deciphered so that no one else would understand their full message. Only then did I assemble them once more, when I knew the power contained within their symbols. They told of how potent were the powers of the mind, how they could be developed, channeled . . . how they could *create!*"

He swayed, his eyes remaining closed. Khayed reached out as if to steady him, but seemed afraid to touch.

Kline's voice became deeper in tone. "They taught the delights of perversity, the superiority that comes from corruption. I learned, you see, learned well, became an avid student. They instructed me in the ways of terror, they showed me how to seek out the evil in others and use it for my own ends. They revealed how I could escape the degenerating process, the wearing away of flesh and muscle, the shriveling of body and mind, how the decay could be transposed to others. They spoke of the secret link between the mind and the earth's own energy, how they could be coupled, and used together. And I feasted upon the knowledge!"

Kline's eyes sprung open, and the blackness in them almost filled the sockets.

"The price of it all was easy to pay," he whispered. "Dissension, wherever it could be spread. Atrocity, wherever it could be encouraged. Malevolence, wherever it could be nurtured. I learned to disperse my disruption, took it to many countries and let it fester. Because that was *his* way, and I am his disciple!"

Kline's hands were raised to his chest, palms upward, fingers curled into claws. He shuddered, a movement that threatened his collapse. But he righted himself, his mouth open in an agitated grin.

"There was another part to this bargain." Now he was stooping, twisting into himself. "An alliance between us. I was to keep Bel-Marduk forever with me, to sustain his bodily self, to keep it living."

A shiver ran through Halloran. There was nothing here of the Kline that he knew. The thing before him was unrecognizable in voice and body. Halloran felt weakened.

"You'll see," said the form opposite. "You'll understand how we breathe together."

Kline moved away, tottering as if about to fall. Yet still the Arab by his side was reluctant to take hold of him. Kline walked awkwardly to an alcove behind the altar, and the others watched, all of them motionless.

He entered the shadows.

Halloran heard something being opened.

Shuffling footsteps.

Kline returning, carrying something clutched to his chest into the candlelight . . .

45

NETHERWORLD RISING

Away from the bubbling lake they ran, throats roughened by harsh breaths, disarray in their stride. Two of their companions had been lost to the lightning-seared cauldron, and these remaining three had no intention of joining them; clumsy their flight may have been, pounding rain rendering earth and grass slippery beneath their feet, but their progress was determined, panic lending its own pace.

Despite himself, a terrible fascination tempted Danny Shay to look back over his shoulder, and he uttered a single alarmed cry at what he saw; he stumbled, went down, the man at his heels sprawling over him so that they both rolled in the soaked grass, kicking out at each other.

Shay sat up, rain streaming into his open mouth, while the other man, Flynn, beat at the earth in pain. McGuire realized he was alone and stopped, searching behind for the others.

"Glory God . . ." he moaned when he saw the lake.

Shay scrambled to his knees and Flynn reached out to grasp his shoulder. *"I've done my ankle, Danny!"* he shouted over the downpour. *"Give us a hand up!"*

But Shay stayed motionless, staring into the rain. Flynn followed his gaze and collapsed back into the grass.

A shining came from beneath the boiling surface of the water, a milky greenness that spread to the shoreline. A curling mist rose from it, turning in on itself like vapor reaching cooler air. Geysers popped and spouted, foamy liquid showering down to create ripples, more turmoil. But something else was disturbing the center of the broad lake. A great mass, hindered by its own weight, was slowly emerging like some huge sunken wreck pushed to the surface by an eruption on the seabed.

This was nothing man-made, though. It might have been regurgitation of a long-lost island, the waters finally relinquishing their claim. Except it was a living, pulsating thing. A mass that swelled and writhed, a gathering in oozing mud of all those nebulous creatures the men had glimpsed earlier beneath the unsettled ceiling of the lake, the forms clinging together as if congealed. Pieces—*living things*—dropped away as this ill-shaped mountain grew; lake water drained off to fall with the rain. Monsters of immense size were among that curling, viscous mass, while leaner shapes wriggled and clung like parasites, the ascending heap never still, constantly bulging and quivering as it rose.

As the three frightened men watched, a bolt of lightning struck the top, sizzling and charring its uppermost layer as if it were flesh. Steam rose as the whole mass shrunk in spasm. It stretched once more, continuing to ascend. They thought they could hear a shrill wailing beneath the roar of thunder.

"What is it!" Flynn shrieked close to Shay's ear, the grip on his leader's shoulder tight.

Shay could only shake his head in a stupefied gesture.

"Let's leave this heathen place, Danny! There's no good for us here!"

The leader climbed to his feet, bringing Flynn up with him, his eyes never leaving the monstrosity growing from the lake, this seen through a screen of driving rain. McGuire joined them, afraid to be left standing alone. He clutched at Shay's other arm.

"There's no turning back!" the leader yelled. *"Whatever devil's work this is, it doesn't matter! It'll not stop us doing our job!"*

"No, it's a bad business, Danny!" McGuire protested.

Shay hit him with a back swipe of his hand. *"You'll do as you're told! The house is close, an' he's in there! We'll not leave until it's settled!"*

He shoved both men from him, forcing them to turn their backs on the lake with its phenomenon that could only be some kind of illusion—there *couldn't* be any reality to such a vision. Although . . . although didn't he see for himself two of his own men dragged down into its terrible depths?

Shay began running, cutting out further thought, intent on one purpose alone, urging McGuire and Flynn to follow. They did for, scared though they were, disobedience was unthinkable.

They did their best to ignore the squishy gurgling of the sinuous island as it heaved itself from the water, resisting the temptation (it was as though there were whispered *entreaties* in their minds to do so) to turn around and watch. They kept their eyes on the manor house that was now but a short distance away.

Most of the lights were on, a welcoming relief despite the duty they were bound to perform, a glorious beacon in the darkness they had traveled through.

They found themselves on firmer ground, gravel crunching under their feet as they dashed forward, no caution in their untidy gait. There was a porch at the front, an entrance like a darkened cave. Flynn strove to keep up with the others, the pain in his ankle a handicap, his hand tucked into his parka pocket, touching the revolver there for comfort. He suddenly slid to a halt.

There were headlights coming toward them!

A car on the road, moving fast, freezing them in its searching beams. It skidded to a stop twenty yards away. Doors were opening. Someone was shouting.

46

TOWARD DESTRUCTION

Candle flames flickered and dimmed momentarily, smoke curling from them, as Kline came closer, his hands livid against the blackness of the robe he wore. In them he held a black chalice, a cloth draped over the top.

All eyes were on the shuffling figure emerging from the alcove, and instinct told Halloran that this was the time to make his move. Yet he could not. Like the others, he was mesmerized.

Kline faltered, as though the weight of his burden was too much. But after drawing in a deep, grating breath, he continued to approach.

Thunder grumbled in the distance and it seemed to come from below, from the earth itself rather than the atmosphere above.

At last Kline, or the disfigured thing that Kline now was, reached the stone slab. He attempted to grin, perhaps in triumph, but his lips merely wavered, his stained teeth bared only partially. His hands were trembling when he placed the chalice on the altar. He removed the cloth, allowed it to fall to the floor. Then Kline dipped both hands into the vessel, the object he removed still unseen by the others. He held out his prize across the furred belly of the paralyzed bodyguard.

A husky whisper: "His disciples, his loyal priests, preserved his poor mutilated body. They hid Bel-Marduk away, a deep place where no one could find him. Hidden in darkness, his secrets around him, waiting out the centuries for one such as I . . ."

He placed the object on the stone beside the bodyguard, and there it rested for the others to see.

A blackened, crisped shell. A thing almost rotted away,

shriveled stumps that had once been tubes, but which now had no function, protruding.

And as they watched, the ancient withered heart pulsed.

Just once . . .

Mather had jammed on the handbrake and was opening the driver's door even before the car had rocked to a halt.

"Stop there!" he shouted, but the three figures either did not hear him over the storm or had no intention of heeding his command.

"Draw your weapon, Phil," he ordered. "Whoever they are, I don't want them to get inside the house."

Both men used the car doors as shields, the operative clenching a Browning with both hands, using the triangle between passenger door and frame as an armrest.

"Hold it!" he warned, but one of the figures, someone who appeared to be limping, whirled around, bringing something from the pocket of his parka as he did so. Flame spat out into the rainy night.

"Pacify him!" Mather yelled at his man as a bullet scythed sparks off the car roof. The operative would have preferred to have "retired" the gunman, a more permanent condition, but he knew better than to disobey an order. He took quick aim at the enemy's shoulder; unfortunately the target had changed position, had tried to follow his companions. The Shield operative knew by the way the man violently jerked, then dropped like a stone, that the bullet had taken him in the head or neck.

He muttered a curse but didn't take time to shrug an apology at Mather, for the other two intruders were disappearing into the porch.

He gave chase, skirting around the vehicles parked in front of the house, flattening himself against the outside wall of the porch, keeping out of sight until he could position himself. Realizing Mather had not followed, he looked back at their car. The Planner was facing the opposite direction, toward the lake.

They had noticed a strange shining from that area when they had broken free of the woods moments earlier to descend into the valley, but the rain had been too heavy to see clearly. Even this close it was difficult, for there was a mist rising from the peculiar incandescence that was the lake itself, creating a swirling fog that the rainfall failed to disperse. Mather tore himself away and began limping toward his companion, body crouched, cane digging into the gravel.

"What is it out there?" the operative asked when the older man reached him.

"I've no idea," came the breathless reply. "Some kind of disturbance in the lake, that's all I can tell. Let's worry about our immediate problem."

"Here comes the other patrol." The operative nodded toward the beams of light descending the hill at a fast pace.

"We can't wait for them. Check inside."

The other man ducked low, quickly peering into the tunnel of the porch and drawing his head back almost immediately.

"Shit," he said. "The door's open. They're inside the house."

It was a dream. It could only be a bad dream.

Yet Cora knew it wasn't. The nightmare around her was real. She tried to focus her mind, desperate to understand what was happening, why Monk, that bloated, repellent creature, was lying naked on the stone, and . . . and . . . Shock broke through the haze.

The black-robed figure standing on the other side of the bodyguard was obscene in its deformity. Only the eyes allowed some recognition.

"Felix . . . ?" She imagined she had said the name aloud, but in fact it had been no more than a murmur.

She held up her hands to her face, not because of the unsightliness in front of her, but to clear her thoughts . . .

. . . While Halloran's mind was sharp by now, all grogginess gone. He stared disbelievingly at the blackened object lying on the stone altar.

"It can't be," he whispered.

"But it is. The only part of Bel-Marduk that survived his mutilated body's entombment. His heart."

"Impossible."

"Naturally."

"Kline, let's stop this nonsense. Let me walk away with Cora—"

Kline screamed across at him, a furious cry that might have been anguish. The wire noose around Halloran's neck jerked tight, and he was dragged backward by Daoud, away from the altar, his legs giving way so that he fell to the wet floor, the

Arab crouching behind him, maintaining the pressure. Cora took a step toward them, then collapsed back against the stone.

"There's still more to be done, Halloran!" Kline screeched. "Especially now, in this era of awesome power, when we hold the very weapons of our own genocide. *Don't you understand that he directed mankind toward this point, he set us on this road!* A few more decades, that's all it will take. A microsecond in earth's lifespan. A few more years of disruption and dissent, of famine and disease, of wars and violence. A culmination of evils, when the balance between good and bad has been tilted irrevocably toward *his,* Bel-Marduk's, way! I showed you the lake, Halloran, allowed you to see its contents. A residue, like many others around the world, of our own corruption, a manifestation of our evils in living form. *You saw them, you recognized your own culpability, your own vileness!* We're not unalike, you and I, Halloran. You just have a little further to travel."

Kline was leaning over Monk's body, sucking in air, exhausted, drained by his own beliefs. "I could have made you one of mine, Halloran. A little encouragement, that's all it would have taken. But I can't trust you. I don't have time to." He calmed himself, or perhaps weariness did it for him. "She'll join us in our communion, Bel-Marduk's and mine. Cora will help us and be one of us." He levered himself up from the body. "Asil . . ."

The Arab stepped forward, and from beneath his robes he drew out a long blade, one edge thickened for weight so that it resembled a machete. The metal glowed in the candlelight.

He raised it over Monk's chest and the bodyguard's hands twitched frantically. His lips parted. A sobbing came from them.

Khayed brought down the blade with a short, sharp movement, minimum effort in the blow, for he needed only to pierce the breastbone so that the paralyzed man's ribs could be pulled apart, his heart exposed.

Monk shuddered. His hands and now his feet quivered as the finely honed blade was drawn down his stomach. The cutting stopped when muffled gunfire was heard from above.

47

ACROSS THE COURTYARD

"Hold 'em there, McGuire. Don't let anyone through the door."

McGuire looked at his leader apprehensively. "An' where the hell will you be?"

"Finding our man. He'll not escape."

"Are you fuckin' insane, man? There's nothing we can do now except mebbe get away ourselves."

"You'll do as I tell you, or it'll not only be me you'll answer to."

"An' what if he's not here?"

"Oh, the bastard's here all right, I can feel it in me piss."

"I'll give it five minutes, Danny, no more than that."

Shay decided it was pointless to argue. McGuire had always been the yellow one, enjoying the killing only if he was with a mob or guaranteed a safe getaway. Besides, five minutes should be enough; then he'd leave McGuire to his own fate. He turned away from the main doors, one side of which remained open, and quickly scanned the hall, taking no note of its grandness. It was a damned cold house, to be sure. And there was nothing good inside these old walls.

Shay ran across the stone floor, expecting someone to appear at any moment through one of the many doors that opened out onto the hall. He kept an eye on the stairs and landing too as he went, sure that anyone in the house would have heard the din outside.

Into a corridor he ran, revolver held before him like a pointer. He stopped and listened. Gunshots from the hall. McGuire was keeping whoever had driven up to the house at bay. Had they nabbed Flynn? he wondered. Things were going bad. He almost smiled. Things were fucking terrible.

A door was open at the end of the corridor, rain pouring in. What was this? The house couldn't be that narrow. He hurried to the doorway and looked outside, suddenly understanding the layout. A courtyard, filling up with rain by the looks of it. And what was that?

Light from another doorway opposite. Somebody there, like him, peering out.

Shay did not hesitate: he was through the door. Something was bubbling to his right, but he paid it no mind, realizing it was a fountain, the storm causing its basin to overflow.

He kept running as the other person spotted him, was backing away. The fool's attention must have been on the fountain before, not on the shadow bearing down on him through the storm. It had been Shay's luck that lightning had not struck during those few seconds.

He burst into the hallway and was able to reach out for the man who, too late, had attempted to flee. He pulled him around, clamping a hand over the man's mouth, then ramming the barrel of the gun beneath his captive's wire-rimmed spectacles so that they rose off his nose, the weapon hard against his closed eyelid.

48

BLOOD RITES

The Arab was murmuring an intonation that was breathless, his excitement conveyed through the wire that vibrated against Halloran's throat. Daoud watched the figures at the altar, fretful that he was unable to join them, but chanting the incantations learned from the cuneiform writings so that he was at least part of the ceremony.

A breeze swept down from the corridor above, bending the candle flames as it swirled around the underground chamber, ruffling the light so that shadows danced and weaved as though they also belonged to the rite.

At the stone slab that served as an altar, Felix Kline, aware that his strength was fading, his will weakening with it, urged Khayed to hurry. Tissue was breaking from him, falling onto the robe he wore, onto the open body lying below on the stone. He could feel fresh lesions forming, the flesh ulcerating and rupturing beneath his clothing, skin weeping pus, dribbling wetness. The pain was intense, as though every joint in his body was on fire, and his scalp was tightening around the skull, splitting apart as it shrank. This agony was like never before, and it was the significance of that which frightened Kline more than anything else. The torments of his sleep, the panic that had lingered afterward, the sense of deep foreboding—these were feelings he had not experienced since discovering the hidden tomb so many years before. *Why now, O Lord? Have I failed you in some way? Are you failing me, Bel-Marduk?* The questions were silent, his spoken invocations uninterrupted, for those ancient words were important to the ritual, their tonal values an inducing cadence for affinity between the psyche and the spiritual realms.

Khayed's hands were bloodied beyond the wrists as he

pulled at the sliced sides of the body to expose Monk's innards. The bodyguard's eyelids fluttered as life dwindled, receding within him so that it could expand outward through another dimension. The Arab tugged at Monk's exposed sternum, bending the ribs upward, then pushed sweating organs down toward the gut, reaching for the heart and dragging it clear, stretching arteries and breaking veins until the feebly pulsing organ was revealed. All a familiar and well-practiced ritual.

Kline took the other heart, the old shriveled husk that represented—that *was*—the existence of his deity. With one hand he lifted this shell, while with the other he reached for Cora's wrist. She was too numbed to resist, incomprehension still misted in her eyes.

But when Kline plunged both their hands into the gaping wound, the dried, withered thing held between them, she whimpered. When he settled the remnant organ against the fresh, bleeding one, using their hands as a vise, she screamed.

Cora felt her whole self being drawn down into the huge open wound, blood spurting along her arm, her hand disappearing into the quagmire. And it was the ancient petrified heart that sucked her in.

Kline was lost in a delirium of sensations, a euphoric rebirth without trauma, a vigor beginning to pulsate through him. All this ceased for him when the girl pulled her hand free, bringing with it the parasite heart.

Cora held the relic in her bloody grasp and stared loathingly at it for but a moment. Turning away, she cast it from her, a violent and sudden movement that neither Kline nor Khayed could prevent.

The brittle shell scudded across the stone floor and came to rest in a puddle of blackened water.

Now it was Kline who screamed, a piercing cry that echoed around the walls of the chamber.

And it was Halloran who took his chance.

With Daoud's attention on the dark, blood-soaked mound lying in the water only a few yards away, his grip loosened on the wooden handles of the garrote. Halloran, half-kneeling below the Arab, swiftly brought the point of his elbow up into the other man's groin. Daoud hissed, releasing one of the handles to clutch at himself, the wire cutting across Halloran's throat. The operative grabbed the Arab's ankle and pulled, sending his opponent crashing onto his back.

Despite the pain, Daoud kicked out at Halloran, toppling him as he tried to rise.

They came up together, but tears blurred the Arab's vision. Halloran's stiffened fingers jabbed at the front of Daoud's neck, striking for the thyroid cartilage. If his balance had allowed a greater force to the blow, the Arab would have been killed instantly; as it was, Daoud crouched over his knees, choking and gasping. Halloran half-rose, turning as he did so, ready to launch himself at the Arab's companions.

Cora had sunk down against the altar, blood from the open body above spilling over the edge to stain the shoulders of her white robe. Kline was stumbling around the stone slab, one hand against it for support, the other stretched out, fingers spread, as though reaching for the relic lying in the wetness of the floor some distance away. Khayed's gaze was fixed on his choking lover. Rage burned when it shifted to Halloran. Khayed lifted the long and broad chopping knife.

But others had entered the chamber.

Janusz Palusinski, whom Kline had ordered to investigate the earlier sound of gunfire, had returned. A man in a rain-drenched parka gripped the Pole's collar from behind; in his free hand was a revolver pointing at Palusinski's head.

Danny Shay was dismayed by what confronted him in the gloomy, candle-lit room. Dismayed, then fiercely angry. There were robed figures below him, one wielding a long, bloodstained knife, another in black wearing a hideous mask of some kind. There was a girl resting against a stone slab, her legs exposed, blood soaking her clothing. And the stone resembled an altar, and on that altar—oh dear God in Heaven! —there was a mutilated body, blood pumping from it like red springwater. There were moving shadows, dark alcoves that might have hidden others involved in this atrocity. Shay thumbed back the hammer of the .38.

And then his eyes came to rest on the man he had been seeking.

"Halloran!" he yelled.

The operative looked up toward the top of the stairway, as did the others in the chamber. Khayed became still, while Kline leaned heavily against the stone, a wildness in his eyes. Cora barely reacted, for the moment too disoriented to care.

The man with the gun shoved Palusinski away from him, and the Pole staggered down a few steps before cowering against the wall, folding himself up so that he was small, a poor attempt to make himself invisible. The weapon came around to point at Halloran.

"You've given the Organization a lot of grief, man," Shay said.

Halloran straightened slightly, his body remaining tensed. The man above him had spoken with a thick, southern-Irish accent, and a hint of the truth began to dawn in Halloran's mind.

"You killed three good men, Halloran. Valuable men to the cause, they were. Shot 'em before they had a chance. You should have known we'd find you, you must have realized the IRA would never stand for that!"

Halloran was stunned. So it was *he* who had been the target all along. This bastard had tortured Dieter Stuhr to find *him* . . .

The man on the stairway felt uneasy with the strange smile that had appeared on Halloran's face.

Shay spoke to cover his own inexplicable fear. "There'll be three Provos, good an' true, smiling in Heaven this night," he said, raising the .38 so that it was aimed directly at Halloran.

"There's no such place for killers," the man below said, and his voice was mild, the lilt of Irish there as if he'd not been gone too long from the old country.

"That you'll be knowing yourself," Shay replied. "God only knows what Divil's worship you're involved in here. Ask His forgiveness, if you've a mind to, an' do it now."

Thunder rumbled as his finger curled against the trigger of the revolver.

"*Liam!*" Cora screamed, and just for an instant the gunman was distracted.

That was all the time that Halloran needed to make a grab for the collapsed Arab.

The gun roared deafeningly in the confines of the underground room, but Halloran had already hoisted up Daoud to use as a shield. The Arab shuddered as the bullet struck his forehead and lodged inside. The operative fought to control the twitching body, his hands beneath the dead man's shoulders, holding him upright. The second bullet entered Daoud's stomach, and the third went through his side. Halloran felt this last one nick his hip as it emerged and, although most of its force was spent, the shock was enough to make him drop his cover.

More screams filled the air, but these were from Khayed, who had witnessed the slaying of his lover. He ran toward the stairs, the long blade raised high, a continuous screech now rising from deep inside his throat.

Shay was obliged to turn to meet the attack, and he was hardly aware of the person who had led him to this ungodly place brushing past. Palusinski was too afraid for his own life to tackle the gunman; he made for the safety of the corridor at the top of the stairs.

Khayed was almost on the bottom step when Shay fired the gun at him. A hole appeared in the Arab's chest, its edges immediately spreading blood. He staggered backward, his arms waving as if for balance, then came forward once more, his face not contorted with pain but with outrage. He reached the second step and seemed to sense he would never get close to the one who had killed his beloved Youssef.

The huge knife was already leaving his hand as the next bullet tore away his throat.

Shay fell back against the stairs, the blade imbedded at an angle in his stomach, the heavy parka he wore no protection at all. His vision was already beginning to dim as he turned his head toward the man below, his target, the Irishman turned traitor whom he and his group had been sent to assassinate as an example to others of how the Organization always avenged itself. His hand wavered as he raised the Webley .38, for the weapon was suddenly very heavy, almost too heavy to lift.

Once again he aimed the gun at Halloran.

49

RETURN TO THE DEATH HUT

"We can't waste any more time with this one," Mather remarked.

"Find another point of entry?" his operative suggested, looking up from his kneeling position against the porch wall.

"No need," Mather replied, raising a hand to the other two Shield men running toward them. He went to meet them, keeping out of sight of the main doors inside the porch from where the gunman held them at bay. He tightened his coat collar around his neck against the drenching rain.

"In the mood for target practice, Georgie?" he asked when the two men reached him.

"Always, sir," came the answer, as all three moved in close to be heard over the storm. "What's the problem?"

"We're being refused admittance. You see the Mercedes parked in line with the porch? You'll have a clear view of the house doorway from the rear passenger seat, or at least you can see some of it in the darkness—our friend appears to have switched off some lights. The vehicle's ours, so use your spare key if it's locked."

"How much damage?"

"Just hit the bugger."

Mather limped away, followed by the second operative, who crouched low and used the Mercedes as a screen to reach the opposite side of the porch. The man named Georgie doubled over also, going to the car and trying the door handle. Halloran must have left it in one hell of a rush, he thought, when he discovered the doors were unlocked. The keys were in the ignition. Georgie switched on the system, then crawled over to the backseat and pressed the button to lower the passenger window. He raised the Browning, keeping it clear of the rain that spattered in, and waited.

He watched as the operative with Mather crawled on his belly on the porch, keeping to the shadow of one wall. The Planner reached inside with his cane to tap the floor, hoping to attract the attention of their quarry.

It worked. Georgie squeezed the Browning's trigger as flame flashed from the doorway ahead. All he heard was the bark of his own weapon, but he assumed Phil, inside the porch, had fired at the same time, aiming slightly left of the gun flash. They waited a few seconds; then, as lightning seared and thunder shook the sky, he saw Mather rush inside, Phil rising to accompany him to the doorway. He bundled out of the car, taking up position on the opposite side of the porch to his other colleague, their weapons pointing inward at the entrance.

Mather pushed the door back farther and flicked the Armalite away from the motionless gunman with his cane. Soft light from an open door across the spacious hall and from the landing above lit the area, and Mather breathed a sigh of relief when he ascertained that no one else guarded the main doors. Rushing forward like that so soon after the enemy was hit had been a calculated risk, but it had saved some time.

Mather pointed at the slumped figure with his cane. "Check him, then send one of the others after me while you search upstairs." He was already limping across the hall making for the lit doorway as he gave the orders.

He entered a corridor at the end of which was a door swaying with the draft that blew in from outside, rain puddling the floor beneath it. He hurried forward, glancing into other open doorways as he passed.

From ahead, Mather thought he heard a scuffling.

Palusinski came out into the courtyard, the pounding rain welcome on his face and head, even though huge droplets spattered his glasses and distorted his vision. Lightning pearled everything before him, dazzling him through the water spots on his lenses so that he blinked rapidly. Whipping off the spectacles, the movement accompanied by a peal of thunder, he hurried across the flagstones. The Pole had no desire to find his way through Kline's private rooms in order to reach the main doors of the house: this way was more direct, and the sooner he was away from the madness inside Neath, the better he would like it. His own acute sense of survival told him some kind of reckoning was at hand for Kline—*mój Pan*, oh Lord and Master!—and he, Janusz Palusinski, did not want to be around for the consequences.

But as he passed the center fountain, a burning liquid sprayed his face.

When he stopped to brush at the stinging with his hand, he felt a stickiness on his cheek. He could feel it eating into his skin. He peered shortsightedly at the fountain, and there seemed to be shapes contorting from the stonework, rising from the brimming basin, writhing among the ornamentation.

Palusinski uttered a startled cry and began to back away. *Gówno!* This couldn't be! The fountain was a dead thing, defunct, slimed and blocked, an extinct spring! Yet he could discern a bubbling outflow catching reflections from window lights around the yard. And liquid dribbled sluggishly from the carved spouts that, in their decay, resembled gargoyles. And these monsters themselves were *moving*, twisting as if to tear themselves free from the stonework, hatching from wombs of masonry, spitting their bile of burning substance, the whole structure gushing unnatural life.

Palusinski slipped as he turned to run, his knees smacking sickeningly against the flagstones. His spectacles flew from his grasp, one lens cobwebbing fine cracks as it struck.

The Pole scrabbled away on hands and knees, too much in haste to search for his broken glasses and too afraid to look back at the quivering fountain. He sobbed when something touched his leg, a curling caress that somehow scorched even though there was no firmness, no strength in its grip. He pushed himself up, moving forward all the time, blundering toward the open doorway on the other side of the courtyard where light was shining outward.

He blinked away wetness. There was someone else in the corridor, limping toward him. Palusinski reacted instinctively and with his natural sense of self-preservation. He drew out the metal bar he always carried inside his coat and launched himself at the advancing figure.

Mather noted the crazed wildness in the other man's eyes, and saw light catching the shiny weapon being raised, ready to strike. He came to a halt and pointed his cane at the bald man's chest.

Palusinski sneered at the other's ineffectual weapon, realizing there was nothing to fear in this old man confronting him, the only real terror being out there in the courtyard and the underground chamber he had just left. He grabbed the end of the cane and pulled it toward himself, sure that it would be easy to wrench it from the frail grasp. The metal bar had reached its zenith, was trembling in his hand, ready to plunge downward against the man's skull. He barely heard the faint *click*.

Mather had pressed the tiny button in the handle of the cane, and the wooden casing slid from the long, slender blade, his would-be assailant unsheathing the sword himself. The Shield Planner took no chances, for he could see the murder in this wild man's eyes.

He lunged forward, the sword piercing the bald man's chest, melting through, entering his heart and still not stopping.

Palusinski looked in surprise at the other man. The pain came only when the sword was swiftly withdrawn.

He sank to the floor, a casual gesture as if he merely wanted to rest for a moment. Janusz Palusinski lay down and, as his mind wandered toward death, he felt he was among other recumbent bodies. He was no longer inside the corridor of the house, but in the dimly lit hut a long, long way from there, and a long time ago.

Those skeletal forms around him were sitting up and grinning their welcome, for they had been waiting many years. One even crawled over to touch the young Janusz's face with bony fingers. Janusz lay there, unable to move, and he wondered why unseen hands were pulling at his clothing. And he wondered why there was no pain when teeth gnawed into his plump belly.

No, there was no pain at all.

Just the nightmare that he knew would go on forever...

50

SHADOWS AND IMAGININGS

Halloran remained perfectly still, staring up into the eyes of the dying gunman.

The weapon wavered in the air, trying to home in on its target. But the exertion was too much, and too late. Danny Shay rolled onto his side to make one last determined effort, but the gun was far too heavy for someone with only seconds to live. For a moment his arm hung over the stairway, the weapon loose in his grip. Then Shay's eyes closed and he knew he would never open them again.

"Dear God..." he began, the plea cut short when even his voice lost its strength.

He toppled from the stairs onto the damp floor, his landing relaxed, for he was already dead.

Wind tearing in from the passageway above ruffled Halloran's hair. The light stirred, shimmered, many of the candle flames snuffed by the breeze so that shadows stole forward from the alcoves. The ancient worshipers watched on, stone eyes dispassionate. And there seemed to be other onlookers within those darkened arches, but these were forms of no substance, observers that could never be defined by light for they were of the imagination even though they existed outside the mind. Halloran was intensely aware of their watching.

He turned toward the altar where the bloated corpse continued to pump blood. Cora had moved away, her shoulders soaked a deep red; she looked imploringly at Halloran, as if silently begging him to take her away from this madness. When she saw the coldness in him, Cora became inert.

Halloran would not allow emotion to hold sway. Not for the moment. He was confused, uncertain of his feelings for Cora. She had touched him, made him vulnerable once more.

And naturally, he had paid the price. He told himself she was an innocent used by someone who existed only for corruption. Yet . . . the thought persisted . . . yet there had to have been some part of her that was susceptible.

"Don't dare to judge me, Liam." She spoke quietly, but with defiance. "Not you, not someone like you."

He understood her meaning.

Thunder rumbled through the passageway, the sound spreading out into the chamber, seeming to tremble the walls. Dust sifted down from the ceiling to congeal in the puddles on the floor.

And in one small slick of black water lay the dried husk that was an embalmed heart.

And those unseen but fearfully imagined forms were emerging from the alcoves.

Halloran sensed their movement at first, and only when he looked did they take on a nebulous kind of reality. These were as the things from the lake, and they shuffled forward, eager to embrace. They were of him, the creatures mere reflections of the dark side of his inner self, manifestations of his own frailty, his own corruption. Hadn't Kline, himself, explained that to him?

He felt weakened. He staggered as if struck. He spun around.

More of these creations of the subconscious were slipping from between the statues, winding their way through, advancing on him. Yet each time he focused on one, it became formless, a swirling, vaporous nullity. His mind seemed squeezed, as though invisible tentacles had insinuated themselves into the orifices of his body, clogging them, sliding inward to capture his thoughts.

He clapped his hands against his temples, shaking his head to free himself of these tenuous intruders. He twisted, bent under their weight. Cora was trying to reach him, but something had hold of her, something not visible that tore at her robe, exposing her shoulders, her breasts that were smeared with blood. She was screaming as she struggled, but he could not hear her.

Halloran stumbled forward, desperate to help her, wanting that more than anything else, heedless of his own plight, the invasion of his own body. But it was useless. He was being dragged down by these seeping infiltrators who sought their own origins.

He could not hear her screams but he could hear Kline's laughter.

Its cracked sound mocked him, tormented, as Kline overwhelmed him with imaginings, the thoughts swelling with all the badness that had been drawn into that underground room, the malignancy that had dwelled inside the dead men, released now by someone who acted as instigator and catalyst, someone who knew the ancient secrets of the Cabala, who understood their potency. Felix Kline . . .

Where was he? Where *was* Kline?

Where else but inside your head? came the silent reply.

"That can't be," denied Halloran aloud, his hands over his ears as though they could cut out the sly voice that was, indeed, inside his head.

Oh, but it can. A familiar snigger. *I can be anywhere. Didn't I demonstrate that the first time we met?*

"I can stop you!"

You can? Please try. A good-humored invitation.

Halloran's legs buckled as white-hot irons pressed against the back of his eyeballs.

There. Painful? I can do more than that. You deserve to suffer more.

Halloran looked up from his kneeling position. Kline was standing a short distance away, facing him, eyes closed, scarlet hands tight against his own head, its skin all but gone, the flesh that had been beneath exposed and livid. He was unsteady as shadows that were something more than shadows writhed around him. Kline's mouth was open in an agonized grimace.

"It's too late!" Halloran managed to shout. "You're weak. Your power isn't the same." And as he said the words, Halloran felt the slightest easing of pressure, the merest cooling of the fire. Pain immediately came back to him.

You're so wrong, Halloran, whispered the insidious voice inside his head. *My only problem is whether I finish you quickly or take my time, enjoy myself a little.*

But there was a gasp, a sound only in Halloran's mind. Kline was reeling, his hands leaving blotches of scraped flesh as they ran down his face.

"Halloran!" A piercing scream, and from Kline's lips.

The psychic's eyes opened, blackness filling them. They rested on Halloran's. "I can hurt you," Kline rasped. "I can make your heart seize up with the horrors I'll show you." His eyes closed once more and the snigger was back inside Halloran's mind.

Nightmares began to form, and gargoyles drifted from them. But these were tangible, on the outside of his thoughts, for when they touched him their fingernails were like razor blades, and he could smell the stench of their breath, dank and foul, like the old sea caves where mammoth creatures of the deep had been abandoned by the tide to die. They clung to him, and their lips—not lips, they had no such things as lips—their *openings* pressed against his face to kiss.

He felt the aching in his arms. The tightening of his chest, as fear began to win through. No! They were in his mind—in *Kline's* mind! They couldn't hurt him!

But they could.

For where they touched him, so they drew out his life. He could feel living beings inside his veins, blocking the flow, expanding so that they burst the tubes and his life's liquid poured uselessly into the cavities of his body. He sagged, slumped on his haunches, and he acknowledged Kline's assertion that he could coax a victim's mind to murder its own host. Halloran was unable to resist, the images of Kline's creation were too strong, too *real!* His forehead bowed to the wet stone floor.

This time the roar was not thunder.

It jolted Halloran into awareness, a confusion of senses muddling his brain, a bedlam of emotions causing him to cry out. Now the worst of his pain was from his hip where the bullet that had passed through the Arab had scraped his own flesh. Blood there was soaking his torn jacket. And the soreness around his throat was a relief rather than a discomfort, for it was, like the throbbing pain in his side, an indication of true reality.

Halloran opened his eyes and looked up. The monsters had fled. The shadows were but shadows.

Kline was lying on the floor, and there was no movement from him.

Halloran pushed himself to his feet and stood for a while, his body bent forward, hands resting against his legs, waiting for his strength to return. He searched for Cora.

He found her crouched over the dead gunman, her robe in tatters around her waist, marks and bloodstains on her pale skin. In her shaking hand was the revolver, smoke still curling from its barrel. She was staring at Kline, eyes wide, her expression lifeless.

"Cora..." Halloran said as he staggered toward her. He knelt on one knee and took the gun from her, laying it to one side. "I think you used his last bullet," he told her as he gently pulled the remnants of her robe around her shoulders. She turned her face to him, and apprehension filtered through the numbness. She murmured something he didn't quite catch, but it did not matter. He raised her to him and held her close, kissing her matted hair, his arms tight around her.

"It's done, Cora," he assured her quietly. "Finished. I'll get you away from this place, as far away as possible."

She sank into him, and the wetness from her eyes dampened his collar. He ran a hand beneath her hair and his fingers caressed the back of her neck.

He felt her stiffen.

He heard the slithering.

Halloran turned.

Felix Kline was sliding on his belly through puddles on the floor, leaving a trail of decayed skin and blood in his wake, the raw flesh of his skinless face and hands puckered and cracked, a glistening redness oozing from lesions. Facial muscles were clearly defined in grouped ridges, and tendons stood proud on his hands, with veins stretched as bluish rivulets. His breathing came as a strained, animal-like coughing as he pushed himself toward the blackened lump that rested in filthy water at the center of the room.

He was almost there, one hand extended, quivering as it reached for the relic that once was a heart within a body, his breath becoming harsher, a drool of spittle sinking to the floor from his gaping mouth.

Three feet away from the pool in which the ancient heart lay.

Push.

Two feet away. A piteous moaning from him as his pain-wracked body scraped against the flagstones. Tears as the suffering became too much to bear.

Push.

Through the wetness.

Halloran rose, softly taking away Cora's hand from his arm as she tried to cling to him.

Push.

Not far now.

Desperation gleamed in Kline's dark eyes.

A few more inches.

Push.

Nearly there.

His fingers stretched, sifting through the dirty water, almost touching the withered husk.

A shadow over him.

A lifted foot.

Kline sobbed as Halloran crushed the heart into the stone floor.

51

END OF THE STORM

Mather peered out into the courtyard.

Thank God the storm's easing, he thought. Lightning flashes were mere reflections, with thunder following long moments after as distant rumblings. The rain had lost its force, had become a pattering. He could just make out what must have been an impressive fountain in an age gone by, its structure now misshapen, worn by time. It glistened from the rain but had no vitality of its own.

He was naturally concerned over the dead man lying behind him in the corridor. Mather realized that the man he had just killed was Janusz Palusinski, one of Kline's own bodyguards. The Planner had met Palusinski earlier that day, but the mad-eyed creature who had rushed at him in the corridor bore scant resemblance to that person: without his distinctive wire-framed spectacles and because of his drenched condition and the sheer lunacy of his expression, the Pole was another character entirely.

Why the devil had the man tried to attack him? He surely must have known who the Planner was. Unless, of course, the reason was that Palusinski was in league with the intruders, yet another traitor within the Magma organization. There had certainly been no doubt about his murderous intent—Mather was too experienced in the ways of combat not to have recognized it. Well, the matter would be cleared up soon enough.

There was activity across the courtyard. An open door there, vague light glowing from it. Shadows, figures. Someone was coming through the doorway.

Mather's grip tightened on the sword-stick. He ducked back inside when he heard footsteps behind him. One of his operatives was hurrying along the corridor. The Planner raised a finger to his lips and the operative slowed his pace, approaching quietly. He examined the bald-headed man whose chest was weeping blood.

Mather returned his attention to the two people who had stepped out into the courtyard, one of them apparently supporting the other.

"Wait there," he instructed the operative when he recognized the couple as they made their way through the drizzle. Mather limped out to meet them, movement awkward without his cane; he quietly called Liam's name.

"Oh, good Lord," he said when he realized the state they were in.

Halloran expressed no surprise at finding Mather at Neath. In the light from the courtyard window, his face betrayed no emotion at all.

"Get her away from here," Halloran said curtly, pressing Cora into the Planner's arms.

"What's happened, Liam?" Mather demanded to know. "I've just been forced to kill one of Kline's bodyguards, the Polish fellow."

There was the slightest hint of a smile in Halloran's eyes. "Trust me like you've never trusted me before," was all he said. "It's over now, but I want you to take Cora out of the house. Wait for me by the main gates."

"Liam, that's—"

"Please do it."

Mather paused. "And you?"

"There's something I have to take care of."

With that, he turned away from Mather and the girl to walk back through the soft rain to the doorway from where he and Cora had emerged.

52

THE BATTLE OVER

Halloran closed the double-doors of Neath, then strode along the gloomed porchway out into the cleansed night air. The clouds had broken up, the moon dominated. Dampness still lingered, but there was no violence left in this night. Across the lawn he could see the lake, a low-lying mist hovering over its calm surface.

He climbed wearily into the Mercedes, switching on engine and headlights. He looked back at Neath once more, studying it for several moments before swinging the car around and heading up the road into the trees.

As he drove, he wondered about Felix Kline and his terrible and unique powers. He wondered about the story the psychic had told him, of the Sumerians, of Bel-Marduk, their devil-God, the Antichrist who had *preceded* the Christ. He wondered about the truth of it. And Halloran wondered about himself.

He thought that perhaps he understood.

They waited for him by the big iron gates, the four operatives puzzled and somewhat agitated by the abrupt ceasing of action, while Charles Mather stood with the girl, who wore one of the operatives' jackets draped over her shoulders. Although barefoot and cold, Cora had refused to wait inside one of the cars; her eyes never left the drive leading to the house. She hadn't spoken a word since Mather had brought her away from Neath, despite his questions. Had Liam instructed her to remain silent? Mather wondered.

Cora caught her breath and Mather, too, saw the approaching lights, the car emerging from the tunnel of trees in the distance so that moonlight struck its silver bodywork. It came toward them at a leisurely pace, an indication that the danger really was past.

They watched as the Mercedes drew near, its headlights brightening the road.

But it stopped. By the lodge house.

They saw Halloran lean out of the car window and drop something onto the ground in front of the two strange-looking guard dogs that had been prowling around their dead companions as though disoriented.

One of the animals warily came forward and began to devour whatever it was that Halloran had offered.

He watched the jackal chew on the crushed, blackened meat and waited there until the ancient heart had been swallowed completely.

Only then did Halloran start up the car again and drive onward to the gates themselves.

He climbed out of the Mercedes and Cora took one hesitant step toward him. He raised his arms and she came all the way. Halloran pulled her tight against him.

Mather was bemused. Such a demonstrable show of emotion from his operative was unusual to say the least.

"Liam . . ." he began.

Halloran nodded at him. "I know," he said. The Planner wanted answers, and what could he tell him? Halloran's tone was flat when he spoke. "His bodyguards had turned against him. Monk, Palusinski, the two Jordanians—he'd treated them too badly. He's quite insane, you know. They finally had enough of him. None of it's clear, but I think they worked out a deal with the Provisional IRA to kidnap him. I guess they didn't want to live out their lives in servitude, and the proceeds from the ransom—or maybe just a Judas fee from the kidnappers—would have ensured that they no longer had to. And they got away with it. All except Palusinski and those two outsiders I saw you'd put down. You can alert the police, get them over here, have them watch air and seaports."

"Wait a minute. The IRA . . . ?"

"They were responsible for Dieter Stuhr's death. I suppose the idea was to make sure no one suspected it was an inside job, that information on the Shield cover was tortured out of our own man. Incidentally, Kline's gate keeper was attacked by those animals back there. What's left of him is inside that lodge house."

There was disbelief in Mather's eyes, but Halloran steadily returned his gaze.

"They took Kline," Halloran continued evenly. "But he was badly injured. I think he'll die from his wounds."

"We'll see if we get a ransom demand. We'll insist on having evidence that he's still alive."

"Somehow I don't believe that'll happen."

"Shall I get on to the police now, sir?" one of the other men asked briskly.

"Uh, yes," replied Mather. "Yes, I think that would be appropriate, don't you, Liam? God knows how they'll take all this shooting, but we've been in similar predicaments before. Such a dreadful thing that all our efforts failed."

Not once had he taken his eyes off Halloran.

"Let's sit in the car until the police arrive, shall we?" Mather suggested. "Miss Redmile is shivering. And then you can tell me more, Liam. Yes, you can explain a lot more to me."

There was something chilling in Halloran's smile. He looked back at the brooding lodge house. Then along the road that disappeared into the darkness of the smothering woods, winding its way to the house itself. To Neath.

"I'm not sure you'll understand," Halloran said finally.

He took Cora's arm and helped her into the car.

SERPENT

Lights all around. Soft-hued glows.

Shadows, pretty, never still, constantly weaving their secrets.

Ah, the bliss of lying here. A fitting place, this altar. Peaceful. And no pain. Not yet.

Is this how it was for you, O Lord? Did your priests minister drugs to suppress the hurting? Or was your cask, your vessel, dead before it was entombed, your spirit trapped within to wait out the years, the centuries? Your heart had not died, I know that.

So tired, so exhausted. Sleep will be welcome. Yes, yes, even eternal sleep.

It's cold in this chamber beneath the earth. And damp. Yet why can't I shiver? Why can't I move?

Oh yes. I know why.

So finally he believed. Halloran finally accepted the truth of it all. A triumph in some ways, wouldn't you say?

But why didn't I understand that he was the one conditioned to ruin me? Why, with all my perceptive powers, didn't I realize it was Halloran who was the threat? Is that the one weakness that comes with the gift of seeing, O Lord? The vulnerable point, the blindness to one's own destiny, the unforeseeableness of one's own fate? Is that your answer to me? Quite a joke really, don't think I don't appreciate it.

Even funnier if it was something more than that. It couldn't be, could it, Lord, that he came at my own invitation? Surely not. That would be nonsense, too perverse for words. Yet we enjoy perversity, don't we? Well, don't we? Constant evil can be wearing, don't you agree? But I tried, I did my best for you. The decades were so long though, Bel-Marduk. Surely you, above all, can appreciate that? But that doesn't mean I'd close my mind to my own impending demise, does it?

Does it?

DOES IT?

No, I was happy with the task you set me. Evil for evil's sake. Harm for the sake of doing harm. Corruption for you! Entirely for YOU!

It doesn't hurt yet. What Halloran has done to me doesn't hurt. Not yet. And it shows he believes, he believes in you! I wonder if the drugs were his idea of mercy, maybe to demonstrate he isn't as wicked as I. He seemed to understand, though, when I told him there are no absolutes, that no one—not even I—could be totally evil. Nor totally good. Yes, that appeared to make sense to him. Perhaps that was why he softened my pain with drugs, perhaps he'd already realized that.

(And was that imperfection in me my failing, O Lord? Did I fail because I was not perfectly evil? But I tried, oh, I tried.)

It had to be someone like him, didn't it? The other Lord, your eternal enemy, had to send someone like Halloran. Someone who could be cruel, someone who would carry it through. And someone who might seek a kind of redemption—shit, how I detest that word!

And I was the one who told him how. Should I be laughing, Bel-Marduk? Are you disappointed in me, will I be punished when I finally succumb? Or will we laugh together throughout eternity?

Ah! A twinge of pain at last! Sweet though, very sweet. I wonder which will kill me first? The loss of blood or the agony when the drugs wear off?

At least I'm not lonely here. I have my servants around me, just as you had yours in the secret sepulchre, their lives willingly given up to be with you always. But my servants were not so willing. No, they gave themselves up grudgingly. Still, their reluctant spirits are with me now. Listen how they whine.

Will I have to wait as long as you, Dark Lord, before my body is discovered? This, my own sepulchre, is well hidden, as was yours, and I don't have the strength to call others to it. In fact, I have no strength, no power at all. I'm sure Halloran sealed the entrance well, and no one would hear me even if I could scream.

Aaaah! Hurting!

And it's darker now. Are the candles burning low? Will I be left on this altar in total darkness; unable to see, unable to move . . .

Spare me this pain, please, Lord. Take me before the opiums weaken. Forgive me for failing you.

If I turn my head I can see the knife he used on me. Its blade is rich with my own blood. Isn't it funny, Lord? If I could reach it, I could use it against myself, I could hurry along my death. But see there, one of my severed arms lying in a puddle next to it? The other is probably close by. And my legs. Where are they, I wonder? It's not important.

Can there be another time for me, O Lord?

No. Of course not.

What good is my limbless form to you, with my spirit forever entombed inside, my body now my soul's own sepulchre. Say you'll forgive me!

Darker now. Becoming very dim. I can still see the eyes though, those huge unblinking eyes watching from the shadows. They'll watch over me forever, won't they?

Even when the darkness is complete, they'll still be there.

Watching . . .